THE *Mist* OF HER MEMORY

SUZAN LAUDER

Meryton Press
OYSTERVILLE, WA

Also by Suzan Lauder

ALIAS THOMAS BENNET
LETTER FROM RAMSGATE
A MOST HANDSOME GENTLEMAN

This is a work of fiction. Names, characters, places, and incidents are products of the author's imagination or are used fictitiously. Any resemblance to actual events or persons, living or dead, is entirely coincidental.

THE MIST OF HER MEMORY

Copyright © 2019 by Suzan Lauder

All rights reserved, including the right to reproduce this book, or portions thereof, in any format whatsoever. For information: P.O. Box 34, Oysterville WA 98641

ISBN: 978-1-68131-031-2

Cover design by Janet Taylor
Graphic layout by Ellen Pickels

Dedication

To Mom, one of the most dedicated mystery and suspense novel readers of my acquaintance, who shares the love with other readers.

And, as always, to Mr. Suze, who rode his bicycle so I had time to write.

A brief note on the spelling and language in
The Mist of Her Memory—

To help with the authentic feel of this novel, a genuine effort was made to avoid the use of words developed later than 1812–13, the years in which this novel takes place. In addition, many British English spellings of the time period were chosen because the story takes place in England. Because British English spelling changes took place after the American Revolution (with the Americans keeping the old spellings), some words may look misspelled to American readers (colour, honour), while others may look misspelled to modern British readers (apologize, realize).

The author's list of non-Regency, non-British words is in excess of eight hundred and growing, but the author and editors still may have missed a word or expression or two from later than 1813. Hopefully, readers won't be distracted out of the Regency moment alongside Elizabeth, Mr. Darcy, and friends in *The Mist of Her Memory*.

It was a gloomy prospect, and all that she could do was to throw a mist over it and hope, when the mist cleared away, she should see something else.

—*Mansfield Park,* by Jane Austen

Early October 1812
Gracechurch Street, London

Elizabeth held her breath as she sneaked towards the servants' entrance of her uncle's home. She had but a moment before she would be missed, barely enough time to slip from her chamber down the servants' stairs. Stepping gingerly to avoid the noise made by the loose board on the seventh stair, she made her way to the bottom and opened the door to the rear vestibule only a crack so no one would hear it creak.

Did she remember correctly? She had seen a cloak of sorts hanging in the back entrance as she wandered up and down stairs whilst her aunt made calls in the mornings. On those days, they did not walk in the park, and her aunt refused to allow Elizabeth to take her walks on her own. Could they not understand how valuable her exercise and time outside of the stale air of the house were to her? She would be perfectly safe—she had never fallen faint on her own.

But as much as she tried to stay out of the servants' way on the days when she ambled about the house for exercise, her presence here had been reported at some point. Uncle Gardiner told her he preferred that she not walk about on the back stairs lest she get in the servants' way.

She peeked through the crack in the door. A woman's hooded cape was suspended on the hook near the doorway, just the thing she would need when the time came to escape. The drab, homespun servant's cape made her skin itch whenever she imagined wearing it, yet the pathetic garment was a symbol of hope—if she dared fetch it. Its distance from her situation taunted her, a reminder of how she was trapped here against her will.

A wave of nausea hit her, and her vision blackened and blurred a mite. She shut the door silently and, closing her eyes, leaned her head against the door frame until the moment passed and she was able to make her way back up to the family rooms.

"Elizabeth?" Her aunt emerged at the very moment when she was able to make it appear as though she was about to enter the family dining room.

"Forgive my tardiness, Aunt. I had a loose seam that needed mending."

It was a lie. But her slow ability with the needle would not be questioned, and her maid had been dismissed a good quarter of an hour ago. Elizabeth pursed her lips. She was so frustrated! Not that she intended to escape right now, but the sensation of freedom had wrapped itself around her and given her hope, if only for a moment.

"Come along, dear."

Her aunt preceded her as she took her place at the table. Conversation at dinner was sparkling, enhancing a tasty meal in the cosy dining room. The Gardiners were nothing if not excellent hosts and interesting conversationalists. It was truly a step above the inane prattle of her sisters and mother at home in Hertfordshire. She smiled as her uncle told a particularly humorous anecdote from earlier that week.

"The fellow insisted he had stacked the latest shipment in the drapery section," said Uncle Gardiner. "No matter how much we looked amongst the yard goods, no matter how carefully we queried, he insisted. Finally, old Grouse got it in his head to ask the driver to come and show us where he had dropped the packages. It turned out his reading skills were not the best, and rolls of fabric were located atop an old sign from the building's earlier life as a dairy! Dairy, drapery—the carter had misread the sign."

Yes, there was laughter, safe reminiscences, discussions on history, reports of the children's antics, happy accounts regarding daily life—nothing ill to complain about. One could do much worse than be a perpetual guest at a refined family member's home. Words flowed, all of an intelligent yet light and comforting nature as was usual for the Gardiners' dispositions. Except that once in a while, the whole tone would make a momentary change.

Tonight, it was surely the fault of a gap in the discourse. During a quiet moment, her aunt appeared thoughtful as she chewed her peas, swallowed, and said, "I shall be calling on Lady Oliver tomorrow." She did not look at anyone in particular when she said this and seemed distracted. "She is acquainted with the lady her husband spoke to you of yesterday, Mrs. Bastion."

Uncle Gardiner stopped eating and stared at his wife. He was clearly as surprised as Elizabeth was that his wife would reveal the details of her call in front of their niece. At least twice a week, her aunt would leave for a few hours in the morning, giving vague excuses about the reasons for her absence. But Elizabeth was no fool. Her aunt was making calls, and Elizabeth was not welcome to join her. The Gardiners were kind people doing their best to protect her fragile mind, though at times like this, it felt more as though she was in captivity and not a family guest. But inasmuch as she would prefer to return to her usual routines, she must develop more patience with her recovery.

On several occasions, she had overheard discussions through supposedly closed doors. Her uncle and aunt were wilfully hiding information to keep her ignorant of anything that occurred outside their safe little corner of Cheapside, and they had no idea how hurtful their concealment was to her lively mind. Whenever current events were mentioned in her presence, the conversation became stilted and roundabout—presumably, lest any items were mentioned that could cause Elizabeth unease in her ill condition. She was not allowed to read periodicals or go out of the house in case she became upset, and with the cold air that had beset the dining table this evening, an embargo was clearly set upon Lady Oliver and her friend as well. But why? What information could they have that would possibly cause her harm? At times like this, she could not, for the life of her, understand them. She groaned inside as her aunt and uncle shared a look of mutual discomfort.

Her uncle put down his silver fork and knife and cleared his throat. With a nervous frown crossing his brow, he looked directly at her aunt. "Perhaps we can discuss your plans after dinner."

Aunt returned her husband's steady gaze, apparently bemused. A pea dribbled off her fork. "Yes. Yes, of course. I do not know what I was... Yes, of course." She pursed her lips in understanding and lowered her eyes at her error.

Once Aunt returned to her meal, silence ruled the dining table until it harried at Elizabeth's nerves. How to return to the easy air they had been entertaining just moments before her aunt's faux pas? "I have almost finished the novel I am reading. Might we take a trip to Hookham's so I may choose another book to pass my time?"

The air of the room became brighter as soon as she asked her question, as if the weight of the secret had been swept away by her innocent suggestion. Her aunt's pleased expression faced her; Elizabeth had saved her all the mortification of her inadvertent disclosure by changing the subject. Her heart became light again.

"I shall do you one better, my dear." Her uncle wiped his mouth and returned the cloth to his lap. He leaned back into his chair and said with a half-grin, "I shall purchase something new for you, a first edition. That way, you can keep it and reread it at will. Mayhap you will loan it to me or your aunt to read as well."

Elizabeth congratulated herself on the change in tone and her role in improving the comfort of her aunt and uncle. How might she use this tactic in the future to obtain something she wanted: wait until there was awkwardness then lighten the day with a request? In fact, why not now? Irrationally and wildly hopeful, Elizabeth held her breath for a moment before she leaned forward, unable to stop the grin from spreading over the whole of her face. "May I join you and help select the book? I should like it to suit us all."

In response, the corners of her uncle's lips turned up even more. But her aunt broke into the discussion. "Not this time. We shall see how your headaches improve." Her words were quick, but her voice was not sharp; rather, Aunt sounded apologetic.

For a moment, the brittle emotions that those words imparted made Elizabeth's body seem fragile, as if it were going to crack into a thousand pieces before it crumbled onto the floor in a dusty pile about the feet of the tastefully matched dining room chair. Thankfully, she was able to halt her indignant rejoinder and hold a practised smile firmly across her gritted teeth. How could she convince them that even though their love was appreciated, it stifled her freedom to excess? She still had the odd spell of pain behind her eyes, yet that was no reason to shield her from the rest of the world!

At least she had learned to never ever mention Lydia's elopement and marriage. She could not keep her calm when they refuted her sister's marital situation, as they always did. In voices dripping with patience, they insisted on the worst rather than trust she knew the truth of the matter. Had they

The Mist of Her Memory

tried to acquaint themselves with the details of Elizabeth's narration rather than close their ears and minds, they would have a good many positive and grateful sentiments, just as she did.

None of it mattered any longer. As soon as she could verify that Miss Darcy was in town, she would take action and slip away to call upon her. The prospect of a renewal of their friendship was a goal just as fulfilling as the possibility of seeing Mr. Darcy during the call where she could thank him as he deserved for all his assistance to her and her family. Heaven help her for her hopes, but if he had the chance once again, perchance the opportunity would present itself for the man to clarify what he had said that fateful day regarding his addresses—if he did not mind Wickham as a brother-in-law. Of course, her escape and visit would be fully inappropriate, but her relations had left her no choice.

Elizabeth had expected she would have to wait until after Christmastide to ensure the Darcys would be at their house in town for the Season, but that all changed when her young cousin Harriet's interest in the *ton* caused the child to pilfer an old news-sheet and bring it to the schoolroom. Starved for news, Elizabeth read it eagerly, and that was when she made her discovery. The *Times* declared that Mr. Fitzwilliam Darcy was resident in Portman Square with his sister.

Elizabeth had the good fortune that no one knew the details of her attachment with Mr. Darcy; therefore, her aunt and uncle did not know why Mr. Darcy had come to Lambton that fateful day in August. They may have wondered at Mr. Darcy's and Elizabeth's feelings given the way they admired each other at Pemberley, and they may have even guessed at the question he wanted to ask her. Elizabeth was certain he must have meant to do so, for she distinctly remembered hearing the words "my love" before her world went black. However, the Gardiners never would have known that he had all but asked for a second time. But had she answered? She could not recall. She knew what her answer would be, and she had to tell Mr. Darcy as soon as possible.

All the Gardiners knew about was her accident and that Mr. Darcy had attempted to save her. When she tried to clarify the details, Aunt Gardiner's lower lip would start to tremble, she would shake her head, and then she would usually start to speak of the children. Clearly, Aunt did not want to revisit that terrible time. And who could blame her? Although greatly

13

improved, the amnesia, the headaches, and the dizzy spells all persisted and made Elizabeth's life a misery, and Aunt was sensitive to others' pain.

Certainly, the children made Elizabeth's new home in London significantly better than the foolhardy distraction of her family at Longbourn. When the Gardiners' governess had to leave to tend to her sickly mother, Elizabeth had persuaded her aunt to let her perform those duties. Although Harriet and little Martha proved to be good students, a few topics in the schoolbooks were difficult for her to decipher. Why was that? Was it possible that she had never been trained in these particular subjects herself? It did not seem likely, yet she had no recollection of the basic principles whatsoever, and if she strove to remember, the painful headaches occurred. In those cases, she would simply move on to another area of schoolwork for the girls. The governess could take them in hand when she returned.

Oh yes, the bookshop! She had allowed herself to become distracted and was now frowning from her internal musings; it would not do! Her demeanour must change to convince her aunt and uncle that she be allowed that specific trip. It would gratify her more than a half-dozen walks in the park!

"The headaches are not that common anymore," she said, trying very hard to keep an uplifted voice and air about her person. "It has been an age since I had one."

"It has only been two months since the injury," her aunt stated with a nod, closing the discussion.

Why must everyone always try to protect her because of her injury? Could she not understand how stifling her present captivity was—to be kept away from everything in the world that was interesting, sequestered in this house in Gracechurch Street with barely a chaperoned walk available to her most days, entertaining herself with nothing of interest to divert her busy mind a great deal of the time?

She needed a reprieve. What harm could there be in asking again? Direct eyes. Solemn, trustworthy countenance. "Please."

"No, dear. No bookshop."

Tears threatened to leak from her eyes. She stifled the impulse to brush them away as it would draw attention to her weakness and ruin her chances. Instead, she stretched a tight smile across her lips and turned towards her uncle, attempting to implore him with her eyes. "Please."

"Elizabeth—" he began.

The Mist of Her Memory

Her aunt interrupted. "It is not safe."

She could no longer control the pressure of the injustice within her and had to restrain herself from sobbing by breathing in short gasps as she looked from one to the other. How could she convince them of the importance of this? Was there no way to show them of her recovery from her contusion? Should she prevaricate about the spells she still experienced from time to time? What else was important to them that she could use to sway their decision? Should she offer never to ask again about Mr. Darcy's help with Lydia and Mr. Wickham? No one said anything for the longest interval, nothing at all, and Elizabeth continued her efforts to regulate her demeanour. She inhaled deeply, wiped her eyes with her handkerchief, and then schooled her features to the calmest she could manage while knotting her hands together under the table. Her remaining nervousness required some outlet for expression! Her aunt was still gazing at the ceiling, eyes shining with tears of her own, when her uncle finally broke the standstill.

"In a few weeks' time, if you have not had another spell, we shall discuss it again. In the meantime, you may select any book in my library. What about some poetry to help your spirits?" His tone was one of a begging pup rather than the firm law-laying uncle that he could be under such circumstances.

Her uncle's library was good but small. Though a successful businessman, he still did not have the resources to stock anything nearly as comprehensive as her father's library, which had been acquired over the years—never mind that which she had seen at Pemberley. With her memory as it was, she could not always recall which books she had read, so there existed a large opportunity for what seemed like new reading experiences.

How could she not agree? Persisting in obstinacy would make her almost as cruel as they sometimes seemed to be. Besides, he had not fully agreed to take her to the booksellers', so she did not have to make the pretence of an offer to abandon her knowledge of the truth about Lydia. She would just continue to avoid the topic—for now.

Aunt and Uncle were kind people to be offering her a home here, and she had no right to be disrespectful or churlish. After all, they were caring for her, protecting her, keeping her from where the people in Meryton thought she belonged—Bedlam.

A month earlier
En route to London from Pemberley

This was going to be the trip from hell if he kept seeing her face at every turn. Darcy looked towards the inhabitants of the coach, away from the blasted window and its reflective surface. Georgiana smiled, but her lips trembled just a little, and Mrs. Annesley was attempting to ward off sleep, her head nodding, oblivious to his glowering mien. His sister was trying to be encouraging, and it was not easy for her in the face of his ill humour. He checked himself and removed his scowl, his reaction to the constant reappearance of a face that was not really there—Elizabeth Bennet's lovely countenance reflected in the coach window.

Elizabeth. The smile faded from his lips. He missed her, and every recollection brought the pain back.

Her presence at Pemberley, his estate, now haunted him. Her special smile—the smile he had believed was a loving return of his affection—lurked in every corner, in the low light of every wall sconce, in the reflection of every mirror, and around every turn. The way she looked at him after Miss Bingley had tried to upset her had secured his belief that she reciprocated his affections. That smile was now gone away, and he had no excuses to pursue her.

He wiped his hand over his face. That harridan Caroline Bingley, in trying to erase Elizabeth's pretty smile by mentioning the decampment of the ——shire militia where Mr. Wickham served, succeeded only in upsetting

Georgiana and drawing Elizabeth and his sister closer, not to mention what it did for his already high approval of Elizabeth. Then, when he attempted to pour out his gratitude through his eyes, the returning curve of her lip—well, it gave him more hope than he had ever had before, including that disastrous proposal back in April when he was so foolishly self-assured as to believe she had been expecting his addresses. Yes, he had not considered at that time whether or not she had affection for him. Instead, he assumed she held him in esteem, and that would be enough. Lord knew, he had enough love for both of them.

Lust had driven him to ask for her hand that day at Hunsford, yet he confused that dreadful, overwhelming desire with the passion of love. He wanted her badly, and being the honourable man he had always been, he thought of only one way he could have her: as his wife. Not that he loved her less deeply—he simply did not love her in the right way until it was too late. His love was not strong enough to think of her before himself, resulting in his damaged pride.

What a tongue-lashing she delivered! Their verbal wrangling in the past had showed her to be a spirited adversary, yet when an argument arose that he was unprepared for, he became offended and said things that should not have passed the lips of a steadfast lover. Her dismissal was painful and delivered with such fervour and succinctness that all he could do was feign a change of heart. Nonetheless, his heart held a tremendous pain inside. Worse than that, his pride and self-importance were damaged. Her words stung yet could not be easily refuted.

The months without her had taught him to change his ways, and little by little, he began to show those closest to him their importance rather than define his interactions based on *his* wants and needs. So, for the height of the season of 1812, Fitzwilliam Darcy was a little more kind, attentive, and generous in the dining rooms and ballrooms than the cold, haughty demeanour he had previously displayed. As a result, the sort of ladies who hovered about him changed somewhat. Was he different, or was it just the practise of a ruse that would be more attractive to the kind of young lady that Elizabeth Bennet was? Was he, inside, still a cold, haughty sort of man?

Before Elizabeth had turned up at Pemberley in August, he could wish away those doubts about any negative traits intrinsic to his personality, yet they were never far from the surface of his sensibilities. At times, he almost drowned in self-pity over the faults he attributed to himself. It had been a dark and lonely time despite all his efforts to improve himself and the positive responses of others.

He still yearned for Elizabeth, even knowing that it was near impossible he should ever see her again, or that she would welcome his attentions if he did. And he could not but expect that she might find a man better than him in her estimation. At least his letter would help steer her from any hopes in Wickham's direction if not turn her away from the blackguard forever. Yet she was vivacious and spirited, and she would attract many men. How many would lack his vanity and pride and treat her as she wished to be treated, with respect and love? Of course, those fears were dashed, at least for a time, by her presence at Pemberley.

Now that she had been to Pemberley, now that he had been able to walk with her on the grounds, take tea with her in his home, and show her who he was in essentials, he would never doubt his ability to please her again. His pride and conceit had grown out of hand for a short while, that was all.

Even so, the cruel reality lingered. She was gone, those closest to her doubted him for unkind actions he had little ability to disprove, and he had not the ability to speak with her to help clarify that awful day to her relations. How was he to go on living within Mr. Gardiner's ultimatum? Nevertheless, he had to do something to escape from the memories of her at Pemberley. Thus, as soon as his guests, the Bingleys and Hursts, made their way north, he decided to go to town, taking Georgiana along with the promise of a little autumn shopping diversion.

The carriage nodded along whilst the scenery changed from the rugged wildness of the Peaks to the rolling hills of the country to the south, and each time he looked out of the window, instead of seeing his reflection pasted over hedgerows and fields, he was haunted by her gentle grin, that one with eyes that—

"I should like to buy green gowns this time." His sister's soft voice broke through his thoughts.

"Pardon me?"

Georgiana was bright eyed in contrast to her companion, Mrs. Annesley, who was asleep with her lips apart. "Almost all my gowns are one shade or another of blue. Lady Matlock and Lady Catherine both seem to think it is best to match my eyes, but I am tired of blue gowns. I must appear boring, always wearing a sapphire-trimmed, lapis-sprigged, or cerulean silk gown or the like. I want green. Olive green. Pomona green." She was slightly forceful in her final statements. What had brought this on?

"You may have whatever colour gown you would like."

Miss Elizabeth Bennet had worn green the day she called on Georgiana at Pemberley. Perhaps that is where she got the idea. It was a lovely gown printed on a base colour he would call sea foam. The fashion papers probably had another name for it. Beryl? In any case, the delicate, pale blue-green tone made the fabric appear oh so soft. Oh, that he could have reached out and touched it.

"I want to pick my own patterns as well. They always pick patterns that make me look like some boring, bookish sort of girl. I shall not fit in with the other young ladies about to come out if I always have such ordinary gowns with self-trim and childish flounces. I want satin and lace, lots of lace, and a more abbreviated bodice."

Abbreviated bodice? That would not do. How had he entered into a conversation of this sort of detail with his sister? He must speak to his aunt about this. But he did not want to discourage her too much at the moment. "Yes, yes, lace is fine. As long as your gowns are appropriate, you may choose the designs for yourself."

"Thank you." Georgiana had her hands clasped, and she straightened her arms towards her knees and rolled her shoulders towards the front whilst she beamed.

Darcy paused to consider how forward his sister had been in asking for this choice. Most of the time, she was passive and seemed to accept the decisions of the elder ladies with whom she shopped. Had Elizabeth's strength of character worn off on her? Another reason to be thankful to the woman he admired. Georgiana had needed to realize that it was not always impolite to speak out one's opinions.

Lord knew he loved it when Elizabeth edged on impertinence with him! It was their arguments that first attracted him to her mind, and during a pause in one of those little skirmishes, he considered all her personal attributes, finding himself overwhelmed by his attraction to her individuality, both inside and out. She was as unusual in her cleverness as in her beauty, and they both suited him well. It was not long after a few more verbal challenges that he began to dream about her, to covet her in his less-than-wakeful hours, and to want her more than anything else. In those days, her fortune and family made him take pause when he was conscious enough to consider reality; however, daydreams forget negatives, and his obsession began. He could not turn away and took chances meeting up with her when others were not around.

He glanced over at his sister. She had been quiet for the last few minutes. It turned out that she had settled herself and closed her eyes for a rest, leaving him alone in his ruminations.

The carriage passed through the turnpike at Ware near Longbourn with the heat of the late summer sun beating down upon them, and he swore he could sense Elizabeth's presence. She would be at home with her family. Was she well? He was anxious for her health. Little knowledge of her situation had reached him since she had left Lambton. Before that, he had faced those horrible days when he had been allowed to know only bits regarding her condition. He was still certain they had been holding important information from him. What was the secret they would not share?

He checked himself; with Mr. Gardiner's banishment, he was supposed to be trying to forget her. Yet how could he cast her from his memory when he yearned to know her fate, longed to see her again even if it were just a passing glance? He released a puff of breath through his nose. He could barely stand to see her image in the window or in his memories without a great deal of pain and retrospection. How heart-rending would a true glance become?

Crowding carriages along the road and the smells of baked pies, smoke, dung, and cesspools indicated they were at the outskirts of London. Georgiana had now awakened; she had been sleeping with her head on Mrs. Annesley's shoulder for the last hour.

"I had a message sent to Mrs. Parsons last night; we shall have roast pheasant and fresh tomatoes for dinner as you requested," he told his sister.

Georgiana smiled brightly.

"And peach tart." He could almost taste the fresh fruit.

"Thank you!"

It was not long before said housekeeper and staff were greeting the Darcys at the door of their Portman Square home. He gazed about the neighbourhood. The park was rather pretty this time of year with the trees and flowers out in their fullest beauty just prior to their descent into autumn. Was

Elizabeth enjoying a similar view? Oh, that she could be here with him so he could share this moment with her and enjoy her effervescence once again.

As Georgiana stepped up beside him, he was reminded of their conversation in the carriage regarding gowns. Was he projecting Elizabeth's boldness onto his sister because he could not stop thinking about her and the good influence she would be on Georgiana? Or was it possible Georgiana's confidence was nothing more than her beginning to mature? In any case, he would rather have Elizabeth by his side while dealing with such matters!

Early November 1812
London

Through a thick rain, drops of water quickly accumulated, trickling in wavy rivulets down the glass and making it difficult to see out from the windows of Uncle Gardiner's carriage. However, the vehicle slowed in front of a haberdasher's long enough for Elizabeth to notice a figure step out in the cold downpour. The bearing and movement of the man could not be mistaken. Mr. Darcy! It was truly him. She had a powerful feeling in her breast upon the sight of him, one that tied her to him with a string so taut and strong, nothing could break it. He did not see her, though, or at least he made no show of recognition. A moment later, he was rushing through the heavy downpour towards a large carriage pointed in the opposite direction, towards Mayfair. He must be on his way home. As the carriage began to move, the sensation of being tied to him was pulled so tight, her heart threatened to crack.

How could she contrive to see him? Would he even want to see her? Why would a man go out of his way to pay court to a woman whose brother-in-law was his worst enemy? The embarrassment Lydia's situation had caused her family could not be overlooked, but his arrangement of the marriage proved he must still have feelings for her. No other explanation could exist for him to save her family's reputation when he was otherwise a disinterested party.

The tightness in her chest and throat threatened to overwhelm her. She blew out a breath of frustration and leaned her head against the cool glass of the carriage window whilst the busy city rushed by, indifferent to her qualms.

"Is aught amiss?" her uncle asked.

She raised her head. "No, sir. I am merely wool-gathering on what might have been."

Her uncle's face pinched into a pained expression. There was silence before he hesitantly responded to her vague statement. "What do you mean—'what might have been'?"

"Had Lydia not done what she did, that is all. I had some hopes…" Her throat closed.

The edges of his lips turned up, but the pain never left her uncle's eyes. "You must not dash your hopes in life, my dear; you must merely re-form them to suit your current situation. You are young. I am sure you will have a promising future if you can be patient until this all passes."

Ah yes. Her problems from the fall, Lydia's loss of credit within society, and her sisters' losses of marriage prospects as a result. Oh, why must they all repeatedly tell the same story as if she were a ninny? Of course, she had a blow on the head and had forgotten a few details. However, that was no reason for her aunt and uncle to tell tales and behave as though the events were horrific. It made no sense. She knew the truth, was settled with it, and it was not so bad. Lydia was married, after all.

She returned her gaze to the spot where she had seen Mr. Darcy. They were far away from it by now, and other shops rushed past the window of her uncle's carriage, just like the busy Londoners hurrying along the streets. Her aunt claimed Mr. Darcy had no knowledge of Lydia's behaviour and their family's embarrassment other than through gossip that might have reached his ears. What about Jane's letter? She had told him about it when he called on her, had she not? She must have. Why else would Mr. Darcy have paid Mr. Wickham to marry Lydia—saving her reputation, and by association, Elizabeth's?

Unfortunately, the events at Lambton were a haze in her mind, misted over like the glass of the carriage. Today was the first time she had seen him since Pemberley. Elizabeth had recognized no one when she woke from her ordeal, she was told. She was required to learn her family members' and friends' names again as well as many little details of her life. Slowly, her memories returned to her, but she was still recalling things to this day. But she always remembered Mr. Darcy. That dear, handsome face was as familiar to her as her own.

The memory of her accident, however, still remained locked away in her mind. And it had something to do with Mr. Darcy. Her aunt's eyes were always shadowed when she mentioned his name. It was not stated precisely, yet a strong implication was made every time she mentioned her visit to Pemberley: she must not speak of Mr. Darcy. It seemed to her that she was to avoid everybody who was not carefully vetted by her aunt and uncle in order to shield her from any shock associated with outsiders in her delicate state. Had she stayed at Longbourn, her social circle would not have been strict, which was exactly why she was sequestered here in London with the Gardiners.

This she remembered well: the taunting stares and rude shouts from townspeople, the shunning and throwing of rocks and tomatoes, the chuckles when she asked why they were tormenting her, the unabashed laughter when she corrected their false story about Lydia, the horrified looks on her sisters' faces the first time it happened, the endless lecturing from her family members on this belief that she was wrong.

The ordeal seemed almost formed to make her stand out and appear the fool. Elizabeth had become exhausted from reminding all and sundry of the truth and being ridiculed. Whenever she thought too hard trying to fill the gaps in her memory or to justify why she remembered the history any differently than did the others, she developed a sick headache with only dear Jane to tend to her. As a result, she quickly learnt that she must rest when a rush of new memories came into her mind. Letting the recollections come naturally over time rather than forcing them was the only way to prevent the debilitating headaches. She must accept what she knew now as the truth and take great care when questioning her reminiscences of Lambton in particular. Yet her righteous indignation rose at her family's wilful misunderstanding of Lydia's situation. Why would they allow such a falsehood to remain the topic for every vulgar gossip's discussion when they could tell them what really occurred? Why would they open themselves to such ridicule when the truth was a much less mortifying tale?

Of course, they would not think well enough of Mr. Darcy to believe he would be so generous. They resisted her explanations of his misplaced pride and good character. Wickham was surely a rake, but at least Lydia had been made respectable by marriage—could they not see that?

After her disputes with the village gossipers, her parents sent Elizabeth away. First Lydia, now Elizabeth—each cast out of Longbourn in shame.

London was a decidedly better place to be exiled than Newcastle, though, and at least she was not stuck with that scapegrace Mr. Wickham for a husband.

After a longer journey than usual due to the rain, the carriage turned down Gracechurch Street. Her uncle's house loomed in the dark shadows created by the storm in the middle of the day, and the carriage slowed to a stop in front of it. The home was a handsome edifice, tall and imposing, made of pink stone carved in an ornate yet tasteful style, the largest on a street full of stately homes owned by the new class of business people making their way among the elite of London.

She and her uncle set aside their rugs, and the footmen, undoubtedly soaked to the skin despite their oiled cloaks, held umbrellas over their heads as they alighted.

Inside the warm house, Elizabeth shed her outer garments and made her way to her room to change from her morning dress. Muffled voices reached her ears; her aunt and uncle were distressed anew, likely concerned she was once again thinking of the accident and its aftermath. They were always concerned about the delicacy of her senses now as if she were as fragile and nervous as her mother.

It must have been terrifying for them when they returned from their walk in Lambton to discover her unconscious and lying in Mr. Darcy's arms whilst he shouted out orders to the maid to fetch a surgeon. Apparently, she had been reading a letter from Jane when Mr. Darcy was announced, and in her haste to stand and move towards him, her chair tipped, and its noise made her unsteady on her feet. Or was she already standing when she darted to the door? She tripped on the table leg—or was it the chair? In any case, the chair was overturned, and she fell, striking her head upon the floor. At least, that is what they thought happened—what they said. No one knew for certain, and no one wanted to discuss with her what they did know.

She had been senseless for the best part of three days. Simply imagining it gave her chills. The surgeon had bled her repeatedly. A war veteran, he had even suggested boring a hole in her skull. The idea was so shocking to her aunt that the poor woman fainted dead away, and by the time any additional discussion had taken place, Elizabeth was muttering a few words and appeared ready to awake, her eyes moving beneath her closed lids. It was enough proof that she would recover and that no further drastic measures needed to be considered.

They said Mr. Darcy had called more than once daily to ask after her, yet he was not allowed to see her. She was sure he had come to the inn before her fall in order to make some sort of a declaration to improve their connection. At least, that is what she hoped after the fact. When a vision of him came to mind, he was usually saying those magical words, "my love," just as he had done at Lambton.

The journey from Lambton to Longbourn was not memorable, other than taking a long time, and her headache was terrible no matter what potions she took. Soon after their return, her aunt and uncle left her in the care of her closest family.

For two full weeks, she was forced to stay abed at Longbourn. She became severely weakened from the bed rest. At first, to keep up her strength and not wither away into a mere shell of herself, she took to walking back and forth within her room when no one was about. When that period was over, she was allowed to be wrapped up in blankets in a sitting room and to take callers. That painful time was used to help to restore her memories: names, events, places of her lifetime, all dashed from her head by that one fateful stumble back in Lambton.

Freedom was found in walks to Meryton and along the local paths, although by then, the falsehoods about her family had started to spread. She tried hard to correct them to no avail, which only encouraged more gossip about what her family and friends termed "her delusions." Her family resorted to sending her to the Gardiners' in London. Her life now consisted of teaching the girls, reading, and infrequent walks in the park with sufficient chaperonage to protect her from anyone who might mistreat her owing to her supposed mental infirmity.

Today's trip to the booksellers' had only been allowed because Uncle was not convinced of his ability to select material for her to read and enjoy.

Opening one of the books, a history, she flipped through it, enjoying the scent of leather, ink, and paper. How she looked forward to losing herself in its pages! Before she could, a call at her door made her drop the book to her lap as her heart leapt into her throat. It was nothing so shocking; her aunt wanted to speak with her, and she beckoned her aunt Gardiner to come in. Her aunt took a seat on a chair near Elizabeth's bedside and begged her to sit on the bed.

A permanent fretful expression was etched upon Aunt's face these days.

The Mist of Her Memory

"Uncle tells me you were concerned about your future today."

Elizabeth nodded. "My future, yes, but also the restrictions placed on me. I wish to walk more, see people other than our family, and discuss what happened to me. I do not want to be treated as a child or infirm. I wish to be myself again, and the exercise and sociability will assist in my recovery and lift my spirits."

"I see. Did something on the ride cause you to have these feelings, or are they long-standing?"

"They are of long duration, but…I saw Mr. Darcy on the pavement during our ride today. I wished to speak with him but knew Uncle would not allow it even if I asked."

Aunt's brows rose. "Did he see you? Did he try to speak with you?"

"No, I saw him from the carriage, but I do not believe he saw me. He was moving briskly from a shop to his own carriage."

Her aunt's expression relaxed again. "Your uncle and I have tried to keep you from any distress since you've been with us, but in doing so, we seem to have caused more. If you believe you're strong enough, we will attempt to tell you more about our time in Lambton." She paused for a moment as Elizabeth nodded eagerly for her to continue. "When we agreed to take you in here, your parents and Jane helped us understand the way your mind worked following the incident. Jane told me how you had argued with Mr. Darcy when he tried to impose an engagement upon you in Kent earlier this year. Do you recall this?"

"Of course. But he did not oblige my agreement in any way other than to assume I was of the same mind and had been anticipating his addresses."

"When you were recovering and asleep yet no longer fully insensible, you would shout out from your dreams: 'my letter,' 'Jane,' 'Mr. Wickham,' 'Lydia,' and 'Mr. Darcy.' Because we had read Jane's letter, we assumed you were agitated by its contents. The only item of your nocturnal exclamations that was not in that letter was Mr. Darcy. We realized that the contents of Jane's letter caused you a great deal of fear and agitation, and we believe that contributed to your unease and lack of equilibrium. It could be that Mr. Darcy caused a similar response in you."

"Agitation and fear? He has never made me feel such… What I mean to say is he was, at first, quite proud, and he made me feel scorn for him, and some of his past actions caused me to feel angry. Once I knew more, I was left full of regrets for my treatment of him. You saw how eager he was to gain your good opinion and mine, and what a good host he was at Pemberley. I remember warmth. Surely my view was more positive then."

Her aunt shook her head. "No matter how well you thought of his manners, we believe he must have tried to impose upon you in Lambton, and you were quite distressed over that and Jane's letter. Did you argue with him? Do you remember any of it?"

They had only argued in Kent, not in Lambton. "No, that is not right. He was not the reason for my apprehension, and I had no disagreement with him. As you know, he was very much the gentleman upon our visit in Derbyshire."

"We have discussed before what you remember of the conversations you had prior to the accident. There was so little, and it was all distressing to you, so I have not let you think too much upon that time. However, Mr. Darcy must have upset you dreadfully for you to recall him along with such an unpleasant letter."

"Could I not have thought he would save us from our shame? I am sure—"

"He did not know about the contents of Jane's letter. We considered that you were planning to ask him to help us, but with the delicacy of the situation, we decided against bringing him into it. We spirited you away early one morning before his call."

"But why? Why would you need to take me away from him?" If Mr. Darcy had been calling regularly, to suddenly find her and the Gardiners gone must have been a considerable disappointment. Elizabeth became excited and her voice rose whilst she spoke. "I did, I know I told him something before I fell ill. And the tea we attended the day before… Mr. Darcy was not such a stranger anymore." A brand-new revelation came to mind, not yet clear to her muddled memories. "Oh, Aunt, there is a matter of importance I need to relate, I just cannot remember it. There was another letter, not from Jane." Her fingers wrestled with each other; her body wanted to go seek the missive immediately but did not know where to begin looking for it. Who was it from? What would it reveal to her?

"Do not become distraught, my dear. This is why we have not discussed Lydia or the letter with you. It brings on memories distasteful to all of us. Let us forget Mr. Darcy, and you will no longer see him and have his face bring up bad memories."

"No, they were not all bad. That is why I try to sort through them. The last time I remember seeing Mr. Darcy before today was when he tried to call and I glimpsed a peek at him through a partially open door whilst we were preparing to leave Lambton. Why…Uncle was arguing with him. It must have been about the impropriety of him calling on me in my sickbed…" All of a sudden, a memory returned to her.

"It must have occurred during my absence from the room," Mr. Darcy's dear voice rang out, filled with distress. "When I arrived, I found her already upset about something, a letter, so I went to fetch her some wine."

Uncle's voice, on the other hand, resonated with fury. "Others heard shouting—"

"The shouts came from within the dining room. A distraction outdoors caused a rush to catch a glimpse of a fellow wanted by the locals for some unpleasant act he committed in Lambton. For that reason, I was delayed in returning to Miss Bennet with the glass of wine. I must have startled her when I entered, and I couldn't catch her before she fell to the floor."

"But how did she fall, Mr. Darcy?" Uncle asked with barely controlled anger.

"A chair was lying on its side, so she must have tripped. It is all I can imagine, sir. I took her in my arms and spoke to her, but she only mumbled incoherently. You arrived shortly thereafter, and I left her to you so I could fetch a doctor."

"I do not believe she tripped, and you cannot make me believe it was so. Her other injuries—a woman's elevated voice was heard—you must have terrified the poor girl with your attack!"

"Attack? I would never hurt her. Please, Mr. Gardiner, do not offend me with such unfounded and impossible accusations! I can at worst be accused of being self-centred when I first entered before realizing how terribly distraught she was. I blame myself for frightening her into the fall. I immediately tended to her, as her head had hit the floor with a great deal of force. She fell hard!"

Although his tone during the argument increased in volume to match Uncle's, Mr. Darcy had tears in his voice, which broke at the end of his speech.

She held her hands over her ears and squeezed her eyes shut to try to rid herself of the voices.

Chapter 4

Portman Square, London

Could a man's heart break worse than his had that day he had been banished? Until today, Darcy would have said no. He had seen her! It was truly her, not merely a vision conjured from the part of his memories he had avoided since that day. For a few precious moments, he stood stunned in the unrelenting rain, rooted to the spot, ignoring the umbrella being pushed towards him by a footman. He stared at her in the idle carriage, stopped along with all the vehicles on the street slowed by the rain.

She was peering into a book. So natural of her, her nose in a book of any sort, the more intellectual, the better—and she proclaimed herself to be not such a great reader. Though her face was indistinct due to the water streaming down the windows, he could still make out her dark lashes upon her cheeks. The moment they fluttered upwards to look out the window, he had to glance away. Under no circumstances could he allow his eyes to meet hers; the ache in his breast was too intense already. If she regarded him with any sort of longing gaze, the sight would destroy him, he was sure of it. So he forced his eyes downward and moved as swiftly as he could to the shelter of his own carriage. A rug was available to warm the cold from his veins, but nothing could fill the vast, empty space within the equipage. He was alone, and she was not with him.

How much did she know? How much did she remember of that fateful day and the days that followed?

Before she had fallen ill, he had been trying so hard to show her he had changed. The memory of his proposal and their argument at Hunsford last April still caused his skin to heat with shame. She likely did not look upon the remembrance of that day with any sort of pleasure either. The conduct of neither, if strictly examined, was irreproachable.

She had read his letter—at least, she had hinted at aspects within it as they walked and talked that day at Pemberley, that blessed day she visited with her relations. He had corrected her regarding Wickham's ignominy, but what of the other complaint she had lain at his door? He had indeed had a part in separating her sister from Bingley, and he could potentially have a part in their reunion—that is, if it were in the best interests of all parties. Had the feelings of that couple endured their separation? After all, it had been nearly a year since they had last been together at the Netherfield ball.

However much that bothered him, the situation at Lambton increased Darcy's ever-present unease enough to make him sick to his stomach at times. He tried to let go of the demons that followed him, but his efforts proved fruitless. Could Elizabeth have grown to love him? If so, how was he to reconcile their attachment with the need to keep distance from her? It was too much for his sensibilities.

Only two days ago, he had gone riding with his cousin Colonel Richard Fitzwilliam, and his frustration caused him to urge his animal to burst forward, racing at a breakneck gallop through the crowds in Hyde Park. He dodged more than one carriage until he was forced to pull his horse to a quick stop. Darcy had been lucky to avoid trampling anyone. He turned back and sought out Richard—who was some distance behind at a more sedate canter to save the pedestrians a certain accident.

"So what is behind your attempting to exorcise demons on a wild horse ride?" Richard asked later as they sipped a well-aged tawny port in Darcy's library. "You might have killed your poor horse if you had continued to push him at such a pace. He was lathered in sweat and foaming at the bit when you returned."

He gazed at the glass before him as he clutched the bowl tightly. "It is nothing of importance."

"I beg to differ," said the colonel. "You have been nothing but cautious all your life, yet today you acted as if you were some sort of rumbustious young Corinthian."

"I do not know what you mean."

"Racing your horse so fast you were certain to mow down those out for a gentle amble in the park. Some state of affairs is bothering you to the extent you have forgotten yourself."

Darcy cleared his throat and tossed back a large swallow of the full-flavoured liquid from his glass. "I did not forget myself. I was merely taking exercise—"

"At the risk of several gentle couples! Tell me, has Wickham been around again? Has Georgiana been importuned? Have you been importuned? What is it, man?"

His cousin's conjectures were worse than what caused the turmoil of his mind; however, that specific knowledge did not lessen the ache in his heart. "Is my misery so obvious?"

Richard nodded.

Without a doubt, his suffering showed on his face. "I am frustrated and have allowed a bit of hurt to my pride. You see, I have been accused of harming a woman."

The colonel's fingers whitened as he tightened his grip on the arm of his chair. "Damn, Darcy! By whom? Am I to prepare to be your second?"

"No, I did not call him out. He is an honest man—rather kind—simply misinformed and protective of his niece."

Richard scowled. "Do I know this fellow?"

"No, he is an acquaintance of mere months."

"Not a close acquaintance if he believes you could hurt a woman. Why would he think you capable of such a heinous act?"

Why indeed? If only her uncle had viewed the situation in the same manner! "She had an accident and, whilst nearly insensible, spoke of an argument between the two of us. This led to the assumption that I contributed to her injuries."

The colonel's eyes opened wide as he leaned forward, obviously acutely affected by Darcy's revelation. "Good G-d, that is terrible!"

Darcy shook his head and blew out a heavy breath. "The uncle is unaware that our disagreement occurred some four months earlier and that we mended our differences. After her injury, the lady herself was unconscious and therefore not in a position to clarify; thus, I became vilified for the action of another man."

"Do you have any idea who attacked her?"

"Not at all. I found her…" The memory made him choke on bile once again. Rather than hurl his glass into the fireplace, he cleansed his throat by finishing his drink before he could describe Elizabeth's state at that horrible moment. "I found her as she was falling towards the floor, but I was not quite in time to catch her. At first, I thought she had merely tripped over a chair and obtained a cut on her face. She uttered my name, waved a letter, mentioned her sister, and then collapsed. Her uncle claimed her injuries were not accidental and blamed me for them."

The colonel leaned back into his chair and contemplated his lap for a moment before he spoke once again. "The old disagreement you spoke of… for you to have a row with a lady implies a close acquaintance."

Darcy's face heated as his warm feelings burst forth in his heart, emotions he could not disclose. Nevertheless, the question reminded him of all he had lost, and all he, as a gentleman, needed to hide. "She is well known to me."

"What I mean is, you must care for this lady to allow yourself to be so open as to argue with her."

Darcy pressed his lips together. No matter how vigorously Richard pushed, he would not reveal such intimate knowledge even though the colonel took his time with a sip of his port to allow a revelation of Darcy's ties to Elizabeth.

Richard sighed and leaned forward, his elbows on his knees. Apparently, he had decided to take the hint, and he would not pressure Darcy on this point. "What caused you to differ with this lady?"

"I am afraid it was Wickham's smooth ingratiation with her as well as an interest of Bingley's."

Richard's brows lifted as he frowned. "One could not imagine two more opposing topics for an argument. How did you come to be discussing both?"

"They were separate arguments. I enlightened her on the truth of Wickham's nature after the fact. On the second issue, I was never able to resolve a problem to her satisfaction, and she received a letter immediately before her accident that left her distraught though I never learnt the sender or its contents. I can only suppose that this recent correspondence stirred her ire against me and she mentioned it to her family; otherwise, I know not what else to think. Yet she did not seem angry with me, merely distraught about another matter. I cannot make sense of any of it."

The colonel's expression hardened. "I hope it was not related to that business from last year."

Of course, Wickham's attempted elopement with Georgiana the previous summer would come to Richard's mind. "No, that was not part of the problem at this time though I did mention it without disclosing the particulars."

"Estate business?" He started at Georgiana's girlish voice. How long had she been standing in the doorway in her pretty green gown? Richard's fidgeting indicated he wondered as well.

"If only all men's troubles were that simple," said Richard, neatly avoiding further discussion.

Darcy followed his cousin's lead. "This is true."

Richard finished the dregs of his goblet and rose. "I must leave you to your brother, Georgiana. Please be patient with him, for he is in a state of agitation today and will require your good humour." He levelled a hard look at Darcy whilst he put on his gloves. "Darcy, this is not over. I want to talk more on the subject."

"Of course." However much he agreed, he was determined to avoid the topic altogether from now on, but his hope would likely not match Richard's doggedness.

They exchanged bows, and his cousin left.

His sister took the chair Richard vacated and stared at her brother in such a way that he had difficulty holding her eye. "You have something on your mind?" she asked.

"I am trying to understand the hearts of women."

She smiled in a demure fashion. "Of one in particular?"

Could he have a discussion with her and not reveal his deepest secrets? He could, but only with regard to a woman in a different situation that had been troubling him—Miss Jane Bennet and his friend Bingley.

"There is, but not in the way you imagine. Let me put it to you as a potential situation." Darcy paused. How could he approach the story he wished to tell her without divulging it all? "A young couple were in each other's company a great deal for about two months' time. The gentleman is a friend of yours, and you know he falls in and out of love easily. Nevertheless, he appeared to be well on his way to an attachment with this lady. In contrast, you yourself had not observed any partiality on the part of the lady. Another lady, an acquaintance who had also witnessed their time together, told you that the lady in question, a close friend of hers, had tender feelings for the gentleman. What would you do? Would you believe that lady acquaintance, or would you make an effort to observe the two together to see for yourself?"

"Is this Mr. Bingley? Who is the lady? When did this take place? Recently?"

Darcy chuckled. "But how...ah, do not try to trick me with your suppositions! You ask too many questions, and I cannot divulge the names of the individuals. I merely seek a young lady's perspective on love." She flushed, and immediately he cringed at his mistake. Her only experience of love was with that villain Wickham, and she had seen such disappointment.

Nevertheless, she responded, "I should believe the lady who says her friend is in love. Ladies observe much more than gentlemen do, and if they were close friends, she probably would have shared more of her heart's desire than she would ever show in public. We are taught not to show our partiality lest we be seen as less than ladylike. Depending on her situation, she may also not want to appear as if she were seeking Mr. Bingley's fortune." She clasped her hands together. "I do hope it is Mr. Bingley and he loves her too."

He was taken aback by the maturity and thought in Georgiana's speech. "Ladies observe more than gentlemen do?"

"You forget, Brother, we are taught to be passive rather than active. You have your sport; we have our needlework and painting. Neither takes one's full attention, and we learn to watch others for their expressions and movements to understand their feelings. Are the ladies close?"

"The best of friends," he said.

"Then it is likely they would share confidences as well."

Since he had little knowledge of sisterly interaction, her comment showed insight that had not occurred to him. With whom did Georgiana share confidences? She had no close friends. As far as he was aware, no young ladies had ever spent any great deal of time with her since she had been taken out of school. Perhaps that is why she had been manipulated so easily by her former companion, Mrs. Younge; the older lady acted as a confidante, putting her in a better position to convince Georgiana to be receptive to Wickham's overtures.

At least they were fortunate that the scapegrace was no longer in their life. Wickham was probably in Meryton again for the winter. Hopefully, the knave was being soaked to the skin through his red coat by this bitter rain.

"Do I know her?" asked Georgiana.

"Whom?"

"The lady Mr. Bingley admires. Do I know her?"

"No, she is not someone who frequents superior society." His fingers had been tracing the carving at the end of the chair arm, and he stilled the nervous movement. "I suppose I should pen a letter to Bingley."

Two weeks later
London

DARCY ACCOMPANIED BINGLEY TO HIS CARRIAGE. THE YOUNGER MAN, UPON learning the news that Miss Bennet held him in some regard, had come to London forthwith to extend his lease for Netherfield Park. He now prepared to depart for Hertfordshire again.

"I regret that a pressing matter prevents me from accompanying you, but I am certain my assistance is unnecessary," said Darcy. The pressing matter was his agreement with Mr. Gardiner, but that need not be mentioned.

"You are certain I should go to her?"

"Unless you no longer hold tender feelings for the lady."

"Of course I still love her! She is an angel!"

"Then your responsibility is obvious given the attentions you paid her last autumn."

"I am not quite sure what you imply." He blinked a few times. "Are you saying I should make her an offer?"

"Good Lord, yes! What do you think I meant?"

"I do not know." Bingley's eyes flicked from side to side as he appeared to consider the situation. Darcy could not believe the inanity of his friend in his hesitation if he was truly committed to Miss Bennet, but Bingley could vacillate for an age, relying on his sisters and Darcy to make decisions. This time, Darcy was not going to interfere any more than he already had. Finally, after a few moments of irritating quiet, Bingley added, "And I have your blessing?"

"The decision is yours and yours alone, but if you wish to take Miss Bennet as your wife, then, yes, I fully support your choice."

A smile burst forth on Bingley's face, and he seized Darcy's hand and pumped it. Elizabeth would be pleased. If only he could speak to her to know the truth of his own situation. However, Mr. Gardiner had vehemently warned him off, which was why he would not be travelling to Longbourn this week. He was not self-righteous enough to be spared any sensation of guilt, however, and spent a great deal of his time wallowing in it as well as a fair dose of self-pity.

A few days later, Darcy received a quick note that crowed of Bingley's engagement to his "dearest love" and requested a meeting to discuss the current situation of the Bennet family without any detail as to the latter. What could he possibly wish to discuss? Perhaps Bingley would bring news of Elizabeth. Was she still in London? It had been three weeks since he had seen her in that carriage, and it stood to reason she would still be here.

No, it was folly to think any connection could come of Bingley's news. Mr. Gardiner was much too clear with his scathing accusations. The news regarding the Bennets was probably something of a more ordinary sort. He should be grateful Bingley did not attempt to pen it in the letter as it would just mean more blobs, smudges, and gaps to sort through to understand the poor penmanship of his good friend.

Chapter 5

Early November 1812
Gracechurch Street, London

Elizabeth's heart beat wildly out of control as she panted for a breath that never fully filled her lungs. For once, there was clarity, yet why did it frighten her so? The shouting voices belonged to Mr. Darcy and her uncle! She opened her eyes to the shocked face of her aunt.

"Oh, Elizabeth! I am so sorry I told you about what happened in Lambton!" Aunt Gardiner said.

The voices faded, and Elizabeth's breathing returned to its usual pace. "I am well. Do not become agitated on my behalf," she said. "At least I know more of my history now."

Aunt ran the backs of her fingers over Elizabeth's brow. "All the same, I suggest you have a rest and think about Mrs. Bastion's visit and her ability to help you. I shall have some headache powders sent up just in case. Is that all right?"

Elizabeth agreed and went to her room. As might be predicted, the dull ache began to grow in her head, accompanied by some nausea. She decided to take the powders. They would give her an opportunity to think.

She had not told Aunt she remembered the argument, which meant it could be her secret. Perhaps one day she could even convince her aunt to allow her to visit the Darcys so she could apologise—once she dared broach the subject with her aunt and uncle again. She missed the society of acquaintances other than her aunt and uncle and their children. Having

The Mist of Her Memory

something in the future to look forward to provided such a comfort.

In two days, she anticipated a different sort of visit. Mrs. Bastion was one of the few people she had been allowed to meet during her time with the Gardiners. The lady had a son who had been injured in the war, including a terrific blow to the head that caused him an even longer period of amnesia than Elizabeth had. She had listened and learned from the excellent physicians from whom her son was fortunate to receive treatment, and therefore, she knew a great deal about the brain and the vagaries of recovery. Uncle had heard about Mrs. Bastion through a business associate and had arranged for her to visit once a week to talk to Elizabeth. Elizabeth welcomed Mrs. Bastion's knowledge and her sympathetic ear as she tried to make sense of her own memories.

The first time they had met, just a fortnight ago, Mrs. Bastion had encouraged her to describe all she had forgotten from before the accident and later recalled. Interruptions in her memory were noted whenever she became aware of them, but she often found herself agitated beyond sensibility when she could not recount events. Even so, little things in life brought back new recollections, particularly when her senses were overcome with some sight or smell.

On some occasions, her aunt joined them on their long walks in the park near Gracechurch Street. Mrs. Bastion also encouraged Aunt to help by filling in small details as long as they helped to prompt memories and not serve to replace Elizabeth's natural recollections. The last time they had been together, Elizabeth had recalled the previous autumn when many new characters had come to Longbourn.

The week before

"THERE WAS AN OFFICER IN THE ——SHIRE MILITIA NEAR MERYTON WHO deceived us as to his character—he was not at all a good man. He told a story I later found to be false in which he maligned a gentleman who was his better," Elizabeth had said as they walked among the skeleton-like trees with the last of the autumn leaves clinging to them.

"Dear, are you sure it did not happen the other way around?" her aunt asked gently. "You and I had some conversations at Christmas about the officer…"

Elizabeth stopped and spent some time looking into the space around her, not truly seeing it as she struggled to sort the memories rushing into her brain. Several stories that had been mixed together seemed to separate and become individual pieces of thought, almost as if the events became lists of activities she was indifferent to rather than situations in which she had taken an active part. Some days, she wanted to howl in vexation as the depths of her exasperation overwhelmed her, but other days—like today—the satisfying thrill of discovering lost memories elated her.

"No, it did not. I believed the officer at first because he was charming and the other man had given offence to all of us in Meryton. I even challenged the gentleman on more than one occasion about his role in the story. But when I read his lett—"

Her face went hot. She had a letter from Mr. Darcy from Hunsford! How could she have forgotten something so important, so full of truths about Mr. Wickham, and so helpful in her improved view of Mr. Darcy? Yet she could not allow anyone to know about that letter. Without an understanding between herself and Mr. Darcy, it amounted to an inappropriate communication, and her acceptance of it rendered her complicit in what could cause her ruin. No, Elizabeth could not share this part of her past. If she did, she would divulge extremely private situations, embarrassing to both.

"My apologies," she said. "However, when the truth was before me, I became annoyed over my foolishness in believing the officer. After all, I truly did not know him well. Later, I discovered the officer had twisted his story, disguised the truth, and left out some rather heinous acts he was responsible for. None of us really knew him, and we all believed him a better man than he was."

A distorted face darted towards hers, red and angry with fierce-looking teeth in a twisted mouth. Spittle flew from that mouth as it shouted in indignation: "Stupid cow!"

She shook her head to shed the ugly, blurred image.

"Are you well, Lizzy?" Aunt Gardiner asked.

"I am fine. Just a bit of a dizzy spell." The excuse was a lie, of course. She had no dizziness, but—oh!—the bitterness that filled her mouth would be more difficult to disperse. This voice made no sense, yet it was frightening.

Mrs. Bastion took her arm. "I am sorry. We have bothered you too much for one day. It is best if the reminiscences come on their own so they do not overwhelm you all at once. Let us return."

The Mist of Her Memory

A week later

DRESSED IN A PRETTY PELISSE AND HER NEWEST BONNET, SHE WAITED BY the door. At length, her guest arrived, and Elizabeth eagerly rushed forward to grasp the gloved hands of her new friend.

"You seem particularly animated today," Mrs. Bastion said with a laugh.

"I am pleased to see you."

Since the day was sunny, Aunt Gardiner and her children joined the ladies on their walk in the park. Once she had asked after Elizabeth's spirits, Mrs. Bastion suggested she speak of more recent events, no doubt to avoid the unpleasantness of their last encounter. Proud that she had no trouble describing activities that had taken place during the last week, Elizabeth was about to mention her trip to the bookshop when little Andrew pulled on his mother's sleeve.

"Mama! Ducks!"

"Do you mind if we go to the pond?" asked Aunt Gardiner. "I am sure you can do well enough without me."

"We shall stay on the path whilst we chat," Mrs. Bastion said.

Elizabeth's aunt agreed and left the two of them as she and the children proceeded to the water's edge with their bag of breadcrumbs.

After a few moments of laughing at the children feeding the ducks, Mrs. Bastion asked whether Elizabeth had anything new to say. More thoughts poured into Elizabeth's head, and rather than hold them in, she allowed herself the comfort of telling Mrs. Bastion whilst they ambled slowly along the path, their breath making mist in the cool air.

"I saw someone I knew this week—the day it rained."

"Someone who came to call?"

"No, I saw him in passing whilst we were in the carriage. The gentleman I knew in Lambton." Elizabeth had not expressed her hopes to Mrs. Bastion, and all the lady knew about Mr. Darcy was that he had been present when she had fallen and that he had called the surgeon. For some reason, Elizabeth had been unable to share more of that painful part of her past; those issues were especially private.

"Ah yes. Tell me, did you know who he was upon sight, or did your uncle point him out?" Mrs. Bastion was clearly attempting to understand which of Elizabeth's memories were natural and which had been dictated to her. She always preferred Elizabeth's point of view over the stories Elizabeth had been told. That alone had persuaded Elizabeth to like her during these visits.

"I recognized him myself." She hesitated, then burst out, "I must tell you some important memories I have of him."

"And you are not afraid that these memories will hurt you rather than help you?"

She shook her head, confident of Mr. Darcy's character in essentials; thoughts of him only brought her happiness and warmth. "On the contrary, now that I have seen him, my thoughts are clearer than ever before, and I am not afraid of him. I believe it strengthens me to know exactly the course of events related to my history with him, his care for me when I fell, and his rescue of our family afterward."

"He cared for you?"

"When he arrived, I was terribly upset about Jane's letter. He went out into the saloon, which was in an uproar, to procure me a glass of wine. I fell just as he returned, and he lifted me in his arms and called to me until I succumbed to my injuries and fell into a faint. I remember little of the next few days with the exception of the times I heard his dear voice."

"His 'dear voice,' is it? How is it so familiar? Did you have an understanding?"

"No, but I believe that was the reason he came to call so early. He started to speak of declaring himself when he realized I was unwell."

"How could he broach such a subject? Tell me the words he used."

"I do not remember the exact words. I remember that he spoke about last April, and if my feelings were still as they were when we had argued."

"What about when you were ill? You said you heard the gentleman's voice, yet he never would have been allowed to visit you. Do you think you heard his real voice or a dream caused by your injury?"

"I think he had called to see whether I had improved and was allowed to speak to me to help revive me. 'Tis the only explanation I have for hearing his voice, which was full of concern. He offered all he could. His surgeon tended to me, you know, and we had been placed in the best rooms the inn had on offer—all of it his doing."

"Not your uncle?"

She glanced over to Mrs. Bastion, whose head tilted with an air of curiosity. "No, I heard Uncle thanking him before—" She broke off and continued in a whisper almost too soft to be heard. "Some time before, he fought with Uncle Gardiner." She looked downward so Mrs. Bastion would not see the tears in her eyes, but the waver in her voice must have alerted her friend. Mrs. Bastion came to a standstill and took one of Elizabeth's hands in hers while she lifted her chin.

She searched Elizabeth's face. "You are agitated, my dear. Let us take a seat whilst you tell your tale."

Mrs. Bastion led her to an ornate metal bench near a copse of oak trees. Elizabeth stumbled and nearly burst into tears. Mrs. Bastion brushed away some damp leaves from the bench and they finally sat.

"Breathe deeply. There, there, Miss Bennet. It is never easy to remember all. Some thoughts are less pleasant. Were you recalling the cause of your injury?"

Elizabeth shook her head.

"Then what has upset you so? Relate it to me. Speaking out loud will help take the pain out of your mind."

"My uncle and the gentleman had a loud argument after I regained my senses. The door was ajar, and I heard all they said." And there was more than she had recalled before. "They were arguing over me, and Uncle refused to let him see me—ever again!" Their voices became fresh in her head as if they were occurring just at that moment. Her lips quivered and her chest ached. She was so close to crying! "I am sorry. Perhaps it is best to talk of a different time."

Mrs. Bastion's gentle hand brushed her brow. "If you like, though you will have to return to the unpleasant recollections some time. You will find it easier when you are supported and have another person to remind you that these memories reside in the past and that you are now safe."

"It is reasonable that I become disheartened when the mist of my memory prevents me from seeing things clearly. However, these vague recollections also allow me hope for better and clearer ones to come. I thank you, but for now, I should like to remove that gloomy prospect from my thoughts and think on experiences that are pristine and encouraging." She did not add that this was the best alternative to the abundance of emotional discomfort she was experiencing this moment.

Mrs. Bastion smiled and nodded. "Now, you mentioned that the gentleman saved your family? What was that about?"

Elizabeth could not help but smile. She was grateful to narrate the history of Mr. Darcy's generous service to her family after Lydia's foolish fall from grace. She recalled the story well.

Lydia had been allowed to go to Brighton with her particular friend, Colonel Forster's young wife, even though Elizabeth had advised her father that Lydia, a hopeless flirt, could readily embarrass herself and her family if not checked. Her family's ill manners had already affected Mr. Darcy's good opinion of the Bennets, but her father teased her about losing suitors due to Lydia's poor behaviour and still waved Lydia off with the Forsters.

While Elizabeth had recently learned that Mr. Wickham was a seducer and fortune hunter, she was hesitant to share her knowledge of Mr. Wickham's perfidy with her family. She and Jane agreed it unlikely that he would importune someone without fortune, and they did not want to blacken his name in Meryton for little reason. In light of the events that occurred, Elizabeth blamed herself for keeping quiet.

"You see, the gentleman in Lambton and I bear some resemblance to one another—taking responsibility for others' recklessness. And what fools they were, running off to elope with no funds. The officer wanted to marry for fortune, and Lydia did not care one whit; therefore, the gentleman solved the entire problem."

"Is this the sister your aunt mentioned? The one who has never been found?"

"They insist upon another story, yet I know they married and were sent to Newcastle. The gentleman I mentioned paid for it all: the officer's debts in Brighton, a position with the regulars, even the marriage settlement—which was really a bribe to marry such a girl."

With a slight frown and downturned brows, Mrs. Bastion chewed on her lower lip. *She does not believe me either!* This woman was supposed to understand what happened to those who had been hurt in the head; instead, she thought—much like the others—that Elizabeth laboured under the spell of a false story brought on by her accident.

"This history is above the expected for a man not associated with your family," Mrs. Bastion finally replied. "No wonder you sustain such respect for this gentleman."

Oh! Perhaps Mrs. Bastion was not averse to the truth of the matter after all. "So do you understand that it is reasonable to believe he planned to declare himself again in Lambton? Yet now…how could he be the brother-in-law of such a man? This is why I have not seen him since, though I would dearly like a chance to thank him on behalf of my family for all he has done for us. He helped them marry and paid for it all."

"In a certain light, it does make sense."

"Except that it is not true." Aunt Gardiner had come back with the children. "None of that story is true, Lizzy. I am sorry, Mrs. Bastion, but we have gone over this time and again."

But it was not time and again! She had tried not to mention the truth in order to avoid raising arguments!

Mrs. Bastion said, "Are you certain? Memories do come back in bits and mixed around, but Miss Bennet seems a good reporter of the history."

"Except that instead of Lydia and Wickham being forced to marry, we never found them." Her aunt's tone was apologetic as she spoke directly to Mrs. Bastion, glancing occasionally at Elizabeth. Tears pooled in her aunt's eyes; they appeared frustrated and hurt during those glances. "They were traced as far as Clapham and never seen again. They could both be dead for all we know, but over this length of time, with no wedding, Lydia is nothing better than a fallen woman. The people in Meryton mock the Bennet family for that reason. Elizabeth insists that her happy story is true, but there is no evidence to suggest it is so. No white knight has saved our family."

Aunt Gardiner's indignation continued. "That so-called gentleman contributed nothing except pain to this family. He hurt Lizzy and pretended to be her saviour, but we know better. *That* is the real story."

Chapter 6

December 1812
London

Bingley had just returned from his successful visit to Netherfield, and Darcy was about to leave for Pemberley, but they managed to find an opportunity to speak at Darcy's home in town. Once they settled themselves, Darcy asked after the Bennets as an excuse to eventually shift into a discussion regarding Elizabeth. Darcy was keen to know how she fared. Had she fully recovered? His unease over her gnawed at his heart, especially with the upcoming wedding. At first, all Bingley could do was express the virtues of his intended. When Darcy insisted on knowing about the rest of the family, Bingley's face immediately clouded over, and Darcy's insides clenched.

"When I first arrived, some sort of difficulty was clearly taking place within the household. Neither Miss Lydia nor Miss Elizabeth was present, and Mrs. Bennet was strangely mute. I must say, Darcy, it was odd—very odd. I have never known Longbourn to be quiet, yet you could hear a pin drop on a carpet. I was astounded to learn that Miss Lydia had left her family and eloped with Mr. Wickham in August."

Good G-d! "Wickham!"

"Yes, and there is more. Miss Lydia was never recovered," Bingley's voice cracked as he spoke. He was deeply unsettled. "They were traced as far as Clapham, and no one has found anything of them since. Mr. Wickham's friend Mr. Denny offered some connections in London, but none had seen the man, and many of them were looking for him as well in order to be recompensed for debts."

His heart had leapt into his throat by this time even though his knowledge of Wickham should not have made it such a surprise. "As you are aware, Wickham has an affinity for shaking his elbow. His gaming away more than he could afford is no surprise to me." Wickham always did acquire more debts than he could afford. It also was likely he… Darcy cringed. "I suppose they are not yet married." With Darcy's awareness of the man's tendencies, the answer was obvious, yet for some reason he needed to hear it.

"It is doubtful they ever married. No announcement ever appeared in correspondence, much less in the papers. Mr. Denny believes Wickham's main reason for running off was to escape debts of honour with his fellow militiamen."

"If he and Miss Lydia went to London, it would not be difficult to vanish. I should expect Wickham to insist Mr. Bennet cover his debts and pay him a significant sum to encourage the marriage."

"You do not know Mr. Bennet well," said Bingley. "He would laugh it off and tell Wickham he lacked spare change for disreputable young men. Her marriage portion is too small to entice a fortune hunter; thus, as I said, I doubt Wickham has married the girl."

Darcy pursed his lips as he nodded. "I would say they absconded into the bowels of the city."

"A deserter running from debts of honour with a sixteen-year-old girl in tow. That cannot be a good situation."

"No indeed." Darcy shook his head. He was sympathetic to the young lady, but a curiosity near and dear to his heart came to mind immediately. Elizabeth had not been herself in Lambton, and Bingley had mentioned he had not seen her at Longbourn. He closed his eyes as he struggled to find the words. "But what of Miss Elizabeth? What happened to her?"

Bingley shook his head. His body fell from its usual composed stature, and he dropped his eyes to the floor and pursed his lips. Such a downcast appearance was not in his disposition. This troubled Darcy. What did it mean? "I know little of her situation. I am afraid Jane became strangely protective whenever her name was mentioned. Perhaps I can discover more when I am once again in Hertfordshire."

"Of course."

Bingley continued, "Oh, and Darcy? Will you stand up with me?"

Could he safely accompany Bingley without earning ire from Mr. Gardiner for coming in such close proximity to Elizabeth? Gardiner had not divulged Darcy's banishment to the family if Bingley was asking this of him. He wanted to be of service to Bingley, particularly since, at one time, he had been the means of separating him from Miss Bennet. It was worth the risk, but he needed to know more—much more!

"Of course, old boy. So Miss Elizabeth? Where is she now?"

"She is on a trip with her Aunt and Uncle Gardiner—you remember, the ones we met at Pemberley. Miss Catherine mentioned they were now on the continent. When I questioned the danger, Mr. Bennet spoke up. Even though they travel in areas well protected from Bonaparte's armies, communications are slow, and I am told a letter could not have reached them in time for them to prepare to return swiftly and safely for the wedding. Jane is quite upset as you can imagine."

His heart hurt knowing she was now so far away that he could not see her. Yet something in him said the tale was wrong—that he would know if she was far away. "A pity. They were close, she and Miss Bennet."

"The best of friends. I am sorry. I wish I knew more. I suspect that an affair of some importance is being hidden. Jane shows a great deal of unease whenever Miss Elizabeth is mentioned; therefore, I do not push the matter. She would attend our nuptials for Jane if she could, but she cannot be present. Miss Mary will stand up with Jane."

Yes, the affair of importance would probably be that Miss Bennet did not want Bingley to know that Elizabeth was still not recovered from her fall. As much as he wanted to see her, Darcy had to respect Gardiner's edict to stay away from her.

Besides, they were no longer in England and would not be for some time. Perhaps Gardiner had arranged things that way.

Boxing Day 1812
Lambton, Derbyshire

"Best o' the season to you as well, Mr. and Miss Darcy," the innkeeper's wife said as she led them into the modest parlour of their residence. She offered tea, which was gratefully accepted to stave off the deep chill of the day. A short period of pleasant conversation ensued that allowed Darcy to learn more about the community and confirm which families had the greatest need. They had done well in their choices of contents within the Boxing Day baskets.

As he was readying himself to make their excuses—they had many homes to visit that day—Mrs. White asked a question that stunned him for a moment. "Beggin' your pardon, sir, but have you seen the old steward's boy, George Wickham, lately?"

Darcy sat with his mouth agape. When he recovered from the shock, he glanced over to Georgiana. Her eyes were wide, and her face matched the innkeepers' surname. Wickham's name still had a dreadful effect on her though more than a year had passed since their intended elopement to Gretna Green.

Darcy reclaimed his calm enough to say, "No, we have not. When was it you last saw him?"

"It be a long time, sir. Word had it 'e was sniffin' around Lambton last August," Mr. White said. "But I'm no' convinced it were 'im."

His wife added, "There were a rumpus the same day that young lady from Hertfordshire were hurt, but we never saw 'im ourselves, so we let it be. Hobson be the man who saw a fella what looked like 'im, but 'e were 'alf in his cups that morning already, as is 'is habit. Excuse me, Miss Darcy."

Darcy was shaken to his core, and though he had closed his mouth, his hand trembled as he placed his cup on the little table. Then Mr. White said what Darcy was thinking.

"I don't know, but it coulda been 'im what pushed that lady down."

Darcy ground his teeth. Yes, it could have been. But why would Wickham hurt Elizabeth? She had always taken his part—unless she had challenged him with the facts from Darcy's letter at Hunsford. It had told the truth about the living Wickham claimed Darcy denied him and had revealed how Wickham tried to elope with Georgiana for purposes of gaining access to her generous fortune. In short, Elizabeth was well aware of his true nature, and she would be wary.

Yet Wickham had importuned too many residents of Lambton and could scarce show his face there. Darcy expressed his doubt. "Even if it were him, that was months ago. I think he would carry on to some place where fewer people would know him."

A cynical bark of laughter came from the old man. "You mean where 'e is

49

able to get money from the locals more easily than Lambton. But were that true! Oh, sir, we have heard more. Word has it, 'e were spotted in this area off an' on for nigh on a month now, an' those sayin' so be reliable sorts. I know of no new debts, though, so your purse can rest easily in your pocket for the time bein'."

"He is known to cause more trouble than debts," Darcy replied softly as he rubbed his chin. If he only knew what Wickham had been up to!

"Nothing bad in any regard has been reported. Just people seein' 'is face here an' there in this part of the country. Cobbler says Wickham been down near Matlock since Michaelmas until these past weeks. No one knows where he been livin' if 'e be near Lambton, though."

The weather had been dreadfully cold and the snow deep. A fire would be needed for warmth; thus, smoke from a disused outbuilding, if that was where Wickham was hiding, should have been noted more often. Tracks should have been seen for the gathering of wood. It was odd indeed that he had been seen but his abode had not been discovered.

"I will make some inquiries around Pemberley. Thank you for the warning. Good day, Mr. and Mrs. White. Happy Christmas." He made ready to leave, but Georgiana stumbled over her curtsey. Damn Wickham! His sister had been making perfect curtseys since she was a small child. For her to lose her equilibrium meant she was severely unnerved.

"Oh, Missy!" Mrs. White said as she reached out a work-worn hand to help steady Georgiana.

"I am fine, thank you." Judging from the deep colour that stained her cheeks, his sister was deeply embarrassed. He offered his arm to escort her to the carriage and away from the others.

The wind blew bitterly, pressing ice crystals into the exposed skin of his face. He and Georgiana settled in the warm carriage.

"Are you well? Shall I return you to Pemberley and continue without you?" he asked her.

A tense smile more like a grimace stretched across her face. "Do not be concerned about me. I am well enough to continue, and the tenants like to see me. It was just…hard, hearing his name, knowing he has been hereabouts."

"Please have faith that I shall make arrangements for you to be protected by a footman for as long as we hear stories of him being sighted in the vicinity, and I shall try to find him and send him packing as soon as possible. That is my promise to you. Ridding Derbyshire of Wickham is my sole priority."

Georgiana's lashes fluttered to where her hands were clenching and unclenching in her lap and back up to gaze at him. "Thank you. That is a great comfort to me." Those knotted hands showed that her relief would not be complete until Wickham was found and away from her for good.

Chapter 7

Late December 1812
Gracechurch Street, London

The patterned hanging papers on the four walls of her bedchamber in Gracechurch Street were her friends and her foes, and today she allowed her imagination to run free in a moment of fantasy that suited her low spirits. Were those vines clambering up the walls to get out and escape? Or were they secretly discussing how to conquer the chamber, strangling all the hope within it? What were supposed to be happy little roses could be red teardrops for all she was concerned. Nonetheless, Elizabeth often preferred this room to any other in the house because she was able to be alone with her own thoughts with no one to dispute her own memories.

Why did she have to remember the events of last summer differently from her aunt and uncle? Many of the memories she retained regarding her life before the accident were clear as a bell in her mind, so clear that she was certain they had to be the absolute truth. They could not be wrong, which was why she always argued—whether silently or not—when her aunt and uncle's versions were in error. The most painful stories of the Gardiners stood in stark contrast to her certainty of what had happened to Lydia. But they would never mention Lydia; they believed the worst of her fate. The reason Elizabeth pushed for her memories' swift return was to convince her family of a more positive consequence for her youngest sister.

Not only did her version of events redeem Lydia, but it also placed Mr. Darcy in the best light. The people of Meryton had thought him rather proud and disagreeable, but with such an important man supporting the young couple, everyone would be more likely to look upon their union with favour. Yet, her uncle and aunt were so set against such a noble and respected gentleman as Mr. Darcy, so intent upon believing he would do wrong towards her! It could not be true, could it?

His eyes, which had gazed upon her with such admiration at Pemberley, were haunted outside the haberdasher's as the rain poured down in sheets around him. Was her uncle's injunction against him the reason for his demeanour when she saw him all those weeks ago? Did he miss her? No, he could not be thinking of her any longer. Her heart was lost to him, yet how could she expect his ardour to endure without communication and with scandal and obstacles in their way? She loved him so dearly. She knew that now when all love must be vain. With no one else with whom to share those tender sentiments, she moped over him whilst alone.

He was such a good man, saving her family even if it meant Lydia was married to Mr. Wickham and living in Newcastle. And she was certain of Mr. Darcy's involvement—despite her aunt and uncle's insistence on his ignorance of the situation—and certain that she knew the whole story of Lydia's folly. It was so clear to her as though the person who had told her had been more than convincing, and she had no choice but to believe it. Or was the person pleading with her?

"This is in your sister's best interest and protects me as well."

What? Where had that thought originated? Elizabeth pushed deeper into her memories, trying to understand why those words had been revealed to her. Who would this protect? Mr. Wickham? He was not the best bridegroom for her sister, but perhaps he would mend his dissolute and spendthrift ways now that he was married and in the regulars rather than the militia, earning a better keep for his family. After all, he would leave a wife behind when called to the continent the next time there was action in place for his regiment. But his income would support them in a better fashion than before, and Mr. Darcy had provided a generous amount for their children. At least, that is what Mr. Wickham had said.

Mr. Wickham! It was he who had told her about Lydia and about Mr. Darcy's help!

But when did Mr. Wickham tell her what happened to him and Lydia, and why ask her to tell others so they would understand the truth? Why did she believe Mr. Darcy would support them so generously when he had numerous reasons to think poorly of Mr. Wickham? The last time she could recall seeing Mr. Wickham was the regiment's final evening in Meryton before moving to Brighton. But she was sure it was true—he *had* told her. This was not mental derangement; she remembered it as though it had happened yesterday, and this new memory, though not perfect, had to be correct. The pounding in her head began to grow merely by thinking of it, so she turned to more easily managed thoughts in an attempt to alleviate that pain.

Her heart rejoiced that Jane and Mr. Bingley were soon to be married. It was a happy thought, yet bitterness surrounded it as well. Her eyes stung and her heart hurt at the thought that she would not be there to participate with her favourite sister on such a happy day. Her uncle's time was consumed by business, and Aunt's approaching confinement made travel an ill-advised undertaking. She would miss the most important day of her sister's life, and the pain of regret tore her apart.

"Please, Aunt. Please, Uncle," she had said, palms pressed together. "I beg you from my heart to allow me this trip to see Jane marry. I can go with Davis."

"My lady's maid cannot be released at such a time for me, Elizabeth. You know this," said her aunt.

"What about Sal? She is very responsible. You have thought about taking her out of kitchen work because of the pain she has in her hands. This would be a good situation for her for a time."

"A scullery maid as chaperone? No, that would not do," replied Uncle Gardiner.

"You are not well enough in any case," Aunt added. "Such a distance in a carriage may bring back your headaches, not to mention we have no idea how so much cold air might affect you."

Uncle continued, "You were also a victim of nasty deeds when you were last in that neighbourhood, and your sisters still bear the brunt of ill treatment due to Lydia's disappearance."

"But Lydia…" She thought the better of arguing *that* difference of opinion. "It has been months since I left Longbourn. Surely, some new gossip has drawn interest away from our family? Besides, Jane marrying a gentleman

The Mist of Her Memory

as respected as Mr. Bingley will help our status as well."

"It has been decided. There are too many reasons against your travelling at this time, so you must remain here with us," said her aunt. She smiled and leaned in towards Elizabeth. "Why don't you write a nice, long letter to Jane saying how dearly you wanted to be with her on her day of joy?"

"Jane would have wanted me at her wedding, and no letter will compare to my actual presence. I am sure she wishes me to stand up with her." Elizabeth had been told that Mary was to stand up with Jane. The idea hurt quite a bit. Had the two become close in Elizabeth's long absence? And Mr. Darcy—without a doubt, he would be at the wedding and likely standing up with Mr. Bingley. The denial of travel to Longbourn represented another lost opportunity to speak with him.

No amount of begging from Elizabeth would alter their plans. Aunt and Uncle were firmly convinced that none of them would be at Longbourn for the wedding.

She had excused herself to her bedchamber complaining of fatigue. She had learned not to use a headache as an excuse since they equated it with her injuries and inability to heal, and the last thing she wanted was to be held back for those reasons. Now she was disparaging herself when she should be dwelling on naught but Jane's happiness. But what were these four walls of her chambers best for but to shed her blue-devilled tears over what had been lost to her due to this cursed head of hers?

Her aunt's voice through the bedroom door caused her to quickly draw out a fresh handkerchief to smear away the newest wetness from her face. When had she become such a watery-headed fool?

"Elizabeth, dear, are you well?"

She rose and poked her head through the door opening then offered her aunt a shaky smile and nod. She had no way of hiding her reddened eyes or nose.

"I have just the thing to cheer you. We have a visitor you might like to see."

Was it Mr. Darcy? No, he would be gone now—to Pemberley for Christmastide and then to Jane and Mr. Bingley's wedding. No use in hoping he would call on her now. That was over. Her time was better spent dwelling on the present, so she pinched her cheeks to brighten them and perhaps distract from her red eyes whilst she followed her aunt to the pretty little parlour that faced the back garden.

The guest turned out to be a rather lively lady friend of Mrs. Gardiner whom she had met once before. In the past, she had not been allowed to join her aunt's calls for the most part, so any chance to talk to a friendly and animated lady was a favourable turn of events.

"Shall I pour?" she offered when the tea came.

"Thank you, Elizabeth."

"You are fortunate to have a pleasant niece to help you. It is such a busy time of year, and with your impending confinement and the children, you must be overwhelmed. The presence of a dear family member must be a blessing," Mrs. Fraser said.

"I agree. Elizabeth is an accommodating young lady, and the children idolize her."

"I expected a much younger girl."

Why would she think that? Of course—Elizabeth had not been present for ladies' calls when she first arrived in Gracechurch Street and had not been introduced to London society before. That was the only reason she could surmise.

Mrs. Fraser turned to address Elizabeth. "I hope to see you at evening events during the Season, Miss Bennet."

"My niece is a godsend, and it will be even more evident once my confinement takes place. She will be occupied with the children at that time, and I shall not be in any position to chaperone her at balls and concerts."

"Then you must accept my offer to accompany her to a ball or two," said Mrs. Fraser. "Would you like that, Miss Bennet? A London ball is livelier than your little assembly balls back in Hertfordshire. Do you like to dance?"

Did she? Of course! Excitement ran swiftly through her veins at the prospect. She would go to balls; she would dance! Perhaps she would see Mr. Darcy at one—even if he did not much care to dance.

But a cautious glance at her aunt caused Elizabeth to check those thoughts in light of her all but recent sequestration. Instead of an enthusiastic response, she offered her opinion with care. "I relish dancing, but I must defer to my aunt's wishes regarding my activities this winter. She may need me to an extent that I am unable to fill a grand calendar. But a ball would be welcome if she agrees."

"We could delay your events until later in the Season. The first few balls matter little. And I would not impose upon you for more than a few private balls, and maybe a soirée or the opera. Oh, do agree for your niece, Madeleine!"

"We shall see when the time comes. First, we have to ask Mr. Gardiner's permission, and there is my lying-in to consider," Aunt replied with enough of a slight smile to make Elizabeth hopeful again.

"I am certain a young lady has enough energy for both assisting her family and a few private balls!" said Mrs. Fraser. "I shall treasure Miss Bennet's company." Elizabeth had a strong notion that it would be a great deal of fun to join Mrs. Fraser at a ball; she was such a spirited, vivacious lady. Mrs. Fraser made it sound as if it were a given that Elizabeth would join her. As she was leaving, she once again reminded Elizabeth's aunt of her offer, and Mrs. Gardiner gave a more positive reply.

After Mrs. Fraser had gone, her aunt patted the seat of the sofa next to her. "Come, sit with me, and have another cup of tea."

Elizabeth complied. Before she could ask about the upcoming Season, Aunt brought up the topic of her children and a possible trip to shop for some new toys for them. She also suggested a dress or two for Harriet, who was outgrowing the ones she now wore. The conversation was full of cheer and helped improve Elizabeth's mood almost as much as their recent visitor had. Keen as she was to speak on Mrs. Fraser's chaperonage, she was disappointed when her aunt stood.

"I must make my excuses now, my dear, as this time with company has worn me down. You should go and rest as well. A caller with so many topics of animated discussion was surely as tiring to you as to me."

She was not tired, but she supposed she should be grateful to get out of the house for the impending shopping trip. How she longed to know about the balls, though! As she climbed the staircase to her chambers, those thoughts threatened to put her into a mood of megrims once again. Halfway up, she spun around to see her aunt about to disappear into the mistress's offices.

"Aunt," she called out, "do you suppose I might be allowed to attend a ball or two during the Season? That is, if I am sufficiently recovered by then. Of course, if I am still in town and not at Longbourn again by spring. The height of the Season is months away."

At first, Aunt Gardiner's lips formed a grim line. But Elizabeth discerned a contemplative light in her eyes, and she finally replied with a slight smile, "Perhaps. Let us be hopeful that you will be well enough. But you know

57

that, due to my confinement, it cannot be in the early part of the Season, and with care for a new child, it is unlikely I shall be able to accompany you. We can discuss it more seriously towards Easter. You are very lucky to have Mrs. Fraser's offer."

Elizabeth was so elated, she could barely keep her composure and burst out an enthusiastic, "Yes, Aunt, thank you so much!" Her aunt's head went back as she chuckled about the outburst. No chastisement was made. It seemed Aunt Gardiner was sympathetic to Elizabeth's desire to re-enter the rest of the world.

She scampered to her room, and after she closed the door behind her, Elizabeth pressed her back up against it whilst she hugged herself. Finally, she had something to anticipate with pleasure. Perhaps soon they would hear more of Jane's wedding too. Suddenly, she recognized how fortuitous it was that she had not brought up Mr. Wickham. Until she could better remember the details of her new recollection, she would keep that information to herself. Better to speak of it when her memory returned in full—when the discussion could be positive based on the facts she knew to be true.

Perhaps if she could re-read Mr. Darcy's letter from Hunsford, it might give her a clue as to Mr. Wickham's character and spur a memory in her muddled head. This would help her certainty that Lydia was safe and not lost as everyone seemed to believe. Hope now filled her, making her mind open like a flower, all light and heady, and she laughed blithely. She would search for the letter. She would go to a ball, dance, and perhaps even see Mr. Darcy. She would remember more details about Mr. Wickham and Lydia. She would be well again.

Sitting upon her bed, Elizabeth gazed about the room. The paper on the four walls no longer appeared as a crushing, strangling entity. Instead, lively, merry, beautiful roses climbed up towards the radiant sunshine.

Chapter 8

January 1813
Pemberley, Derbyshire

It should have been easier. With so many trusted servants and such an exemplary level of loyalty among them, Darcy would have expected them to have mentioned Wickham's presence to him at any time he had shown his face near Pemberley, yet the Whites' account was the first he had heard of the rogue's movements around Lambton. He was wrong.

Most of the senior servants had known Wickham all his life. They would have spoken to Darcy directly had they any notion that Wickham was in the vicinity—at least, those who were aware of his perfidy to some extent. Indeed, that description would be suitable for the majority of the servants now at Pemberley. But his silence and lack of warning to the newer and lower-placed servants had allowed the cunning Wickham to spend time and spin his tales whilst avoiding detection by those standing members of the staff aware of his ignominy and lack of welcome at Pemberley.

An under-gardener new to Pemberley heard the account that Wickham liked to tell. "'E sayed you owed him some money, sir, and that's why 'e come back to Pemberley."

"And when was this?"

"Last summer. Think it were August? 'E asked about work. That made me wonder. We had no need of 'elp. Any man who knew gardens would know August needs no new 'elp."

"Thank you," said Darcy. "Should you see him again, please report to me or Mrs. Reynolds immediately."

"Yessir, Mr. Darcy. The fella were shifty. I shoulda said something before. But 'e never showed 'is face again, an' we get fellas askin' after work on and off all year."

A young groom reported Wickham asking about the living at Kympton, the identity of parson, and his personality. When the servant became suspicious about questions of whether the Darcys were at home and when they were expected, Wickham was away in quick time, never to be seen in or near the stables again. Yet this was also in August.

Mrs. Reynolds discovered one of the housemaids had entertained a flirtation with a fellow named George whose picture was on a miniature with the family portraits so, in the words of the girl, "he couldna be so bad." Upon detailed questioning, the maid was vehement that she had not been importuned in any way, but she admitted to letting him sleep in the cellar on particularly bitter nights. Besides, she was uncertain that he was the same man since he had the look of someone who slept in his clothes and had no heavy coat for the cold, so she procured one from storage. The severe line of Mrs. Reynolds's lips and the closeness of her brows showed her distaste for the girl's actions, and she immediately had the miniature delivered to the attics to put the blackguard's image out of sight.

This last sighting had not been during the summer but only a few weeks earlier. As the Whites had implied, Wickham could still be near Pemberley.

The cur's appearance in Lambton last summer was an inordinate concern to Darcy. Wickham's possible attendance near the inn at the same time Darcy had come to see Elizabeth made it entirely likely that he was the miscreant who had hurt her. His first instinct would consider Wickham incapable of physically harming a man or a woman. Women he romanced; men he fleeced. If he was indeed the person who had inflicted such grievous injuries on Elizabeth back in August, he held a violent disposition no one—not even Darcy—knew he possessed. What could have caused Wickham and Elizabeth to quarrel—Miss Lydia's disgrace?

Rage simmered inside him. If Wickham was the culprit, he had not only damaged Elizabeth physically but also separated her from Darcy.

Darcy took a deep breath to settle his anger. The circumstances that seemed to point to Wickham were not necessarily true. And why would he have left the militia and come to Derbyshire again? Had he accumulated as

The Mist of Her Memory

many debts in Brighton and Meryton as he had in Lambton? Why would he return to Lambton in that case? No one could positively confirm it was Wickham at the Lambton Inn or near Pemberley recently. They had merely seen a man who resembled him, dressed in gentlemen's clothing.

But it must have been him! There was simply no one else. In fact, up until now, Darcy had striven to imagine that Elizabeth's injuries came from a simple fall. They had first assumed she had tripped on a chair, and for that reason, Gardiner had accepted Darcy's help, even allowed him in the sick room for a few private, precious moments with Elizabeth.

Oh, those moments! He had poured out his heart to her, sworn his love, and begged her to come back to life. He had to know whether her feelings and wishes had changed since last April.

She had been bundled in the bedclothes, a nasty bruise marring her face. She had been bled; his own surgeon was supervising the case. The fellow had said that, although he was in general not in favour of bleeding, bad blood could be keeping her from waking.

The door remained ajar when he was allowed his private time with her, and likely Mr. Gardiner heard his most personal thoughts and feelings, but Darcy did not care. Elizabeth had to know that he needed her more than he needed air to live.

But if Wickham had been in the area, perhaps he, too, had heard Darcy's pleas for Elizabeth to return to him when he first found her in the parlour. What were the chances Wickham had poisoned Mr. Gardiner's view against Darcy somehow? A simple way to punish Darcy would be to separate him from Elizabeth. Could he have swooped in when Darcy was away from the inn and fabricated a story to ensure Darcy would be blamed and kept from Elizabeth? *This* bore a closer likeness to his childhood playmate. Lies, tales, vindictive behaviour—this Darcy believed more than he believed Elizabeth's wounds came from Wickham's hand and not a fall.

Wickham had to be found and the truth forced from him in any way possible. Darcy could not allow Wickham to get away with inflicting so much pain and suffering.

Longbourn, Hertfordshire

THE MOST ANNOYING FEMININE LAUGH WAS FAR TOO CLOSE. COULD HE term it a bray? No, too grating. Gah! He would never escape in time! Darcy winced before he turned to face the harpy who owned the harsh voice.

Miss Bingley had sought him at the wedding feast following the marriage of her brother to Miss Jane Bennet and now clutched his arm with a tight grip. Darcy shook loose from her grasp and brushed his sleeve. His skin crawled.

"I can speculate that it must be a trial for you to face this family, Mr. Darcy. At least we do not have the brash flirtations of the youngest or the strident remarks of Miss Elizabeth to further offend our sensibilities, do you not think?" She continued to speak into his ear, low and oppressive, oblivious to his discomfort with her closeness.

Given the little he knew about the fates of both young women, Darcy stiffened and clenched his fists at his sides, ready to verbally lash out at Miss Bingley. However, could such an infamous gossip have some additional intelligence to share with him with regard to Elizabeth's fate and location? Had Miss Bingley heard of the Bennets' problems?

Miss Bingley looped her arm through his and leaned close. The touch heightened the sensation of agitation within his body. Since he did not want anyone to hear what she might say, he walked with her to a quieter part of the room whilst the others enjoyed Mrs. Hurst's astonishing technique on the pianoforte. Of course, he was reluctant to be seen in a private tête-à-tête with her, but it was better than letting her derisive observations heard by the wrong ears.

As anticipated, Miss Bingley was all too willing to speak at length. "These people are much more tightly knit than those of our class, Mr. Darcy. Usually, when I am invited to an event with the peerage or others of higher class, it is but the work of a moment for my maid to discover the secrets necessary to negotiate the difficult path of the connections and learn which topics to avoid or to use to my own benefit in conversation. 'Tis quite vexing, but the higher-placed servants at Netherfield Park will not gossip."

His shoulders collapsed with disappointment for a moment before he gathered up his pride and stood tall again. His hope for word of Elizabeth and the expectation that Miss Bingley would enquire of her was for naught. "So you have learned nothing?"

"No, I do not give up easily, nor does my maid. Poor dear Duguay had to speak with the kitchen maids, who should have been below her notice, to discover anything. All they would reveal was that Miss Lydia ran away from Brighton and disappeared and that Miss Elizabeth is travelling with relatives from London and would not be able to return for the wedding.

"Mr. Darcy, I am beside myself with anger that my brother neglected to inform me that the Bennet family has been tainted by Miss Lydia's disappearance. Charles will help to restore their reputation, but what will associating with such a family do to my standing in the *ton*?"

He shrugged. "They are hosting a grand wedding with little difficulty, so the Bennets must have enough friends left to stand by them."

"Or who want a free meal and chocolate," Miss Bingley responded, her cat's eyes rising to match the tone of her statement.

How rude! Yet Miss Bingley was nothing less than a known gossip, and Darcy needed to know as much as he could about Elizabeth. But how could he ask of her absence without revealing his heart? A vague statement rather than a direct assault might be his best strategy when it came to Miss Bingley. "I did not expect to see Miss Mary stand up with your new sister instead of Miss Elizabeth."

She narrowed her eyes and pursed her lips. "I cannot but think you seek information on her whereabouts."

Miss Bingley's perception fell too close to the truth, and he had no choice but to demur. "Not at all. I merely missed seeing her at this happy occasion…"

"Is your wistfulness merely a means to conceal your admiration for the current Miss Bennet's pert opinions and fine eyes?"

If he followed this direction in their conversation, he risked interminable goading on his impending nuptials—not that he had such different opinions—and he hated hearing her intentional slights of his beloved. Yet perhaps baiting Miss Bingley might gain him valuable information. Darcy took the hint and leapt into the area of the tease. "In contrast to Miss Mary, Miss Elizabeth Bennet always seemed amused by everything."

"Pitiable woman. Do you not recall how she tried to make fun of you? It is not easily done with someone so noble, Mr. Darcy."

Why did she use his name in practically every sentence? She had always disgusted him with her ingratiating approaches. As was his wont, he ignored the indirect compliment. "It is unfortunate she is unable to be at her sister's nuptials. There must be an important excuse."

"You are correct. I have heard she is with an aunt and uncle—that tradesman from *Cheapside* whom we met at Pemberley in the summer—on yet another journey abroad, in Italy this time. Supposedly, they are too far away to bother returning for one day. Mr. Gardiner must have significant funds available to him to travel so frequently and so far."

"Perhaps. You know no more?"

"Nothing for certain. I have my suspicions. I believe the younger sister's folly may be the reason they have distanced themselves from her family. If so, I can hardly call them charitable. Can you believe it, Mr. Darcy? To avoid a dear sister's wedding because of another sister's"—she leaned in to whisper—"debauched behaviour? Yes, it is true. Miss Lydia ran away with a man. However, this trip speaks more ill of Eliza Bennet than Miss Lydia's folly."

Darcy's gut twisted at her maligning the woman he loved. The retort burst from his lips before he had given the words much thought, and it possessed a sharp tone he should have tempered. "Since we do not know all the specifics, it is difficult to lay any blame. Usually there is a great deal more to a story than what is shared by gossip." When he glanced to the side, Miss Bingley was gawking at him, her large eyes nearly popping out of her head.

"You do continue to have interest in that lady, sir, do you not?"

Hmm. "Sir." It was a change, though no improvement. Miss Bingley tossed her turbaned head back, the impossibly tall, tinted feathers bouncing as if in agreement.

"You once said she was handsome, but her manners are less so. Remember, Mr. Darcy, how she and the Gardiners failed to appear at the formal dinner your sister had at Pemberley. Miss Elizabeth planned some sort of little fall, if I recall, and created enough drama to change everyone's plans. What a terrific insult to Miss Darcy."

He could not commit himself to too much sensibility to the accident without inciting additional curiosity on Miss Bingley's part. However, he could not help himself and moved to correct her. "It was a bad fall, an accident. Miss Elizabeth suffered a concussion and was insensible for several days."

Miss Bingley sniffed and fanned herself. "Please, Mr. Darcy. The results were not that grave, as I recall." She released a low chuckle as if amused by the situation. "A country girl is of a sturdier sort and will survive a mere bump on the head. I speculate she merely feigned a swoon for the attention she would gain."

Darcy's ire was up before the insult, a slow burn inside him that threatened to burst out. He swallowed his gall. "Still, it seems unfortunate that she was not able to be here for such a favourable occasion."

"If you can call this marriage favourable. Oh, Mr. Darcy, I hate how Charles was taken in by the smiles of a Bennet girl! They are such fortune hunters!"

"They have a love match. Nothing can be superior to such a marriage."

"From my brother's side, perhaps. But he should know better, always falling in and out of love. Now he is tied to one of his infatuations for life due to the cunning of the mother."

He would not let Miss Bingley continue to malign the Bennets! "Mrs. Bingley is skilful at hiding her true feelings," said Darcy. "She is a decent lady and *does* care a great deal for your brother. He is closer to her than either of us is, and he assures me there is no other for him. I am satisfied with the match." He pursed his lips and levelled her with a severe glare. The topic was closed.

"You are too apt to be pleased with the Bennet family today, sir. Pray, what has happened to you?"

All Darcy could manage was to stare at her with his mouth slightly open. How dare she attempt to insult him in this manner? True, he had not shown himself inclined to approve of the Bennet family in the past. His feelings for Elizabeth had helped him see them through her eyes. "The Bennets are tied to your brother. You are family with them now, and Bingley is my closest friend. Of course I am more inclined to like them than when I first met them."

"You must admit, Mr. Darcy, it is still great entertainment to make light of their shortcomings."

"I prefer not to, Miss Bingley, out of respect for your brother."

"At least Eliza Bennet is not here importuning us with her comments. I can tolerate anything but that woman. Her sister found a man in her own way, but no one would deign to marry that impertinent Eliza Bennet."

Darcy crossed his arms and scowled at the vexing lady who remained at his side. The direction the conversation had turned irritated his intelligence too much to continue. Though he had learnt some new information, Miss Bingley proved less than reliable in most cases, given her prejudice against the Bennets and especially against Elizabeth.

Fortunately for him, Mr. Collins sidled over to join them and wasted no time telling Darcy about his excitement that such an important person attended this blessed event. He rattled on without taking a breath, expounding with foolish grovelling and self-aggrandisement whilst his arms waved in the air at random. Here was the embarrassing relative: the heir. Elizabeth was above him in both deportment and perspicacity.

Miss Bingley agreed with his praises of Mr. Darcy and then rolled her eyes a few times at the fellow's genial yet ambitious praises of the newlywed couple before she slunk off to continue her whisperings with her sister. Even though he still had to gently settle Mr. Collins's obsequious ramblings, her absence was a relief.

THE MORNING BEFORE DARCY PLANNED TO LEAVE FOR PEMBERLEY, HE encountered Bingley awaiting him in the stables, ready to join Darcy on his ride before breakfast.

Not long after they started their ride, Bingley offered the information that Darcy had been ruminating upon these last days. "Since you have shown a great interest in the Bennet ladies' fates as of late, I thought you might like to know Jane told me more about Miss Elizabeth…er…Miss Bennet." He stopped himself from holding his breath as Bingley continued, "It seems she is still suffering from the ill effects of the shocking fall she had in Lambton. At first, she had severe amnesia and had to be told most everything about her life. She still forgets quite a bit and has frequent headaches."

It was all Darcy could do to hold back a rant, but such a grand level of distraction would not do. He took a steadying breath. "The events sound difficult. I feel for Miss Bennet." Good, his response was calm and controlled just as he had intended.

"Of course, Miss Lydia's indiscretion caused the family to be shunned locally, but though it is difficult to imagine, their situation became worse.

"You see, Miss Elizabeth thought she remembered events that were clearly untrue. When she became agitated at the truth of the matter and spoke of her beliefs, the people of Meryton mocked her for it. I am not aware of the particulars, only that people considered her to have mental derangement. Of course, such an affliction makes good folks fearful at best and often cruel. Some tradesmen are simply no longer open to the family, causing them to travel to other towns for goods. My Jane was even pelted with tomatoes when she walked with Miss Elizabeth. Yet, from the Gardiners' letters, Miss Elizabeth still insists her recollections are what really occurred."

Darcy could not respond immediately, he was so affected by the news. He squeezed his eyes shut and controlled the release of a sigh so it came out as a shuddering breath. Elizabeth's treatment was unbearable.

"As I related earlier, the Bennets' situation was truly a mystery to me when I arrived in November, and still would be, had Jane and I not become engaged. The attitudes of people towards Miss Elizabeth's infirmity and its effects on the family necessitated her being sent away for her own protection. I fear I do not know more than what Jane says, that Miss Elizabeth is safe but could not attend our wedding. You know that Kitty mentioned travel on the continent, but Janey will not even confirm she is there. She has asked me to ask you to tell no one. I can trust in your discretion, can I not?"

"Of course. You may depend on me." Darcy's stomach seemed leaden with the weight of the news. She may not be on the continent? Then where was she?

He swallowed to ease the anguish that had settled deep in his gut. He would have to abandon such shaky feelings if he were to try to forget her in an unreserved endeavour. Yet there was no way he could erase his love for her from his heart, and that, combined with the frustration of the unknown, threatened to swallow up any small hope he still retained of a future with Elizabeth.

He adjusted his gloves' clutching grip on the reins, which was indicative of the tautness in his entire body. Poor Elizabeth, who had amnesia consume her mind last summer. Was she recovered, or were they protecting her because of her unstable mental state? Good G-d, do not let it be the worst! Do not let her be incarcerated!

Chapter 9

February 1813
En route to Meryton, Hertfordshire

The search for Wickham had taken place over the course of a month with the available servants from Pemberley as well as men from Lambton. No further sightings had occurred since those reported in December. The best they had found was a remote stable on the Pemberley estate—thought abandoned—that had been made into a rudimentary home for someone. Signs of a fire, some crusts of bread, and blankets from Pemberley—likely from the same sympathetic maid who had purloined a coat for Wickham—showed it had been made more comfortable for its inhabitant, and a small nosegay of dried flowers sat on one table, indicating a more feminine touch. This was a matter of some concern given Miss Lydia's continued disappearance alongside the bitter winter weather.

But the resident of the stable was nowhere to be seen, even upon watching the building on a regular basis for several weeks. Where was the blackguard? Without any sign of him, Darcy was forced to admit defeat. Somehow, Wickham must have caught wind of his investigation and left the area. Darcy was quite certain he must be the force behind the serious injuries that Elizabeth had incurred in August. Yet why had he returned to Derbyshire in the first place? One could surmise familiarity with the area as a safe haven, but why return to the scene of the crime?

Darcy adjusted the fur rug draped over his knees, but his feet remained chilled. The bricks had cooled at least a half-hour ago. By the end of the day, he would see the happy faces of Mr. and Mrs. Bingley at Netherfield, where he would stay for the night before continuing on to London. He would be required to school his own features to appear more positive than he felt these days.

The scenery of Hertfordshire now appeared through the windows of the coach, its lushness hidden under a blanket of snow that seemed as though it had been there for some time and meant to stay. Yes, this winter had been awfully cold. Bare trees twisted above the snow, ending in limbs covered in sparkling frost. He shivered. Even within the confines of his carriage, it was frigid.

As anticipated, his mid-afternoon arrival had been heralded by a messenger; his hosts waited upon the front stairs to meet him. Both were in fur cloaks. Mrs. Bingley's hood almost hid her face entirely, and her gloved hand made a brief appearance to wave then returned quickly to its muff. Encouraged by their sunny smiles, he alighted from the carriage with the swiftness one uses to greet dear friends.

"Darcy! Welcome!" his friend said whilst shaking one hand and slapping the other arm.

"I thank you, Bingley. Mrs. Bingley, how do you do?"

"We are well, I thank you. But do let us hurry inside for we are about to become as frozen as the pond if we remain out of doors any longer!"

As could be imagined, they made short time of entering the house, which was warmed by fires in all the main rooms, and Darcy's toes tingled in the newly found heat. Bingley had done well: no chimney at Netherfield showed the tendency to smoke, and the windows fit well. The house was stuffy but not smoky in the least.

"Your usual chamber has been readied, and a bath is being drawn. Once you have had time to refresh yourself, please have me called, and we can meet for a drink before dinner," offered Bingley.

"Splendid."

Two hours later, washed, rested, and dressed for dinner, he took light sips of brandy whilst awaiting Bingley's arrival in the library. He slowly swirled the liquid in the glass, noting the golden hues drifting languidly around the curved walls, leaving their filmy shadows behind. Shortly thereafter, Bingley entered, and once they had passed the initial pleasantries and verified in general platitudes how the families of each were faring, little time was needed for him to apprise Bingley of all that had taken place with Wickham.

"I too am angered with whomever inflicted harm upon Miss Bennet," Bingley said. "She still suffers, and the nature of her injuries has made her believe strange stories. Of course, her family knows none of them are true, yet it is hard to argue that she is still of sound mind."

"It is regrettable that I have not found Wickham yet. Perhaps, he would have revealed the true history. But then, he would likely not confess to any wrongdoing pertaining to Miss Elizabeth, which I would like to know about most," said Darcy.

"Jane receives regular correspondence from her sister and says Lizzy is progressing well, recovering her memories. You would never know it here, though. She has been away four months, yet just this week, I overheard some scoundrel joke about crazy Lizzy Bennet disappearing. The men he was drinking with all laughed. They make sport of Miss Bennet as if she is a fool, and I abhor it. She is one of the cleverest women I know, yet the locals think she is bound for Bedlam."

Darcy's hackles were up just as much as Bingley's. He possessed little tolerance for tittle-tattle. "Do you know where she is?"

"The Bennets still insist she is travelling on the continent, but someone is posting letters for her in London. I shall not ask Jane about it since I would rather protect her from thinking ill thoughts no matter where the truth lies. My wife was terribly upset over Lizzy and the Gardiners being unable to attend our wedding, and I know she misses her daily. If she were here, I would take her into my home and protect her. At least Jane can be confident in that."

"I am certain I saw her in town once last November in the Gardiners' carriage. The letters point to her being somewhere near London at the very least."

Bingley pursed his lips and shrugged. "I do not know. Jane says little. However, I know my wife well enough to discern that the situation bothers her a great deal."

"What about Miss Lydia? Do the people in Meryton still gossip about her and Wickham?"

"Interestingly enough, that is a less noteworthy story to the public these days since another young lady who used to live in Meryton was rumoured to be shamed by Wickham since Lydia's disappearance."

"Another? Of course, that should not surprise me."

"She is in a family way and claims it is by Mr. Wickham. She has been moved to the north. All ills are healed in the north, it seems. It must be why you live in Derbyshire, my friend."

Darcy managed a smile at his friend's jest. This is what endeared Bingley to everyone: he could lighten even the most solemn of discussions. But Darcy was not made in such a way. He pressed his lips together and glanced around the room, gathering his thoughts once again. "Do you know anything of what happened to Miss Lydia? Has there been any correspondence to the family at all?"

"No, and I realize my hopes that she has found a good situation in spite of her absconding with Wickham are foolish, yet I cling to them for Jane's sake. Jane will always look at things on the brightest side possible."

Darcy lifted one eyebrow at his friend. "You are well matched."

"I am still more of a realist than my wife. In all likelihood, no matter how much I do not want it to be so, Miss Lydia is fallen whether she has remained with Wickham or not. There was no sign of her in Derbyshire?"

"She was not seen at all though I could not exactly ask after her as we searched, but no one mentioned a woman in any of the sightings. Staying with Wickham would have made certain her reputation was thoroughly ruined rather than leaving any possibilities of redemption alive."

"Indeed." Bingley shifted his weight within his chair as he changed the subject. "So, you are to town for the Season. I expect you would rather delay that trip and stay here as long as you can."

"I admit the anticipation of some aspects of the society I shall meet and the balls I shall attend give me a terrific headache, but I shall enjoy some of the artistic performances I have time to see."

"I do not know a more awful object than you at a ball."

March 1813
London

As he had been most evenings for the last few weeks, Darcy was impeccably dressed and handing his outer garments off to an attendant at yet another cloak room, this time in a fine home in Mayfair. He schooled his features into a neutral expression as he approached the wood-panelled ballroom, readying himself for his inevitable ritual.

In the light of a thousand candles, he cast his eyes around, seeking to determine who was and was not present. As usual, a dark-haired lady caught his attention until he was able to determine it was not Elizabeth Bennet. This happened to him at least once at every function. His breath inevitably quickened and his palms dampened within his gloves until his hope was dashed by the wrong set of curls, the wrong colour of eyes, and the wrong timbre of laughter. He should know the specifics of the hair and posture of each dark-haired lady in London by now.

Whilst this perusal took place tonight, he was able to note the attendance of two very different acquaintances he could not avoid. One, his cousin Richard, was welcome; the other, not. The latter was, of course, the first to approach him: Miss Caroline Bingley, whose flaxen tresses and shrewish eyes were not the sort he sought. His teeth began to grind at her cloying tone before she even reached him and spoke.

"Mr. Darcy, how do you do?"

He bent over her hand but made certain his face did not come within half a foot of her fine kid opera glove. "I am well, Miss Bingley, and you?"

A false-looking smile accompanied her response. "Marvellously entertained thus far. The Brunsdons put on the best functions. I do believe this is one of the largest ballrooms in London and so well appointed."

"It is a fine home."

"Of course, the guest list is the best of the best. You could not expect anyone from any lower than the cream of the *ton* tonight, could you, Mr. Darcy?"

"I suppose not," which was why he should not be searching in vain for Elizabeth at these functions. Her family simply did not carry the same rank as those he could expect to see at most of the balls and soirées he was invited to attend. But ever since he noticed her outside the haberdasher's in the autumn, he was constantly in search of another glimpse of her.

"For example," continued Miss Bingley in an affected drawl, "I was just speaking to Countess Lieven, and she almost said she would promise me an Almack's voucher. I do hope she meant it. I cannot be shamed into asking for the invitation outright. Do you not agree, Mr. Darcy?"

"You will have to stay home at all times until your invitation arrives in April." Darcy did not mean to tease, but Miss Bingley took it as a flirtation and slapped him with her fan.

"You, sir, are a devil. You know it is not apropos to stay at home at the height of the Season! A lady has calls to make. She must be remembered by all her friends!"

His jaw immediately tightened. Ha! If they were true friends, their bonds would not suffer from the lack of formal calls; instead, they would regret the short duration spent together at those visits as well as the lack of familiarity they foster and strive to find circumstances where they could spend more time together. Darcy hated formal calls for that very reason; he preferred his time with Bingley and Richard and those of a similar ilk.

He doubted Caroline Bingley knew that type of friendship. However, no sooner had the idea crossed his mind than they were approached by two young ladies who seemed acquainted with her. She introduced them with a bit of a grating tone to her voice, and he bowed. Of course, Miss Bingley's haughty expression was meant to show these supposed friends how she had admirable connections. One of the ladies actually suppressed a giggle, covering her grin with the tips of two fingers. Was she a fool, or was she laughing at Miss Bingley?

"Of course, *you* have many friends, Mr. Darcy," said Miss Bingley. Her little friends nodded enthusiastically.

"A few. I like to keep the best of my friends close to me."

"I am glad to know my brother is one of those few. Am I correct, sir?"

"Yes, Mr. and Mrs. Bingley are dear to me."

Miss Bingley rolled her eyes. "Mr. Darcy is truly a gentleman. My brother married a lady who is not well known, and he strives to help raise her position in superior society."

The jaw clench reappeared. "In fact, Mrs. Bingley is a gentleman's daughter." The two ladies' faces moved as if one from him to Miss Bingley and back again during the interchange, causing their ringlets to bob.

"Quite true, Mr. Darcy, though she is unknown to our circles." Miss Bingley tossed her head such that one could look up her nostrils.

"What is her father's name?" asked one of the young ladies.

"Bennet, of Longbourn in Hertfordshire," said Darcy for the sheer joy of saying part of Elizabeth's name.

"I do not know them," the young lady said with a quizzical expression that quickly changed to a cultured smile towards Darcy. "But if they are your friends, they must be a suitable sort."

"Hardly," said Miss Bingley. "It is a small estate entailed on a distant cousin and of no real concern to Mr. Darcy. There are five daughters, and the only one of any quality is my brother's wife. The current Miss Bennet is a shameful, impertinent hoyden who was sent away because she is not in her correct mind. The youngest sister…"

The orchestra played the introductory notes to the next dance, signalling to anyone promised for the dance to join the lines within the centre of the throng and saving Miss Bingley from continuing to make untoward comments about the Bennets. He had suffered more than enough of the three ladies' sycophantic behaviour, and he was relieved when they were collected by their respective partners. Miss Bingley tried to tarry as long as she could, but her dance partner wanted a prime spot in the line and led her away while she gazed over her shoulder at Darcy. He turned away.

He himself had not committed to any lady other than relatives tonight, and those sets would be later on in the festivities. As the current dance commenced, he procured some mulled wine and wandered the edges of the ballroom, nodding and acknowledging acquaintances and stopping to speak briefly to those he called friends. Few of these conversations took place, and Elizabeth's words rang in his ears, challenging him to practise his skills of speaking comfortably to strangers. He took the easy course and began with his cousin Colonel Fitzwilliam.

"I feared I might have to extract you from the situation you became entangled in near the entrance," the colonel said. Richard could be counted upon to divert an awkward moment in any situation.

"It was brief, thanks to Mr. Dahl's quickness in collecting his partner for the best spot in the formations."

The colonel smirked. "Ah, Dahl. His estate is entailed, and his tastes never fail to be more expensive than his income. A bit of love for wagering on sport, as I understand it. He needs an infusion of money from a wealthy lady, and Miss Bingley is not so difficult to look at."

"I did not know you were well acquainted with him."

Richard's head jerked back as if he were affronted. "I am not. I merely like to keep abreast of what is happening in the world. I must save myself by deflecting ladies like Miss Bingley towards men like Dahl."

Darcy nodded. "So merely a distant acquaintance then?"

"Indeed. Speaking of such, I have no new information for you on the old acquaintance you seek. I do not believe you wish to call him friend."

The light mood was done with. "I am sorry to hear it."

"On a similar bent, another acquaintance appears to be missing, which causes me some grief, and I cannot, for the life of me, figure out how to deal with it."

This caught Darcy's attention. His frame stiffened, and he sat a little straighter. Did the colonel speak of Elizabeth? After all, she was supposedly on the continent, yet also believed to be in Bedlam. Richard knew of Miss Lydia's disappearance with Wickham. Who else could be missing?

Fitzwilliam continued, "Sir Frank Nelson-James of Mellonleigh in Sevenoaks was courting my sister all season last year."

"Yes, I recall seeing him dance with Lady Margaret as much as propriety allowed."

"He has not been seen for nearly a seven month. Maggie is crushed, alternately thinking she has fallen out of favour with Sir Frank and blaming herself, and other times, thinking the worst has happened. Some said he was at his country home, but he was expected at Matlock after a critical race with his driving club. He was last seen on his way north in early August."

Darcy rubbed his chin. "That does not sound like Sir Frank." The gentleman in question was well respected and reliable, and the Fitzwilliams had held the expectation of a brilliant match with the quiet and unassuming Lady Margaret.

"I probably should have mentioned it earlier, but I half expected him to show up out of the blue. Yet it has not happened. No one wanted to cast aspersions on his character, as if he were doing something nefarious rather than following through on expectations. Although he likes games of chance as much as Wickham does, he has no real ties to him that I am aware of, so I doubt we have to wonder over a connection."

Sir Frank and Wickham? No, that made no sense. They had moved in very different circles at Cambridge. In addition, he had no reason to believe Sevenoaks was an area Wickham had ever visited—unless he stopped there on his way to town from Brighton. Yet Sir Frank's estate was not on the road commonly taken. No, no other connection with Wickham came to mind. Mellonleigh was closer to Rosings; Lady Catherine and Anne knew Sir Frank as well and would be shocked at his being missed. "I am surprised you even considered the possibility. I find it unlikely they would know each other. Where could they have crossed paths once they left Cambridge?"

Richard nodded. "I doubt it as well, but they disappeared at the same time, and my army intelligence experience has taught me always to consider even the most unlikely alternatives. I am suspicious that it is no coincidence."

"For Lady Margaret's sake, I hope he is well."

"He is not the sort to be waylaid by any vice. He enjoyed gambling but never lost more than he brought to the table, and driving fast was the only passion the man seemed to have that could be considered immoderate. He is a good sort, not at all the type to have run with the crowd Wickham preferred, which makes his disappearance more of a curiosity to my mind."

He did not like it, but he could only agree with his cousin. The two similar disappearances made him circumspect and only begged more questions on the utmost issue upon his mind: How did Elizabeth's fate fit into this tangle?

Chapter 10

Late February 1813
Gracechurch Street, London

"Good morning, miss," the cheerful maid called out to Elizabeth as she peeked into her chamber.

"Good morning, Davis." She smiled in return whilst she rose from where she had been reading by the window when Davis entered her chamber. Elizabeth had already been awake for a while and had finished her ablutions. She shared Davis's assistance with her aunt, but she was always attended second since her aunt had unrivalled dedication to her young children and wanted to see to their needs early each morning. The maid helped her into her stays and petticoats whilst she chattered to her about the rumours in town.

"Of course, all I can tell you is what Mrs. G. read out to me whilst I was doing her hair. There could be more that you would be interested in, miss. If you want, I can bring one of the papers to you so you can read it yourself—after your aunt is done with it, of course."

She perked up. Elizabeth enjoyed reading the broadsheets but did not get an opportunity all that often. She settled for the news her aunt and uncle told her, which at least made for an interesting conversation most days. More news of the outside world would be more than appealing. Parliament was sitting, and many of the fashionable set had returned to town. "Oh, could you? I would be terribly grateful," she said.

"I shall try to fetch one before the paper is used for wrappings." Davis continued her cheerful stories, and Elizabeth attended though slightly distracted. How she longed to read the reports for herself! She had gooseflesh over the anticipation of news of Mr. and Miss Darcy.

The wait proved frustrating since it was the next day before Davis was able to deliver the papers to her. Even then, only a portion found its way to her hands, with some pages already removed to wrap some trivial item. While those pages were of little consequence, exactly what mattered most was found within the pages Davis delivered: a comment on Mr. Darcy attending a ball. If he was in town, perhaps she and her aunt could call on his sister.

She sighed when she imagined their meeting. Would he gaze upon her much as he had always done, with that intense scrutiny? Speaking to him would be awkward with others around. They would have to find some time alone together, and she knew somehow that, if he still loved her as she loved him, they would find the moments they needed.

But this was all a projection of the possibilities of one visit—though one of the most important calls she could make in her life. Perhaps Miss Darcy was not in town, but if she was, how could they ensure her brother remained whilst they made their call? She expected him to wish to stay, given the strength of the admiration he had spoken of at Hunsford. Of course, she had abused him badly in her refusal at that time, all because she had believed Mr. Wickham's lies.

Oh! Mr. Wickham was a despicable man! Where were her letters? She had to see her letters again!

She kept all her correspondence in a wooden box, and Jane's missives were on top, carefully tied with a ribbon. She suspected Jane took a prodigious amount of care in what she included in her letters. They seemed bland in comparison to the daily routine she expected from Longbourn and Netherfield. Jane had been a much better correspondent before the accident, but like everyone else, she withheld the truth of life, supposedly to protect Elizabeth's shattered mind.

His letter was tucked at the bottom where she kept it hidden from prying eyes. She unfolded the missive carefully, as its worn creases showed signs of being folded and unfolded many times, and the wear was beginning to make certain parts more difficult to read. But there it was—Mr. Darcy's account of Mr. Wickham's attempt to elope with his sister for her large fortune.

The Mist of Her Memory

Elizabeth tried to untangle the threads of memories she had recovered. Mr. Wickham had told her Mr. Darcy paid for his wedding to Lydia. Why would Mr. Darcy do such a thing after he and Miss Darcy were so infamously treated by Mr. Wickham? And when did Mr. Wickham have the opportunity to share with her that important information about Mr. Darcy paying for her sister's redemption? Was it in Meryton after her accident? No, Lydia and Wickham left for the north right after the wedding. Her brain began to hurt as it attempted to grasp those elusive memories.

A light knock came on her door, and she nearly jumped out of her skin. She rapidly folded her letter and returned it to its place as her heart settled into her breast once more.

Aunt Gardiner called out from the other side, "Elizabeth? May I come in?"

"Of course."

Her aunt's eyes rested upon the box of letters nestled atop the bedclothes. "Re-reading your letters from Jane?"

"Yes. I miss her." She did not want to reveal Mr. Darcy's letter to her aunt. Thank goodness, her aunt did not notice her blush, or if she did, she did not mention it.

"Perhaps she and Mr. Bingley will come to town soon, and you can visit at that time."

The heat burning her cheeks disappeared when her aunt mentioned the possibility of seeing Jane, and her spine straightened. "That would be nice. Do you think they will come for the Season?"

"Well, I am not certain. As you recall, he does not want to stay with his sister Mrs. Hurst. Miss Bingley voiced her opposition to his wedding, and she lives there. The Bingleys would have to take lodgings somewhere. Our house is too crowded to allow for a couple who have not been wed long." Elizabeth sagged from her previous energetic position as the possibility of seeing her sister vanished as soon as it was mentioned. Her aunt's head tilted, and her eyes became soft with sympathy. "I shall ask your uncle whether he can help Mr. Bingley to find a suitable house for them to lease—not too far from here but in a fashionable area," she said. "Jane must be shown off as she deserves, a gentleman's daughter married to a wealthy man who will soon have property of his own."

"Then we can visit them!" Elizabeth clapped her hands together with glee as her face nearly split from the smile that burst forth upon it.

"Yes, yes, though only on days when she is not receiving other callers. We do not want strangers disrupting your thoughts whilst you are still recovering your memories."

"I am nearly well, Aunt. I can tolerate one or two ladies of the *ton*."

"Well, I came to ask about a pleasant excursion."

"The opera?" Elizabeth recalled the promise of a night out to see *The Marriage of Figaro* with her uncle in two weeks' time.

"No, this is a different event. Would you like to go to the booksellers' with Uncle today? He plans to take you to Gunter's for sweets afterwards."

"Of course, I would love to go! Oh, Aunt!" She leapt to her feet and rushed to hug her.

"He will be returning around half past eleven, so you must ready yourself by then."

"I will, I will." She perused her person. Her hair was done simply, so Davis would have to adjust it for a special excursion after breakfast. Her morning gown was a pretty one, suitable for this type of occasion, but it was cold outside, so she needed warmer undergarments and boots for the trip. "There is enough time."

A shrill shout and a cry of "Mama" caused her aunt to take her leave.

The promise of such a trip lightened Elizabeth's heart a great deal. What a delight to anticipate! Aunt and Uncle must trust her recovery a great deal to allow her this much time out of the house. It gave her hope for other calls.

Her mood was so positive, she was extra chatty over breakfast with the children, indulging them in discussions about fairies and other imaginings particular to young ones. She had a gift of reacting to their childish statements so they felt noticed and important and thus was a favourite with the four Gardiner youngsters. This always lightened the load for her aunt and the nurse as the children could be a challenge for two grown ladies, particularly when one had less energy due to her recent lying-in with a new babe, never mind picking up a small boy who had tripped and fallen and needed his mama.

Soon, the time came to ready herself for the afternoon out. Once she was dressed, Elizabeth gathered her best bonnet and warmest gloves whilst she awaited her uncle's return.

Her aunt joined her in the sitting room and told Elizabeth that the new babe was finally sleeping, providing some time for her to catch up on her correspondence. She seated herself at the writing desk provided near the fire for the purpose of her writing or enjoying the view whilst seated there. "Perhaps if this trip turns out well, I shall bring you along on a call to Mrs. Fraser to discuss her offer."

Elizabeth's day could not possibly get better. "Oh, Aunt, attendance at a ball would fulfil the best part of my dreams!"

Her aunt continued, "We shall have to arrange for some gowns to be made, but it will only be for small, private affairs with families known to us."

Elizabeth was so excited, it was all she could do not to fly across the room and embrace her aunt as she had earlier, but she maintained the decorum of a lady whilst she replied, "Oh, thank you, Aunt!"

Just then, her uncle returned, and she rose to join him. His face was pink from the cold outdoors, and he grinned widely at the ladies, asking Elizabeth, "Are you nearly ready?"

"Yes, just a few minutes to put on my outer garments."

Uncle warmed himself by the fire whilst Davis helped Elizabeth on with her merino cloak and handed her the fur muff. Gloves alone simply would not do on this frigid a day. It had been an exceptionally cold winter thus far.

When they entered the front hall and were about to leave, she recalled the broadsheet she read that morning. Given all the faith her family had shown towards her ability to be in public without embarrassing them with what they considered inappropriate statements, perhaps she should take this pleasant permissiveness as a signal. Was this a good time to ask for one small indulgence? She addressed her aunt, who stood in the sitting room doorway.

"Do you think it would be possible to make a call to day soon? I have thought a great deal of her and should like to renew the acquaintance."

Uncle's cheery smile faded into a frown, mirroring that of her aunt's. What could be wrong with such a request? Aunt replied, "She may not be in town."

"Mr. Darcy is in town, and I am sure we could find out whether Miss Darcy is as well. Please, Aunt. I should apologize for missing dinner when I had my accident."

The Gardiners looked warily at one another before he spoke. "I am not certain we should continue a familiarity with that family after what happened in Lambton."

"But Mr. Darcy provided a surgeon to care for me and was all attention to my well-being; you told me so. He was quite solicitous to us before I fell as well, inviting us to a dinner we did not attend. If he were at home, I could thank him for that and for—" She could not mention specifically his aid to Lydia and Wickham lest that anger them again, so she stopped speaking.

The air in the room became heavy. But why? Elizabeth looked from one to the other. What was it about the Darcys that caused such a change in their happy demeanours? Should she have used the coarse woollen cloak in the back hall to sneak off for the call? The deception struck her as so unseemly, and they had been showing signs of allowing her to make such calls. Her uncle turned towards her aunt, who nodded. Both had grim expressions.

"We must tell her all," said Aunt Gardiner.

"Very well," replied her uncle, and he stepped forward to take Elizabeth's hand. "We learned more about Mr. Darcy from the surgeon's report after you awoke, and that is the reason we quit Lambton so quickly despite warnings you should perhaps lie still for a few more days."

"But why? What was it about Mr. Darcy?"

"Mr. Darcy was the cause of your injuries."

"No, no, I fell. I tripped. That is what you told me."

"No, your injuries were much more extensive than those you would have obtained in a simple fall. You were beaten and thrown to the floor. Since you were found alone with Mr. Darcy, we could only conclude he was the man who hurt you."

"No, no! It cannot be! He came to see me. He spoke words of…of… attachment. He could not have hurt me any more than he could have hurt his own sister. You must be mistaken. It must have been another."

The voices, the shouting, loud and fierce in her head, came back to her along with a sharp pain in her head.

Her packed trunks sat waiting near the foot of the bed as they were set to leave within the hour. Even with doses of willow bark and laudanum enough to make the journey, an easy day's trip to the closest coaching inn on the way back to London, how was she going to stand the bumping and rocking of the carriage? Each successive leg would be as short as possible and move slowly for her comfort. She carefully made her way to the parlour room and situated herself upon a divan, waiting to be beckoned for the journey.

The door to the apartments swung open a bit, and her uncle's voice came through the gap loud and clear as the door swung towards its jamb once again, but not before she caught a glimpse of Mr. Darcy. Though the men were no longer visible, their voices were as strong as if they were in the room. There was a booted foot in the door as if someone tried to hold it open, yet for some reason, no one entered.

Uncle was speaking through his teeth. "Do not press me, sir. I have had to send you away with gentle admonishment too many times, merely in deference to your stature in the community. I am tired of doing so. You are not welcome here, Mr. Darcy. Please leave."

"I do not wish any discomfort for Miss Bennet or your family, but I understand she is lucid, and I have something important I wish to ask her. If her response is as I expect, I shall be wanting to speak to you of it as well." *Could he be wishing to make his addresses? His words implied enough to allow her to hope.*

"You cannot be expecting to declare yourself after your actions." *Yes, Uncle was incensed! The harsh tone of his voice was dreadful!* "We are aware of what you have done. You tried to force yourself on her. The bruises tell the story my niece cannot."

What?

"Bruises?" *Mr. Darcy's voice carried not only confusion but hurt as well.* "Yes, she fell. I found her in that state."

"That is what we have been saying but only because it is the story you told us. The truth is easily seen from the facts we have since been presented. You attacked the poor girl! She bears marks on her arms and neck—finger marks, from a man's hands! A bruise mars her cheekbone in addition to the knock on her head! You beat her and threw her to the floor!"

"I did no such thing! I would never hurt Miss Bennet! Perhaps before I returned—"

The door drifted until a wider gap showed the two men who meant so much to her. Mr. Darcy was biting a knuckle, agony lining his handsome features. Uncle stepped in the parlour whilst he shouted, "Make haste and leave, I say. I care not that you are the most important man in the county! Do not bother us again! You are banned! Do you hear me, Mr. Darcy? Banned from Elizabeth, banned from my home, and banned from my family. Keep your distance!" *Spittle flew from his mouth as he spat out Mr. Darcy's name, and his arm barred the door when Mr. Darcy lurched forward to gain entrance.*

Mr. Darcy's wide eyes met hers through the open door as he tugged on his cravat. "Elizabeth, I did not—"

The door slammed in his face.

Chapter 11

Her eyes leaking with tears, Elizabeth was ready to collapse to the floor when her aunt took her in her arms. She gasped huge gulps of air but could not seem to fill her lungs. Oh, hopeless situation! Uncle had banned Mr. Darcy from seeing her! He was certain Mr. Darcy had…had beaten her! Yet she was certain he had not. His whispered words, whilst he held her after her accident, were of hope with the promise that his love had been sustained after all those months.

She had behaved her worst to him when she denied his petition for marriage at Hunsford, but he barely raised his voice to her then. From the set of his lips, the torment in his eyes, and the trembling of his hands, he was angry and hurt. His letter showed his good breeding, containing compliments to her and Jane even with his obvious pain and disappointment. Its adieu was charity itself.

He could not have hurt her in Lambton. Elizabeth trusted her own instincts, and they told her the Mr. Darcy she knew would never do such a thing, even in anger or frustration. This situation differed drastically from her foolish first impressions, those assumptions that had caused her to refuse him when he made his addresses at Hunsford and so cruelly reprimand him for his supposed faults.

Even when she did not like Mr. Darcy, she would never have believed anyone who said he could hurt a flea. No, no, there must be another explanation. Another man must be the culprit who inflicted those bruises upon her. But who? Why did this have to be so difficult? She turned her tear-stained face skyward as if in search of something written there to help her with this conundrum.

Mr. Wickham had been in Lambton. He had told her about marrying Lydia. They must have been on their way to Newcastle in a roundabout way to be in Lambton, but Mr. Wickham claimed to fear for his safety in his hometown. So why would he go there? She recalled his agitation and rushed words, making him appear more desperate than angry.

But where was Lydia? Would she not want to stop and see Elizabeth and the Gardiners? Perhaps she did not realize they were there. Mr. Wickham had professed he did not know they were in Lambton before he had accidentally seen Elizabeth looking out the window of the inn.

The window! Mr. Wickham had talked to Elizabeth through the window. He had not entered through the main door but through a back entrance to the servants' stairs after talking to her through that open window! She stepped back, and he grabbed her arms, insisting she hear him out. Then he described his marriage to Lydia. Oh, this was a new memory! She had to tell her aunt!

She pulled back in Aunt Gardiner's arms and accepted the offered handkerchief to wipe the tear streaks from her face. Calmed somewhat, she took a breath to bolster her fortitude.

"If I had a mark on my arms, it was caused by Mr. Wickham holding them earlier that morning. Perhaps it was with enough force to leave a mark. I am not certain. I have only just now remembered it."

"Mr. Wickham? He was not in Lambton," said her aunt.

"But he was. I saw him through the window, and he came in through the servants' entrance." Her aunt looked at her doubtfully, but Elizabeth rushed on. "Please, let me explain. My memories continue to return, and I may soon possess additional clues as to what happened that day."

"Mrs. Bastion said you may never remember it all," her aunt said softly. "By forgetting, you are able to hide from the fear."

Uncle Gardiner nodded, his eyes sympathetic. Their concern, despite her reference to Wickham and Lydia, was gratifying since mention of her sister and the man usually perturbed them.

"I know that," she said, "but this is as clear in my mind as if it happened just yesterday. There was mist on the meadow nearby, but the sun shone brightly that morning, threatening to burn it off, and the sky was free of clouds. Mr. Wickham caught my attention as he walked through the garden. I called out to him, and when he saw me, he spoke to me through the open window of the apartment's parlour. I was not kind to him in my response since I knew his reputation as a rogue, but he pleaded with me to hear his story, to aid him in his travels. He appeared to be alarmed, so I agreed to listen. Then he surprised me by entering through the back door."

Aunt and Uncle exchanged a concerned glance but said nothing.

Elizabeth continued, "He told the tale I have been telling you. I finally remembered where I heard how Mr. Darcy had helped him and Lydia. Mr. Wickham insisted upon Mr. Darcy's generosity, though he also said that Mr. Darcy would claim that it was Uncle who gave so much towards their marriage."

Aunt Gardiner pursed her lips. "The tale of the funds for her settlement and his commission."

"Yes, and that Mr. Darcy paid off his debts of honour. Mr. Wickham was very concerned that I accept his story as true, and when I told him he was lucky to have Mr. Darcy's help, he seemed relieved, yet he repeated the news again." She thought about it for a moment more. "I believe he…he grabbed my arm—my right arm—when he said I must not doubt him. He was quite agitated. Then he grasped both of my arms. This is probably why that memory, the one about their marriage, stayed so present in my mind despite the contusion on my head."

"Did he strike you? Throw you to the floor?" asked Uncle Gardiner with a tone of incredulity.

The question caused her dismay. The lack of remembrance caused her frustration to reappear so quickly after it had been removed. "I do not know. I can barely recall him grabbing me; it is all so vague. The feelings come in bits of clarity among the memories." She shook her head. "No, I am unable to say. It does not seem possible that I would forget such a dreadful act, but I have no recollection whatsoever of that type of injury at his hands." She paused and ran the scene through her mind again. Had Mr. Wickham hurt her, even a little? "No, I believe he merely held me until I agreed to tell his and Lydia's secret whilst keeping their reputations clean. Mayhap he shook me. I am not certain. A pained look came over his face, and he stopped."

Clouds gathered on her uncle's countenance. "Although the grasping and shaking does resemble some of your wounds, your explanation does not account for all of them. Please, try to remember. If it was truly Wickham who hurt you, I have placed myself in a terrifically nasty situation by blaming Mr.

Darcy and banning him from our family. I may find it difficult to recover our standing with that particular gentleman and his family."

"I will try though sometimes it is still as if a fog is hovering just over the truth." The mention of Mr. Darcy buoyed her spirits. Perhaps, once her uncle made friends with him again, she could see him, thank him, and maybe gain his favour once more.

"What about Mrs. Bastion? Perhaps the next time she comes, she can help Elizabeth remember," said Aunt Gardiner as she rubbed her husband's arm, soothing his disappointment.

Mr. Gardiner nodded. "This is a great deal of distressful news for one day. Perhaps we should defer our trip to the book shop."

She had to agree that it had been a trying conversation, but surprisingly, no headache had resulted from the new memories. She would attempt to discover the reason later, but for now, she still felt well. "I believe I am recovered well enough from the new memories, and you are so very busy, you may not find another day that is as suitable. If it is acceptable, I would still like to take the trip."

Her aunt and her uncle both managed sincere smiles and nods, so Mr. Gardiner held out his arm and they went off to enjoy a much better conversation. She vowed to studiously avoid upsetting conversation for the rest of the day to keep from returning to the unsettled feelings they had just released; instead, she focused on the books and the sweet ices they would enjoy afterwards.

A week later
Gracechurch Street

Mrs. Bastion was not expected until teatime. Elizabeth stayed in her room all morning, trying to read, but her mind was too busy to concentrate. The situations she remembered from Lambton played over and over in her head, especially the discussion with Mr. Wickham and the argument between her uncle and Mr. Darcy, and she had tried all week to open her mind to more memories. Oh, how she hoped more clarity on the former would turn around the animosity created from the latter!

Finally, her friend arrived, and the ladies took a walk in the park, a location Mrs. Bastion suggested was more conducive to regaining the past due to its relaxed and happy atmosphere. They chatted about their previous discussions for a while; then Elizabeth finally spoke about the matter pressing most heavily on her.

"Do you recall me speaking of Mr. Wickham?" Elizabeth said.

Mrs. Bastion's mouth opened as if she was about to speak. She hesitated and closed it again.

Aunt Gardiner leaned in. "She said there was an officer of the militia who had deceived the people of Meryton."

Mrs. Bastion nodded with rather pursed lips, frowning slightly. Elizabeth must have ensured a negative opinion regarding Mr. Wickham when she spoke of him before. As Elizabeth completed the recitation of what she recalled, trying to maintain herself as a distant observer so she could limit her emotions and avoid the headache. Goodness knows she had experienced her fair share of tumultuous feelings during her declaration to the Gardiners the week before. She told Mrs. Bastion of Mr. Wickham's visit to Lambton, his story about what happened with Lydia and him, and Mr. Darcy's involvement. Mrs. Bastion had heard this tale before, but this time, Elizabeth was able to relate some of Mr. Wickham's exact words, though she had to admit it was a somewhat broken account with holes and gaps. At points, the report made little sense. Perhaps some memories were missing or out of sequence. However, Aunt Gardiner and Mrs. Bastion listened patiently.

"Of course, I do not remember how all my suffering came to be. But this recent elucidation may be the clue to those injuries my uncle has formerly ascribed to Mr. Darcy and a possibility to discover the full truth of who is responsible for hurting me," she concluded.

Mrs. Bastion was silent for a moment. "This Mr. Wickham—is his Christian name George?" she asked.

How did she know? "Indeed it is. Are you familiar with him?" asked Elizabeth.

"Only by reputation. You see, my sister has a boarding house. She complained to me just this week that one of the men—though otherwise a reputable lodger—had been found playing at dice. Worse, the fellow asked whether there was room for an old friend at her house—and it was a George Wickham, claiming to be a gentleman from Derbyshire. My sister, having known Mr. George Wickham in the past, made it clear she was not interested in having him as a boarder—or anything else, for that matter."

"Was Mr. Wickham gaming with this lodger or was he expected in the future? Perhaps he and Lydia planned a visit to town."

Mrs. Bastion tilted her head. "My sister thinks he is either already in town or well on his way here. This occurred a few days ago. If it is the same man, he is not in Newcastle."

"If he is in London, then perhaps Lydia is too."

"Oh, my Lord!" said Aunt Gardiner as she glanced at Elizabeth. "If we could find Mr. Wickham, perhaps he could shed some light on Lizzy's experience—that is, if he is willing to explain when he could be held culpable for her injuries. We could also lay to rest this situation with Lydia and answer so many questions about where she has been these last months and how she fares."

Mrs. Bastion's brows moved together, and her lips thinned. "I do not believe you can expect a candid revelation of facts from such a man. Respectfully, Miss Bennet, this man is a rogue."

"I am somewhat aware of his actions prior to his marriage to Lydia, but I had hoped that, with Mr. Darcy's help, he had changed his ways," said Elizabeth. "If your sister knows more about his current activities, then I must bow to her superior information."

"I doubt he can change. Two years ago, he had a business agreement with my sister that went foul. My sister should have known better than to enter into such an evil situation, but she is a silly woman who loves money."

"Do not fret, Mrs. Bastion. She is not the only person he has duped, and my sister is not the first lady he tried to elope with. The only difference is that Lydia has no fortune, and according to Mr. Wickham himself, Mr. Darcy was required to create a monetary incentive of sorts so Mr. Wickham would marry her."

"Indeed. My sister's folly was to assist Mr. Wickham in an elopement with another young lady, an heiress. I am mortified to admit that she could have found herself in gaol for her part in it. And there is more. His debts of honour and intrigues run into every county where he has lived. He needed the money, and she was susceptible enough at the time to think she would gain from the association, so she contrived to have him follow her to Ramsgate and mislead a lady in her care."

"Is your sister called Mrs. Younge?"

"Why yes, that is her name!" replied Mrs. Bastion. "How do you know?"

She could not tell the whole of the history since she had been entrusted with the knowledge through Mr. Darcy's letter, which she was loath to share. She would protect Miss Darcy's good name and lend the privacy she knew he expected of her whilst saying enough to let the others know it was a valid claim. "I am aware of the attempt to seduce the heiress in general terms. I know the family." Mrs. Gardiner looked at her in surprise.

"A sad bit of business that was," said Mrs. Bastion. "I am ashamed she allowed herself to be involved with such a reprobate."

Elizabeth shook her head. "You must not blame your sister. Mr. Wickham has ways of speaking and insinuating himself into the wants of others. He makes friends easily but is not capable of keeping them once he has duped them. I listened to his pretty words at one time as well."

"He is a spendthrift and profligate."

"Poor Lydia. I should like to hear how she is faring—whether I am an aunt yet. Perhaps if your sister can find his direction—"

Mrs. Bastion raised her palm. "My sister does not trust him and has cut all ties. You must see, Miss Bennet, he cannot be depended upon for the truth if he can contrive such evil schemes."

"But he may be my only chance!"

Aunt Gardiner took one of Elizabeth's hands in hers. "Shush, dear. Do not fret. We do not have to solve this all today."

"B...but if Lydia is in town—" She broke into a sob.

"She will come to us," said her aunt in a gentle tone as she put her arm around Elizabeth and rubbed her other arm. "If they are indeed married and Lydia has no reason to be ashamed, I am certain she would like to see her aunt and uncle, and she will be doubly pleased to find you at our home."

It was the first time Aunt Gardiner had given any indication she might trust in Elizabeth's version of what happened to Lydia. The possibility calmed Elizabeth enough that she could dry her tears. Perhaps she would soon see her sister and get a chatty version of how she and Mr. Wickham came to be married. It would be half the marriage mystery solved, at least.

Oh, to speak to the one person she knew could solve the rest of the puzzle—not Mr. Wickham, but Mr. Darcy. One rogue and one good man—or so it seemed.

Chapter 12

April 1813
London

Once again, as in past seasons in town, the ballrooms had already begun to look the same by the time the Almack's vouchers were awarded. This evening's hosts, the Richardsons, had made an extraordinary outlay on the best candles, and the room was bright and hot. The ladies had spared no expense on the latest fashion in gowns, and a rainbow of silks was interspersed with the clean black tailcoats of the men. The fragrance of their toilet water mingled in the air as they went down the line of the dance, changing hands with dandies sporting cravats in a sophisticated and complex mix of bows and loops that tumbled down from their throats like waterfalls.

The other aspect of balls that did not escape Darcy's notice was the presence of two young ladies, both of whom bore a remarkable resemblance to Miss Elizabeth Bennet. The ladies had the same natural curl to their hair, allowing for curly tendrils that crept down their necks. They had light and pleasing figures and walked in a blithe, playful way. Both excelled at dancing and appeared to be favourites amongst the gentlemen. One of the two ladies even possessed similar facial features, but the lack of a tiny mole just above the graceful curve of her upper lip and her smallish green eyes gave her away. The second proved to be quite different upon closer inspection: a long, pointed nose on her narrow face contrasted sharply to Miss Bennet's little pert one.

Everywhere he turned, his heart leapt at the sight of one of them, only to be disappointed when he realized she was not the woman he sought. After a few such occurrences, he actually made the acquaintance of both ladies, and since he had promised himself to try to practise more conversation, he danced with each once. Green Eyes, or Lady Althea, chattered and giggled incessantly about gowns, bonnets, and her previous dance partners. Pointy Nose, or Miss Hartricke, spoke nearly as much as the other, trying to impress him with her list of acquaintances though she had something sharp to say about every second person she mentioned. Her gossip was not as bitter as Miss Bingley's, but she certainly intended to boast of her superiority within the *ton*. When she was done with that part of her conversation, she began to compliment him in a grovelling manner. Neither was able to manage a sensible conversation for two dances. How he longed for Elizabeth!

Damn! He was supposed to forget her! Mr. Gardiner had made it clear he would never be allowed near her again. No matter how ill advised the decision, it was fact, and Darcy's own pride revolted. He was nothing like Wickham, a man who would pursue without scruple a woman who was banned to him by her family.

Thinking of his ignoble childhood friend brought to mind two things that still required further investigation: first, Wickham's sighting in Lambton, and second, Georgiana's odd breakfast conversation the day before. Her words reminded him of all kinds of ills from the past, even when he began to search for ways to assist her in overcoming her painful shyness and lack of confidence.

The day before

"Perhaps you should speak to Lady Matlock about joining her for some calls?" he suggested to his sister at breakfast. "You will undoubtedly meet a few more ladies and reacquaint yourself with some friends from school. The practise will be of great aid next year when you come out."

Georgiana's brows rose, her eyes became wide, and she touched her hand to her throat. Then she carefully dotted at her mouth with her linen, her features becoming neutral. "I am not all that easy with calls. Only a few ladies of my acquaintance do not discompose me. They are the handful with whom I am comfortable enough to speak at all."

"I remember some advice given me in the past regarding ease with strangers. As with the pianoforte, you will not achieve success without practise."

Georgiana hesitated as though considering the advice but eventually countered his suggestion with one of her own. "Perhaps I can wait until the autumn to practise."

"That would offer an additional opportunity to expand your circle of friends, but it is not a good reason to put off the exercise. Besides, we may not come to town in the autumn. It may not be worth the long trip for such a short duration of a season if there is a sitting of Parliament."

His sister silently played with the eggs on her plate, shuffling them around between the kidneys and beans.

Poor Georgiana! As one who was uncomfortable with strangers, he sympathised with her situation. How was he to improve her comfort with ladies of the *ton*? "Perhaps it would be less intimidating if you started with acquaintances with whom you are more at ease. Once you have conquered your disquiet, you may be introduced to those of Lady Matlock's choosing for additional practise. She will not expose you to anyone who would have cause to alarm you."

"You do not know this! What if someone knows Mr. Wickham and makes mention of him? I could not bear it!"

Of course, her old fears would surface at a time when she felt vulnerable. Yet Darcy could not accept the discomfort as legitimate in this situation. "No person of our circle would want to speak to you of our old steward's son. He is no concern of theirs."

She stubbornly lifted her chin. "Miss Bingley tried to agitate Miss Bennet by speaking of him at Pemberley."

Ah, now her fear made sense. "I assure you, Lady Matlock will not expose you to the likes of Miss Bingley."

"*You* have."

She had a point. As Bingley's sister, Miss Bingley and Mrs. Hurst had been part of their group of acquaintances even though they would not be of his choosing under other circumstances. "You are more likely to encounter Mrs. Bingley than Miss Bingley now that Mr. Bingley has married, and Mrs. Bingley is kind-hearted. Besides, you have already mastered the art of dealing with Miss Bingley and Mrs. Hurst! You have demonstrated the ability—you just need to learn to expand it."

"But I would be nervous around Mrs. Bingley. She sounds so perfect."

"In many ways, Mrs. Bingley is not unlike you or me. She is quiet and shy, but rather than hiding her feelings behind cool reticence, she uses a smile and gentle words. I think this comforts her when others say or do things that bother her. She is loyal almost to a fault."

"She is Miss Bennet's sister, whom I should like to visit. It is too bad *she* does not come to town."

Darcy nearly bit his tongue in his surprise. How he wished he knew where she was! He was startled when Georgiana spoke up again.

"What about Mrs. Gardiner? Remember how much we liked the Gardiners last year at Pemberley? I would be at ease with them, and it would be an excellent way to practise. Do you think I should call on them?"

How could he face Mr. Gardiner whilst banned from seeing Elizabeth? No, this was not a good idea under any circumstance. "I do not think their address is one you could convince Lady Matlock to visit."

"It cannot be so bad. They were people of fashion. If Aunt does not like their area of town, then you can take me. You would like to renew the acquaintance, would you not?"

"Dearest, as kind as they were at Pemberley, you should not be exposed to the part of town through which it is necessary to travel to arrive at the Gardiners' home. You see, even though they live in a respectable neighbourhood, it is within some rather unsafe ones."

"I have ridden through disagreeable sections of London before, Fitzwilliam."

Darcy gave her as stern a look as he could before he began to counter her argument, but Georgiana was faster.

"We could send a card and have Mrs. Gardiner call on us here. Then I would not be required to pass through untoward streets."

Darcy shook his head. "The last I heard, the Gardiners were in Italy. I do not know when they are expected to return, particularly since the recommencement of battles on the continent. I do not know any common acquaintances with whom to enquire about their situation."

"We know Miss Bennet. I could write to her and ask her."

"Unfortunately, dearest, she travelled with them."

Georgiana huffed and stomped her foot under the breakfast table. "Why does my best chance at a safe call end in nothing?"

"Do not fear. We shall speak to Lady Matlock and have her make a list of potential calls, then you can organize the list in order of those least intimidating first."

"Fine. However, I wish to be able to refuse any that are too frightening."

Darcy shook his head. "No, that is not acceptable. Instead, you will place them later on the list so you have had adequate time to become comfortable with closer friends before you are faced with a call to a stranger."

"But why?"

"By the time you come out, there should be no respectable lady in town whom you are not prepared to see. You will want the best of connections if you are to make a good match. Your friends are only a start. Lady Matlock knows people who will open doors for you."

"I expect I should be grateful for her patronage."

"Indeed."

"Could you discover when the Gardiners are to return, Brother?"

Even if he was able to find out, they really could not make the call until he convinced Mr. Gardiner of his innocence and they reconciled their fledgling friendship. Yet, no way existed to do so; Mr. Gardiner had stated his decision.

What was it about Elizabeth's injuries that had caused Mr. Gardiner to believe Darcy had attacked her? And how could she have come by those injuries whilst he fetched her a glass of wine? He was at a loss. The sighting of Wickham around the same time was suspicious, but Darcy had been out of the room for but a few moments! Try as he might, he could not recall seeing marks on her, other than a scratch and bruise on her face that she may have sustained in the fall. Perhaps something had happened whilst Elizabeth laid in her sickbed; however, she was attended at all times by his own surgeon or assistant, and in no way would they have wilfully injured a woman under their care. Darcy was wild to find out, yet he had nowhere to start.

Georgiana spoke his name questioningly. She sat waiting a rather long time for an answer whilst he wool-gathered, and guilt filled him until he burst. "I shall try." Damn! How could he possibly succeed with so many obstacles in his path? He could not dwell on it at the moment, not when he should concentrate on his sister. "For today, would you fancy a walk in the park?"

With a satisfied smile, Georgiana agreed and excused herself to prepare for the walk.

Once alone, he sipped his coffee. Where could Elizabeth be? No doubt remained that it was Elizabeth he saw in the autumn; there was a powerful feeling in his breast that told him it was so. It would be easy to assume she was on a pleasure tour with her aunt and uncle and that they had been preparing for the journey when he saw her last autumn. By now, they could be hundreds of miles away. But he would feel her absence, and instead, he felt certain she was nearby and safe. The Bennets claimed she travelled on the continent, but his doubts about the veracity of the information her family was sharing overcame any potential to believe their tale. All his senses said they were hiding something. The stories spread in Meryton disconcerted him.

If the Gardiners were in London, he must discover a means to find out for certain. Yet even if they were, Mr. Gardiner was not going to waver on allowing him to see Elizabeth. He told Georgiana he would try to discover when they returned from the continent, but no visit could occur unless he managed to convince Mr. Gardiner he was innocent. And that meant strong proof Mr. Gardiner had no choice but to believe, which seemed the most doubtful possibility in the world right now. But he told Georgiana he would try, and in his heart, he knew that was what he wanted to do.

Chapter 13

Darcy had used various connections to discover whether Mr. Gardiner of Gracechurch Street was conducting business in London at the moment. He also had begged his aunt Lady Matlock to make discreet queries as to whether Mrs. Gardiner was open to callers. At first, it was not easy to convince his aunt of the Gardiners' worthiness, but his assurance regarding the couple's appearance of fashion and impeccable attitudes was enough to satisfy her.

True to her reputation, Lady Matlock was able to reveal to Darcy a few days later that both Gardiners were in town and, indeed, the lady was accepting callers. "Although they are not among the cream of the *ton,* they are connected with some bright stars of our sphere. I believe I might consider including them among my own acquaintance since it has been fairly easy to discover their specific importance in the world. And I must admit to curiosity regarding your interest in them, given how few intimate friends you allow into your closest circles and your fastidiousness for good connections."

"I am not interested in growing my circle of close friends unless I become more than usually partial to a new acquaintance," said Darcy.

"Connections are important in our society. Do not let your sense of importance in the world cause you to pay them too little attention. Your pride keeps you from allowing everyone you meet a place amongst your intimates, and you know it. You will need connections to help Georgiana obtain a suitable husband in both character and position when the time comes."

"Well, dear Aunt, for now, I shall welcome the Gardiners as friends if they will have me. They are known to Georgiana already, and she is comfortable

The Mist of Her Memory

with them. She wishes to pay a call on Mrs. Gardiner before making an attempt with someone who makes her uneasy."

"How did you meet these people?"

"They were touring Pemberley last August with their niece, Miss Elizabeth Bennet, whom I met whilst at the estate Bingley is leasing in Hertfordshire."

"So they are friends of Mr. Bingley?"

"Well, they are the aunt and uncle of the Miss Bennets, and the eldest Miss Bennet is now Mrs. Bingley, so that is the connection. The young ladies hail from a neighbouring estate in Hertfordshire, and I had the pleasant opportunity to be in Miss Elizabeth Bennet's company several times whilst I was Bingley's guest, and I have met her closest relations. I encountered her again in Kent when I was visiting Lady Catherine. Miss Elizabeth introduced me to the Gardiners last summer at Pemberley. Mr. Gardiner is her maternal uncle."

"I presume you will be calling on them?"

"Georgiana and I shall call tomorrow."

"So soon?" His aunt's brows rose. A strange expression came over her face as if she had a revelation. "Oh! Is there any significance to your friendship with this Miss Bennet?" Before Darcy could compose himself, heat rushed to his complexion. He crossed his arms and tried to school his expression to one of neutrality, but it was too late. His aunt had caught him. "Ah, then I must meet her. I shall have to drop my card at Mrs. Gardiner's."

She did not waste time swooping out of Darcy's house. The woman was on a mission.

The following morning

DARCY WAS ON A MISSION AS WELL. ALTHOUGH IT COULD BE DEEMED A fool's errand, he was all pins and needles at the possibility of finding out the answers to his questions about Elizabeth even if he may have to be somewhat impolite in bringing the topic up as more than merely a polite inquiry. But he had to know, and this visit to Gracechurch Street would be the best opportunity he had since he had heard the conflicting rumours. His reputation in the eyes of Mr. Gardiner stood to be improved by any kind of friendship he could contrive between his family and theirs. That alone would make the discomfort worthwhile. In addition, a call to Mrs. Gardiner would help Georgiana begin the necessary practise of making calls before she came out. Hopefully, Georgiana's presence with him today would ease his entry into their home and allow him to learn more about Elizabeth.

He should not have been astonished that the Gardiners lived in a respectable neighbourhood or that their home was a large and well-appointed one—much like the houses surrounding it. He still stretched his neck to view the significance of the place in comparison to his expectations. The home was smaller than his own house in town but not by a great deal. The exterior stone and trim were not gaudy nor uselessly fine; in fact, had he been a man of less consequence, he would not mind living in such a home.

Across from him in the carriage, Georgiana struggled with the fidgets. As they drew up to the Gardiners' home, she spoke in a small voice. "I am nervous."

He reached out and rubbed between her shoulder blades, where he also harboured anxious stiffness. "Do not be so. Recall how friendly and unassuming Mrs. Gardiner is. That will take away the fear to a great extent. You will be automatic in your courtesies, and she will be a gracious hostess, interested in pleasing you. You need only to be yourself."

"Thank you." Her words were sincere, but the set of her lips showed she remained uncertain. Darcy was less concerned. His past experience with the lady of the house led to expectations of welcoming kindness—unless she had been influenced by the husband's prejudice.

The butler greeted them at the door and immediately informed Darcy that he would lead him to the library to speak with Mr. Gardiner. This was an unexpected turn of events, and he glanced at Georgiana to determine whether she was ready to run like an untrained colt or to shore up her strength and join Mrs. Gardiner alone in the room where she was receiving callers. But his sister raised her chin and smiled as if to reassure him. He would need her reassurance for his own fortitude. Speaking alone with Mr. Gardiner? He was not certain whether to be frightened or heartened at the prospect. The last he knew, the man despised him.

When he entered, the anxious expression on the man's face was quickly erased and a rather blank, unapproachable, haughty mien remained. Darcy was not unfamiliar with putting on such a mask. The expression was, no doubt, to hide the emotions Mr. Gardiner really felt. He had to tread carefully with his approach if he wanted the opportunity to convert the firm distance of their association towards acceptance.

Formalities restricted to a polite greeting were shared before Mr. Gardiner spoke of his position. "I do not know what you are playing at, Mr. Darcy, but you must be well aware that, before today, you were not welcome in this house."

"I hope I do not sound impertinent when I say that my intentions are good ones, sir."

"And you had no thoughts of trying to see Lizzy?"

"Is she here? Is she well?" he blurted out without thinking. A man with lesser feelings would have been more discreet and gently nudged at the topic, but he had managed to ruin it before he ever had a chance to win Mr. Gardiner's approbation.

Mr. Gardiner's crossed arms and the haughty lift of his nose strengthened the sense of his unapproachability. "Why should I tell you? You were banned from her company some months ago. Must you insist once again on trespassing on my goodwill?"

"That was not my intention. I come as a friend and to ask after the health of Miss Bennet."

Gardiner went to a side table where he poured himself a drink of some sort and took a large sip. The slight of not being offered the refreshment was intentional. But the man revealed his emotional state by tugging his cravat away from his neck as he spoke. "She is improved. Recently, she read a broadsheet that said you were in town, and I have struggled to contain her pleas to visit Miss Darcy and speak with you."

Relief and hope washed over Darcy. "She is here? She wishes to speak with me?"

Gardiner shook his head. "That is none of your concern at the moment."

"Sir, if you please, perhaps if I described exactly what happened that morning in Lambton, you would find it easier to believe my version of the events. You must understand that I have as much interest as you do in knowing the truth—in knowing how she obtained such severe injuries."

"I saw the bruises with my own eyes. But she now asserts you were not the only person who visited her that morning, and she is convincing in her tale. But if another hurt her, I do not understand why you did not see the wounds yourself. You claim to know nothing of them, but due to the timing of the incident, they must have been present when you were attending her."

"I did not look for harm done, but I was intent upon my own words of comfort for Miss Bennet's benefit. Once again, my self-interest made me forget her, and I have endured remorse to no end. In addition, to be indelicate, the nature of her morning gown would have hidden most of the injuries. Allow me to share my account with you."

Gardiner pursed his lips and barely inclined his head in agreement.

"As you are well aware, during our meeting at Pemberley when I first made your acquaintance, Miss Bennet and I were enjoying a reunion of sorts following a quarrel. What you may not know is that the difference of opinion was in regard to my proposal of marriage and her refusal of me in April of the year twelve."

"Lizzy has spoken of your disagreement, but not at any great length. I did not know an offer had been made. I am surprised that this is the first I had heard of such an eventful conversation when I thought the two of you only knew each other a little. Lizzy has been circumspect."

"I had not made a good first impression or worded the proposal well; however, I believed during the days preceding the accident, Miss Bennet's opinion of me had improved. That morning I arrived with the full intention of renewing my addresses. When I found her, she was weeping and waving some pages of a letter. She was so overcome with grief, she was unable to speak coherently, and I decided to fetch her a glass of wine. It took much longer than I anticipated, so I was out of the room for quite some time. I fretted for her during the whole of it.

"The reason for my delay was some sort of altercation outside of the inn; the barkeeper had joined some fellows at the window. He later told me the disturbance was a fisticuffs with a young man who had left a craftsman's daughter in a family way—a common reason for a fight but a distraction nonetheless. More recently, I discovered there might be a connection between this person and Miss Bennet's injuries. However, at that time, their local issue was nothing of my concern in comparison with her distraught demeanour. I was so taken up with Miss Bennet's misery, I thought little of the situation outdoors at the time."

It was a long speech already and yet there was still more to add.

"When I returned, she was falling to the floor. I tried to catch her, but failed, spilling the wine on her. I lifted her up and found her conscious, but she was not well. Her eyes were large, and she rocked her head to and fro in a strange manner. She said my name and then lamented something unintelligible about her sister before she fell into a fit of sorts. The surgeon later said that, in addition to the cut on her cheek, she had suffered a contusion on the back of her head from her fall. I blamed myself. I thought perhaps that I had surprised her when I came back. I entered without knocking on the door, you see, so she tripped over a chair."

"Those were not the full extent of her injuries," Mr. Gardiner interrupted.

"In no way did any of her injuries come at my hand! My regard for her is too tender to ever hurt her in any way."

Mr. Gardiner stepped towards him and leaned in, but his brows had dropped on the outside and his voice was tremulous. "Finger marks, Mr. Darcy. On her arms and throat!"

Darcy's hand rose to his mouth. No matter that he knew of this before, it was still a horrifying detail! "I am equally as upset as you are. I do not understand how I had been gone long enough for such an attack to take place. Who could have acted in such a vile way?" As if mirroring his own suspicions, Gardiner brought up the very man.

"She thinks she spoke to Mr. Wickham that day, and if it were not for her recent and very convincing description of that event, I would not have spoken to you at all this morning—I would have had you removed from my household. In fact, Mrs. Gardiner convinced me, upon seeing you alight from your carriage, to have the butler send you to me so your presence would not alarm her. I was to discover whether you had knowledge of Mr. Wickham's presence in the parlour at Lambton."

Darcy could hardly believe his ears. "She is here?"

"Visiting with your sister as we speak."

A feeling of gratification swept over him. He had known she had been in London all this time as if he could sense her presence. And, more troublingly, having become increasingly certain that Wickham had had something to do with her injuries—and that Wickham had been at the inn all those months ago—he now discovered Gardiner had the same suspicions. "I have evidence from others that Mr. Wickham was in Lambton at the same time. I am convinced he was the one who hurt Miss Elizabeth, and I will do anything to find him and influence him to tell the full truth."

"Do you think it possible?"

"My friends and I have not had success in apprehending him thus far. But we have had more information on his whereabouts recently."

"Any clarification of the correct history could help my niece, who cannot remember all of the events."

Poor Elizabeth, and likewise, her aunt and uncle—the daily reminder of her injuries must be taxing. More than ever, he was determined to find Wickham and have him correct any misunderstandings as well as he could be coerced to participate in settling the matter. "I wish for everyone's peace of mind."

Mr. Gardiner strode over to the door, opened it, and gestured for Darcy to depart. "I believe you do, but my niece is still fragile. Therefore, I must now ask you to leave without seeing her. I do not want Elizabeth agitated today."

"I shall leave immediately, but I still intend to make my addresses eventually. For that reason, I am resolved to win her good opinion and yours." Gardiner wiped a hand down the side of his face as he sighed and looked away. "I hope we shall soon have a resolution that suits us both." With those words, he quit the room.

He forced a careful smile as he collected his sister in the hall. She was in good spirits from a successful visit and did not hesitate to tell him all the wonderful things that she had experienced, chattering away as the carriage took off.

"And Miss Bennet is looking very well. She was clearly unhappy that you were unable to join the ladies. She expressed her apologies for missing the dinner at Pemberley and asked after your health. Mrs. Gardiner was so kind! She kept asking me questions when I was too shy to speak, and…"

He was listening no longer. Without a doubt, he now wore a smile to rival Bingley's! She was asking about him! He had to discover a way to prove himself to her uncle since, without Mr. Gardiner's trust and approval, he could not approach her unencumbered by the disturbing history at Lambton. But for the first time since that dreadful day, his heart found some semblance of peace.

Chapter 14

Every part of Elizabeth's being wanted rush out to the carriage before Mr. Darcy climbed inside, but restraint was imperative. By the time she had become aware of his presence in the house, all she could do, without a great deal of dramatics, was helplessly continue a polite visit with Miss Darcy and her aunt. She could not act as if she were some sort of wild, spoiled child and run to him. It would be much too ill-mannered for a proper lady to appear in the middle of a gentlemen's meeting uninvited and unannounced.

When her uncle came to the parlour, she had to bite her tongue to refrain from querying him on the conversation he had had with Mr. Darcy. Instead, she picked up her work and tried to concentrate upon it whilst her uncle and aunt discussed the last quarter-hour with each of their guests.

"Miss Darcy was all that was pleasant even though she is still so shy. Elizabeth and I had to carry most of the conversation. How did your discussion with the brother proceed?"

All Elizabeth's attention to little yellow flowers came to a stop as she stared at Uncle Gardiner, waiting for his account of Mr. Darcy's visit.

"He told a detailed story about what happened in Lambton." He proceeded to outline much of what she already knew: that it was supposed she was hurt by falling over a chair, confirming that Mr. Darcy had tried to help her, and that he seemed genuinely distraught over her condition.

"Each time we quarrelled, Mr. Darcy's response was an impassioned speech about his tender feelings and how he could not have hurt Lizzy."

Elizabeth could stand no more. Mr. Darcy's presence had agitated her vigour, and words flew from her mouth in a rush, closely resembling one of her mother's fits of nerves rather than her own well-mannered habit of discourse. "It is true! Mr. Darcy could never have hurt me! He is the best of men." She inhaled a deep breath to relax her attitude before she continued. "As you said, I learned of his goodness not only during our time at Pemberley, but also by the recommendations of those who call him friend. I do so want to see him and talk with him again. Perhaps it would help recover more of my memories. I have not had a headache for ages, and recently I have recalled so much more."

Aunt Gardiner smiled gently. "Perhaps, my dear. But let us hear what else your uncle has to say about their conversation."

Uncle Gardiner continued, relating that Mr. Darcy believed Mr. Wickham had been in Lambton at the same time Elizabeth was hurt and that Mr. Darcy was still looking for him without success. "This business with Mr. Wickham has me questioning my understanding of the facts."

Her aunt turned to her. "If Mr. Wickham can be found and convinced to speak the truth about himself and Lydia, do you think you would remember more clearly?"

Wickham had pushed his tale on her, the one she had at one time been certain was true. But he also said she had to tell it because no one would like his and Lydia's actions—or some such statement. Wait—had he really made such a comment? This was new to her. She concentrated on that moment, willing herself to remember.

I am counting on the benevolence of Mr. Darcy and yourself to see fit to honour her with this version of her future. You are going to tell him this story. This is the truth.

He had tried so hard to influence her—no wonder the facts he was hiding were erased from her memory. "I already recall more. Mr. Wickham said his story was a *version* of the future to help him and Lydia, but I do not know what he meant by saying such a thing. I do not recollect what happened to them in truth." She paused, her mind racing. "Perhaps they did not marry after all. I believe he told me all of this, and he somehow convinced me to tell his side of the story."

"Mr. Darcy spoke of an altercation near the inn when he went to fetch wine for Lizzy. There is a chance it involved Mr. Wickham," Uncle said to his wife before turning to Elizabeth. "Was he there whilst Mr. Darcy went for wine?"

Altercation? Had something occurred other than her own injuries? No matter how much she strove to reach any new recollections, only the conversations with Mr. Wickham and Mr. Darcy came to mind. "I do not know," she said slowly, trying to sift through her memories.

Aunt Gardiner looked into Elizabeth's eyes. "Try, dear. Did Mr. Wickham speak to you before Mr. Darcy? Were men chasing Mr. Wickham when he came into the room? Was he angry?"

Elizabeth closed her eyes, concentrating. It was all such a muddle! Mr. Wickham—window—upset—pleading—hiding—Mr. Darcy—fetch you a glass of wine—gone—noise—window—shaking her—hurt—Mr. Darcy—my love. "I think the encounter with Mr. Wickham occurred before Mr. Darcy came, but I cannot be certain. He may have returned. I do not know. I cannot…it happened so fast…I…I think so, but…" All the faces, actions, and words swirled around in her brain in a confused tumult. But she refused to get a sick headache or burst into tears. She took calming breaths and then opened her eyes. "I want to remember, I do! The memories are so mixed up; I cannot make sense of all that happened that day."

"Do not think on it any longer," her aunt urged with concern in her eyes.

"But I must! If my memories can show that it was not Mr. Darcy who hurt me, you will allow me to see him again!"

"Oh, dearest, do you think your heart may be misleading you?"

"No, I do not," she said in a firm voice. "He was not in the room when I was hurt. I am certain that is what he told Uncle as well."

"Yes, yes," said her uncle. "That is what Mr. Darcy insists upon."

"Perhaps that is why he offered me wine. He saw how badly I was injured."

"I am sorry, but he has admitted not to seeing your physical ills, only your anguish. He did say you were falling when he returned to the room with the wine."

"So perhaps I was injured whilst he fetched the wine."

"He did not see the bruises before or after. He merely recalls your fall and how he tried to catch you before you hit the floor. He thought the mark on your cheek was from the fall."

"Yes, and he spoke to me then, but I was dizzy and unable to answer him. I have no idea how I obtained the drastic injuries you describe." How could any person treat her so harshly? And why?

Her aunt took Elizabeth's hand and patted it to soothe her. "Well, you must wait until your thoughts are less excited before you try to solve this mystery, my dear. It may come to you again soon, but do not try so hard. Just like your other memories, this will be recovered too. Allow yourself time."

"I am convinced we shall find out more when Mr. Darcy finds Wickham," her uncle said. "He will not hesitate to try to speak with me again; I know it. His feelings for you seem quite strong, my dear."

Elizabeth was heartened but still upset. "Does…does he know where Mr. Wickham is in London?"

Her uncle scratched his head. "I do not know. He said he was seen at Lambton."

"Mrs. Bastion said Mr. Wickham was probably coming to London," said Elizabeth, "so he may have moved. He had asked her sister about coming to her boarding house, but she turned him away."

Aunt Gardiner added, "Mrs. Bastion was reluctant to request information with regard to his current lodgings. It seems her sister is no friend to the man."

"This is too important to continue to heed her wishes," he said. "We must approach this sister for Wickham's direction. Hopefully, she will change her mind once she knows these facts and his perfidy. It could lead us to Lydia as well."

Elizabeth nodded. "Mrs. Bastion's sister knows him well. She was duped by him in a near-scandal involving the stealing of an heiress."

Uncle Gardiner's heavy brows shot up. "I was referring to Wickham's actions towards *you* if indeed he is the one who beat you. But stealing an heiress! He is a worse knave than I knew! In any case, she must be convinced to help us and to realize it is in her interests as well. If she knows where he is staying, that will be a start."

"He is probably somewhere less than acceptable, I would think, if he requested a room at her boarding house and was turned down," said her aunt.

Another memory crossed Elizabeth's mind—a memory of the man as he stood in the room at the inn, pleading with her. He was not Lydia's scarlet officer at all; rather, he wore a tailcoat too short and loose. Why would he not be in uniform? She blurted out, "He must not be in the regulars as he insisted. He wore no uniform of any sort but gentlemen's clothes instead. He would not usually wear clothing that fit him so ill."

"Borrowed clothes. That is a help," said her uncle.

If only her memories were clearer! But how could she force those events to return to her mind? Even with Mrs. Bastion's help, her memories never simply revealed themselves fully. Did Mr. Wickham hold the key to what occurred in Lambton? And was he now in London? As much as she wanted to find him to fill in that important missing piece of her history, she dreaded it as well.

"I am concerned about Mr. Wickham," she confessed. "I hope he is found and can tell us what I cannot remember, but I fear that he might try to hurt me again. I do not know why on earth he would have done so before, though. I agreed to tell his story, even though there was no corroboration. I wish Lydia had accompanied him to the inn instead of picking out a stupid bonnet."

"Lydia was with him in Lambton?" asked her aunt.

"I do not know for sure. I assumed, because Mr. Wickham was in Lambton, she must have been as well since they had eloped together only days before. You know Lydia—always wanting a new bit of lace or frippery that she cannot afford. But at least part of his story was a deception, so I do not know how much of it to believe. I cannot trust him for the truth of Lydia's whereabouts. For all I know, she was in Newcastle or even still in town."

Her uncle shook his head. "Lambton is not on the way to Newcastle. I suspect, if he had the chance, he did not take her with him. We did track them both to Clapham and they were said to be planning to travel on to London. Even if he took Lydia with him, the reprobate has ruined her reputation, and I am afraid for her safety after what he may have done to you."

"So you agree with me: Mr. Wickham was the one who must have hurt me, and Mr. Darcy is not the villain you believed him to be?" she asked.

"I am beginning to see your point, yes. As I say, we need to find Mr. Wickham to settle all this. But I have a feeling I will be eating humble pie before long."

"Since we are no longer of a mind to blame Mr. Darcy, I believe it would be prudent for Lizzy to join me when I return the call to Miss Darcy within the week," said her aunt.

Oh! Maybe Mr. Darcy would be there!

"I agree," said her uncle. "I no longer have qualms about a call where Lizzy and Mr. Darcy are in company with others."

Aunt Gardiner touched Elizabeth's arm gently. "Dearest, you were supposed to be attending a ball with Mrs. Fraser tonight, but under the circumstances, I wonder whether you should take some powders and rest instead."

Her uncle agreed. "Let Elizabeth have a chance to calm herself after the assault to her senses these revelations must have caused. No one should have to hold a brave face at a ball."

This would not do. She was fully capable of enjoying the evening out. In fact, despite the difficult topic, the conversation had heartened her more than a little about the future. "I shall be fine. I have so looked forward to this event, and we rushed my gown so it would be ready. Let me attend. I shall be fine, I assure you."

Aunt gazed at Uncle with a slight smile. "It is not as though she will be harmed by enjoying the few dances Mrs. Fraser has arranged for her. In fact, her heart could be better eased if she has a bit of indulgence tonight."

"Yes, a distraction would be just the thing after so heavy a discussion," Elizabeth added.

"Perhaps, if you have your supper on a tray, you will be spared the additional excitement caused by the children," said her aunt.

She agreed. "But only if they are allowed to see me in my gown. Harriet and Martha have been anticipating my 'princess dress' all week."

"Very well," said her uncle. "You may have your ball as planned. I am relieved to know this is a small, private ball and you are well chaperoned."

Elizabeth could hug herself; she was so pleased. She turned her mind towards the ball. Although she might know a lady or two beyond Mrs. Fraser, she had not attended such affairs in the past, so she would not have many acquaintances. Still, Mrs. Fraser had chosen this ball for exactly that purpose—helping to ease her into superior society and meet a few members of the *ton*, yet not expose her to too much on her first real event of the Season.

Oh, but she could imagine the ballroom with its elegant décor, the flickering light of the chandeliers brightening the night, the gentlemen in all their formal finery clasping hands with lovely ladies in supple, swishing gowns across the palette of colours whilst they shifted down the lines of the dance in perfect formation. Elizabeth took delight in anticipation of the smells of a sumptuous supper, the tickle on her tongue from cool refreshments, and the pleasant exhaustion from a very late night of amiable activities. It had been too long since she had enjoyed a ball. And she would enjoy one again tonight!

Yes, tonight she would create happy new memories. And she would dance!

Chapter 15

Darcy would have been content to miss the Powell ball, but Frederick Randall, Lord Powell, had been a dear friend from as far back as Eton, and his shy wife was completely unlike the man-eating devils constituting most of the ladies of so-called superior society. Though the ball was a small, private affair, Darcy still struggled with the precise time to arrive at such a function. Should he arrive early and fit into a small crowd, so he would be engaged with them by the time the people of fashion appeared much later in the evening? Or should he delay his appearance on the stairs to lessen the painful eternity he would have to posture and communicate with those he considered a waste of time? Neither enticed him. Really, he would rather be at home with a book, occasionally taking the time to ponder the mystery of Elizabeth Bennet's situation.

Of course, he was always thinking of her, and as he quietly entered the small but well-appointed ballroom, he espied one of the two ladies who resembled her on the other side of the room. Any moment now, he would realize which one it was, and he would be disappointed that it was Green Eyes or Pointy Nose instead of Elizabeth. He sighed. Not every slight lady with dark curls would be his love.

The lady turned, and he halted so abruptly he nearly fell on his face. It was her—Elizabeth!

Nothing had prepared him for this moment. Now, when Elizabeth Bennet appeared before his eyes, he refused to believe it could be her. And yet it *was* her—here—in *this* ballroom! Suddenly, all the promenading couples on the dance floor stilled, and the din of the guests' chatter became dull noise.

Nothing else in the room mattered but *her*. His heart throbbed almost out of the confines of his chest. Elizabeth had not yet seen him, which gave him a few moments to merely stare at her, his mouth slightly agape, forgetting all about his habit of schooling his features. She moved with such playful grace as she spoke to her companion, he could swear he had only seen such whimsical delicacy within nature. Beyond that, the unique, unrivalled beauty of her face enhanced the brilliance of her fine, dark eyes in a manner that he had never seen in any other lady. How could he have mistaken the other ladies with their dull, wiry hair where hers glowed? So focussed was he upon assembling a list of the vast number of Elizabeth's attributes that the presence of a friend at his side completely escaped him.

"So which of the ladies has the fastidious Fitzwilliam Darcy's full and rapt attention? It cannot be the widow Fraser, even though she is still handsome for an older lady," Lord Powell teased.

Darcy steeled himself for the playful jibes. He knew better than to let down his guard! Powell was a great deal like Elizabeth in his cleverly worded mischief. A brief recollection of his encounters with her made Darcy crave her intelligent attention. He always would. Nothing was more provocative than the brilliance of that lady's eyes as she coyly matched wits with him.

Those dark orbs met his from across the room, and Lord Powell faded away. She was too easy to admire and, had he not known he was being watched, Darcy would have poured all the love in his heart through his expression of admiration. The delicate, rose-embellished silk of her gown was almost the same colour as her skin and made her appear as if she were some kind of faerie, and its abbreviated bodice allowed a significant glance of her best assets where her topaz cross lay nestled. Her hair had been fussed over to an extent he had never seen before—a complicated set of curls and plaits tightly arranged as was the fashion these days—yet the nape refused to stay within its pins. With lips of the loveliest rosebud shape and her sweet cheeks a comely blushing pink colour, no other met her match. Oh, how he wanted to steal her away and kiss those lips until they were quite red, run his lips down her throat, and more!

Lord Powell cleared his throat, and Darcy started. "Miss Bennet it is!" said Powell. "Would you care for an introduction?"

Gardiner had said he did not want her upset by him…but she was at a ball, meeting with all sorts of gentlemen and surely ready to dance at any time. He glanced around. Gardiner and his wife were nowhere to be seen, but the lady who stood with Elizabeth must be her chaperone—the very respectable widow of Mr. George Fraser, a gentleman from Derbyshire as well. He had known the couple in Mr. Fraser's lifetime. Mrs. Fraser vetted the requests for dances and whispered to Elizabeth behind her fan as members of the *ton* entered the ballroom. She would certainly approve of him.

"Miss Bennet and I are old friends," he replied. "However, you could be of assistance. I need an excuse to approach her with more ease than I could manage on my own. I do not desire her to see me as unforthcoming, and I am afraid that my tendency to be restrained will do me a disfavour."

"Ah, the great Darcy deprecating himself! I believe this lady has cast a spell over you!"

"I believe so too, Powell, and anything you can do to forward me in the lady's favour will be well appreciated."

"Since when have you been on the marriage market? I am used to seeing you dance with few and notice no one!" Powell's bushy brows rose as he smirked. "Very well. I shall reacquaint you, and then you can use your proud, cold expression to entice her to dance."

"I am not that way with Miss Bennet. She is a lively sort of friend."

"I am a lively sort of friend too. Does she also enjoy making sport of you?"

"Something like that, yes. Her playful manners are quite charming, and I enjoy the banter we share. And I believe I could surprise you with how flirtatious I can be with the right lady."

Powell chuckled. "And this is the right one, then? I should like to see what Fitzwilliam Darcy deems being flirtatious. I imagine you might actually burst into in a real smile once in a while. Perhaps flatter her on her choice of ball?"

"You well know I am amiable enough with those I know. I am merely awkward among strangers."

"True, and most ladies fit among the latter, or at least, they do not recommend themselves as more than indifferent acquaintances. But perhaps this Miss Bennet is distinctive. Though I have met her only today, she seems cheerful and engaging without false airs."

"And I am wasting my time speaking to you of her whilst her available dances are being filled." Darcy waved towards a grinning buck obtaining a promise for a dance with Elizabeth. "Will you assist me, or are we off in different directions? I should like to re-establish the connection."

"I shall come along and vouch for your good character."

Darcy was not sure whether to laugh or scowl at the offer, but Powell was a good fellow, and the friendly discussion they had just held was the sort of light conversation that would bode well for a reunion with Elizabeth.

He moved with as much dignity and grace as possible given that he wanted to rush to be by her side. A bow was met by curtseys from the ladies. "Mrs. Fraser, Miss Bennet, how do you do?"

He could have practically floated away when Elizabeth replied she was well, her thick lashes lowering, not in a coy or flirtatious way, but with natural modesty. When they rose again, she made much the same inquiry of him. The lady at her side echoed the pleasant greeting, but he barely noticed Mrs. Fraser as he was staring at Elizabeth.

"I am quite well," he replied, a small smile coming more naturally to him than he had anticipated. This was how he reacted in the presence of a friendly lady.

"And Miss Darcy?" Miss Elizabeth inquired. "I was pleased to see her earlier today."

"As was she to see you. She is well."

"I am glad to hear it." He made a friendly enquiry of Mrs. Fraser, and she spoke positively about her time in town then took up a conversation with Lord Powell about his family. Darcy's agreeable feelings made him abandon his resolve to merely talk to Elizabeth, and he ventured for more. "Miss Bennet, would you do me the honour of dancing a set with me at some time this evening?"

"Indeed, sir, it would be my pleasure."

Her response was positive enough in tone that he attempted to gain more than a mere half hour of her time. "Have you availability for the supper dance?"

Mrs. Fraser grinned like the cat who got the cream as she watched them make their arrangements, and Powell's smile was not far different. To his dismay, he was unable to make any more conversation with Elizabeth as her next dance partner came to claim her and they took their place in the line.

The time until their dance was interminable! He spent most of his time watching her as she danced with other gentlemen, her soft gown swaying with her graceful movements.

He, too, stood up for a few sets with ladies unlikely to read much into his attention, including Mrs. Fraser. As had been his recent habit, he practised his skills of friendly discourse with these ladies as Elizabeth had advised that the effort would help him in performing to strangers. Mrs. Fraser was kind about telling him the benefits of a friendship with Miss Bennet, amusing him since he could only smile his approval and state his agreement in the most general of terms.

Finally, the time came, and he was able to claim her. His greatest hope was for Elizabeth to be receptive to him for all the same reasons as he was inclined to renew his addresses. For now, he would settle for polite time to converse with her regarding any topic she chose. The bustle of the ball, the cadence of the music, and the pounding of his own heartbeat in his throat vied to overthrow his sensibilities as he struggled for something to say. His scattered nerves and inability to produce the simplest of conversation topics brought to mind their dance at the Netherfield ball and her teasing manner that coaxed him into conversation—*"One must speak a little, you know. It would look odd to be entirely silent for half an hour together; and yet for the advantage of some, conversation ought to be so arranged, as that they may have the trouble of saying as little as possible."*

"May I ask after the health of your family?" he began. Damn! It was barely more interesting than speaking of the weather. Her presence had affected him to such an extent, no interesting subject of discourse came about in his brain.

"They are all well, I thank you." Her voice was small and her eyes, though warm, had an appearance of distraction about them. Of course, little else existed to sustain a discussion, as she had already asked after Georgiana.

His every desire was to have her expression become content once again and, even more, demonstrate her admiration for him. It moved him to make more of an effort to speak even though he was still at a loss. How was he to fill the unnerving lack of topic in his mind? Her advice at the Netherfield ball came to mind.

"I am aware you believe that observations on dimensions and numbers at a ball are more important than discussions of books. Therefore, I must note how very many couples there are for the size of this room."

Her head snapped in his direction as if startled. A bright smile appeared upon her lips, enhancing every feature on her face. Her fine skin glowed with the slightest blush as she replied, "You tease me, Mr. Darcy." She remembered!

"If I were to gain such a remarkable change in countenance by doing so, I should tease you every day for the rest of my life." Oh, what a declaration! But he was a man in love, and he simply could not be sensible.

Her eyes sparkled in the flickering light of the candelabras, but the forms of the dance separated them for a short time. When they were reunited, her reply was swift. "Do not provoke a lady who enjoys making sport of others, as it is tantamount to throwing down the gauntlet for a competition on who can make the greatest mockery of the other."

"I do not dare!"

Laughter bubbled from her mouth like the brook at Pemberley, rolling from her in trickles of mirth, yet subdued enough to be called ladylike. For his part, he merely grinned in wild happiness as her humour vanquished all his misgivings and fears about his ability to engage her in the way he had come to love when they had first made each other's acquaintance. Her comfort seemed to be equally affected as a lift of one brow preceded her witty retort.

"A pity this is not a Scottish air. You do owe me a reel," she replied.

"I owe you? You were the one who declined my offer!"

"But you were not in earnest at the time."

"Indeed I was. I wanted very much to dance with you even if it would have meant struggling through the forms with fewer in the group than is customary."

"You cannot be recalling it correctly. You did not like me then."

He merely shook his head and smiled.

"You liked me then?" Her lips twitched as if hiding a smile, yet her eyes shone, betraying her similarity of mind with his.

He nodded, his smile broadening. He had not smiled so much since she had been at Pemberley, and then he had all but made a fool of himself with his mooncalf face whilst she helped Georgiana with her music.

"Oh! Heavens!" She let out a little burst of laughter, and her cheeks turned a pretty pink again.

He could not help but widen his grin.

"Then I am a terrible person because I so enjoy dancing with you now. That evening at Netherfield would have been a good chance to do so had I not been influenced by the untrue tales I heard from your enemy."

The mood darkened her looks ever so slightly, but the ill-natured moment was short-lived when she directed a reassuring smile his way. He had probably mirrored the gloom when the thought of Wickham crossed their pleasant discourse.

She surprised him with her next statement.

"Sir, I must thank you for all you have done for my poor sister. It was not deserved, and you must trust that I shall not broadcast it any further." As she spoke of her gratitude, she stammered and looked aside as if her confidence was abandoning her.

The dance separated them for a few moments precisely when she had finished her statement. What had he done for her sister that required such an uncomfortable speech? No more than was deserved. When he learnt that her eldest sister still carried tender feelings for Bingley, he had struggled for a way to tell him without any promises that Bingley would be received by her sister after he had all but jilted her.

Her hand was offered up to him again and they continued down the line. "I do not deserve your gratitude. Their situation was my fault. All I did was correct the error."

"I was not positive of the truth of it, and I thank you for clarifying. But you cannot for a moment blame yourself for their folly, for his taking advantage of her innocence, or her dreams of love and marriage before she even had an offer. You are the best of men, and my family does not know how much they owe you for your intervention."

This was a rather aggrandized generalization of Bingley and Mrs. Bingley's attraction in the beginning, but he would not insult her by arguing her point. "You must not think I did it for your family. Everything I did for them, I did with you in mind. If you must thank me, thank me for yourself. It was all for you."

A most becoming blush overspread her features and spread down to the enticing glimpse her fashionable ball gown revealed of the tops of her breasts. The knowledge that his gaze had settled there came to the forefront of his muddled mind, and he flinched and forced himself to look away. His eyes rose again to meet her warm and affectionate ones in return of his own intense regard. He tried to show all his adoration for this lady who had owned his heart since nigh on the first moment he paid attention to her, which was immediately after he had insulted her most cruelly. His folly for those prideful words would long be his regret.

The final strains of the second dance played, and their time together on the floor came to an end. Yet, their opportunity for conversation had barely begun, and Darcy meant to make the most of her proximity to him at supper.

He offered his arm, which she took with a playful smile. They joined the queue towards the tables, and he was solicitous as he helped her take a seat next to him.

Mrs. Fraser chose to sit with her most recent dance partner, a rotund gentleman of near forty who owned a reasonable estate. Darcy would not like to see Elizabeth's sponsor taken in by a fortune hunter, so this pairing boded well, not only for its potential for Mrs. Fraser's future but also for his desire to speak privately with Elizabeth on matters not suitable for the dance floor. Those moments would be few, however, since she was popular with the gentlemen. With any luck, a second dance could be procured, and he would be able to produce enough sensible yet charming words to encourage her smiles and give himself something to dream on that night after the ball.

Chapter 16

Their set had given Elizabeth hope that all was not lost between them. Mr. Darcy was making a great effort to please her with his conversation. Their discussion was reminiscent of the verbal wrangling they had shared while she stayed at Netherfield Park, though with less animosity on her part. It surprised her to realize the profound effect he had on her so early in their acquaintance, but she had never paid attention to it until tonight. At the time, she had been certain they disliked one another and that he might be judging her. But perhaps all her unease at that time had spoken to a desire for his approbation.

Now, as he escorted her to dinner, the heat from his body next to hers caused a similar rush of warmth to flow over her skin from the roots of her hair to the tips of her toes. The simple touch of her gloved hand on his strong arm and the occasional brush of her body against his superfine wool coat brought awareness to her every pore, and her breath became quick and shallow as the memory of falling into his arms at Lambton returned to her. The fleeting occasion provided her a brief moment of strength before her loss of consciousness, and his precious words echoed in her head: *"my love."* Oh, if only she could know for sure that his love had survived the argument at Hunsford.

He was most attentive to her needs, offering her the platters beyond her reach, foods he must have noticed were her favourites: minted lamb, braised celery, currant pudding, pickled walnuts. They joined interesting discussions among those seated nearby until the others became quite engaged themselves and he leaned in to speak just to her. "I should like to comfort you by saying that my cousin Colonel Fitzwilliam and I have searched for Mr. Wickham these last few months, and I am only sorry we have not been successful thus far."

He had broached exactly the topic she considered raising herself, and he planned to support her! If she ever held an infinitesimal concern that he could have been responsible for her pain and suffering, she was beyond those imaginings now. He was as much her Mr. Darcy as he had been when he smiled at her across Georgiana's pianoforte that ill-fated summer. "I thank you and your cousin for your efforts on my behalf."

"We have had several occasions when we believed ourselves close, but with no luck. However, we are hopeful that new information regarding his location will be more fruitful."

"My uncle Gardiner is also looking into reports of Mr. Wickham's most recent lodgings. We wish to learn more about his role at Lambton and the truth behind his stories."

"I hope my saying this does not cause you renewed anguish, but he must be taken to task for his attack."

"The information at hand truly points to him as the person responsible, yet it is still confusing. I have no memory of the specifics, you see. Until recently, I remained unaware of the extent of the damage done, and I certainly do not have the instigator's face in my mind. I remember Mr. Wickham being in the room and speaking to me of my sister, but I do not remember how I was hurt." She gave him as meaningful a stare as she could accomplish. How else could she tell him that she never doubted his integrity and that he could never wilfully cause her pain?

Several fleeting expressions crossed his beloved face. At first, he appeared agonized at the mention of her wounds, but when she continued to speak, his countenance softened as if her words caused some kind of new understanding that, until that moment, he had not known. "For your relief, I wish we could prove the man responsible for the wrongdoing and end the multiple conjectures. It must be frustrating not to remember yet have a strong sense of the truth."

Although it appeared he felt vindicated, her faith could not but help the matter. She could not meet his gaze when she made the confession that was meant to help. "I may not remember the truth, but the relative merits of each man involved influenced my beliefs of what probably took place, and

The Mist of Her Memory

Mr. Wickham certainly does not inspire a belief of decency."

A meaningful breath of air escaped him, and her head rose. His noble brow remained furrowed, and his eyes were full of pain. "At the time, I believed it to be the letter that upset you."

"Yes, the letter from Jane did have a part in my concern, but you have since remedied my frustration over that situation. Her troubles disconcerted me." All of a sudden, the timing of something that afternoon became foremost in her mind, and she blurted out to Mr. Darcy, "But when you came into the room, my suffering was caused by Mr. Wickham, and solely Mr. Wickham. I only remember bits and pieces. I suppose providence hid his ill treatment from my memory. Fortunately, this limits my ability to feel regret about the event."

"And my role? What do you recall there?"

His tender words came to mind, but the last thing she could do was repeat them. The heat that flashed over her entire being at the remembrance was such a distraction! "You…you were most solicitous, sir. I am quite grateful for your kindness and your efforts to calm and assist me in my unfortunate situation."

"I wish I had not left that parlour to get you a glass of wine. As it was, I spilled it all over your gown."

"In attempting to support me."

"Aye, but everything I have done related to that unfortunate day has turned bitter." His expression matched his words.

Oh, how she hated that she had changed the tone of the discussion! How could she return to the easy banter of before? Heaven forbid Mr. Wickham to interfere in her life forever! They must stop this now. To assist in brightening his spirits, she touched his arm lightly and smiled when he lifted his gaze to meet hers. "I find I would rather dwell on the positive aspects of my time in Derbyshire, as short as our blissful hours were."

He smiled slightly again. "I shall try," he said. Sadness lurked in his eyes, but she was comforted by the knowledge that he was making an effort to improve his spirits for her benefit.

"I hope the pleasant memories bring you relief."

"If you could remember my words when I was allowed for all too brief a moment to see you in your sickbed, it would bring me immeasurable relief."

Oh yes, she remembered some of them—the best parts! However, she certainly could not quote them at supper during a ball. "I do remember a great deal, sir, and I received them with gratitude no matter how weakened I was when you made your confession. I hope it is not too impertinent of me to state that I hope our interactions this evening show our ability to start anew precisely due to the feelings you so eloquently uttered in that short time." She dropped her lashes. Had she been too candid?

He released another long sigh, and she gazed at him once again. He had put his hand to his chin as if deep in thought. "I wish I had had the time to say more in Lambton, but you appeared to be disconcerted by my attentions, and I was asked to leave. Then your uncle…"

How had everything changed so quickly? Her uncle never thought to say, so perhaps she could obtain the answers she sought from Mr. Darcy. "What happened?" she asked in a soft tone.

His face crumbled. "He was given details by the surgeon of the injuries that became obvious over time, those beyond the blow to your head. He then decided I was no longer welcome in your presence."

She pressed the tips of her fingers to her lips whilst composing herself before she dared speak. Would that he knew a tongue lashing from her uncle was no longer an event he need fear! She could attempt to reassure him herself, though. "I do believe that will alter now we are convinced one man has all the goodness and the other has all the appearance of it. The Gardiners and I are almost certain Mr. Wickham was the blackguard who inflicted those injuries upon me, based upon my returned memories and his reputation for trouble in the past. I clearly recall his arrival that day, and this helped to change my uncle's mind. That is progress, is it not?"

His expression became pinched before he lowered his gaze to his plate of food. "I guessed your uncle's views may have been your own. Had you been set against me, I do not know what I would have done."

Even though he just agreed to dwell on the happiness of the past, his words proved that his suffering lingered barely below the surface. He did not seek her uncle's approbation; he sought hers! What a sweet, sensitive man.

Could she renew his smiles for her alone? "As often as I heard those accusations, I was never once convinced of them. In fact, I always harboured strong doubts. One who spoke such tender professions could never hurt me. I cherished those words although, at first, I thought they were merely a lovely dream that fulfilled my wishes. Yet I hoped that part was real." Although her confession was bold, her encouragement was important to help lift his gloom. Thankfully, she was rewarded by the change in his demeanour; his countenance relaxed from its tortured state, and his softened eyes could not be more indicative of his relief.

He leaned closer and spoke in a whisper barely audible over the din of the room. "You give me hope where I once thought hope was gone."

Her heart was so full, it could barely be contained in her breast, yet she could not meet his gaze as she made a shy reply. "Then I am satisfied we understand each other."

At his laugh, she glanced at his beloved face, and his appearance was enough to hold her regard. He had turned an endearing hue of pink after the outburst, but he continued alternating between grinning with a delighted glow on his face and attempting to school his features in some semblance of dignified reserve as he looked into her eyes with clear affection.

This was the man she loved, the one who was not as proud as he seemed but was merely trying to hold a public image of noble respectability for the sake of his grand name. And illustrious it was to be Mr. Darcy of Pemberley. If any chance remained that she could once again be offered the opportunity to become his wife, she would accept with eager joy. All doubts had been laid to rest that he desired such of her.

"What say you to that, Mr. Darcy?" a countess asked from across the table, interrupting their little tête-à-tête.

He straightened from where he was leaning towards Elizabeth, and she likewise moved quickly to centre herself in her chair. When had they become in such close proximity to one another? The warmth of mortification trickled down from her face to cover her body as she stared at her plate.

Mr. Darcy cleared his throat before responding, "My apologies, I was not attending."

"Lady Powell has outdone herself with her table, am I correct?"

"Yes, of course. Splendid. It has been a splendid ball all around."

She dared look at him through her lashes, and his smouldering eyes rewarded her. How she desired nothing more than to remain by his side! She may have been overwhelmed by him, and their unstated yet understood depth of affection may have dominated her sensibilities, yet she was unable to dwell upon them for the time being. Although she was compelled to attend to the others and the festivities, the evening proved to be entirely enjoyable compared with her months of solitude at her aunt and uncle's house.

The event was far from complete, and not a moment was wasted at the end of the meal as Mrs. Fraser swooped in to gather her for her next dance partner.

Elizabeth moved through the forms by rote. Her mind was so full of Mr. Darcy that she required the uniformity and familiarity of the dance to get through each step. Nonetheless, she was a merry partner to each gentleman she danced with for the rest of the evening. Nothing could spoil her mood.

Chapter 17

As expected after a night that stretched to the wee hours of the morning, Elizabeth slept late the day after the ball. Even when she awoke, her mind was so full of Mr. Darcy that she was disinclined to rise too early. Better to stay alone in her room and reflect on their conversation at dinner. It had ended abruptly, and even though so much had been said, she longed for more information.

How much more did he know about Mr. Wickham? Had Mr. Darcy spoken to Mrs. Younge—he knew her from being Miss Darcy's erstwhile companion—and had the success in finding out more about Mr. Wickham's location, results she had yesterday wished upon her uncle? What about Lydia? Was she in town or was she in Newcastle?

Most of her time this morning was spent reminiscing about their thinly veiled words of admiration and dedication to each other. Did he perceive correctly her intention when she said they understood each other and told him she had heard his words at her sickbed?

"My feelings and wishes are unchanged from last April. Please awaken for me. I hope beyond hope from our time at Pemberley that your affections have undergone so material a change as to be the opposite of Hunsford, yet I need to hear it from your lips."

At length, she made it down to breakfast before noon. She was required to relate her experiences from the night before to her aunt and young cousins—"How many of the ladies wore pink, cousin Lizzy? How many wore blue? What dances were called? Who did you have supper with?"—which prompted Elizabeth to mention having danced the supper dance with Mr. Darcy, a comment that drew a small, satisfied smile from Aunt Gardiner. After Elizabeth had related the remainder of the pertinent details of the evening, her aunt pleased her by stating her intention to return the call to Miss Darcy.

Following breakfast, Elizabeth returned to her room to dress for the call. She was so terribly nervous! She carelessly threw gowns onto her bed. None were really fine enough for a call to the Darcys. In the end, Davis helped her pick a newer sprigged muslin for the purpose.

Even so, her nerves continued to plague her during almost the entire carriage ride to the Darcy townhouse. Thankfully, her aunt reached over at one point and patted her hand, stilling it from its busy writhing.

"Remember, dear, you know Miss Darcy. She is terribly shy, so she will not bite. Think of it as a visit to the home of any shy lady you know. Are there those in Hertfordshire that match that description? It will help you calm yourself."

The idea did calm her, and she breathed deeply in her relief. Yet, what if Mr. Darcy were there? He had been comfortable in her company the night before, so she need not be concerned about him either. She stroked her gown neatly smooth and then folded her hands. Though not fully relaxed, at least she was not excited with her mother's nerves!

When they arrived, Mr. Darcy was away, and part of her apprehension abated instantly, yet she also missed his presence. Instead, they were to see Miss Darcy and her aunt Lady Matlock. Elizabeth had been introduced to the latter the evening before and had been pleased that such a grand lady had been so solicitous towards her during their short conversation. She introduced her aunt, and the two older women soon became involved in an animated conversation about the town of Lambton. Like Aunt Gardiner, Lady Matlock had grown up nearby, and they had many acquaintances and memories in common.

In the meantime, she spoke with her friend Miss Darcy, who was far less diffident than Elizabeth remembered. Had both the brother and the sister practised their skills at conversation, or were they merely quiet upon first acquaintance but actually more gregarious than they seemed? Mr. Darcy had smiled and teased at Netherfield even though Elizabeth had not realized it at the time, and he had laughed often and held friendly discourse last evening at the ball.

As if reading her thoughts, Lady Matlock addressed her. "Did you enjoy the Powells' ball last evening, Miss Bennet?"

"I did, very much."

"Did you dance the whole evening?"

"Very nearly so, madam. Mrs. Fraser made certain of it."

"Fitzwilliam mentioned you danced the supper dance with him," Georgiana said.

The heat of a blush overtook Elizabeth's skin. "I did. Your brother is an admirable dancer, and it was a pleasure to renew our acquaintance."

"Ah yes, you knew Fitzwilliam before," said Lady Matlock.

"Indeed. I met Mr. Darcy in the year eleven whilst he was a guest at Mr. Bingley's estate in Hertfordshire. My father's estate is a mere three miles distance. We renewed the acquaintance the following spring when I visited the home of my friend, whose husband is rector for Hunsford parish near Rosings, and again last summer at Pemberley where I met Miss Darcy."

Georgiana beamed at the reference but stayed silent.

"So you and my nephew are old friends," said Lady Matlock. Her lips turned up at the edges and produced a crinkling about her warm eyes.

At just that moment, the gentleman himself strolled through the door to join them in the drawing room. "Yes, Aunt, I suppose you could put it that way," he said. He kissed Lady Matlock on the cheek and then crossed the room to where Georgiana sat next to Elizabeth to do the same to his sister. He began to reach out to Elizabeth as if he would have liked to shake hands, but settled for a slightly awkward bow. "Mrs. Gardiner, Miss Bennet, how do you do?"

Elizabeth was stirred by his presence but unable to speak. He gazed upon her in a manner that made her want to wriggle in her seat—his eyes were so intense.

Thankfully, her aunt responded for both of them. "We are well, Mr. Darcy, and you?"

"Much the same. Miss Bennet, I trust you slept well and have recovered from the excitement of last night's festivities?"

She straightened and looked him in the eye. "Yes, I am well this morning. Can you say the same?"

His lips quirked up ever so slightly at the edges, lending a softness to his eyes. "I had a great deal to ponder, but much of it put me at ease, so sleep came better than it has during recent months."

"I am glad to hear it."

Lady Matlock spoke at this point. "The ball proved to be a success, then. The Powells can be proud."

"I am pleased it was a smaller ball," said Aunt Gardiner. "Elizabeth was unwell last autumn, and I do have a care for her health."

"Are you convalesced from your illness, Miss Bennet?" Lady Matlock asked.

"I am quite mended, I thank you."

"I hope you are able to enjoy more of the Season as a result."

"As do I."

"Mrs. Fraser sent a note this morning," said Aunt Gardiner, "to say that Elizabeth's success at this ball evidences her ability to enjoy those events that interest her. Mr. Gardiner and I could not be more pleased to hear it."

Mr. Darcy's deep voice broke into the conversation between the ladies. "Her friends are equally pleased to know that she can partake in the Season's pleasures. I do look forward to seeing you enjoy the offerings of town, Miss Bennet."

The warmth that started on Elizabeth's cheeks and spread over her face was as much due to the affection in the gentleman's voice as the affable feelings in his words. A pity the next voice in the room broke the pleasant air. The butler announced additional guests: Miss Bingley and Mrs. Hurst. Elizabeth cringed in anticipation of the ladies' haughty, sharp-tongued antics.

Miss Bingley showed whom she had really intended to visit as she glided across the room directly towards Mr. Darcy. "Mr. Darcy! We missed you at the theatre last night!" Miss Bingley's lips were all a pout.

"I preferred to support an old friend who hosted a private function."

"Yes, I heard about the Powell ball. It was quite a success for such a small number of guests. I did not expect it to be so."

"Your suppositions were incorrect then." Mr. Darcy's face was clouded over so little could be read in his expression, yet a tiny furrow in his brow and a glare in his eyes remained for those who took notice. He had returned to his formal mien as opposed to the friendliness evident only moments earlier with the smaller group, appearing more as he had when Elizabeth first met him. He definitely used this expression to hide his discomfort!

Miss Bingley tittered and glanced around the room as if to decide whether any of the others present supported her proclamations. Before her perusal made the circuit to Elizabeth's side of the room, a glint appeared in her eyes. Elizabeth could just imagine her thoughts: *another important person to acknowledge me!* "Dear Lady Matlock, how good to see you again. I trust you are well?"

Lady Matlock responded with only a modest nod; she did not deign to speak to Miss Bingley. The younger woman stretched her lips over her teeth in an affected version of a gracious smile and looked further about the room for another to engage in conversation.

Her eyes lit on Miss Darcy, who shifted in her seat, then on Elizabeth. Miss Bingley's eyes popped open, the smile momentarily washed from her face, and Elizabeth's stomach turned. However, the disagreeable woman swallowed and chose to return her attention to Miss Darcy. What a relief to be spared Miss Bingley's version of wit!

"Georgiana! How are you, my dear one?"

To Elizabeth's mind, it was an overstatement of an endearment even had Miss Darcy been a family member. Miss Bingley was doing it a bit brown today.

Miss Darcy proved to be reticent as usual, her eyes flitting over the carpet whilst she measured her words with such care that little opportunity remained for conversation. "I am well, I thank you."

This did not stop Miss Bingley. "You are looking lovelier than even your many marvellous talents! I am sure you have many new accomplishments that I do not even know about. I admire you immensely!" She was determined to make a conversation with the young lady, and where else to start but with too many words of flattery?

Yet poor Miss Bingley surely did not have an amiable effect on her, for once Georgiana had given a weak smile and a nod with the simple words of "Thank you," silence reigned for a few minutes.

As if sensing the cold from the noble personages in the room, Miss Bingley then turned to Elizabeth. Her eyes had a severe look about them as she perused Elizabeth in a manner that made the hairs stand up on her neck. Elizabeth ignored the cold feeling and decided she would be amused at the thinly veiled insults she expected. "Miss Eliza Bennet! I hardly recognized you! You are so altered since your time on the continent; I should not have known you again. Yes, you look poorly indeed. Tell me, when did you return?"

This was worse than usual! How could she say such a thing in company?

"You must be mistaken, Miss Bingley." Until her aunt's gentle voice broke the dreaded silence in the room, Elizabeth was unaware that her mouth had dropped wide open and she had said nothing in her shock. "Elizabeth has been in town since our holiday to Derbyshire last summer. She was ill for a time, but she has returned to good health and is now assisting me with the children."

Miss Bingley sniffed, and her eyes flared into something that appeared akin to rage. "Ill? You should be…but we heard you were in Florence or some such place. They said—"

Mr. Darcy interrupted, shocking them all. "It does not do to listen to rumours from the people in Hertfordshire regarding the daughter of the primary gentleman in the vicinity."

Aunt Gardiner added, "They like to believe the most glamorous of respites when she was merely helping me with my confinement."

Oh, thank you, Mr. Darcy and Aunt Gardiner! Elizabeth could feel her courage rise despite the attempt to intimidate her.

Lady Matlock joined in. "How kind of Miss Bennet." Bless her for her positive words.

Mrs. Hurst spoke through tight lips whilst glancing at Miss Bingley from the corner of her eye. "And how are you and the little one faring?"

"Quite well, I thank you."

"Boy or girl?" asked Lady Matlock.

"My third daughter, and I have two sons as well."

Lady Matlock's kindly smile further eased the mood in the room. "You are blessed with a healthy, happy family."

Miss Bingley cleared her throat and rolled her eyes, and her sister's head whipped around to glare at her. Miss Bingley shrugged and opened her mouth to speak but, observing Mrs. Hurst's scowl and subtle head shake, must have thought it ill-advised.

"Just so," replied Aunt Gardiner as she rose, "and I am anxious to return to them. Thank you for your hospitality, Miss Darcy. We must now take our leave."

Miss Bingley bared her teeth in what could only be a smile, the small, even, white line of them pressing tightly against her lips—that is, until

Georgiana turned to Elizabeth. "Do not go without promising me that you will consider joining me for a carriage ride in the park someday soon." Miss Bingley's eyes could have shot fire.

After the few minutes of Miss Bingley's malice, giddiness at the offer of friendship made Elizabeth answer with haste. "Oh yes, Miss Darcy, that would be splendid. I do so love being out of doors, especially now the weather is milder and the flowers are blooming."

"It has been a terrible winter and spring," said Mr. Darcy. "I am glad it is over and we can continue our acquaintance." So many subtle hints in such a short statement.

Miss Darcy smiled and leaned forward slightly towards Elizabeth. "I agree. Can we set a date now?"

They discussed the matter briefly and agreed on three days hence. After a visit of a respectable duration for a morning call, Elizabeth joined her aunt as they gave their best regards to all present before they left the Darcy residence. As they accepted their coats in the front hall, Miss Bingley's drone was audible, though not her words.

"She is not a favourite of anyone, is she?" asked Aunt Gardiner once they were in the carriage.

"No indeed. She does try too hard." Indeed, Miss Bingley was much worse than she could ever recall, and jealousy was surely the reason. Elizabeth flinched, a chill running down her spine thinking of Miss Bingley's treatment of her, as brief as the episode was.

"I am sorry she was so unrelenting in her unkindness towards you. It was unacceptable, and I could barely remain civil with her, nor could Mr. Darcy."

"I thank you for your concern, but do not fret over her behaviour. I expect both sisters to use biting wit and scarcely veiled insults against others, but usually the person is out of the room, and they are not often so scandalous in their barbs. Mrs. Hurst was all sympathy today, but she can be just as vindictive."

"For shame."

"I agree," said Elizabeth.

"For his part, Mr. Darcy reminded me of how much the gentleman he was when we first met him at Pemberley. I have to say how impressed I was after all the time since I had seen him and had believed ill of him. It must have been a pleasure to have supper with him last night. Are you now comfortable around him?"

Dear Aunt, trying to ask a different question while she sought to protect Elizabeth once again. "I am more than comfortable, I thank you. But I was never uncomfortable, you see, thus, you need not fuss on my account."

"Are you certain?"

She nodded. "In fact, I would like to further my friendship with both Darcys. They have been nothing less than kind to us."

"Your conversation with Mr. Darcy at supper last night was a success, then?"

She could not look at her aunt whilst her face was so hot. She clasped her hands together so she would not fidget. "It was. But I prefer not to speak much more about it as the topics were quite private."

"A private word in a public place? That has my interest piqued! Is there an attachment?"

Elizabeth pressed her lips closed and tried to glare at her aunt. They both burst into giggles.

"I shall not importune your private affairs any longer. We do believe it likely that Mr. Wickham was responsible for your injuries, so there is nothing wrong with being friends with the Darcys—especially the brother. He is a fine young man, and we regret thinking him otherwise," her aunt said mischievously. "I will speak to your uncle about allowing him permission to call if that pleases you. Then you will have more opportunities for agreeable words with him."

Had her prayers been the selfish sort, this would be the answer to them. Relief and gratitude poured into Elizabeth's chest, relaxing her after all the disquiet Miss Bingley had instigated. "Oh, yes, I would like that a great deal."

Chapter 18

Miss Bingley's strident tone made Darcy's skin prickle. "Did you notice how ill she looked, Mr. Darcy? I am not one who favours a tan on a lady. She appeared so brown and coarse."

"I noticed no change in her complexion," said Georgiana in a timid voice.

"That is because you look favourably upon all, Miss Darcy. You must beware of people attempting to elevate themselves based on your good heart, my dear." Miss Bingley patted Georgiana's hand. The artifice that was characteristic of Miss Bingley made him ill; however, he maintained his dignity when his true desire was to ask her to leave his sister be.

"Miss Darcy is indeed a genteel sort of girl." Mrs. Hurst's voice was rather sweet though far less cloying than Miss Bingley ever used. "Tell me, how is your playing on the pianoforte? Still as pleasant an experience as in the past?"

Georgiana was covered with the deepest blush, and he almost intervened. But she replied, "I do enjoy playing for myself and my family."

Miss Bingley leaned in towards his sister. "You are such a decent young lady with no faults. Listening to you play is one of my favourite memories. No one I know can come close to your ability to play the specialities of Herr Mozart, let alone the demands of Herr Bach! I do hope I am able to hear you again someday soon."

His sister's returning smile was forced—he was sure of it. She had never been pleased by Miss Bingley, whose words of friendship were always exaggerated. Anybody would guess it was pure fawning no matter how sincere Miss Bingley believed her flattery to be. Georgiana replied simply, "I am not inclined to play today."

"Do not concern yourself. We shall endure," replied Mrs. Hurst.

All enjoyed a little laugh over Mrs. Hurst's dramatic tone, but the moment was short-lived as Miss Bingley interrupted the friendly turn of conversation her sister had attempted. "But Miss Darcy, you must be told that Miss Eliza is not a true friend. Indeed, I cannot fathom how she tricked a whole community into believing she was sunning herself on the continent when she now claims she was on her sickbed. Of course, I cannot believe her little tale, even though she looks so poorly! Then to make her appearance here in such a state and behaving as though she belongs among our fashionable set. How rude!"

The number of those present who inhaled audibly in their shock at her insolence was a topic Darcy would consider at a later time, yet for that moment, he could have sworn that the entire population of Portman Square gasped.

Mrs. Hurst spoke first. "Caroline—"

"It is true!" Miss Bingley interrupted. "She is no one of importance, yet she puts on these pert airs to turn heads. I cannot bear such artifice. I am glad she left."

Darcy could tolerate her antics no longer yet struggled to control his annoyance by unclenching his fists and speaking in a low and measured voice. "Miss Bingley, it is you who must leave at once. If you are bent upon insulting my guests, you are not welcome in my home."

"It is fine, Mr. Darcy. My sister is not in earnest. She did not mean her words to be taken literally." Mrs. Hurst smiled and placed a hand over her sister's, but Miss Bingley was having none of it.

"I do not joke about such matters! Mr. Darcy, that woman hopes to trick you, to lure you into approbation! I have seen it all along, and today was worse! Her obsequious manner to Miss Darcy was inspired by her intention to gain your favour. She wants Pemberley, and that is all. You must beware of such feminine wiles and guard yourself against them to avoid the unspeakable tragedy of her success."

Lady Matlock was staring to one side, her brow deeply creased, her frowning mouth slightly agape. Georgiana and Mrs. Hurst both paled and looked away. Neither seemed quite ready to produce a response to so bizarre an accusation.

That was enough! He pressed his lips closed to keep himself from saying something more vulgar than Miss Bingley's words. Oh, how fortunate he would be if only he could throw flames at her with his eyes. He settled for an enraged glare until his perception of the discomfort among the other guests reminded him of his role as host. Fuming, he crossed the room to pull the bell, and in an instant, Hodges appeared at the door.

"Miss Bingley and Mrs. Hurst have outstayed their welcome," he said. "Please ask for their carriage to be readied and assist them to the door."

"Yes, sir, Mr. Darcy."

Mrs. Hurst wore a mottled complexion, but she did not defend her sister nor did she argue against her. Was she as mortified as she deserved to be? She held her head high as she took Miss Bingley by the arm and attempted to steer her from the room before they were forcibly evicted.

"Louisa, let go of me," Miss Bingley hissed in a low, angry tone whilst she tore her arm from Mrs. Hurst's grasp. "I have not said all I want to say." She spun about. "Mr. Darcy, you must know she has no connections, no fortune, nothing to recommend her. Please do not allow—"

"Caroline, please do not embarrass yourself further," her sister muttered in a low voice from between clenched teeth. "Let us take our leave with dignity and hope our long-standing connection with the Darcys will endure your insolence." She spoke louder with a taut smile, "My apologies, Lady Matlock, Mr. Darcy, Miss Darcy."

"I have done nothing wrong!"

Mrs. Hurst momentarily silenced her sister with a withering look as she once again grabbed her arm and led her through the doorway. When the latch clicked shut, Caroline Bingley's renewed opposition could be heard until she and her sister quit the house. The sound of the outer door closing caused Darcy's whole body to relax.

Lady Matlock was the first to speak. "What a contemptible harpy that one is!"

"I apologise. You should not have been required to listen to her drivel," he said as he took the vacant seat next to his sister. Hopefully, she was no worse off for having experienced such a shocking display. "Since Miss Bennet first met her, Miss Bingley has seen her as a sort of rival for attention. To her disadvantage, she has not considered the wealth of friendship available to her from Miss Bennet, who is the more amiable of the two."

"I agree," replied his aunt.

"I am of a mind to inform Hodges that Miss Bingley is no longer welcome at my house. The only reason I have tolerated her thus far is due to my close friendship with Bingley, but he must understand I cannot allow such insolence to be unnoticed."

"Yes, Fitzwilliam, please do," said Georgiana. "I have never cared for Miss Bingley's company. She is only nice to me because she wants me to tell her about you."

"I hope her exhibition was not too ghastly for you to bear, dear," said Lady Matlock.

"I am well, Aunt, but thank you for your concern."

Darcy pressed his lips together. "Just another reason to ban that woman. Georgiana does not need to be upset by that sort of treatment from callers in her own home."

"I do appreciate the gesture, Brother. It will go a long way towards calming my nerves."

"I do not wish to continue talking of our discomfort; rather, I would like your opinion on our other guests. How did you find Miss Bennet and Mrs. Gardiner?"

Georgiana's eyes brightened as she sat up straighter. "As amiable as always."

"I agree," said Lady Matlock with a broad smile, "and I admire Miss Bennet's courage. She remained gracious in the face of difficult circumstances. Her fortitude implies great strength of heart."

"I am pleased that you have observed them as such and that Georgiana will enjoy their company more in the future. Miss Bennet's friendship is precisely what she needs as she prepares herself for more varied society when she is out next season." He turned to Georgiana. "Perhaps you will also like to call on Mrs. Bingley once they come to town. She is milder in personality than Miss Bennet, but as they are sisters, the similarity between them will bode well for your friendship with the elder sister too."

Georgiana frowned. "Only if Miss Bingley is not at home."

"I doubt she will ever be allowed to live with Mr. Bingley due to her disdain for Mrs. Bingley and her family. She lives with the Hursts."

"A pity for the Hursts," said Lady Matlock. "Mrs. Hurst seemed more amiable than her sister."

"At times she can be, but at other times the two cooperate, and Mrs. Hurst has her fair share of poking fun at others."

"Well, whispering behind people's backs for sport can be expected at functions where the *ton* is gathered. Ladies and gentlemen alike take part as well. I find the practise too common and attempt to extricate myself from those spiteful conversations with good taste, but they cannot be avoided entirely. Georgiana, you had best learn a few comments to calm the talk as well as a few delicate excuses to be removed from the gossips of the *ton*. For example, when a lady like Miss Bingley says something disagreeable, you reply, 'That is very interesting. Why do you say that?' The speaker usually is unable to answer in as untoward a way as their original comment. If you want to leave the unpleasantness of a conversation at a function, you can say, 'Oh, look, there is Miss Grantley. Excuse me, but I must go to compliment her on her design for a little table.' Such graces will enhance your reputation as a kind and well-mannered lady."

Georgiana would be in good hands if Lady Matlock continued to help her prepare to come out in society. No little additional comfort came from the knowledge that Miss Bingley would be kept at a distance and his sister would be friends with his Elizabeth.

RELUCTANT TO GIVE UP HIS HAT, DARCY FINALLY HANDED IT TO THE GARdiners' servant, who was waiting patiently to assist him. What was he supposed to do with his hands now that he could no longer worry the poor hat's brim? They had no better occupation whilst travelling across town, yet let alone, each finger tingled with a need to fidget away his restlessness. Sweat had gathered on his upper lip by the time he relinquished the balance of his outer garments. As soon as he could manage an inconspicuous moment, his handkerchief was employed to dab the dampness away. His back and shoulders were painfully stiff, his vision was not quite right, and his heart wanted to leap into his throat, causing him to swallow more than seemed necessary. He awaited the interview that would lead to the most important private moment of his life. Finally, the gentleman in Mr. Gardiner's study left and Darcy was admitted.

Mr. Gardiner waved to a chair. "I can only give you a few minutes, Mr. Darcy, as there is an urgent situation I must attend to at one of my warehouses."

Darcy glanced at the seat but preferred to stand. He wet his lips. His mouth was so dry! "Thank you for seeing me under such stressed circumstances, sir. I shall not take much of your time. I would like to speak to you of Miss Bennet."

"Yes, I hope that the ladies' call sufficiently demonstrated that we have had a change of heart and no longer believe you were the person who harmed Lizzy at Lambton. I was not as easily swayed as my wife, but her encouragement convinced me of the truth of your character, and we have other reasons to change our suspicions. I do apologise for my accusations. No matter how justified my feelings seemed at the time, they were wrong in consideration of my knowledge of you, sir. Your actions and words confirm your respect for my niece, and Lizzy speaks strongly of your excellent qualities."

He blew out a long breath. "You say *respect*, sir, but I am certain you have long known that that I also hold sentiments of deep admiration and devotion to your niece's well-being."

Mr. Gardiner nodded. "You are correct. I have suspected your partiality since we first saw you together at Pemberley."

"I come today to ask your permission for a private audience with her for the purpose of requesting her hand in marriage." He blurted out the words, which were not at all what he had imagined, but they would have to do. They could not be taken back—not that he would!

"So quickly?"

"I have known Miss Bennet for eighteen months, and I have spent time with her in Hertfordshire, Kent, and at Pemberley last year. My intention in Lambton had been to ask her to marry me, but instead, I found her in distress. So, you see, both of us have had the time to become certain of our own feelings."

"Very well. You have my permission to ask the question, but you must also seek her father's blessing once she has accepted you." Mr. Gardiner strode to the door. "Now, I must be away this instant. You may wait here, and I shall ask for her to be sent to you."

Relief poured over him like the contents of a ewer during a hot bath. "I thank you, sir."

Mr. Gardiner smiled warmly and held out his hand to shake Darcy's. "You are very welcome, Mr. Darcy."

After Mr. Gardiner quit the room, Darcy clenched his hands and released them. He needed something to absorb the agitation inside of him whilst he waited. He wiped them on his trousers, cleared his throat, and sighed, his body wilting at the weight of his thoughts. However, the door opened, and he snapped upright in response. When Elizabeth slipped into the room and greeted him with a gentle smile on her face, his body eased considerably. He could not help but smile himself as he bowed to her curtsey. Oh, what this woman did to him!

"Please take a seat, Miss Bennet." She hesitated then chose a situation on a bergère chair. Once she was seated, he clasped his hands behind his back and began to pace the room. "It has been nearly a year since I embarrassed myself by foolishly phrasing the most important question of our lives. Today, I ask the question again, but instead, you must allow me to clarify my intentions in order to provide you with adequate reassurance that your decision is the right one for the circumstances.

"I apologise for my insults towards your family. I had no right to judge them, and I have every reason to be ashamed of some of my own relations. I recognize the attributes of each of your family members and assure you they are always welcome in my homes."

Were his words tender enough to sway her? No, it would not do. His expression as well as his words had to show how truly remorseful he was for his affronts, as well as impress upon her his utter devotion. She returned the warm gaze with a tender expression, her delicate lips barely parted and pink warming her lovely cheeks. He would hold an unyielding attitude in his neck and shoulders until the moment he recognized her affection towards him! He relaxed them, which moved him to continue.

"I admired you from almost the first moment I saw you, but my pride did not allow me to recognise it as such." He placed one hand over his heart. "I wasted far too much time denying my attraction until my love for you overwhelmed me. I accept all blame for any misunderstandings or grief resulting from my injudicious actions and words, and I yearn beyond expected likelihood that you will overlook those slights and allow me to spend the rest of my life making up for them—*practising*, as you say."

Although his previous discourse was as full of turmoil as hurling down a raging river in a boat without oars, humbling himself before her for the final plea was the easiest part of the speech. He dropped onto his knee, took one of her hands in his, and stroked it gently.

"Today, with the hope that you are more partial to me than in the past, I ask your indulgence in my tender sentiments towards you as I humbly offer myself and beg of you to consent to be my wife."

Elizabeth was quiet, too quiet, as she gazed at their joined hands. What had he done wrong? Should he be dismayed in anticipation that she would once again turn down his proposal? How would he cope if that happened? He rubbed a thumb against the back of her hand. Perhaps she would think it a sign of his encouragement and affection.

When she finally did speak, her voice was soft and caught a bit at the end. "You will align yourself with a woman who is sister to Mr. Wickham?" She was looking at him now, her eyes moving around, searching his face for hints of his response.

What? This was a stunning revelation! He had no idea Wickham had married into her family. When had that taken place? Could it have been whilst they were apart this winter? But why had he not heard it from Bingley? And after Wickham attacked her, to have him as brother! How horrifying if all her memories had returned to her. Which sister? It must be Miss Lydia as no other seemed likely. Some of the rumours from Meryton and Miss Bingley came together and assuaged his confusion, but only a little.

Recovering from his dumbfounded state, he snapped his mouth shut so he would not alarm Elizabeth, though she was looking at the carpet at the moment. He had paused for too long! It must be dreadful for her to await his answer. He would have to speak carefully to draw out specifics related to her question. "I have said that I shall accept all your family though you will understand that it is for both our sakes if I insist that Mr. Wickham is not welcome at Pemberley. Mrs. Wickham may visit us, though."

Her eyes rose to meet his, filled with unshed tears, "I understand. Lydia will be pleased, I am sure, and I am grateful for your understanding on the…ah, gentleman. I do not remember all, but in case the worst is true, well, I… Thank you, sir."

"No thanks are needed, just your response to my question."

Her countenance radiated contentment that spread from the sparkling eyes behind those tears, feeding the expression of a most exquisite smile. "I accept your offer with great pleasure."

He let out a noisy breath combined with a brief laugh. Impulsively, he drew her into his arms, pulling her off her chair and awkwardly onto her knees in front of him. Her expression was wide-eyed. He pressed his lips on hers, and their noses bumped, but it took little for them to reposition and perfect the kiss. Tottering for a few seconds due to the rapid motion and awkward position, they collapsed on the floor side by side and burst into

The Mist of Her Memory

laughter at the same moment. She looked so beautiful with the dusting of colour that crept over every visible inch of her face to the edge of her fichu.

When she paused her chuckles to just grin at him, he could not help but lean in to enjoy another luxuriant taste of her lips. This time, he deepened the kiss to hint at the passion of lovers. When he pulled away, the lack of focus in her veiled eyes and the wistful tilt of her mouth were obvious. The kiss had done its duty. She was as overcome with passion as he, and it kindled additional heat in his already overstimulated body. A small noise outside filtered into the room. How could he have forgotten others were still in the house? Even though no one was expected to enter the room for a while, the impropriety of their position could not be sustained, so he swiftly rose and helped her to her feet. After a quick caress of her warm lips, he stood a respectable distance away.

"I must go to Derbyshire on business. In fact, my servants are already travelling ahead of me," he said. He could not tell her the business was Wickham in case it frightened or discomposed her in any way. "I shall stop in Hertfordshire to speak with your father. Is that acceptable to you?"

"It is. But you must ensure that my uncle has sent a letter ahead of you to pave the way with my father. You see, his impressions of you may be influenced by your earlier time at Netherfield as well as my uncle's misunderstanding of your role in my injuries. That said, I am certain, after all you have done for my family, that he will be welcoming of you as a son."

"As I have said in the past, I do not believe my actions have been that worthy, but if my attempts to make amends have resulted in your father's approbation of our understanding, I shall not complain."

Elizabeth's eyes brightened as she began to giggle. "I cannot believe we are engaged! Oh, how wondrously happy you have made me!"

For a short moment, he braced himself. How he wished to pull her into his arms once again and kiss her senseless. The enticement of her standing so close was simply too strong. After one step forward, he took her hands and tugged them about his waist, which resulted in his arms embracing her in a protective circle. "Will you be pleased to be Mrs. Darcy?"

"Of course I will be delighted to be your wife although it comes with great responsibilities. Aspects of Pemberley are daunting to me, but being by your side in leading that great estate will do me as proud as you are of the Darcy name."

"I thought you warned me against pride and conceit."

"Yet I now find that you have no improper pride. You are a good man with a need to practise your skills at speaking with strangers."

"Ah yes, I remember your admonishment at Rosings. I wanted to kiss that smug expression right off your face." With that, he gave her another brief kiss on the lips, earning as bright a smile as could be expected of a lady newly engaged. How lovely she looked with a delicate blush and kissable air about her! Her eyes sparkled, a hint that she had something brash to say. How he loved that he could now read her expressions so well!

"Oh, goodness! What would Lady Catherine have said?"

"We would not have cared because I believe, had I done just that at Rosings, you would have realized my feelings much earlier and saved us a great deal of grief."

"I do not regret the path we have travelled although the long breaks when I did not see you were painful. We, both of us, needed time to grow and learn to accept the other as an equal partner."

"You are a wise woman, Elizabeth."

"I am a woman with an ample amount of important experience behind my tender years, Mr. Darcy—therefore, beware. I may expect you to defer to my wisdom at least some of the time."

"It depends on the wisdom. Were you to call me Fitzwilliam instead of Mr. Darcy, I would acquiesce to your profound good sense with a prompt demonstration of my approbation."

Her chest rose and fell with an interesting sort of a sigh. What could it mean? "Of course. I shall just have to get used to calling you by your name."

"Try it."

Her lips went into a small "o" shape as a light pink colour once again overspread her cheeks. "Fitzwilliam."

He pulled her into a firm grip, and his mouth closed down on hers without any hesitation or unfamiliar delicacy. It took a knock on the door for them to come up for air, right their clothes and hair, and invite an elated Mrs. Gardiner in to confirm the news from her husband. What a superior day it had been! If only Darcy did not have to travel so soon after the engagement! Yet, he would not have put off the question any longer even if Gardiner had placed an impediment before him. He had simply waited long enough.

Chapter 19

The voice that occupied her head was hideous, and its invasion was unexpected, given her pleasant thoughts of yesterday's kisses. A dream! It had to be a dream! No, no, she was awake. Thank goodness she was alone in the sitting room, for others would surely notice her discomposure as the voices clambered over themselves within her mind, fighting to make their way to the fore. Elizabeth dropped her needle onto her lap and covered her ears in an attempt to block out the voices.

"You vile, ungrateful wretch!"

She did not understand. Why?

"Yes, you should be surprised to see me. No one warned you I would be coming here to see you, to stop you." Her persecutor sneered, mocking her.

They argued. She denied the charges against her. Then came the hurting, the pleading, the crying. No, no!

Her tormentor shouted. "Listen to me! Stay away—he will do you no good!"

A lady screamed in agony and fear. Was that her? How could she hide? How could she make it stop?

"Do not try to ignore me," the low-pitched voice roared in her ears. "And do not dare tell anyone I was here! I will deny it."

She had to make it stop! She would agree to anything. Anything.

"I will kill you if you tell them the truth, do you hear me? Stupid wench." The low growl sent a shudder down her spine.

Her body collapsed. The chair! Grab the chair. The back of her head exploded in pain. A creak echoed through the room. Was it the door or the back stairs?

Suddenly, Mr. Darcy's deep voice came from close, very close, beside her.

"Good heavens, what has happened?"

An arm slid under her shoulders and lifted her. She was safe, protected within his arms.

"Elizabeth, Elizabeth, my love. Are you well?"

She strained to open her mouth, to say anything at all, but she could not speak.

"What happened? Who did this to you?"

The voice that ended the "dream" was full of concern, but it was altogether too much for her equanimity. The other voice, the one that spit with rage and claimed in a low, cruel tone that she was horrid and should not be noticed… was the bad man in her head Mr. Wickham? He must have been overcome to speak so maliciously and then…then…he…he…grabbed her arms painfully! He shook her until her brain rattled in her head. Then he struck her face when he released her. It stung so badly! When the door began to open, he pushed her away so that she fell to the floor. All this she remembered, just not the face of her attacker. Why could she not see who had forced this injury upon her? It was as if a mist had been thrown over that person to confound her.

Or was it even a memory? The experience could just as easily be something conjured by her confused mind, much like Mr. Wickham's story. But no, she had not dreamed those particulars! She was certain Mr. Wickham had told her the words he wished her to share with all and sundry. His tone was so clear; pained, not cruel, it was pleading not only as he related the tale but also as he insisted she repeat it to everyone as if it were true.

As if it were true.

She had remembered it as if it were true only because that is what he commanded, over and over. She recalled Mr. Wickham's visage bearing just enough anguish that it seemed he would burst into tears if pressed; then, in the next moment, he was trying not to shout crossly. However, the expression she recalled upon his face made no sense for someone who was so wrathful and intent on harming her. Yet, whose voice could be so angry?

So the story was just that: a story Mr. Wickham made up—as everyone thought she had—and he had formulated the lie. Could he have been using her emotions to sway her, behaving in a contrite manner to increase her sympathy? Or was he truly remorseful? And for what? What was the secret she could not put her finger on, the other part—the truth—of his tale?

The Mist of Her Memory

She had to speak to someone about it. Thank goodness Mrs. Bastion was expected to call later today.

"When my son began to recover his memories, some remembrances were mixed together, and some dream-like thoughts were not exactly true," Mrs. Bastion said when Elizabeth explained the latest developments in recalling her memories. "Almost as if his mind tried to make sense of it all and filled in the gaps with imagination to soothe itself."

This was particularly disappointing. How could she be certain of reality? Who was villain and who was friend? The weight of this uncertainty caused a sinking feeling. "So, parts of what I remember may not be true?"

"That is correct. Parts may also be out of sequence. I know this because my son related to me some of the conversations we had when he first returned, and he had them all muddled."

"But what I now remember is not pleasant. It is not as if the memory comforts me by alleviating my anxiety about what happened to me. The wicked voice is vivid and real and cruel. When will I understand why this happened and why this person wanted to hurt me? How can I conquer the voice and have peace in my head?"

Mrs. Bastion tilted her head, her expression encouraging. "My son forgot the most painful memories for a long time. When he was ready for the facts, they came pouring back. It is my belief that you are stronger now, and that is why these thoughts are filling your brain."

The expectation that she would recall even more of that voice made her recoil, yet to solve some of the mysteries behind Mr. Wickham's tale and discover Lydia's whereabouts made her wish for more knowledge. How perplexing it all was! "I just wish I knew how to allow the important memories and prevent the disagreeable ones."

Mrs. Bastion was quiet for a few moments as if thinking it over. "You must remind yourself that they are in the past and understand that some of your remembrances may still be distorted to protect the sensibilities of your dear heart. I suggest you be curious about them rather than dread them. They are only thoughts. They cannot harm you."

The suggestion was interesting, but was it practical? She did not know whether she could remind herself of this when the frightful voice came again. "But they are so real and terrifying!"

"If you are truly terrified of the thoughts when they come to you, I suggest you do something pleasant, like spend time with the children. If that is not possible at the time, try to think of some activity that makes you happy. Can you recall a place and time when you were most contented?"

Of course she could—walking next to Mr. Darcy along the river at Pemberley. That memory had never disappeared and still caused a sort of fluttering in her belly. She would dearly love to repeat the encounter or something similar so she could relive the wonderful sensations it excited. However, she could not tell this to Mrs. Bastion; it was too private. With so many missing memories regarding her youth, she could not help but struggle for a short time, yet it was but a moment before she recollected a situation in the past that gave her pleasure.

"Yes, with kittens in the hayloft at Longbourn." Blessed, fuzzy little imps with mixed coats like Joseph in the Bible. Now, that she could share.

"Whenever you are overwhelmed by dreadful thoughts, close your eyes and remember that day. Cheerful memories will then overrule the unpleasant ones." The older lady paused then continued, "I believe you possess a strong mind that will overcome your apprehension about the past."

Elizabeth sighed before responding. "I do not know what I would have done without your advice. I could well have remained bemused without understanding myself or my experiences at all. I am very grateful for all your assistance."

"I am pleased to give it. As you know, I learned this by helping my own son, and to understand the methods of healing the injured mind is a gift that must be shared. Sometimes G-d in His mercy gives the gift of forgetting things that are too frightful to remember."

"Perhaps someday I may be able to help someone else as you have helped me."

"I do not wish injuries of the mind on anyone, but I do believe you have excellent strength of character based on how well you have survived your physical and emotional injuries. You will use your own experiences well in helping others should you be faced with such a situation."

A great deal was still upsetting, but time would be her remedy—at least, she hoped so. "That is a happy thought."

"Indeed. Shall we return to the house?"

They ambled the short distance from the park to the Gardiners' home. On the way, Mrs. Bastion waved her hand expansively in the air before her, causing

Elizabeth to notice the landscape encompassed by her gesture. "Look at the pretty scenery that surrounds us! The fresh new spring flowers and trees in bloom, and the fragrances that envelop our senses as we walk by! What a lovely time of year. I enjoy spring better than any other time as it is so full of rebirth."

Elizabeth agreed. The scents of the park and the heat of the high sun reminded her of springtime walks in her youth, almost as a picture in her mind. "We are fortunate to enjoy this fine day, to walk out in comfort, and to enjoy the beauty of nature. To think, when you first started coming to see me, it was winter and quite cold for our walks. It is the first time I have been able to use my new parasol this spring."

Once they reached the house, Elizabeth offered for Mrs. Bastion to join her aunt and herself for tea, a ritual that was part of their meetings.

"I cannot stay long as I have an appointment later this morning, but I would love to have some refreshment with you and Mrs. Gardiner."

The tea things did not take long to be readied, and the ladies were soon engaged in light conversation.

The parlour door opened as Mrs. Bastion stood and began saying her goodbyes. Mr. Gardiner was home and joined the ladies.

"I am sorry I have not the time to talk with you, sir, but I had plans to call on my sister today," said Mrs. Bastion.

"That is a hopeful event for us," replied her uncle as his eyes connected with Aunt Gardiner's. "We wish to ask a favour of you regarding your sister. For urgent personal reasons, we should like to speak with Mr. Wickham, and we were hoping your sister had some information, any information, that could help us to find his direction."

"I do believe that, despite her ill opinion of the gentleman, she would be most willing to share anything she knows of him if it is so important to your family," Mrs. Bastion said. "I assume the interest is to help Miss Bennet with the recovery of her memories regarding Mr. Wickham and her sister?"

"He may be able to tell us the truth of the matter and clarify what he may have said to Lizzy," Mrs. Gardiner answered.

"Would either of you be interested in joining me on my visit today?" Mrs. Bastion asked Mr. and Mrs. Gardiner.

Her uncle and aunt shared a glance of corroboration, and her aunt nodded to her husband. Uncle spoke to Mrs. Bastion. "I would be grateful to meet with your sister," said Uncle. "I shall have a boy sent to call for my carriage whilst we obtain our outer garments."

"Miss Bennet and I were remarking that the weather is good," said Mrs. Bastion, and her aunt and uncle agreed with the lady. "Not so many warm clothes are needed now."

Ah, the weather as a conversation topic for diversion, allowing Elizabeth time to consider her thoughts. What would Mr. Wickham reveal to them? If they found him, could she face him? A part of her protested loudly. The idea of the man made her tremble with terror. And what had he done with Lydia? She was so desperate for news of her youngest sister! All of it was overwhelming. Even so, she believed she could question Mr. Wickham at least as well as, if not better than, her uncle. After all, she had been there, not Uncle, and could ask Mr. Wickham which parts of her recollections were true. For a moment, she was about to speak up to tell them she wanted to accompany them on their visit to Mrs. Younge. After all, her mind was stronger and her memories of Wickham's visit were clearer.

However, good sense prevailed, and she let Mrs. Bastion and Uncle Gardiner go off to begin the discourse. Perhaps they would be able to find Mr. Wickham and Lydia and confirm the truth of their history.

Chapter 20

April 1813
Meryton en route to Derbyshire

The interview with Mr. Bennet was foremost in Darcy's mind as he rode into Meryton, but it was soon overcome. The town was busy with people going to market, and the ——shire Militia was performing drills as his carriage passed their encampment. His burning questions about Wickham surfaced, and his blood boiled. How could he find the man and make him pay for his evildoing? His suspicions were more than enough to inspire him, and if he were to confirm what he thought Wickham had done—well, in his estimation, no punishment severe enough existed to deal with the reprobate. Wickham's immoral actions once again impinged upon Darcy's world, but he had gone too far this time. The situation had become a reckoning of wills. Clearly, Darcy had helped him elude legal repercussions one too many times.

Someone in the corps must have some idea of the libertine's destination before he was discovered missing and, perhaps, even more recent news of his whereabouts. The colonel of the regiment, Forster, might have some helpful knowledge. In addition, Darcy recalled a Mr. Denny, who had been friends with Wickham, and resolved to speak with him as soon as an opportunity was availed for a meeting.

After he refreshed himself with a quick wash and change of clothes, he boarded his carriage once again and hastened to Longbourn before it was too late in the day for a call. This part of his agenda must not wait until the morrow to be completed.

As might be expected, Miss Catherine's face peering through the window was the first sign of a Bennet at Longbourn. The delicate fabric of the curtain snapped back into place. They did not know him well, but the nervous, noisy chatter amongst them would not be restrained by lack of familiarity, and the younger Bennet ladies and their mother were famous for their inability to curb their tongues. He smiled to himself. If he were to take them on as family, he would have to become accustomed to behaviour he had complained about in the past.

But he did not come to call upon the ladies of the house, and upon admittance, Darcy requested an audience with Mr. Bennet. As expected, the gentleman was found in his library, his bespectacled nose in a book, when Darcy was announced. As he entered, the older man held up one finger as he finished whatever passage held his interest. While he waited, Darcy perused the room he had seen only briefly in the past. It was small but lined with rich mahogany shelves containing many books of high quality. In fact, there was a lack of space, and piles of volumes stood among those neatly shelved with stacks nestled in corners on the floor and upon the large desk of a library too small for its owner's collection. The scents of leather, paper, and dust mingled in the air.

After a few moments, Mr. Bennet placed a leather marker at his page and closed the tome whilst viewing Darcy over the tops of his spectacles. Following Darcy's bow and formal greeting, Mr. Bennet rose and offered his hand in a gesture of friendship.

"This is a gentleman's library, not a parlour. We are less formal here," the older man said with a mild smile as he waved the volume in his hand towards a chair.

"Are you enjoying your book?"

"Indeed. I am rereading an old favourite." He passed the copy of Shakespeare's plays to Darcy.

"Ah yes, a preferred book in my home as well. I also enjoy seeing the plays performed in the theatre." Darcy returned the book to him.

"I am seldom in town, so I must rely upon my imagination for that aspect. I am not wistful about it, though. I do enjoy the country life in preference to all that noise and bustle," replied Mr. Bennet. "So what brings you here so early this morning, sir, and without your friend? Though I suppose whenever you have attended with Bingley, it was while he was making eyes at Jane, and he no longer needs to come to Longbourn for such a thing."

"I have come to ask your blessing on my engagement to Miss Elizabeth, who has consented to marry me."

The older man's bushy brows flew towards the receding line of his white hair, and his eyes became impossibly wide for a few seconds. "Oh!" was all he said before he peeled off his spectacles, bit the earpiece, and seated himself again behind the desk.

Darcy started at the loudness of the exclamation then waited for a response, but Mr. Bennet sat silent. Darcy began to notice sounds in the distance that accentuated the absence of one gentleman's much-desired reply: a clock, high-pitched voices, a service bell. All were muffled as if far away, yet they pierced his ears nearly as much as the one word full of emotion and surprise had done. Should he fill the air with explanations on how he and Elizabeth were well suited? Would Mr. Bennet want to hear how he would only give her the best life possible? Should he attempt a simpler approach? "I love her dearly, and she has assured me her sentiments are as strong. The best sort of match."

"As a rich man, you could have any lady you want, yet you choose one whose name is blackened by rumour and innuendo. You must indeed have strong feelings towards my Lizzy."

"True, sir, and I shall do all I can to restore a positive public opinion towards her by sharing the *facts* of her illness rather than the myths. As you know, there is talk that she has been travelling for her health or in Bedlam, yet she has been living a quiet, isolated life in town."

"We did not argue with the rumours of her pleasure trip since her months in town gave my daughter time to recover. In truth, I think it was invented by her mother though I have nothing to prove my conjecture."

Darcy continued, "Lately, she has been taking her part in the enjoyments the Season has on offer. This proves there is nothing to mock of the lady; she is as worthy of respect as any gentleman's daughter. All of this she can claim after having endured such a difficult time."

Mr. Bennet's lips formed a thin line as his brow contracted. "My respect goes out to you for wording the situation so carefully when we both are well aware the devil is behind her treatment."

Mr. Bennet's expression alarmed him. Could he once again be blamed for attacking Elizabeth in Lambton? He must ensure her father knew the truth of the matter. "That devil's name is Wickham, and I intend to find him and make him pay for hurting Miss Bennet."

Bennet's nod was almost fierce in its abruptness. "As well as my Lydia."

He recalled a piece of information that had been bothering him for some time. "Mr. Bennet, Miss Bennet said Wickham was wed to her sister, and I gleaned it was Miss Lydia. Can you confirm this?"

"No, I cannot. I know that spiteful creature eloped with her but only took her as far as London. Lizzy claims you paid for a wedding that I am certain never took place as well as providing better funds for the marriage settlements and a position with the regulars in Newcastle for Wickham. She was proud of your philanthropy; however, I believe she has some recollections confused within her mind and will soon come to a better understanding. I hope her admiration goes farther than gratitude."

What a revelation! It explained a great deal of why Elizabeth wanted to thank him when he assumed it was nothing more than his repairing the damage he caused to the Bingleys' potential courtship; that misunderstanding had indeed been his fault. "Good Lord! I had no idea! I did not support him with Miss Lydia at all though, had I been aware, I would have provided whatever aid was sufficient, given the necessity. Of course, it is easy to claim potential generosity when the deed was not done in the first place. I know nothing of what happened to Wickham other than his attack on Miss Bennet in Lambton. I doubt she is beholden to me for her perception of my munificence. The attachment on both sides is of long duration, I assure you." His mind would not quiet, and the repetition of the false history caused him regret. What he would have given to know more about Miss Lydia's situation and to be able to aid in recovering her reputation, as Elizabeth believed! Yet, how could she have conceived of such a thing? Had someone lied to her—set her up for false hopes? In his rumination, he nearly did not hear the next thing Mr. Bennet said.

"Yes, my brother Gardiner wrote his view that, due to Lizzy's latest recollections, they are now convinced that Wickham attacked Lizzy in Lambton. He once thought it was *your* fault. I, however, had trouble believing that such a punctilious man could beat a woman. I am glad to know I was not mistaken and Gardiner was incorrect in his assumption."

Darcy pinched the base of his nose. He should never, ever have been suspected, and it rankled to have the issue broached. "This must make your agreement easier." He tried to temper the brusque tone of his words but failed. At least he had not been sarcastic.

"Do not get your hackles up, sir. You must understand that, until Lizzy came out of her forgetfulness, we did not know what to believe. You were the only one there, and as Gardiner says, he found blaming you difficult to swallow given your seeming partiality towards her in the previous days, but he felt he had no choice. Although we no longer hold this misgiving, an issue still holds true that my neighbours would say impedes your offer: Lydia's elopement. Unless my youngest daughter has been with Mr. Wickham all along and the scoundrel actually married her, she is lost to us forever and has brought her shame to her sisters. Our family has become social outcasts in the neighbourhood even with the help of Mr. Bingley's marriage to Jane. Are you certain you wish to join yourself with such a family?"

Social outcasts. The situation proved worse than Bingley had indicated. "No family is devoid of relations to embarrass them," Darcy said in as convincing a manner as he could muster. "I have my own. My love for your daughter means I shall lend the best part of my character and reputation to help make amends in your family whilst I work to discover what happened to Miss Lydia and that useless scoundrel who stole her from her friends."

"Indeed, sir. I shall rest more soundly knowing you are in agreement with me."

"I am more committed to avenging Elizabeth's injuries than one could obtain in a simple agreement of guilt." He clenched and unclenched his fists at his sides. "I intend to find Mr. Wickham and have a reckoning with him."

"In your best interests, I do hope you are not intending to pursue any measure that may not be the best and safest way to deal with him."

He understood Mr. Bennet's concern. "Do not torment yourself. I will not challenge him, and if I did, I am confident I would prevail. No, instead I will see him brought to rights by any legal means I have available to me. Tomorrow, I intend to speak with his former friends in the ——shire. I hope for information to help locate the scoundrel as well as learn what exactly happened with both of your daughters."

"If you are able to do all that, my Lizzy will be marrying the best of men. You have my blessing." He reached out his hand, and Darcy shook it. At the very least, he could count on Mr. Bennet.

Colonel Forster was not in camp at the time Darcy arrived, but Wickham's old friend Mr. Denny was, so Darcy sought him out and asked what he knew concerning the elopement.

Mr. Denny was not a great deal of help. "I do not know much of what happened to Wickham once he deserted the ——shire whilst we were stationed in Brighton. I do know half a dozen militia men and shopkeepers who would like to find him and receive reimbursement for debts he incurred."

"You do not have any idea of where he went or whether he married Miss Lydia?"

"No, not at all. Your presence here asking these questions confirms he is a rogue of the worst sort, though." Mr. Denny stood firm, his hands clasped behind his back, and looked Darcy in the eye as he spoke. "I should have liked to believe Miss Elizabeth and her story that you supported them. I am of the belief that he has gone to neither Scotland nor London. He wanted to marry for money, and Miss Lydia would have been an inconvenience of which he would quickly rid himself. He has enemies in town and, consequently, has only a few places he can hide to avoid them."

"He is better at making enemies than keeping friends."

"Perhaps. When I first came upon him after I joined this militia, Hertfordshire was ideal for him. He could spin tales to gain friendships in a place where his past exploits were unknown. As for a destination now that he no longer holds a militia post, I could foresee him returning to Pemberley. It was almost all he spoke of amongst the men, about how it was the best place he had ever lived." Denny was a good reporter of facts and opinions. "It is also far enough away that it would be easier for him to hide from the ——shire militia. You see, Colonel Forster intended to send him to the Fleet prison for debts before he disappeared. I am almost certain the colonel had not yet gone through with it unless it is the reason he is still not serving for duty. But it is only a matter of time, given the mounting knowledge of how many men he owes."

"Wickham was seen near Lambton and Pemberley last summer and autumn and has as many foes there as he does in town. A more recent sighting near Lambton causes my cousin Colonel Fitzwilliam interest, and at this very moment, he is in pursuit of Wickham. Until this latest description of a gentleman in ragged clothes near my property, I was of the view he may have moved on, but it would be impossible to know. He is quite adept at hiding."

The Mist of Her Memory

"He is a strong sort who is able to find resources, including money, where he has none. Unless he has fallen upon particularly good luck, I could see him settling in another village in that vicinity," said Mr. Denny.

All the information put together was useful but not sufficient enough for Darcy to be convinced Wickham remained anywhere near Derbyshire. Even so, he would continue towards Pemberley with Colonel Fitzwilliam. "I am grateful for your honesty as I thought you were friends with Wickham and would have hidden his direction."

"I ceased being his friend when I saw what he did to the Bennet ladies." Denny lost his military posture and shuffled his feet as he gazed at the ground. "First Miss Lydia, taken away to the loss of her credit, then Miss Elizabeth, being exiled as a defective because she so firmly believed you knew of the elopement and intervened to have them married. Wickham trod on her good nature far too extensively if she thought him honourable enough for such a marriage!"

Darcy wished she had not had this significant misunderstanding, yet no one could understand the complex changes her mind still endured. "Yes, I heard from Bingley of her expressing her misconceptions some months ago, but no particulars until this week. I had no idea it involved my reputation nor how extreme was the difference in facts."

"Her mortification was never-ending. The townspeople did not give her worthy reputation one moment of notice. Instead, they chose to dwell upon what they saw as weakness of mind and, therefore, character. She was tormented because she insisted on a story to protect her poor sister. Those poor ladies."

Darcy's disappointment matched Mr. Denny's. "Although it is not exactly reasonable, I feel a certain amount of responsibility for Miss Elizabeth's beliefs. I wish I had been able to act as she reported. Had I known, I would have helped in any way possible."

"You take too much on yourself, sir, but I understand the sensibility."

"I was on my way to Pemberley to see whether I could discover more about Wickham's location. Am I correct to confirm you know nothing for certain? It is all merely supposition?"

"That is true. My information is simply conjecture based on how he spoke of his childhood and his dashed hopes for his future. You are probably aware that he often maligns you to anyone who will listen to his sad story. I believed it at one time until I saw how quickly he accumulates debt and woos then abandons poor young girls. I'm certain he has at least one by-blow in each of Brighton and Meryton."

"Lambton and Kympton as well," he replied with a heavy sigh. This was definitely no surprise. In fact, he had planned to examine the situation before he left the village. "As for what he owes, if you could direct me to the correct people, I shall attempt to make amends for his debts here."

"You are truly a better man than he paints you."

He shook his head. "I deserve no such praise. In my pride and silence, I allowed Mr. Wickham to prey upon this community with no warning of his proclivities. Besides, if I hold his debts, I have the power to send him to debtor's prison. He must change his ways or deal with my resentful nature."

Mr. Denny opened his mouth as if to speak then closed it again.

What could Mr. Denny want? "If I can help you, you need just name it."

Mr. Denny raised his palms to Darcy. "I do not wish you to pay what he owes to me. I would like my own chance at the man."

"You do not intend a duel?"

"No, mere fisticuffs will do. Wickham is a coward and a poor fighter. I aim to disfigure his pretty face. With a flattened nose and some sheep's teeth, mayhap ladies like Miss Lydia will no longer be so easily duped by him."

He could not help but smile at the prospect. "Then I shall honour your ability to settle the debt on your own terms, and thank you in advance for the service you wish to give to ladies in general."

Chapter 21

The sound of a carriage stopping in front of her aunt and uncle's home had Elizabeth rushing to peek out of the window. Her uncle had returned alone. Her body relaxed ever so slightly, a reminder of how she had been secretly fearful that Mr. Wickham would come with him. That man had ways of insinuating himself into every place he was unwanted. She hoped her uncle would include her in the discussions regarding his discoveries at Mrs. Younge's home, yet she doubted the information she wanted to hear would be forthcoming. Would Mrs. Younge know Mr. Wickham's location? Would she tell Mrs. Bastion and Uncle Gardiner? Would they find him? Would he lead them to Lydia? All were possible, but suppose Mr. Wickham held the information back? Would someone need to pay the rogue to verify what had happened in the past? He did not give the impression of a man who would help without some sort of benefit to himself.

The irritating part of the whole situation was that she now remembered so much more from Lambton, though not enough to discover what had happened to her sister. She was certain the story Mr. Wickham had told her about Mr. Darcy was a ruse—a complete untruth—but even if he had not married her in fact, he had not told her Lydia's whereabouts. Or had he? She still could not recall. In any case, he had seen Elizabeth at Lambton, promoted the false story about Mr. Darcy helping him marry Lydia, and told her that her family would be harmed if she failed to repeat it. And Mr. Wickham had hurt her. His hands on her arms had been painful, and he had struck her and thrown her to the ground too. Her skin crawled every time she thought of the vicious man who frightened and injured her so badly. If he could do such a thing to her, what would he do to Lydia? Was she in danger?

Elizabeth did not have long to wait. A scratch came at her door. "Enter!" she said.

Davis appeared in a crack wide enough for her face. "The master and mistress would like to see you in the small sitting room, miss."

"Thank you. You may tell them I shall be down directly."

She could barely manage the patience necessary not to run down the stairs, and she burst into the room. Her uncle was kind to her exuberant anticipation and, without a pause in his greeting and no waste of time with niceties, got to the point. "You will be anxious to hear our news though not necessarily pleased. We were unable to find Mr. Wickham or Lydia. I am sorry."

Her spirits collapsed at once. Every prickly feeling she had been carrying since Uncle and Mrs. Bastion had left the house for Mrs. Younge's had subsided, and the sensation of a heavy weight replaced them. What was she to do now?

"The gentleman who had been enquiring about a room for Mr. Wickham was a Mr. Symonds. With Mrs. Bastion alongside me, I was able to convince Mrs. Younge to disclose what had been said. The difficulty was in convincing her to share how to find said gentleman, a favourite of hers, and she appeared apprehensive about why we may want him. I indicated I could merely sit outside her establishment and question every man who walked inside with an air of residence, and my simple threat was enough to make her cooperate. In the end, we learned he was working in the role of clerk for a barrister, and we were introduced to him when he arrived home.

"Mr. Symonds concurred that he had asked about a room on Mr. Wickham's behalf. Mr. Wickham had written to him asking such, yet he was not in town. At the time, Mr. Wickham was travelling with a friend from Cambridge, and Mr. Symonds knew not where to find him."

"He could find him through the friend," said Elizabeth, full of anticipation once again, "and you could seek him that way."

"Curiously, no. I began to understand then that Mr. Symonds was not at all forthcoming: he had formulated the story to appease me. He claimed to have forgotten the name of Wickham's acquaintance, said he never knew the man well, and that he had burnt the letter. In effect, my opinion is that he was prevaricating to lead us *away* from Mr. Wickham. He could not look us in the eye at any time during the discussion."

"Even so, could you not have an investigator watch Mr. Symonds to find Mr. Wickham?" asked Aunt Gardiner.

"I have made such an arrangement, but due to my questioning, I doubt Mr. Wickham will approach Mr. Symonds again. The latter will find some way to get a message to Mr. Wickham, and he will disappear."

This was not helpful. Elizabeth racked her brain for ideas that might convince Mr. Symonds to be more obliging. If the right person spoke with him, they could find all they needed. "What about Mrs. Younge? Is there no more help to be found there?"

"According to Mrs. Bastion, her sister has no more loyalty to Mr. Wickham but a great deal for Mr. Symonds. He was put out at some of my questions, and Mrs. Bastion feared for the potential loss of any future hope of help from them regarding Mr. Wickham if we agitated Mr. Symonds. He most certainly has something to hide. On the basis of his comments, it is impossible to say whether he is protecting Mr. Wickham or not, so we cannot know whether Mr. Wickham is out of town as the man says."

No longer could she hold back and hide her worst fears. Tears began to form in her eyes, and she tried to wipe them away quickly with her fingers. "If Mr. Wickham is in town, he could come here. What would he do to me? What harm may have befallen Lydia?"

Aunt Gardiner rushed to her side and put an arm around her. "Hush, dear. All will be well."

"Of course it will. You will be well protected until he is found," said her uncle.

Elizabeth took the handkerchief her aunt offered, but despite the encouragement, her body still trembled. "In what way? Will I be forced to hide once again—not because of my illness, but to conceal me from Mr. Wickham?"

"No, nothing so terribly drastic. We do not even know whether Mr. Wickham is in town or knows you are. We shall still allow you the sorts of enjoyments you were promised upon regaining your health. But Ralph will be with you no matter where you go. You will become much like a diamond of the first water with your footman at hand every moment." He smiled. Ralph was a giant of a man: well over six feet tall and close to eighteen stone.

She let loose a shaky breath. "What of Lydia?"

"That part of our questioning was difficult. We did not want to risk her reputation worse than it already has been compromised. We asked Mr. Symonds whether Mr. Wickham mentioned a lady in his letter, and he said he had not. But still, he avoided looking at us when he said so, which means he likely has something to hide. It is my belief he knows something, if not all, and is hiding it from us for some nefarious reason of his own. If we could discover why and encourage the man to talk, that would be helpful.

"If Mr. Symonds is a gentleman and knows Mr. Wickham, it could be that one of their friends is in a position to learn more." Uncle Gardiner rubbed his eyes. "If only I knew the supposed gentleman from Cambridge."

Mr. Darcy went to Cambridge with Mr. Wickham! Was it possible that he could help them with Mr. Symonds? "Uncle, what about Mr. Darcy? Perhaps he knows this Mr. Symonds."

Aunt Gardiner gave her a squeeze of comfort. "How clever of you. I suppose you think of Mr. Darcy a great deal, and it is natural to think of his help."

A light warmth covered Elizabeth's face at the inference. She certainly thought of him often. "I also believe Mr. Darcy may have means of convincing Mrs. Younge to help. You see, she was once his sister's companion. If any close connection between her and Mr. Symonds truly exists, her influence may induce the gentleman to be more forthcoming."

"Since you have heard all there is to hear and have a close acquaintance with Mr. Darcy, I believe that you are the better of us to write to him. You are affianced now, and there are no concerns about impropriety," her aunt said.

Elizabeth brushed the tips of her fingers over the cheek that had become heated again whilst she rose and went to the escritoire. She must get over this blushing every time her association with Mr. Darcy was mentioned! Usually she was invulnerable to such abashment, but maybe her maidenly sensibilities were heightened with the newness of the betrothal. She prepared her paper and pen, and the task at hand calmed her somewhat.

Aunt Gardiner rose. "I shall go to the children for now. Your uncle will remain nearby in the library to help you with details of Mr. Symonds's assertions should you need assistance."

Mr. Gardiner nodded, and they both quit the room.

Starting the letter proved difficult, and she chewed on her lip a little. It was the first time ever writing to her affianced. Others would see it, so she could not write a true love letter. Nevertheless, "My dearest Fitzwilliam" and "I send my hopes for all the blessings you deserve" were important to include to ensure he understood her fidelity and to demonstrate that, although the perfunctory form of the letter was necessary, her feelings were more profound than a mere statement of facts could portray. She loved him with a depth of emotion impossible to write, no matter who would read the missive. This was her best effort in spite of the letter being intended for the eyes of others.

Once she had penned a few lines beyond the greeting, she was a faithful scribe of the information her betrothed would need were he to help them on his return to town. The letter was supposed to relate the urgency of the situation well enough to encourage him to come back straight away but without alarming him beyond necessity. In the end, the intent was written within and her letter was completed. Given her haste, she had not employed her best penmanship, but it was readable and free of blots.

Now, all she could do was hope that the missive would reach Mr. Darcy soon and he would make a quick return to town. If he could help them to find Mr. Wickham and Lydia, it was possible that the whole truth would become known. To be free of her past would be a welcome change. Then she could give herself leave to commence with her future, no matter what it held.

Chapter 22

April 1813
Matlock, Derbyshire

The business of assisting Colonel Fitzwilliam to look for his sister's missing suitor whilst the colonel supported Darcy in his quest to locate Wickham was not what Darcy would have even foreseen for the early days of his engagement to Elizabeth, but it could not be avoided. For that reason, the two cousins now finished the day with a glass of brandy by the sitting room fire. The Fitzwilliams' manor house was closed while the earl was in town for Parliament, so they occupied a guest cottage where a tidy set of chambers had been prepared for Darcy as well. The rooms were decorated in dark tones, giving a warm feel to the place. It was as if he and Richard were in a cocoon where they could talk frankly without interference.

"At least Wickham has been sighted off and on by reasonable people," said the colonel, drumming his fingers on the chair arm. "Sir Frank has not been seen at all since last summer and has disappeared from all those areas of England he would frequent under ordinary circumstances. Maggie now wears black trim on her gowns and muddles about her day bleary-eyed. She has lost hope he will return and believes there is some evil behind his loss."

"I do not understand how a gentleman like Sir Frank could just disappear," replied Darcy. "Unless for some reason the press gangs got him. As a baronet, he could serve in the militia in his own region, though. In either case, he would be allowed to write to his family."

"Yes, and that is why Maggie believes he must be dead. She feels that if

Sir Frank were alive, he would have written to her by now, which is why she is convinced he was overcome by highwaymen despite the lack of evidence to support her conclusion."

"Did they have an understanding?"

Richard nodded. "Sir Frank had not yet gone to Father although he was expected at Matlock two days after he was last seen."

"And the circumstances around his disappearance are odd, to say the least."

"Yes. His curricle had broken down, appearing as if it had been in an accident, with no evidence of why the wheel was broken. He was not racing, or at least no second equipage was evident. In addition, the man and his horses went missing. He could have ridden away on one, but what about the other? If he wanted to hide, it would make no sense to take it along."

"Horse thieves can cover their tracks only so well," said Darcy. "Sir Frank had a stunning matched pair of greys. I am surprised they have not appeared at auction or on nearby farms."

"Ah, but one has been found. I saw the mare just yesterday and confirmed its markings."

Surprise was an understatement for Darcy's feelings, and he leaned forward automatically. After all this time? "Where?"

"At a coaching inn in Rowsley. It has been in use since the autumn with Sir Frank's brand barely visible under the new mark. The innkeeper feigned shock and blamed a head groom who had left his employ around the time the horse was purchased. However, when pressed, he stated that a gentleman sold it to him. But I described Sir Frank to the man, and it was not him."

Darcy shook his head. "One would think Sir Frank would have just come to Matlock rather than selling his horse so close by."

"Remember, Sir Frank has not been seen. Besides, this man was tall and slender and wearing an ill-fitting coat. Definitely a thief."

Darcy nodded. This was not a description of Sir Frank. "To sell a valuable horse pretending it was his own was cunning and planned, not to mention brazen."

"Whoever abandoned it was familiar with this inn's lack of care. He was probably from the area."

The hairs on Darcy's neck stood on end and his jaw dropped at the disclosure. The stable where they had found remnants of a vagrant was within a half-day's ride from Rowsley. "So the person who stole the horse brought it to the Peaks."

The colonel took a sip of his brandy before he confirmed Darcy's thoughts. "This could be our tie to Wickham."

Darcy blew out a huff of breath. "This could *be* Wickham. No wonder you summoned me on urgent business. Do you believe Wickham has harmed Sir Frank, or do you think they were in collusion?"

"I do not know. But I believe he is involved in Sir Frank's disappearance and that of the horse that was taken. Wickham has been seen in this area; Sir Frank has not."

"But Wickham is accustomed to certain comforts in life. How could he have spent the winter hiding in the conditions of an impoverished person?"

"He must have a great deal to hide," Richard said.

"Like the events at Lambton and the location of Miss Lydia Bennet?"

"Miss Lydia Bennet?"

"The young lady he absconded with from Brighton. I did not mention it before since I wanted to preserve what was left of her good name. Do you recall Miss Bennet from Rosings at Easter? Miss Lydia is her sister." His heart lightened, and he smiled at the recollection of his betrothal. "By the way, Richard, you must wish me joy."

Richard stopped halfway in the motion of taking a sip of his beverage. "A lady has accepted you?"

"Miss Elizabeth Bennet."

Richard leapt forward and shook Darcy's hand. "Well, congratulations! I am quite relieved at your choice since the only ladies you have spent any time with as of late have been Miss Bingley and Anne."

Darcy's brows could not have reached higher. "You have lost standing in my eyes if you assumed I might offer for either of them!"

Richard chuckled. "I suspected you may have admired Miss Bennet back in Kent. Why did it take you so long?"

"It did not. She turned me down the first time I proposed, just over a year ago."

"She denied your proposal? Well, well. I suspected she did not hold you in near the approbation you held her. She once asked me why you stared at her so often, and she was convinced you were judging her ill."

"As I discovered. In addition, I was a horse's ass in the way I worded the initial proposal, and she gave me a good piece of her mind. I saw her again at Pemberley last summer and was about to repeat my addresses when she had her accident. Do you remember when I told you about the lady who was hurt and the misunderstanding that caused her uncle to blame me?"

"That was her? Good G-d!"

"Her uncle, Mr. Gardiner, banned me from her company for many months. However, recently, based on the content of Elizabeth's returning memories, he changed his mind. She recalled speaking with Wickham in Lambton, and he now believes, as I do, that her injuries were caused by Wickham."

"I always thought of Wickham as a lackadaisical sort but never harmless. Ramsgate proved he could be evil though I did not expect him to become violent," said Richard.

"I do not believe anyone expected it, least of all Elizabeth. I look forward to being rid of his spectre over our lives. For myself, I am relieved that my time as suspect is over and cannot wait to return and begin marriage preparations."

"So you managed to convince her it was advantageous to become Mrs. Darcy this time?"

"She remembered some of my words from last summer, and she was anticipating my declaration. Her heart had changed, and she is not one to have her mind altered by anything other than a true attachment."

Richard grinned and leaned forward. "So she no longer believes you a horse's ass. How did you manage it?"

He laughed. "When she visited Pemberley, we had time to speak, and I used the best of my manners to improve her impression. During that visit, I showed her I had tried to heed her criticisms and become a better man."

"You have always been a good man."

Although he appreciated Richard's faith in him, it was another reminder of his feelings of self-importance when he first met Elizabeth. His gratitude to her overflowed for her role in helping him understand the changes he needed to make. "Nay, I was proud and conceited, and Elizabeth felt it well. In addition, Wickham poisoned her mind against me."

"What of the sister? The one Wickham disgraced?"

"My good name will support the Bennets in regaining the standing they lost when Miss Lydia ran off."

With a slight grimace, Richard said, "You take on a great deal. But you now have even more reasons to want to capture Wickham and see him taken to task for his wrongs."

"I sent a couple of men to check the area where we thought he may have lived last autumn, but it appears the person has long abandoned it."

"So he has been seen near Pemberley but came from Brighton."

"He and Miss Lydia Bennet were tracked as far as Clapham and then never seen again until his appearance at Lambton at the time Miss Bennet was attacked."

"Heaven forfend! Sir Frank's curricle accident was at Battersea Bridge Road! They're barely more than a mile apart!"

Darcy ran his fingers through his hair. "Then the tall, lean man *must* be Wickham. But how are they related?"

"I cannot say. However, with one young lady missing, another badly injured, and Sir Frank missing, it sounds like Wickham is far more dangerous than expected given his petty crimes of the past. Since that horse was found at Rowsley, I suppose the search should be widened once again to include the areas farther south of Pemberley. But it has been so long since he sold that grey."

"And he was seen near Lambton around Christmas."

"Matters could not be more complicated."

At this point, the door opened and the butler entered, bearing a salver with a letter. "An express for Mr. Darcy," he said. Darcy thanked him as he retrieved the missive. The handwriting was unfamiliar, but it was clearly a woman's hand, and he could think of only one woman who was familiar with his travel plans other than his sister. He excused himself whilst he opened the letter with eager anticipation to look for the signature. His mouth went dry when he read who had written to him, and his heart leapt at the sweet closing words.

"It is from Elizabeth," he told Fitzwilliam before he quickly perused the rest of the letter.

"Ah, a love letter so soon, and by express. I anticipate your asking my leave to respond before we get down to business," Richard replied with a smirk.

"No. The letter is about business." He leaned back in his chair whilst the hand that held the letter dropped to the side. Her words were so certain, yet how could it be? This changed everything. "She writes that she believes Wickham is in London."

Richard's mouth dropped open. He quickly leaned forward. "But how can that be if he was sighted in Derbyshire? It is a great distance to travel for one who is supposed to be in hiding, but over a long duration, I suppose it is possible."

"I know you feel disbelief of sorts. So do I, and unfortunately, she does not say for certain he is in London. From what she and her uncle have gathered, they conclude he has been there recently." He perused the letter again and expressed his thoughts to his cousin. "How could he be in two places at once?"

"Recall that Pemberley is not a recent sighting. But have they seen him in town? Spoken to him or the young miss he eloped with?"

"Miss Lydia. No, they do not say that much. But do you recall Mrs. Younge?"

The colonel's deep scowl expressed all he needed to know. "Indeed I do. She is nearly as terrible a person as Wickham in my estimation to dupe a young girl like Georgiana into a near elopement. Was she involved with Miss Lydia Bennet as well?"

"Elizabeth does not say. But Mrs. Younge had a gentleman boarder who requested a room for a Mr. George Wickham. Mrs. Younge made it clear she was not at all interested in Wickham as a guest in her establishment. Mr. Gardiner—Elizabeth's uncle—and a lady friend of the family looked into the matter further to try to glean more from this boarder, but Mrs. Younge would not divulge anything—she had been sworn to secrecy and was partial enough to her lodger to take Wickham's side."

"Damn. So close."

"Finally, they were able to obtain the gentleman boarder's name and employer. Mr. Gardiner believes this clerk was hiding part of his story about speaking to Wickham, but he had been told the clerk received a letter from someone that made reference to their having studied at Cambridge together. Elizabeth hoped that I knew the fellow from Cambridge and could convince him to tell the truth about Wickham and Lydia. Unfortunately, she seems to have written this in a hurry and neglected to recall she needed to share his name. I am asked to go up to town as soon as my business is completed so I might try to convince Mrs. Younge and this man." He held his hand out in plea of understanding. "They seem to think I may succeed where Mr. Gardiner's efforts have failed as I might have some sort of sway over both due to my past connections."

In response, his cousin's eyebrows knitted together. "You do have the option of having Mrs. Younge prosecuted for her part in Wickham's attempting to elope with an heiress, even if the action was incomplete. Your word will defeat hers every time, though, and her intent and near success will put her in a negative light with the law the way it is interpreted. Are they aware of this?"

"No, unless Elizabeth knows more of the law than she has divulged to me. I suspect they believe my closer connection and name will influence the dratted woman."

"As is likely true, though your dismissal of her without a character could make her resentful and less forthcoming to you as well."

"It is worth the chance, and I believe that is the reason Elizabeth has asked my assistance."

"Fortunately, your betrothal permits her to write to you in such a way." Leaning forward on one elbow, Richard grinned and winked. Despite all Darcy had just divulged, did Richard believe the letter was full of secret messages due to their recent engagement?

A quick perusal showed it was worded so he could share it with anyone he trusted with the intelligence within, though the opening and close tugged at his heart and could give his cousin cause to persist with his teasing. "Her words are not those of a love letter, Richard. They are very serious indeed. Behind them, I suspect she is terrified. He was brutal to her in Lambton."

The colonel withdrew to a more solemn attitude. "Then we must take her seriously. You must return to town and question Mrs. Younge as your lady suggests. I shall go to Pemberley in your stead and lead the locals in a wider query for any hint of Wickham's presence in that area of the Peaks and towards the south."

"What of your search for Sir Frank?"

"Somehow, I believe we have just started on this mission of discovery, and Wickham is the key to it all. And the key to Wickham, unfortunately, is your ability to prise information from Mrs. Younge." He raised his glass. "Godspeed, Darcy."

Darcy toasted him in kind. "The same to you."

Chapter 23

May 1813
Portman Square, London

The moment he arrived in town, Darcy sent his card over to Gracechurch Street. After he refreshed himself from the journey, all he could do was to sit on needles and pins while he waited for Mr. Gardiner to respond.

At length, the man's arrival at Darcy's London house was announced, and a handshake was exchanged in greeting. Mr. Gardiner suggested that they leave at once to speak with Wickham's friend, and soon they were on their way to Bond Street.

"I thought it best that we speak in the carriage on our way to Mr. Symonds's place of employment," said Mr. Gardiner.

"Symonds?" asked Darcy, hair on the back of his neck rising at the name. "He is the man who asked after accommodations for Wickham?"

"Do you by chance know him?"

"I suspect who he is, but I cannot understand why he would use another name. But perhaps…" Darcy said, considering another upsetting possibility. To assuage his apprehension, he asked, "Mr. Gardiner, have you met Wickham before? The man you met was not Wickham posing as another man who met with some sort of nefarious end?"

"I met him briefly at Christmastide in the year eleven when he was stationed with the militia in Meryton, and no, this was a different man altogether. Mr. Wickham is tall and of slim figure, and this fellow is average size, fairer, and bespectacled. He is taciturn where Wickham is loquacious, clearly avoiding our questions."

Darcy nodded. "I happen to know a man called Sir Frank Nelson-James, who has been missing since last summer. Though it could be another Symonds, it is likely no coincidence that Symonds is the family name of Sir Frank's mother," he said. "With the exception of the spectacles, your description resembles that of Sir Frank. This man was courting my cousin Lady Margaret Fitzwilliam until his mysterious disappearance south of the Thames at around the same time Wickham and Miss Lydia Bennet departed from Brighton. Can you enlighten me on the details of what he told you?"

Even though he should have experienced relief for Lady Margaret's sake, Darcy was concerned at the prospect of seeing the man and obtaining the information he needed about Wickham, especially since Mr. Gardiner had been unsuccessful. He was unable to reconcile the modest, humble peer as a friend to Wickham. As before, he could not make out any commonalities between them, yet the two men were obviously familiar with each other. Mayhap Sir Frank was not all he seemed.

Gardiner wiped his hand across his face. "Elizabeth thought you might know him from Cambridge, but we could not have imagined…" Mr. Gardiner then described much the same as Darcy had read in Elizabeth's letter: Symonds claimed to have had a recent letter from Wickham that said Wickham was travelling with a friend from Cambridge. He had not mentioned the name of his travelling companion, and Symonds had supposedly burned the letter. Mr. Gardiner believed the story to be fiction and that Symonds had seen Wickham in town but had no proof for his allegations. He also mentioned Elizabeth's contribution to the analysis: since Darcy had gone to Cambridge at the same time as Wickham, he may know Mr. Symonds.

"Wickham would know of Sir Frank for certain, but they were not close associates. I cannot fathom why they would vanish at the same time." Surely, Sir Frank had no reason to cause Wickham's demise.

"That information is what I hope you can prise from Mr. Symonds."

When they arrived at the address on Bond Street, Darcy spoke with the barrister briefly to ensure a private audience with his clerk; then Mr. Symonds himself entered the office. Immediately upon seeing Darcy, he tried to rush from the room, but Mr. Gardiner stood in front of the door, barring his exit. The man wore the slightly dishevelled, worn garments of a man who could not afford better clothing or a valet, as well as metal spectacles, but he was still instantly recognisable to Darcy.

"Hello, Sir Frank," Darcy said. He tried to control his vexation, but his tone was more antagonistic than was his intention.

"This is about Wickham again, is it not?" Sir Frank asked, looking at Mr. Gardiner. He crossed his arms, a sullen frown covering his face, and turned to Darcy. "You must know, Darcy, it was not my fault. I...I...damn that cur! I wish I had never set eyes upon him in my life!"

It was easy enough to concur with the exclamation. "You will be neither the first nor the last to express such a sentiment. Now, Mr. Gardiner here tells me you were looking for a room for Wickham with Mrs. Younge, but she would not have him as a boarder. You seem to be a favourite of hers. Tell me, have you exchanged my cousin for a woman I had to dismiss as my sister's companion for her objectionable ethics?"

The man paced the room, running his hands through his sandy hair. "No, no! If I could go to Maggie, I would. But Wickham...he told me I must hide or he would blame me for it all!"

"I recall you read law at Cambridge, but you are a gentleman. So was this disguise as a barrister's clerk your way of hiding?"

"Why are you hiding?" asked Mr. Gardiner. "Or should I say from whom? Wickham? Why would you request lodgings for him if you are afraid of him?"

"If I tell you, will you promise to believe me? Because Wickham will tell another story. One that puts me in a terrifically bad light, but I swear to G-d, it is not true."

"No need to blaspheme, sir," said Mr. Gardiner. "Just tell us the truth."

Sir Frank gave a slight nod. He took a deep breath before he commenced his speech. "It was the second of August in the year twelve. I was on my way to Matlock and had stopped for the night at a coaching inn when I encountered Wickham and a young lady in the nearby public house. Wickham was dressed in regimentals, and the lady hung over him in a too-familiar manner for a public room, if you understand my meaning. I had thought her a doxy he had met at the coaching inn, but upon seeing the lady more closely and hearing her speak to Wickham, I realized from her clothing, hair, and diction that she was likely a gently bred young lady, perhaps fifteen or sixteen—exactly the type Wickham gravitated towards in Cambridge, and part of the reason I did not spend a great deal of time with his crowd. He referred to her as Lydia though she instructed me to call her Mrs. Wickham. The look the two shared over this, laughing and joking in their expressions, touching each other—I knew no marriage had taken place, but in a baser sense, they had become joined."

Darcy winced at the description. The explanation of Miss Lydia's elopement gave him hope she was still with Wickham. It did seem odd that Sir Frank was telling of her embarrassment, though.

"Wickham was a lively fellow that night, obviously flush for some reason, spending money on ale for the punters. I had seen him like that the odd time over the years, but he tended to be too foolish to stop and rarely walked away without losing more than he could afford. When he asked for the opportunity to win back what he owed me the last time I played against him a year or so ago, I quickly learned he had won at cards that evening. I had not mentioned his debt earlier since he was poor at paying them, and it was only a couple of guineas in any case. However, I am always interested in playing at dice until the point where I am losing more than I can afford; then I quit the game. That evening was no different at first, but the little lady goaded me into staying at the table longer than usual. Wickham looked at her in admiration, and I realized to my amusement that this was how he had managed to win for a change."

In response to Darcy's quizzical expression, Sir Frank elucidated. "He was not cheating, but the young miss seemed to give him better luck, and she encouraged his opponents to stay and play longer, losing more to him— Excuse me, but could I get some refreshment for my dry mouth?"

Mr. Gardiner stuck his head out the door and called to a boy to bring a pint of ale. Sir Frank nodded his appreciation as he continued.

"When I finally bowed out, I was down a dozen guineas. I was ashamed to a certain degree since it is more than I usually allow myself, but I had enjoyed my time playing.

"The next morning, I arose before dawn so I could get an early start to my trip. The lights of the coaching station were behind me, and it was still fairly dark when I espied Wickham and his lady at the side of the road, on foot, as I came towards them in my curricle. I was surprised to find them awake so early, but I attributed it to a desire to get to town quickly. After all, they had a wedding to plan—that is, if he was planning to honour her."

"A wedding was probably the first thing on her mind and the farthest from his," Darcy said in a growl. "She did not have the sort of fortune to attract him to matrimony."

Sir Frank's eyes opened wide. "You know the chit?"

"She is sister to my betrothed and niece to Mr. Gardiner."

"My apologies for my candour as it relates to her behaviour, gentlemen. I had no idea."

Mr. Gardiner spoke, arms crossed, his face bright red. "Of course you did not. She could be anybody's sister." Gardiner's words were terse, and Sir Frank had the good grace to avert his eyes. After a pause of a few moments' time, Mr. Gardiner inhaled deeply and addressed Sir Frank. "Please continue."

"They were having an argument of sorts. She stamped her foot and attempted to turn away from him. He leapt towards her and grabbed her by the arms. Suddenly, he released her, throwing her body away from him, and she stumbled and fell. I…I…was so intent on watching them that I did not give them wide enough berth, and Miss Lydia fell below the hooves of my horses." Sir Frank's voice wavered significantly as he made the statement. The ale arrived, and he took a long draft from his glass.

"Lord, no! Was she injured?" asked Mr. Gardiner.

Sir Frank's face crumpled like that of a lost child. "I am so sorry, but yes, she was hurt quite dreadfully. Her body lifted the curricle and tipped it over, and the back wheel of the curricle actually broke as it took the entire load. You have no idea the remorse I carry as a result."

The accident as described could never have a good outcome. Darcy dreaded hearing the resulting trauma.

"Her body was broken in more than one place, but the worst was that her head—it lay at such an odd angle to her body. Wickham rushed to lift her in his arms and carry her, shouting that we must take her to the inn. I…I stopped him, telling him to put her down lest he do more damage. I told him we needed an apothecary or a surgeon, and he was to go fetch one at once until he decided to ensure she was alive." Now Sir Frank's eyes overflowed with tears, and he produced a handkerchief to wipe across his face. "Forgive me, gentlemen, but I am always overwhelmed when I think of how she appeared all battered from the accident."

Mr. Gardiner offered nothing but a choked noise.

Darcy swallowed, ill to his stomach. "We understand your turmoil," he said.

"She had perished, probably the moment the carriage hit her. Wickham began to shout at me about driving too fast, racing, hitting her as she ran off. 'You murdered my betrothed and you will pay for it!' he said." His hands opened in plea, much as he must have done in front of Wickham. "But I had done no such thing, I swear it! I was alone and had barely urged the horses into a canter. He, however, had pushed her in a way that she fell under my wheels. After the event had taken place and I had more time to consider how things happened, that is how I saw it. But Wickham kept repeating over and over—'You murdered her!'—and I began to fear that he was correct." Sir Frank's hand shook as he raked it through his hair. His eyes were still moist.

"May she rest in peace," Mr. Gardiner murmured.

"He told me I must help him hide the body lest I be charged with murder. I was so shocked that I just stood there as he dragged her off the road and into some bushes." Sir Frank grabbed his ale and took another drink, and then his confession came out in a rush. "We buried her later under cover of darkness by digging into a fresh grave in the churchyard. He then told me we had to go into hiding lest we be caught. At the time, I was not thinking correctly, and he made me fear the worst."

"Wickham is nothing if not convincing." Darcy growled.

Sir Frank nodded and drew a breath, collecting himself. "He insisted that I give him a set of my clothes so he would not be recognized, and he described his plans. He would return to where he could easily be taken care of; he knew of a number of places a man could live without being detected. In addition, he told me I must depart for town and take on a new identity. He knew a lady who owed him who would help me—Mrs. Younge. His countenance was wild, and his voice sounded desperate, so I complied."

"Are you aware of his history with Mrs Younge—of the way they knew each other?" Darcy crossed his arms as he asked the question.

"No. I assumed he had lived at her house in the past. In fact, I did not hear from him at all until a few weeks ago when I received a letter postmarked from Matlock. I thought that maybe Maggie—my apologies, Lady Margaret—had discovered me, and I was nervous yet desirous of communicating with her. Obviously, Wickham had someone else write to me for him as it was in a lady's hand. Her ability with a pen and spelling left a great deal to be desired, so I imagine she was not well educated.

"The letter asked me to have Mrs. Younge hold a room for Mr. Wickham in one week's time. I asked her and she refused, so I replied to the sender's direction that I was unable to meet the requirements of the request. Thus far, to my great relief, I have heard nothing further from him. So, if you are seeking Wickham, look towards Matlock Dales. I am sorry I cannot elucidate further, but that is my best knowledge." Sir Frank drooped in his chair as he finished his story.

"By common report, he was near Lambton and Pemberley in past months, and your horse was sold at Rowsley in the winter. We will indeed redirect our efforts through my cousin's search. But there is another thing I must ask." Despite Colonel Fitzwilliam's inability to find any trace of Sir Frank between his estate near Sevenoaks, Clapham, and his destination at Matlock, the tie to Wickham was damning. Could this be who attacked Elizabeth? "Did you join Wickham on his trip north before you hied off for London, sir? Did you take part in nefarious acts in Derbyshire as well?"

Sir Frank's watery eyes widened. "No, I swear I have not been north since last July. I have been in London since the fourth day of last August. You can ask Mrs. Younge."

"And Lydia? How can we find her remains and reunite her with her family as she deserves?" asked Mr. Gardiner. His voice shook, but whether from grief, anger, or frustration, Darcy found it impossible to tell. He himself was overwhelmed by all three.

"Near Clapham. I can show you. I marked it with a cross of light-coloured stones. The poor young lady. She did not deserve such a demise," said Sir Frank. He released a heavy sigh and dropped his head. "I suppose I shall get what is coming to me now."

How was Darcy to respond to such a statement? The words would have hung in the air, unanswered, had Mr. Gardiner not acted. He grabbed Sir Frank by the collar, putting his face close to his.

"Do not think we shall forget your part in this just because you have finally spoken out. What took you so long? Why did you hide for the better part of a year? Wickham may be a brute, but your actions show you to be a weak simpleton, Sir Frank, and G-d will punish you where the law may not," he growled then tossed the baronet back so he nearly toppled over.

Sir Frank wiped his brow. "You are right. I should have come forward. But I was terrified Wickham would twist things and I would be caught taking responsibility for an accident. How many times has he lied and got off free?"

"Neither of you deserves freedom," Mr. Gardiner spat as he marched to the door. Such honest yet threatening words to be said aloud! Darcy could not disagree with him.

"I do not plan to flee if that is what you are concerned about," said Sir Frank. "I am prepared to defend my lack of culpability."

"We shall be seeking your employer's assurances before taking our leave to discuss the matter. Please do not try to escape as the authorities will find you. Good day, sir," said Darcy as he donned his hat and gloves. Sir Frank called the barrister into the office, and he was apprised of the need for Sir Frank to remain available in case the authorities wanted more from him. An easy enough fellow, the employer agreed, giving Sir Frank a look that indicated an expectation of disclosure once their guests left.

In the carriage on the way back to the Gardiner house, he and Mr. Gardiner were mostly silent. Mr. Gardiner's voice sounded forced as he asked whether Darcy planned to go after Wickham.

"My cousin is looking for Wickham near Pemberley and Rowsley. I shall send an express to request that he question young ladies in service at Matlock and any nearby towns for someone who can read and write but not well. That should help us find the cur."

"And Sir Frank? What of him?"

"I do not know. Lydia's demise seems an accident on his part, but he concealed it rather than reporting it to the authorities. Some sort of retribution is due. The year he has spent hiding from his family and friends should prepare him for a life in the colonies."

"That seems a fitting punishment if he is considered a murderer. We cannot be sure. His reticence is deplorable. Look what her poor family had to go through!" Mr. Gardiner's lips were in a severe line, his countenance as furious as Darcy had ever seen. His own face likely reflected similar sentiments.

They said no more, yet, if his own mind was any indicator of what was happening in Mr. Gardiner's thoughts, there was conflict enough for ten men. Even in his anger, he had sympathy for the meek peer. Both men's disappearances pointed to their guilt, but Wickham's confident persuasion would go far in court compared to Sir Frank's remorseful countenance. It would level their differences in situation for certain.

Despite this, Darcy had worse things on his mind than what to do about the two men responsible for Lydia's death. He did not know how they were going to tell Elizabeth about Lydia. How would she react when, for so long, she had thought the best of the situation whilst everyone else believed the worst?

Chapter 24

Gracechurch Street, London

Elizabeth had spent almost the entire day waiting. How were her uncle and Mr. Darcy getting on with Mr. Symonds? After an interminable amount of time spent distractedly on her needlework whilst glancing out of the front parlour window every few minutes, a carriage finally appeared. She had seen this grand crest and liveried driver before: Mr. Darcy's carriage. Her uncle and her betrothed alighted from the vehicle.

Clutching her hands, she willed herself to sit still. She should have examined their features as they moved towards the house. She had not seen toothy smiles indicating joyous countenances, merely shadowed faces beneath their hats as they rushed through the light mist that was expected during spring in London. *Do not let it bother you. All will be well once they tell you what they have discovered.*

Aunt and Elizabeth rose to greet Mr. Darcy and Uncle, who followed the more consequential man into his home. What was written on their faces? What did the way they held their bodies reveal of what they knew?

Uncle Gardiner stared at his wife with pleading eyes and a frown Elizabeth could not understand. Was he so very unhappy, and what did it mean? He gave a subtle tilt of his head towards Elizabeth, and Aunt Gardiner gazed at her then back at Uncle. She then nodded and shifted towards the sofa where Elizabeth had been sitting.

"Madeleine, Lizzy, please sit," Uncle began, waving towards the sofa. When they were settled, he began. "Firstly, we were able to arrange a meeting with

Mr. Symonds, the man who mentioned Mr. Wickham to Mrs. Younge. He could not lead us to Mr. Wickham, but he did tell us a story that I shall now relate to you. I shall not prolong it, as I find it difficult enough to relate as it is." His voice broke in the middle of the last sentence and his face had an odd quality to it as if he had exerted himself greatly.

Elizabeth's chest was so tight it almost impeded her ability to breathe.

Uncle wiped his face with his hand. "Lydia was in an accident last August and perished. She is buried in Clapham."

Did that shriek come from her? Some part of her had distanced itself from the room as though she had begun to watch from above. Tears were streaming down Uncle's face—had he just started crying this moment? No, he had not. How could she have overlooked it when he was speaking?

Oh, dear Lydia! Foolish, dear sister. She had lost a sister and would never get her back. She had been one of five and now would be one of four. Lydia's bright, unabashed, untamed nature could be a special joy at times, no matter that it sometimes rankled her. How could this have happened? She had been so convinced that Lydia's ill-chosen elopement had been resolved for the better, and her loss was impossible to bear. Pain stabbed her heart.

She could no longer support herself and began to fall forward as if to double over in her seat, but someone's gentle arms caught her and pulled her to the side. The softness where her head landed was her aunt's lap. Those heavy, painful sensations in her chest were sobs. Oh! She was crying harder than she had ever done in her life, and it nearly threatened to suffocate her. The subsequent heaving breaths she had to take were noisy and prolonged. A handkerchief was pushed into her hand. She wiped her face, yet the scrap of cloth did not serve to stop the flow of tears and soon was sopping wet.

A large area of warmth, not part of the hold her aunt had on her, spread across her back. Whose hand was it? Mr. Darcy! He was on his knees beside them, his handsome face distorted and pinched in pain, wetness staining his cheeks.

She stared at him through her tears, and his face broke and bent even more, his lips a trembling, uneven line and his eyes holding the most sympathetic expression she could ever imagine. This was the man she had loved so long, trusted so well, whom she could never believe unkind. Despite the obstacles and contrary evidence, she had faith in him—relied upon his goodness in essentials. Nature took over her impulses, and she slid off her aunt's lap onto her knees in front of him and allowed herself to be wrapped in his embrace as her entire body shook with the harshness of what she had just learned. A sister dead, and so young!

The sensation of his warm hand stroking up and down her back as his other arm held her tightly to his sturdy chest, her face buried in the curve of his shoulder and neck, allowed her to eventually return her sensibility to the room and the deep sobs to calm to a heavy breathing pattern. The occasional shudder of her body broke into the regularity of breath he had inspired by his soothing embrace.

Uncle cleared his throat. Elizabeth leapt from Mr. Darcy's arms back onto the sofa and busied her hands wiping her face. Mr. Darcy rose, but as he stepped away, his eyes would not settle on any item in the room above the level of Uncle's watch fob. She had never seen him so contrite, and the hug in front of her relations must be the reason.

By now, Elizabeth had gathered enough composure and awareness of her deportment to have returned to a position of curiosity as was her wont. Even so, she dabbed her leaking eyes with another handkerchief, this time pulled from her own pocket. "Can you tell me what happened? Mr. Wickham lied when he spoke with me; I understand that well enough now. But what was the truth of the matter?"

"As you know, they eloped from Brighton," said Uncle. "Lydia told Mr. Symonds they were married, but he was suspicious that it was her desire, not a completed event. Mr. Wickham argued with Lydia, and somehow she fell in front of a moving carriage. Mr. Symonds was the driver, and Mr. Wickham frightened Mr. Symonds by implying that he murdered her."

A recollection suddenly entered her head: Mr. Wickham denied injuring Lydia most vehemently. Elizabeth replied in a soft voice, "He said, 'I did not hurt her, Miss Elizabeth, I did not. She pulled out of my hands and ran away. Neither of us could help her then.'"

"What?" asked Mr. Darcy.

"Those were his words, Mr. Wickham's, as he was trying to make me promise to tell the story of you saving them, that they were married. I only remembered it just now. He never said Lydia perished, just that she ran away."

"And he used force to try to make you promise."

"I expect that was what happened next though I do not recollect it for certain." A chill passed over Elizabeth as another memory vividly returned.

"No, what happened next was that you were announced, and Mr. Wickham bolted from the back door before you entered the room. You exclaimed your concern over my fraught state and offered me a glass of wine."

Uncle said, "So, Mr. Wickham had not struck you or thrown you down at that point."

Elizabeth was helpless to respond further. "I do not know, but I do not think so."

"He must have returned later," said her aunt.

Elizabeth squeezed her eyes shut as she tried to recall the rest of the day back in early August, but pictures and sounds only came in bits. She could not force the memories any more than she could change night to day. They had to be left alone and nature allowed to sort through the events that made sense in order for the proper revelation to surface at the proper time. Yet, the missing parts of the story still frustrated her and placed a heavy weight upon her shoulders and a smarting pain behind her façade.

Mr. Darcy spoke. "There was a commotion in the public area of the inn with a lot of shouting, both indoors and out. A man had been seen who was not in favour with several of the gentlemen there, and they were chasing him. At the time, I did not know who he was and did not think to suspect Wickham being anywhere close to Derbyshire.

"Since then, the innkeeper mentioned he had seen Wickham nearby around the date of your attack and suspects the fellow they chased was Wickham. Maybe he had to come back into the room whilst I was gone, to hide from the masses." He ran his fingers through his hair, tousling it a little more than it already had been. His brow was furrowed thoughtfully. Poor Mr. Darcy, to wonder how Mr. Wickham could evade a crowd and yet cause such havoc. The man would have been forced out the back door once again when Mr. Darcy returned. Would Mr. Wickham be resentful that he was unable to hide in that parlour?

"There was more shouting—I know it—but I do not know who or when," Elizabeth said. "Perhaps it was the people chasing him, but the words are strange and do not match a crowd after a rogue."

"Can you tell them to us, dear, those words you recollect? They may help solve this puzzle of who hurt you. Anything you remember." Aunt Gardiner leaned towards Elizabeth and took one of her hands.

Elizabeth shook her aching head as she sighed. "I am sorry. They come into my brain at times, but I cannot quote them. Some of my recollections were Mr. Darcy and Uncle arguing, but another voice bellows in anger. I do not remember Mr. Wickham yelling in such a manner; most of the time he was despondent. Even when he raised his voice, the tone was one of desperation, not hatred. He pressed me to help him as he repeated the story, but he never threatened me with violence. If he returned in anger, his face was not associated with the few words and actions I can remember from after he left. But I cannot recall a face for the man who hurt me."

"Well, if he can push Lydia towards a moving curricle, he is the devil himself." Her uncle's voice held a fierceness she had not heard since his argument with Mr. Darcy in Lambton.

This was confusing. Mr. Wickham claimed he did not hurt poor Lydia. "But he said she ran from him. Perhaps she ran into the path of the carriage," she said. "Or perhaps she fell. But he insisted he was not to blame."

She looked from one to another of those in the room. Aunt's brows were turned down at the edges, tears still in her eyes.

"I do not believe he told you the truth, Lizzy. He lied to save himself," said Uncle. "We have come to know of his evil tendencies from many directions. He is a liar as well as a spendthrift, a wastrel, and a seducer. Now, we may add murderer to the list."

"The man we spoke with, who calls himself Mr. Symonds, claims Mr. Wickham threw Lydia aside, and she fell under the curricle," said Mr. Darcy. "We think something similar must have happened to you—the way you were thrown to the floor."

"There is more," said Uncle. "Mr. Wickham frightened this man so much he was forced to go into hiding. His real name is Sir Frank Nelson-James, and he is a family friend of the Fitzwilliams of Matlock. Mr. Darcy has intelligence to indicate Mr. Wickham is in hiding near Matlock or Pemberley. He used one of Sir Frank's horses in his escape."

Another turn in this peculiar situation. When would it end? "It is almost as if they changed places but not names."

"Not quite. Sir Frank changed his name, and Mr. Wickham returned to the area of his youth, which he must believe to be a place of safety. At least, that is where Mr. Symonds, or Sir Frank, told us to search for him. We also have evidence of a vagrant near those two estates, as well as witnesses who saw a gentleman some months ago, the sale of one of Sir Frank's horses, and the letter that was sent to Sir Frank. Few of the witnesses knew Mr. Wickham by sight, though, and he has been successful at evading those searching for him."

"I hope you find him soon. He is the key to my memories," said Elizabeth. Her head hurt, not like when it had been injured but, rather, just behind her eyes. Lydia's death, the search for Mr. Wickham, trying so hard to remember—it was all too much to take in at once. She would have to wait until they found Mr. Wickham and the balance of the truth was unveiled. Then if she were lucky, clarity around the voices would come naturally. For now, she was confident she had the faith and support of the other three in the room, and that would help her with the remaining grief, doubts, and fears.

Chapter 25

Portman Square, London

Darcy waited in his library with Mr. Gardiner, anticipating the arrival of Colonel Fitzwilliam. Whilst he had been in town questioning Sir Frank and then calling upon Elizabeth, the colonel had discovered the identity of the girl who had written the letter to Sir Frank on Wickham's behalf, an upstairs maid at an estate near Matlock. With her assistance, Wickham's location had been easier to find than anyone had anticipated, and Richard had quickly sent an express to Darcy detailing the discovery. The colonel reported Wickham was ill with the trots and a fever when he found him, and almost incoherent. Desperate to be helped, Wickham let the maid bring a "stranger" for his care, though the last person he would have wanted to assist him would have been Richard Fitzwilliam. Fate had given up on Wickham that day, and the colonel was able to capture the miscreant.

When Colonel Fitzwilliam and Wickham entered the library in Darcy's London house a week later, Darcy hardly recognised his former friend. The gauntness of his figure and face against the decidedly unfashionable hair shorn close to his head made him into a different man. His clothes hung on his narrow frame. An ugly slant, likely resulting from a break, now marred his nose, rendering him much less handsome. Whatever the cause, it took away Mr. Denny's chances of being the man who ruined the libertine's face.

"Good day, Darcy," said the colonel.

Darcy bowed his head to Richard and turned to Mr. Gardiner. "Please allow me to introduce my cousin Colonel Fitzwilliam. Colonel, this is Mr.

Gardiner of Gracechurch Street, Miss Bennet's uncle," Darcy said.

After acknowledging Mr. Gardiner with kind words and a bow, Richard then glared at his prisoner in expectation. Wickham's shoulders were slouched and his head low, a look Darcy never expected to see on him. His hands were tied behind his back and the colonel jerked at them, earning a wince from Wickham. "Address your betters."

Wickham dipped his head and mumbled a greeting without looking up.

Darcy scratched his brow. Should he give Wickham the courtesy of a response or should he simply ignore the prisoner? His ingrained sense of politesse would cause him to offer at least a nod, but his seething anger deemed the cut direct appropriate. Yet, if he hoped to incite a full recitation of the facts, he must at least make an effort at civility. He addressed him with a curt, flat, "Wickham." He would not offer more.

Mr. Gardiner offered Wickham the cut direct, turning away and situating himself on a nearby chair. Darcy waved for his cousin to take a seat before he settled himself at the desk. No indication was given for Wickham to have the honour of being seated, and none was intended.

Richard started the process. "You have summarized your manner of living over the past year to me and the magistrate at Matlock, but these gentlemen require a more detailed accounting, particularly regarding the events of last August."

Wickham cleared his throat, his gaze on the floor to one side of the room. "At this time last year, my unit was performing exercises in camp and preparing to leave for Brighton in May. Once settled in Brighton, we were allowed a great deal of free time. I filled the hours entertaining myself with dice and card games with my fellow officers. After a string of good luck, I found myself well ahead, and my friends pressed me for an opportunity to regain their losses. I foolishly entered some games of chance with some swindlers. I lost it all and more. However, this had happened to me before, and I was always able to get ahead."

Ha! He was always able to leave town and have Darcy pay his debts. Darcy opened his mouth to say something, but the colonel held up one finger to stay his protests. Richard had mentioned this in the letter—they wanted a full report from Wickham, so there would be no interruptions to upbraid him.

"The fellows who cheated me were rough sorts, big men from the lower ranks, and I became afraid for my well-being," said Wickham. His voice was resentful. "I decided to go to town rather than face them and arranged for a carriage in the middle of the night to take me to a nearby post station. I was friends with Mrs. Forster, and I told her of my plans so she could ask her husband to write papers allowing me proper leave under the circumstances. Instead, she told Miss Lydia Bennet my intentions, which is how I found her hiding under a rug in my carriage not a mile from the encampment. She had a *tendre* for me and expected we could get married in town."

"So you did not intend to elope with her or kidnap her? She surprised you when you encountered her as a hidden passenger?" asked Mr. Gardiner.

Wickham looked up for the first time since he entered the room. "That is correct, sir. But I did have a sweet spot for the little lady, who was rather free with her kisses."

Mr. Gardiner looked as if he were about to burst, his face a deep red colour. "Had you cared one whit about her, you would have turned the carriage around and returned her to her friends' home without a moment's consideration. That you continued and dragged her along on your foolish—"

Richard interrupted in a louder, firm voice. "We shall address that after Mr. Wickham has told the entire history." Darcy could not blame the poor gentleman for his outburst. This was his niece who was being discussed as if she were a common trollop. Richard paused and waited for a nod from Mr. Gardiner before he addressed the criminal again. "Go ahead, Wickham."

Wickham stood up a bit straighter and took a peek at Mr. Gardiner with more confidence now. "I could not evict her and chance meeting up with those ruffians. She wanted to be with me, and how could I resist such a sweet thing?" The blackguard dared a lascivious smirk, but Richard's scowling reproof made him drop his gaze once again.

Elizabeth's uncle tugged at his neck-cloth whilst his other hand clenched his chair arm, but he said nothing. His ruddy face spoke of the anger he withheld.

"We continued on to Clapham where I encountered an old acquaintance, Sir Frank Nelson-James. I spent the night at games of chance along with him and a few local fellows and wound up winning, with Sir Frank down the worst of the lot. This was advantageous, since I had owed him a few quid prior to the game. I had some travelling money gained from him and a promise of more once I made arrangements to meet with him in town at a later date." As he spoke, Wickham's demeanour relaxed a little more, but he still did not look any of the men in the eye.

"Miss Lydia and I rose early to catch the first post coach before sunrise. She was unhappy we were going towards London, not Scotland, and expressed her indignation. I argued I did not have the funds for the coach and the inns all that way, but she would have none of it. Even with my winnings, we had very little blunt—we were leaving without paying our bill—yet she still had ordered the best meal at the coaching inn."

"That sounds like Lydia," said her uncle. Darcy did not say that it also sounded just like Wickham to abscond with debts behind him.

"Indeed," said Wickham with a wistful bit of a smile tugging at his lips. So he had liked Miss Lydia after all. "She insisted I use what money she had left—she had been given some by Mrs. Forster—to hire a carriage, but it was a pittance since she used most of it to purchase fripperies the day before we left Brighton. Instead, we were to walk to the next posting inn. She and I were bickering—no, it was a row of colossal proportions—when she pushed me and I landed on my bottom by the side of the road. After I leapt to my feet, our argument worsened."

"Her demise was not an accident." Richard's voice was hard and cold.

"Of course it was," said Wickham. His Adam's apple bobbed as he swallowed deeply. "I tried to reason with her, but she tugged out of my hold—straight into the path of a fast-moving curricle. Her accident could not have been worse. All four hooves and one wheel went over her. The driver was unharmed, but Lydia perished immediately. Sir Frank was the man driving, and he had seen us, but did not expect her to rush out. I shouted at him that he was moving uncommonly fast for his proximity to the inn and accused him of racing."

Darcy broke into the speech with a question. "Was there another curricle? A witness?"

"No, but he was going very fast. He claimed he saw me push her into the path of the curricle, which is false. But I felt it partly my fault for releasing her so abruptly. Sir Frank and I buried her in a nearby graveyard in a fresh grave." Wickham glanced up only briefly. Apparently connecting with the eyes of his accusers was now beyond his ability. His voice was unsteady, and he appeared to be trying to be smaller by rolling his shoulders as much as he could given his bindings.

"You did not push her during the argument as Sir Frank alleges?" asked

Richard. "You did not shake her by the arms and throw her into the path of the curricle?"

"I never hurt her. In fact, *she* slapped *me* before she tugged out of my grip." His voice was quiet but vehement.

Raised eyebrows came from the men around the room.

"Sir Frank implied I would be charged for murder, and I threw the same threat back at him. Since he also owed me money, I had him in a difficult position, so I suggested I would not lay a formal accusation if he gave me a suit of his clothing to travel in and went into hiding in town. I told him where he could stay in London." He glanced at Darcy. "Miss Darcy's old companion, Mrs. Younge, has a boarding house on George Street. No doubt you found him there."

"We did."

"I do not know how you came to persuade him into speaking, but I am certain he twisted the story to paint me the villain. But keep in mind: he had been living under another name and in a low profession so he would not be found. He obviously had a fair belief in his guilt in this case."

"Or you pressed him into believing in it," muttered Mr. Gardiner.

Richard sent another furious glare towards Mr. Gardiner, which Wickham observed with interest. Wickham glanced from one man to the next.

"I, myself, decided the best place for me was to return home to Pemberley," he said, focusing directly on Darcy.

Darcy seethed. What had given Wickham the boldness to gaze about the room as though he had done nothing wrong? Mr. Gardiner's outbursts and the colonel's visual reprimands must have caused him to feel stronger in the moment than before. But the miscreant certainly knew how to irritate him: Pemberley was not Wickham's home! He had been unwelcome there since his elopement with Georgiana at the very least and, in Darcy's mind, since he took money in lieu of the living at Kympton. But he would not point out Wickham's lies and errors, though they were numerous. Instead, he would sit quietly and let Wickham dig his own grave. A full disclosure could aid them in understanding what had happened to Elizabeth. The entire story would also help soothe her fears about what she could not remember. That alone made the process worth the effort of listening to Wickham's story.

"I took one of his horses and travelled off the main road as much as I could so my path was not easily followed. I had not enough funds to feed an animal and stay in decent lodgings, and I was afraid that I would be prosecuted for stealing the horse, so I sold the grey as soon as I was able to find a willing buyer. I still could not stay on the main roads, and what little money I had barely covered acceptable lodgings. So I continued on foot, occasionally getting rides on wagons. When I finally arrived in Lambton late at night, exhausted from the exertion of travelling for four days with little sleep, I had not much more than a few pence in my pockets.

"I considered sleeping in the stables at the inn, but there was too much chance of being recognised there, so I managed a couple of hours of sleep in the back of a shop where I knew the shopkeeper was not an early riser. The next morning, I rose and began to walk to Pemberley. Miss Bennet's voice called to me from a window as I passed the inn." He looked at Darcy again in this calmer part of his recitation. "I pleaded with her not to divulge that she had seen me, but she started waving a paper at me, asking about Miss Lydia and making a fuss. When I noticed a set of stairs to the side, I took the servants' door into the parlour.

"When I entered, she continued to shake some letter at me, asking whether I was travelling to Gretna Green and where Lydia was. That was when I decided I should recruit her help. I told her how Miss Lydia had intentionally joined me when I left Brighton, and that her living with me prior to marriage would ruin Miss Bennet and her sisters. Instead of having tarnished reputations, she was to tell everyone a story I fabricated right then and there. I tried to convince her that Lydia and I were married, that my good friend Darcy had paid for the licence, an enhancement to Lydia's portion, and a position with the regulars, and that Lydia and I were on our way to Newcastle. If Darcy had caught wind of the story and protested, I figured I could always get some money out of him for agreeing to an alternative version of the tale. Darcy has always been good about protecting his honour and the honour of others. I did not let Miss Elizabeth know her sister was dead."

Wickham licked his lips and shuffled on his feet a bit before he continued the story. His speech was clear, but he appeared weary and reluctant in body. Was this difficult for him because of the topic or because he had been worn down whilst in exile?

"You see, I argued with Miss Lydia to stop her from ranting about getting married, and she tore away from me to escape. It is not my fault she decided to dart and fall in front of a moving vehicle, but the law will view it as if I pushed her on purpose. No one but Sir Frank and I know what occurred—and he will keep quiet. I simply needed help with this fabricated story.

"I reiterated the tale to ensure Miss Elizabeth understood, and I was succeeding when Darcy himself was announced. I had no wish to speak with Darcy; I had to escape. I slipped from the back door with as much speed as I could manage."

Darcy grimaced in agitation. Mr. Gardiner fidgeted, but Richard was all calm attention. No one uttered a word other than Wickham, though.

"At that point, a man noticed me and brought some friends from the public house asking me to repay some debts. Then a different fellow claimed I had left his daughter in a family way. I had intended to return to speak again to Miss Elizabeth after Darcy left, but instead, I ran away from the inn. I was afraid that they would beat me if they caught me."

Darcy exchanged a look with Mr. Gardiner. "When did you return to the parlour?" Darcy asked.

"I did not. I hid in a shed until nightfall and then left Lambton for Pemberley, where I slept for a week in the stables until Old John came back. He knew me where the young stable boy did not. It was more of a risk of being caught."

Richard then asked, "What happened to you afterwards?"

Wickham explained that he moved between several places of shelter whenever people came too near. Knowing the area as he did, he was able to slip in and out unseen for some time. Of course, he had to hide his fires, but he managed to obtain aid, including a warm coat and blanket, and food off and on at first from sympathetic maids and farm hands. When his clothing became dirty, he could no longer rely on his gentlemanly charm to get him help. Foraging and fishing sustained him at that point, and the wilderness of the Peaks hid him. He would have starved in the winter had he not stolen eggs and a hen or two.

That was when he convinced a young maid from Rowsley to write on his behalf to Sir Frank under the pseudonym he had suggested for him, Mr. Symonds. Although he had no idea how Colonel Fitzwilliam's men could have located him other than luck, their walking in on him whilst he sat on the privy of his makeshift lodgings near Matlock showed that somehow Sir Frank knew his location.

"You and Sir Frank will probably be charged with murder," the colonel said. His tone was flat, and he bore no facial expression to betray his emotions.

Oh, to be a soldier and have the ability to do such a thing. Darcy's experience at warding off people who sidled up desiring some service or notice had helped him to be well-versed in achieving a neutral expression, but not under circumstances such as these. The ache of spite in his face and shoulders was profound, never mind pain induced from the crescent arcs drawn by his fingernails within his fisted hands.

As for Wickham, every emotion he was likely feeling showed on his face. His eyes were wild, his mouth gaped open, and his brows lifted in the middle. The man should have expected to be charged under the circumstances. Or had he deluded himself in that regard as well?

"She was pushing me to marry her, and I did not want the chit, so she ran away. She should have known better than to run into the road! Sir Frank is the one who killed her! He could have swerved had he been paying attention!"

"You have spent nine months in hiding and have expectations less than the death penalty for killing a young girl and injuring a lady, never mind the outstanding debts and theft of which you are guilty?" asked Mr. Gardiner.

Wickham's body stiffened, and his eyes were wide and full of disbelief. "Injuring a lady? Which lady?"

"Miss Elizabeth Bennet, of course," Darcy said, shaking with fury.

"But I did nothing more than hold her by the arms!" His voice was high-pitched and elevated to the point he was practically shouting.

Darcy stood up, no longer able to hold his tongue. "Hold her? You struck her and threw her down!" He demonstrated the words at the same time as he said them, causing Wickham to stumble backwards and nearly fall. Wickham caught himself in time and responded to the accusation with great haste.

"Miss Lydia? No, I did not! I grabbed her and shook her, so she slapped me and ran away!"

Darcy stepped closer to Wickham and leaned forward so he was face to face with the murderer. "You previously denied shaking Miss Lydia, and now you admit it. It seems to me these two crimes are very similar: you grasped the lady by the arms and threw her off to fall in harm's way, Miss Lydia into the path of a curricle, and Miss Elizabeth to the floor. Did you strike Miss Lydia, as you did Miss Elizabeth? Did you choke her too? You revolting excuse for a man! I wish I could knock you flat right now as you did to that defenceless lady." His stomach churned, and he trembled from head to toe, his hand in the air, ready to strike. Wickham cringed and Darcy returned to his chair, disgusted with Wickham beyond any level of offence he had ever experienced in his life.

"I never touched Miss Elizabeth!"

He spun around, shocked that Wickham had the impertinence to deny it. "Miss Elizabeth herself acknowledges that you gripped her by the arms, and you said so yourself. You held her so hard, it left bruises. She was knocked insensible by the fall, and the surgeon noted the rest of the marks you left on her person."

Wickham leaned forward towards them and insisted, "No, it is not true! I merely held her when she would not listen to me. I…I was tired and could not think straight and wanted her to understand I needed her help. But I assure you, I did not even hold her tightly. She shook me off just as Lydia did!"

Richard spoke up. "Obviously, Mr. Wickham is unwilling to admit this part of his crime. However, enough evidence exists with which to convict him on Miss Lydia's demise alone. We need not involve Miss Elizabeth in this trouble."

Thank the Lord! Dealing with Wickham's continual lies was bad enough, but to fret about Elizabeth's reaction—at least he could tell her in a quieter, safer setting that she need never lay eyes on Wickham again. They could move ahead with their wedding plans and build a joyful life even though the scars would always be there.

Chapter 26

Gracechurch Street, London

While Uncle Gardiner was at Mr. Darcy's house to meet with Colonel Fitzwilliam regarding Mr. Wickham, Aunt Gardiner made slow progress at her needlework. But Elizabeth had long given up on any occupation other than regular glances out the window whilst she fretted. The day was a pretty one, but how could she enjoy the verdant colour of the trees in the bright sunshine when she needed to determine whether her uncle's carriage had returned? She kept knotting and unknotting the corner of a soft silk handkerchief to keep her hands busy. What discoveries had been made? Had they found the man? What did that mean for Lydia's fate? For hers?

When he finally returned to the house in Gracechurch Street, Uncle Gardiner appeared to have aged ten years. He requested a brandy and took a large sip before he seated himself. Although she urgently wanted him to speak on his meeting with the other men, Elizabeth took note of her aunt's forbearance in waiting and held her impatient tongue.

At length, Uncle situated himself on a settee near Aunt. "Mr. Wickham has been caught."

"Thank the Lord!" his wife exclaimed.

"He first claimed Lydia's death was an accident, but when we pressed him further, he could not keep his lies straight."

Yes, just as he told her all about how he had been mistreated by Mr. Darcy. That tale proved to be part truth, part lie, and said in such a way as to damn

Mr. Darcy and make Mr. Wickham look like the injured party. "He is very good at that, and I was one of those foolish enough to believe his lies."

"It is unconscionable to be such a cunning cheat, let alone one who attempts the worst kind of crime." Uncle had tears in his eyes. "After a great deal of questioning and his retracting many aspects of his tale, Mr. Wickham finally confessed to allowing poor Lydia to fall in front of a moving curricle when she broke free of his hold and attempted to run away. I do believe her death was an accident. I am so sorry, ladies."

Elizabeth's lips began to tremble, and her eyes clouded with tears once again at the news. Poor Lydia. Aunt Gardiner was doing no better. The handkerchief at her eyes told of her sorrow at the news.

"Unfortunately, he denies any injury to Lizzy. However, if he grabbed Lydia in the same way he grabbed Lizzy, leaving bruises, then I can see worse occurring. If he could have pushed your sister in front of a moving carriage, he could have pushed you down too, dear. Though we still do not understand the truth of what happened at Lambton, it only makes sense. Can you help us, Lizzy? Does any of this help your memory?"

Elizabeth shuddered. She had no choice. She had only been able to recall pieces of the story and had avoided putting them all together so she was not forced to endure the whole, hurtful memory at once. She must gather up her courage to form the entire story from beginning to end.

She closed her eyes.

Early August 1812
Lambton, Derbyshire

JANE'S LETTERS WERE SHOCKING. LYDIA ELOPED? WITH MR. WICKHAM?

Then, as surely as she had seen a ghost, Mr. Wickham himself walked along the grounds of the inn outside the parlour window of their apartments! She leapt to her feet to see him better. Yes, it was most certainly the blackguard. Was Lydia with him? She called his name.

The shock on his face to see her was apparent. He darted over. "Miss Bennet, you must listen to me—help me on my way," he whispered then glanced around him. Who was he looking for? Lydia? She peered out of the window, but no other person was on the grounds of the inn at that moment.

"Mr. Wickham! Where is my sister? Are you wed?" She held the letter from Jane out for him to see that she knew of his perfidy.

"*Please, you must listen to me!*" *he insisted.*

She crossed her arms. "*I asked you about my sister.*"

"*I shall tell you if you agree to help me.*"

"*Help you what?*"

As quickly as she had seen him, he disappeared, only to reappear shortly after a soft knock on the door from the servants' stairs. He bowed low. "Miss Bennet." His clothing was expensive yet it fit him ill, his eyes were dull, and he was unshaven. Why would he choose such a way to appear in public? Jane's letters came to mind. What sort of wedding apparel was this? He had been a fashionable man even before his militia uniform was fitted to his form. "I did not expect to see you in Lambton."

"I know you left Brighton covertly with my poor sister Lydia. Where is she now?" She stretched her neck around him to see whether Lydia had followed.

Mr. Wickham's hand went over his mouth, and his fingers stroked his cheek. He appeared to be trying to formulate a response. Finally, he deigned to reply. "You deserve to hear the truth of the matter; however, you must swear not to divulge it. Instead, I would like you to tell the others a story. This story will put your sister and me in a better light than the truth."

"What do you mean? Is the truth not something I should wish to share, or would it embarrass you?"

He paced the floor in front of her, rubbing the back of his neck. When he stopped walking, he waved his hand at the chair she had just left. "Please, Miss Bennet, sit. This will be difficult for you."

She huffed out a breath. The last thing she wanted to do was sit whilst he wandered around the room like some caged animal. Instead, she crossed her arms, tapped her toe, and waited. Following a long pause during which he bit a knuckle, Mr. Wickham asked a question. "Is your presence here so close to Pemberley proof that there is something between you and my old friend Darcy?"

She inadvertently stepped back. How could she defend against this? What she hoped and what was true had not been reconciled, and she could not make assumptions of a second proposal. "I cannot speak for Mr. Darcy, but in my case, I am on a pleasure trip with my uncle and aunt. She hails from Lambton."

"I have seen how he looks at you, and you defended him after you returned from Kent. I believe it would be painful to him if any harm were to come to your reputation—say, by my elopement with your sister?"

She gave him a hard look. "It would be painful to any respectable man to know that his profligate friend, after attempting to steal an heiress, would steal a girl who had nothing to recommend her." She spoke sharply, and Mr. Wickham's face fell, proving his shock that she knew so much. "Yes, I consider Mr. Darcy an upright and proud gentleman who would be hurt by the actions my sister Jane relates in this letter."

Mr. Wickham shuffled his feet. "Ah, ill news travels fast. I suggest you try to remember another story, one that will please both you and Darcy in saving your family's reputation. Are you amenable to listening to it?"

"Is it the truth?"

"Not quite," he confessed. "But it will become truth if you hope to put everyone in the best light. Regarding the information within your sister's letter, you are correct. Miss Lydia and I eloped, but our funds ran out before we made it to London. Fortunately, your Mr. Darcy discovered us and was kind enough to offer a decent-sized portion for her so we could afford to marry. He also procured a license so we could be married from her aunt and uncle's home in Cheapside. Darcy purchased me a commission in the regulars to give us a better income as well. Unfortunately, my new wife and I were required to leave immediately for Newcastle without seeing your family. Darcy wants your uncle to receive all the credit for arranging the circumstances I have recited to you, but Darcy provided the blunt. He had to compensate me for the loss of the living he owed me, you see."

She blinked slowly. No one would believe such a convoluted story. "That does not make sense. How could that have happened? My uncle has been travelling this past week and just met Mr. Darcy two days ago here in Derbyshire."

His eyes flitted around as he furrowed his brow for a moment. "Let us assume your uncle's part, as I have described, takes place after you return to London. When is that? Next week?"

"This is unreasonable. Why should I tell such a preposterous lie? Do you expect them to do so? Mr. Darcy would use the opportunity to distance himself from my family's disgrace rather than try to mend it, I think." Her world began to fracture as she said it. Proud Mr. Darcy could not align himself with one like her! After the last two pleasant days, all was lost again!

Mr. Wickham smiled briefly though it did not reach his eyes. "I do not believe you know the power you have over Darcy, Miss Bennet. Besides, if he does not agree to the story, I shall continue to malign his name all over the country, not just here and in Hertfordshire. I shall blame him for Miss Lydia's disgrace too. He really has no choice." His voice held a great deal of confidence.

"How could you even do such a thing? Why would anyone believe you?"

"Darcy's manners have given me opportunities to sway people against him in the past; I could easily do so again."

"It is such an unbelievable tale. Are you going to go to him and ask him to do this for you?"

"No, you are going to tell him this is his story."

"But it is not true. Why should we misrepresent the facts—whatever they may be?"

His brow became creased, and an angry frown marred his good looks. "Because the truth is too awful to bear, and we cannot share it. Instead, we honour your sister with a lie."

Instead of answering her questions, he got his back up and offered another vague comment. All she wanted was the truth. "What do you mean?"

Mr. Wickham assumed a haughty air. "I had accrued a few small debts in Brighton and decided to take leave from the regiment for a short while. It was unfair of the gentlemen to press me as they did, and they did so most cruelly. I had no choice but to take to hiding for a short while.

"Your sister sneaked into the carriage and forced me to take her along to London. Lydia insisted we should eventually marry, and she got it into her head that Gretna Green was as good a destination as any. However, it was not to be. Your sister and I parted ways in Clapham. I went on, and as you see, I am at my old home again, trusting the benevolence of you and Mr. Darcy to honour her with this version of her future. You are going to tell him this story. This is the truth. This is in your sister's best interest and protects me as well."

Except that—not one word of it seemed right. Her heart dropped and her stomach was unwell for her sister, similar to the sensations she had encountered whilst reading Jane's letter. Pursing her lips, she sank down in her chair. "Where is Lydia?"

He looked away from her. "I cannot say. The last I saw her was in Clapham. Who knows what happened to her?"

"Clapham?"

"I did not hurt her in any way, though—but forget I said that. I need you to tell this story rather than what really happened. I depend upon you doing so. Do not be distracted; it is important. As I instructed you before, Mr. Darcy paid for the wedding, her portion, a license, and my commission in the regulars. Your sister and I are now on our way to our new home in Newcastle. Do not forget it." *He was fidgeting, pacing once again as his voice became higher-pitched. He bit his knuckle again, but he would not look at her.*

Of course, she was incredulous. "Can you not speak to my uncle about this, about Lydia?"

He stopped his pacing and held out his hands, palm up. "No, Miss Bennet, I am afraid that news will be up to you to deliver. I am in hiding, do you not see?"

"But why? You say you have done nothing wrong." *Or were his debts really so large? She could not believe his temerity at trying to hide the truth and raised her chin to him.* "If you amassed large debts in Meryton and Brighton, I imagine it to be a habit of long standing. Do you not still have such a problem here?"

"Darcy took care of most of my problems long ago with the exception of a couple of by-blows. The ladies can never resist me, you see. You probably wondered at Mary King's quick decision to leave Meryton. She could not resist my charms and got herself in a breeding sort of way. You yourself were half in love with me, were you not?"

Disgusting man! Guilt ate her insides. Although her heart had not been touched, she had been fooled by him. Had he not transferred his affections to Mary King, what might have happened? She would not have surrendered her virtue so easily, but would she have been able to maintain her credit compared to all the tradesmen's daughters with whom he had dallied? And what about his attempted elopement with Miss Darcy?

"Had your sister been less spirited and more biddable, I should not have had to leave her behind." *His voice wavered again, and he placed his hand over his eyes and turned away. Once again, he was caught between the bravado of telling her what to do and some sort of remorse over Lydia. Elizabeth needed to know more of the latter.*

She stood and approached him. "But it is entirely your fault, do you not see, Mr. Wickham?" *He turned back to face her whilst she continued,* "You did not have to allow her along with you, but you cannot control your base inclinations. Tell me, had you already ruined her in Brighton or were you waiting until you married her?"

He had the grace to blush. His discomfiture did not help her distress, and her ire transformed into despair at the dreadful future of a young woman who had left her family and lived with a man to whom she was not married—only to be abandoned by him.

"I see how things fall." Her voice trembled, and she tried once again to be firm. "Tell me the truth. I shall not recount a made-up story."

He grabbed her by both arms and put his face near to hers. "You will! You will tell it exactly as I said!" he hissed. His voice was not loud, but it was not calm, either. He clearly struggled to control his emotions. His eyes pleaded.

She shook her arms free and gave him a withering look. He had the decency to look ashamed. She turned away from him to walk back and take a seat in the chair, only to change her mind and spin to face him. "You must know something of where my sister is if you must make up such a story."

Suddenly, he leaned in towards her with his hands on the arms of her chair, his brow furrowed, and wagged a finger in her face. "Stop making such a fuss, or I shall tell you exactly what happened to her, and you will not like to hear it!" he said through his teeth.

At that moment, the hair stood up on her neck and tears prickled her eyes. For the first time since he had entered the room, she was frightened. What would he do to her? What had he done to Lydia?

He brought himself back to his full height. But all her fears melted when his face quivered and crumbled into one of anguish. "We are married! Darcy made it happen! He paid for everything, but your uncle has all the credit! This is what you must say! Do not forget it!

"I did not hurt her, Miss Elizabeth, I did not," he said. He held his hands out in front of him. "She pulled out of my hands and ran the wrong way. Neither of us could help her."

What could he mean? She had no time to ask. A knock came on the door, and Mr. Wickham stepped back from her.

"I must go. I am not safe here."

Just then, Mr. Darcy was announced, and Mr. Wickham's eyes nearly popped out of his head before he quickly slipped out by way of the servants' stairs.

Mr. Darcy swore an oath as he rushed to her side—she must have appeared a fright after all Jane's bad news and the confusion of Mr. Wickham's visit.

Her mind was in a turmoil. It was ill advised to speak to him about her meeting with Mr. Wickham today. It could be the first step in losing Mr. Darcy forever. In frustration, she burst into tears, hugging herself. Pain crossed Mr. Darcy's face, and he offered to fetch her a glass of wine then rushed from the room.

Shouting carried in on the breeze from outside, and an unknown man yelled

The Mist of Her Memory

Mr. Wickham's name. She hurried to the window. Mr. Wickham ran past, followed by several men. She stretched her neck but could no longer see them. Then, someone took rough hold of her arm and turned her brutally towards the room. It hurt—so much hurt!

She was falling, falling, and Mr. Darcy's alarmed voice echoed in her ears. Her world went blank as if it were enveloped in a mist that refused to reveal what was just around the corner, almost within her reach but not within her vision.

May 1813
Gracechurch Street, London

SHE STARTED AS SHE PULLED HERSELF OUT OF THE DIFFICULT MEMORY, AS if it had been one of those dreams of falling but never landing. She put her hand to her chest to calm her beating heart; then she sighed. Reflecting on her recitation, she found it less of an ordeal than she would have expected, and now she was terribly frustrated.

"I am sorry, but at that point, I can recall no more of the morning's events."

"Mr. Wickham must have been half mad, expecting that anyone would believe such a tale," said Aunt Gardiner.

"Indeed," said Elizabeth, "and he was lucky I fell and hit my head, else I would have no reason to credit a lie to Mr. Darcy or press the story upon Uncle."

"But we still have no additional information to make a case against him," said her uncle.

Elizabeth nodded. "Mr. Wickham never confessed outright to killing Lydia. He insisted he did not hurt her."

"And yet she managed to fall in front of a carriage and perish," said her uncle. "We lost our dear girl that day, and we remain stifled in our ability to grieve her properly because of all these questions."

"Indeed. Such an unsettled demise causes pain for her family. If only we knew for certain what happened." Aunt's wistful face mirrored all their feelings.

"Unfortunately, I can be of no help to the authorities with what he said. In addition, I am certain I was unhurt when Mr. Wickham left and before Mr. Darcy came into the room. You can ask Mr. Darcy yourself. I was agitated but physically fine. He went to fetch me a glass of wine, and it must have been then that I fell. Nor do I recall a return by Mr. Wickham to the parlour. I saw him running away when someone grabbed my arm and turned me around."

She was in a sickbed being bled. Voices shouted, and her head hurt.

She flinched and tried to think more, but it was over as soon as it began. "I am certain it was not Mr. Darcy who hurt me. I know Mr. Darcy's angry voice from when he argued with you outside my room when I was ill and you insisted he no longer be allowed to visit me. The voice I hear in my head does not match his. But it was also not Mr. Wickham."

She strained to remember the other voice from that terrible time. "I have had dreams that were not dreams. An enraged voice continues to return to me. I do not know whose it was."

A brutal, painful grasp of her arm and a growl through clenched teeth, warning her to keep away from him. From whom? Mr. Wickham?

She shook her head to clear the horrible voice that came with no visions, unlike her memory of Mr. Wickham.

"It was neither Mr. Darcy nor Mr. Wickham—and it was not you, either, if I must think of all the angry voices I know for comparison. Someone else came into that room whilst Mr. Wickham was being chased by the crowd and Mr. Darcy was procuring wine."

Who could have possibly slipped into the parlour to join her? Whoever he was, he had some reason to hurt her. Was it one of the men who chased Mr. Wickham? And why? She may never know.

"Uncle, maybe Mr. Darcy's recollections will help me remember. Is it possible for me to meet with him along with you and listen to his full accounting of that day?"

"Of course. Let us call on Mr. Darcy on the morrow. Today he is engaged with assisting Colonel Fitzwilliam, who is acting on behalf of Colonel Forster in delivering Mr. Wickham over to the magistrate in Clapham for his civil trial prior to court martial."

"G-d help his soul," said Aunt Gardiner, "And Lydia's as well."

"It is also possible that, in discovering the identity of the true villain, I may rest better with no more bad dreams. I suppose I should speak to Mrs.

Bastion again soon," Elizabeth suggested. "She may have some ideas she has not yet disclosed that may help me to remember. And I think I shall speak to her about Lydia. She has a way with soothing words that will help to ease my pain." Opening more of her history with the help of her friend could be just the thing to end this frustration over lost memories and a lost sister.

Chapter 27

The sun was setting, bathing the city in pretty reds and pinks when Darcy returned to his London home from the trip to Clapham with Colonel Fitzwilliam. Wickham had been turned over to the authorities, and the colonel had continued on to a ship bound for Wellington's army in Portugal. Darcy had bid his cousin a difficult farewell. Every time Richard went into battle, it could be the last time he saw his cousin and friend.

As the carriage entered the mews, Darcy's spirits lifted. He was returning to the comforts of his home, and his heart and shoulders rid themselves of the weight he had worn all day. As soon as he entered the house, the butler indicated that a visitor was awaiting him—Elizabeth's Uncle Gardiner.

Mr. Gardiner met him in the library after he had quickly refreshed himself from his trip. Their greeting was more than civil; it was warm, as noted friends. Darcy's address expressed the generous sentiments of one speaking to a most admired member of Elizabeth's family, and Gardiner sat comfortably in his chair, leaning to one side as they spoke. He started the discussion about a topic that was of great concern to Darcy: his betrothed.

"Elizabeth would like to speak with you regarding what happened in Lambton. You see, there is a lady who has been helping her make sense of her memory loss who has suggested that others' memories might help Elizabeth recall more details of her injury. Elizabeth believes that a phrase or a description from your recollection of the events may assist her in remembering who hurt her and how that person happened to be in the room whilst you were procuring wine. She is insistent the man was not Mr. Wickham or you."

Darcy was amazed at this suggestion that someone other than Wickham could be Elizabeth's attacker. Though doubt had been placed on Wickham's renewal of his visit, Wickham had also lied about some aspects of his time spent with Elizabeth and his actions towards Lydia. However, if Elizabeth had ruled out the men known to have access to that parlour and suspected another culprit, he would not argue.

"Who else would have been dissolute enough to have attacked her?" he asked.

"This is what she is hoping your visit will tell her. She indicated she would like Mrs. Bastion to assist, but in my opinion, there may be…delicate subjects you must discuss that you may be reluctant to speak of with a third party in attendance. I suggested she speak to Mrs. Bastion at my home tomorrow morning and, afterwards, accept your call with her maid as chaperone. Is this amenable to you?"

Darcy's face warmed at the idea of sharing very personal words and feelings with Elizabeth during a private audience. He hated to blush in front of the other man, so he turned away slightly and coughed before he replied, "Yes, that would be fine. What time would you like me to visit?"

"Mrs. Bastion is expected at eleven, so any time after noon should be fine. Now, what has happened with Wickham since we last spoke?"

It did not take long to sum up. Custody had been transferred, the rogue had continued to insist on his innocence, he had begged Darcy to help him, and he had threatened to reveal secrets that would harm Darcy. In any case, Darcy did not stay long since nothing new could be discovered from the prisoner. If Wickham's intent to harm Lydia by pushing her in front of the curricle could be proven, the accusation would become murder, not manslaughter, and Wickham's future prospects would be grim. Sir Frank would probably be charged with manslaughter though his help in capturing and convicting Wickham and his voluntarily turning himself in to the authorities would affect his sentence.

The next morning

EVEN THOUGH THE RECOLLECTIONS COULD RENEW SOME PAIN TO HIS intended, Darcy was keen to commence the discussion, which was why he arrived a full quarter-hour early for his appointment.

He moved from one foot to another in the entrance hall whilst fumbling with the brim of his hat before he handed it to the waiting footman. Why was he so nervous? His interview was merely with his betrothed. He stilled his movements. A Darcy must not be so fidgety even when uneasy!

His thoughts were interrupted by an unknown middle-aged lady who beckoned him into a pleasant sitting room. A tight sensation gripped his chest as he nodded. She glanced back at him and offered a sustaining smile that pulled the tautness out of his bones. He smiled in return.

Elizabeth was inside, and after their courtesies acknowledging each other, she introduced him to Mrs. Bastion. Elizabeth's welcoming smile removed any last traces of unease.

"I am extremely pleased to make your acquaintance. Elizabeth thinks a great deal of your ability to aid her," he said.

"Thank you. Now if you will excuse me," said Mrs. Bastion, "I shall fetch the maid who is to sit with you whilst you have your discussion."

The door was left slightly ajar whilst Mrs. Bastion went in search of the lady's maid, but that did not stop Elizabeth from darting to her feet and throwing herself into Darcy's arms. They had not had time for such closeness in the past, and he was overwhelmed at her reaction to him. Just her smile affected the pit of his stomach, never mind what her kisses did to his equanimity. She was such an exquisite creature with unique beauty and a figure that stopped his heart. He was certainly blessed that they shared a love so deep; it boded well for a happy marriage.

"We must be married as soon as is possible," she said. "For I cannot stand to be parted from you now that we are allowed to be together."

"Do you want me to procure a license?"

"No, we should have the banns read. But as soon as possible after they are complete?"

"Yes. I expect you would like to marry from Longbourn?"

"That would be best. My mother will complain to the heavens that she cannot possibly plan a wedding so soon, so we shall compromise with her and give her one month."

"You little mischief-maker, deceiving your own parent!"

"You have seen enough of my mother to know it is necessary and easily accomplished!"

"I shall send an express to your father asking him to make the arrangements at Longbourn parish. My own priest will read the banns at St. George's."

"Thank you."

They sprang apart as a cough at the door preceded its opening. An older,

The Mist of Her Memory

amiable-looking maid called Davis came into the room and bobbed a quick curtsey. The door was shut for the privacy of the upcoming discussion as promised.

"Shall I sit by the window?" The eyes of the lady's maid twinkled as she gestured to a small chair covered with fine embroidered fabric, situated to one side of the sitting room.

"You will have better light for your work there," offered Elizabeth with a playful smile. How clever of her! This arrangement left the large sofa available for Darcy and her, and it would allow them to speak quietly, heads near each other, without being overheard.

"Where do you want to start?" he asked Elizabeth once they had situated themselves on either end of the sofa. "When I first came into the parlour at Lambton?"

"Yes. The door opened and you were introduced," she said. "I now recall that Mr. Wickham was still there. His face went pale, and he immediately darted behind the door so the maid did not see him. He hurried outside through the servants' door from which he came in. That door closed as you entered."

"I had no idea I had missed him by seconds."

"You did not see him, correct?"

"That is true."

"He appeared frightened of you. Now that I know the truth about Lydia, it makes his unease easier to understand. Though I did know of Miss Darcy's history from your letter, I did not equate that situation with his decision to hide from you. But that day I was only thinking of Jane's letters and the story Mr. Wickham had just related to me."

"You were standing in the middle of the room with a letter in your hand. You opened your mouth to speak, but no words came out. At that point, your brows went up, and you held the letter up to me, your hand trembling. You said my name, and then 'Jane,' but no more. You must have been shaken badly by Wickham to be so unable to communicate with me."

She shook her head slightly. "I suppose I was, but not because he hurt me. He frightened me with his insistence that I tell his story." She quickly explained the lie that Wickham had told her was to be represented as the truth, including Darcy's own role.

Of course, he would have given anything to help her as in Wickham's tale, but that was not to be. "I wish I had known about Lydia before her demise. I would have done all I could to convince her to return to her family."

"If you could have been successful with such a strong-willed girl. But we did not know they had eloped until it was much too late. However, Mr. Wickham's irrationality explains that I was mute from confusion rather than fear."

"That is interesting. Then you began to cry. I believed something dreadful had happened and offered to get you some wine."

"You were quite shocked, sir. You swore an oath," she said with that same arch smile from before.

He laughed lightly, looking away. "So I did. I apologise."

A short burst of laughter puffed out of her mouth, easing the clenched heart he did not know he held within. The discussion would be easier if she were to lighten it in this way each time it became heavy, and he was eternally grateful such a woman had agreed to be his wife.

"I cannot recall whether I closed the door when I left the room."

"You did, but the latch did not catch, and it swung open. I had turned away to read the letter again and did not see who entered—there was some noise outside the window that distracted me, and I went there to see what was occurring. In the distance, I saw Mr. Wickham and a crowd of angry men chasing him. Then someone grabbed my arm and squeezed it so hard whilst tugging me to turn around. It pained me a great deal…" Her voice became elevated and sharp towards the end. Suddenly, she began to shake, her mouth wide open and panting as she pressed her palms onto the sofa. Darcy glanced at the maid, who stared at Elizabeth with wide, concerned eyes. She had put down her work and appeared about to dart over.

He covered one hand with his. "Are you certain you want to speak of this?"

"It may be better to skip that part and speak of what happened when you returned," she offered. Her fingers were icy.

"Very well." As much as it pained him to do so, he released her hand.

"I am well, Davis."

The maid nodded and picked up her needle and cloth. "I will depend upon Mr. Darcy to care for you." She returned to concentrating on her work.

Now, on to the difficult part of his recitation. "You were falling, along with the chair. I tried to catch you, but I was too late. That is when I dropped the wine glass. I could not hold it and you at the same time." His face became hot as he considered what happened next. He glanced at the maid. She was seated facing slightly away from them, her face out of view, busy with her work. He leaned forward and whispered, "I collected you off the floor and I…I…gathered you into my arms. Please excuse me, but you were hurt and I believed it would be of help at the time. A huge knot had formed on your cheekbone already. I said, 'Please be easy, Elizabeth. Do not move.'"

Elizabeth had also leaned forward, and their heads were now less than a foot apart. "I remember this part. I was confused and agitated and in pain, but your arms comforted me."

"You were white as a sheet. You struggled in my arms. I thought you were trying to sit. You began to speak. 'Mr. Darcy, he said—' but I interrupted before you could say more."

"I meant to speak of Mr. Wickham's false witness and became agitated. You stroked my hair and helped me relax in your arms in a reclined position. Then you said…" She blushed becomingly from her hairline to the edge of her gown, and her eyes dropped to her lap. "You said, ah…"

Darcy was somewhat mortified to have her repeat those tender words, so he gathered his courage to say them again himself. He whispered just loud enough for her, but not Davis, to hear, "'Elizabeth, Elizabeth, my love. Are you well? What happened?'"

Her eyelashes rested thick and heavy upon her cheeks. Was she too shy to look at him? He would say those words again and again until she became comfortable with them.

"Indeed," she said quietly. "I was not so insensible as to not notice the importance of what you said. The one pair of words—that expression—was the only part of the morning that remained when I suffered from the worst of the amnesia. I tried to tell you more about Mr. Wickham, but I do not recall how I phrased it."

She only remembered "my love"! It spoke a great deal about the importance he held in her mind even at that time. "I am sorry. I did not realize whom you wished to speak about, so I quickly bade you to hush. I should have let you tell me about Wickham then. I do know I said 'Please do not distress yourself. It will wait.' I asked how you fell—whether you had tripped. You did not respond directly. Instead, your eyes closed, and your head fell back." He choked for a moment, near ready to sob. For her sake, he must not break down. "I…I…thought you were lost to me, but your eyes fluttered open again, and you began to speak as if telling me the whole story from the start. 'I had a letter. My poor sister…' you said before your voice disappeared. You began to tremble as though chilled. I stroked your arms to warm you as I noticed the wine that had spilt down the skirt of your gown. I had to apologise; I was so remorseful for not caring for you. I said, 'I only came to declare myself, and look what has happened.'"

Elizabeth's eyes brightened and she leaned forward, palms on her lap. That sensation deep within him came alive again at her agreeable expression. "I told Mrs. Bastion I expected your addresses even though I could not remember it directly—yet now, I remember it as if it were today."

"Good. That is why we are discussing this—to bring back your memories."

"Yes. So what happened next?"

Darcy's heart clenched as he recalled their short conversation. "At that point, your eyes rolled back into your head as you flagged. I was distraught. I called your name and shook you lightly to no avail. I called it again and shook you slightly more. When I had no success, I whispered a prayer for your recovery as your aunt and uncle entered the parlour.

"Your uncle asked me, 'What is the meaning of this?' with great energy because his first view would have been of you in a man's arms. Your aunt instantly recognised what had occurred and corrected her husband's misunderstanding. 'She is hurt!' she cried and called out to you, 'Lizzy, Lizzy!'

"I tried to recover into a more respectable position, but I would have dropped you. I told them I blamed myself for frightening you into the fall. You see, a chair was tipped over, and I thought you had tripped on it when I entered the room. I mentioned it to your aunt and uncle, and they seemed to be of the same mind."

Elizabeth shook her head. "The chair did not trip me. I grabbed for it to break my fall, but my steadiness was poor and it toppled over with me."

"That chair is probably the reason they allowed me into your sick room when you showed signs of awakening since they did not suspect me of any ill-doing then. At that time, they believed the truth." His voice broke like some schoolboy's purely out of his disappointment and pride that they had not believed him. Had it happened at another time, he would have been similarly mortified, but at least he should have been more remorseful regarding her illness than his loss of dignity.

"I do not remember anything of that time. Can you tell me about it?"

"You appeared so small and fragile, your hair dark on the pillow and your face as white as the bedclothes. I knew you had been bled to help remove the bad blood gathering in your brain. I am not ordinarily in favour of bleeding, and neither is this particular surgeon, yet he was convinced it was important with a knock on the head. I knew more by that time—that the mark on your face was not the full extent of your injuries, but the knot on the back of your head was the worst.

"I approached you and wanted so badly to take your hand, to touch your hair, anything. But it was not appropriate." There was a tightness around his heart as if it were almost happening again.

The clearing of a voice broke their little murmured conversation. Davis had risen from her seat and said, "Miss, I hope you do not mind, but I did not bring enough of this colour with me, and it would not do to mend this lace in the wrong colour. Please excuse me. I shall be but a moment fetching the correct thread." She dipped a curtsey and scurried out of the room, closing the door behind her.

What excellent timing! The maid left just as they were getting to the most private of disclosures. Darcy slid closer to Elizabeth, but not so close that he could not swiftly retreat when Davis returned.

"So what did you say to me, the seemingly dead woman?" She was not smiling, but her eyes sparkled. This was the Elizabeth he knew and loved, the woman who brought out the best of him with her wit and light-heartedness.

"Oh, you may make sport of it now to ease my troubled heart, but at the time, I was overcome with pain. It was near intolerable."

She tilted her head and lifted her brows, but said nothing.

"What did I say? I said so many things on top of each other that it is hard to speak of it clearly. Oh, one part—I think I can quote it exactly. I remember it every day, and it is still a valid expression of my feelings now." He looked at her as he repeated the words so important to him. "'You are my only love, my heart, the soul that *my* soul has been seeking, and if you can see fit to open your soul again to the world, I shall dedicate myself to your happiness every day from today onward.' It is rather shallow to beg in such a way."

She shook her head. A delicate blush had appeared on her cheeks.

"Despite you teaching me how I need to improve myself, I can still be a self-centred fool who wants nothing more than to have his love be alive."

He could not bear to look at her, so he studied the floral pattern on the sofa's seat between them.

The tips of her fingers brushed his cheek and he glanced up, gazing into the most poignant eyes. "It is not wrong to wish for our souls to be together, Fitzwilliam," she whispered.

"You are correct, but I spent a great deal of time pleading with you to come to sensibility so that I could have you once again. It was rather selfish of me."

"That is fine. You were in pain. Please continue. A lady likes to hear these words said to her."

"Do you remember them?"

He wanted to kiss her so badly, but she had the good grace to blush and tilt her head down to hide her face. "Not all, but the most important ones."

He whispered, "Like, 'I love you with all my heart?'" He kissed her hair and she looked up at him, wide-eyed. "Or 'You are too generous to trifle with me. If your feelings are still what they were last April, tell me so at once. My affections and wishes are unchanged; but one word from you will silence me on this subject forever.'" He kissed her forehead. "Then, I said, 'Please awaken for me. I suspect it from our walk at Pemberley and hope beyond hope that your affections have undergone so material a change as to be the opposite, yet I need to hear it from your lips.'" He kissed her there as gently as he could muster given his passion for her.

A moment later, her lashes fluttered up to gaze into his eyes and a positively alluring smile formed on her lips. "Yes, those words," she murmured. "They taught me to hope as I had scarcely ever allowed myself to hope before. When I became sensible and recalled them later, I knew enough of your disposition to be certain that had you been absolutely, irrevocably decided against me, you never would have pleaded in such a way to a nearly dead woman."

He smiled at the way she had characterised herself in the same manner once again. "At that moment, you became agitated in your sleep. You tossed and whimpered and your eyelids fluttered. I thought I was frightening you." He reached out and held the side of her face, stroking her cheek with his thumb.

She continued to meet his gaze with eyes that were soft and yielding. "I do not recall that. I must have been trying to speak and became frustrated at not being able to do so."

"That was when the surgeon and your uncle returned, and they ended our meeting." He dropped his hand and took hold of one of hers, keeping his gaze there on the sofa where they were joined. "Later that day, I believe the surgeon spoke to your uncle at length about your injuries, and I believe he said that someone had overpowered you to make such marks. Apparently, in your sleep, you muttered something of an apology for our disagreement, meaning, of course, at Hunsford.

"The next morning when I arrived, your uncle banned me from seeing you ever again. I suppose he had decided for himself that it must have been me since he saw me there with his own eyes and thought we had argued. I was heartbroken, yet I did not fight him as I should have done because I felt such agony over my own culpability."

"But you did nothing of the sort. Someone else hurt me. I know it for a fact. I sometimes have…memories of someone speaking. The voice is a deep, mean-spirited one—not yours at all. I remember that you came in and saved me from the person tormenting me. Yours was the loving voice. The other was likely who hurt me."

"Had I not left the room for the wine, this would not have occurred. Even further back, this was my fault. Had I given Wickham over to the authorities rather than cover for his fiendish ways, he never could have run off with your sister or showed himself at Lambton to bother you."

"My dear, you cannot blame yourself for everything. Please, for me, try to forgive yourself for what you did not know would hurt others."

"I shall, but it will not come easily to me."

She squeezed his hand, and he looked into her eyes. "Yes, you and your unwelcome pride will get in the way of any belief that you are among the best of men in all situations. But you are, Fitzwilliam, and I am proud to be marrying you." She leaned forward and placed a lingering kiss upon his lips. Their separation was simply too much for him, and he gathered her into his arms and deepened the kiss, tangling his tongue with hers in a way that delighted him. The kisses were too short, yet they were panting when they finally tore their lips away and leaned their foreheads together.

They had no sooner broken apart and gazed lovingly into each other's eyes when the door latch rattled as if a person was having difficulty with it. He released his love and leapt to his feet.

Davis returned and held up a small skein of coloured thread. "Silly me, forgetting this. Please continue. My ears are closed."

He found it difficult not to grin, but he addressed Davis in the most formal manner. "We are grateful."

Elizabeth made a little squeak that was clearly a stifled giggle. His serious expression fell apart, and he gave her a wide smile. What a wonderful woman to make him into a better man than he was before he had met her. He was surely blessed.

Chapter 28

After having hoped all Season for Jane to come to London so she would have someone familiar to visit, Elizabeth almost wanted to take back her hopes—but it had more to do with the rest of her family than with Jane. The Netherfield Bingleys and the Bennets had taken apartments together in London so her mother could oversee the purchase of wedding clothes for Elizabeth, and Mama was favourably impressed with the refined Mayfair address that had been selected. Thankfully, Jane and Aunt Gardiner were expected to assist in the shopping endeavour. According to Mama, this support would supposedly ease the pressure on "the future Mrs. Darcy." Of course, her mother would never let her forget her incapacitation of the previous autumn. Mama's weak mind had decided Elizabeth's ailment was no more than an exaggerated case of her own suffering from nervous complaints and, as such, would plague her for the rest of her life.

So, after one reading of the banns at Longbourn parish, Mama had sufficiently basked in the congratulations of her friends for settling her daughter so suitably with a man of ten thousand per year, and the family all travelled to town. Two weeks later, Elizabeth was ready to tear out her hair. Her mother's attempts to show off her daughter's future riches by over-embellishing her gowns to the point of ridiculousness were difficult to manage. Even with fashions that accommodated more lace than in recent years, Elizabeth was thankful she had other ladies in the party to continually count upon. They would overrule her mother's tawdry additions.

Mama, chafed at being overruled on Elizabeth's gowns, was somewhat mollified by being allowed to dress Kitty and Mary as well. Mary stubbornly clung to the simpler gown designs of the last couple of seasons although she accepted the slightly wider bodices in her goal of less revealing costumes. Kitty, on the other hand, embraced the newest fashions with zeal and let her mother choose the most luxuriant patterns with rows upon rows of undulating lace draping at the hemlines of her gowns. Truly, Kitty had become a feminine dandy!

By the time the first set of gowns was made up, the Bingleys hosted a pre-wedding event at their elegant London apartments. The fête, in honour of the engagement, consisted of a reception and dinner party for family and honoured friends.

Kitty's new gown was indeed the most detailed of those on display, but it was covered in the same number of rows of lace as those of several other ladies'. The styles were changing, to Mama's good luck and Elizabeth's relief as she had not wanted her family to be seen as ridiculous. However, Kitty had also decided that a turban with towering feathers was all the crack, a piece of frippery she must have learned from Miss Bingley.

Elizabeth's gown was fashionable enough to compete without being gaudy, and Davis had fashioned her hair tightly to her head in an elaborate coiffure. "The future Mrs. Darcy" had to appear stylish but tasteful, her gown's embellishments demonstrating her forthcoming position among the *ton*. Was she over-dressed? A quick comparison with those around the richly appointed room showed that the apple-coloured frock conformed admirably to the becoming evening dresses of the other ladies. The gossamer overdress was worn over a satin slip, featuring a deep flounce of lace about the feet, headed with silver netting. Pretty white lace sleeves matched the lace about the hem. The effect was lovely and suited her figure well whilst appearing à la mode.

Fitzwilliam—no longer Mr. Darcy to her—had made certain she had met the people she was expected to know best prior to the evening, though there would be too many acquaintances for her to remember them all. Thus, she was not too uncomfortable with the guests whilst they welcomed them in the receiving line—until Miss Bingley appeared at the door. Immediately, the back of her neck prickled, her palms began to sweat, and her spine stiffened. On the basis of the difficult situation in which she had found herself the last time she spoke with Miss Bingley, she expected at best an awkward moment when Miss Bingley arrived in front of her after making

THE MIST OF HER MEMORY

her way up the line and, at worst, a scene similar to the last. She could not help but be chilled as she anticipated eventually being seen. Distracted as she was, she jumped when a gentle hand touched her bare arm between the bottom of her petite sleeve and the top of her buttery soft kid opera gloves. She spun around.

"I need your advice on behalf of the hostess, my dear," said Lady Matlock in a voice as smooth as silk. "Can you step out of the line for a few moments?"

"Oh, of course." Elizabeth came closer to Lady Matlock, who had moved a few paces behind Fitzwilliam, nearly out of sight alongside some rich brocaded silk draperies.

"I do not wish for you to have to fend for yourself with that harridan," said Lady Matlock, her brow furrowed. "Although I am certain Fitzwilliam would like to give her the set-down she deserves, he must not, and he knows it." She spoke just loudly enough to be heard over the din of spirited voices but quietly enough for no one other than Elizabeth, whose back was to the room, to understand clearly. "For a brief moment, I shall be conferring with you on whether the white soup ought to be served before the first course or with it. Mrs. Bingley did not say, and she could not be freed from her duties. I felt I could easily ask you to make the decision on your sister's behalf."

Elizabeth could not help but smile. "Is this a real problem or one you have manufactured?"

"Oh, this chef is a Frenchman. He would not ask; he would tell you what he wanted. I happened to be nearby when your mother asked him when the white soup would be served. He raised his nose and said it would be served at the proper time—before the meat."

Elizabeth had to clap her hand over her mouth to keep from laughing aloud. Lady Matlock remained dignified though the sparkle in her eyes and a slight shudder of her shoulders betrayed her holding in at the very least a chuckle at what could easily be imagined as a battle of wills between two very determined individuals.

Suddenly, Lady Matlock's visage became expressionless, and her eyes shot such a frozen look across the room that Elizabeth practically trembled.

"Do not turn around," said her ladyship. "Miss Bingley is staring at me with an ingratiating smile. Goodness, the woman has too much paint on her face. She appears almost clownish for all the powder and rouge she has applied, and her gown and diadem are positively overdone with more embellishment than even your mama would deem appropriate." Lady Matlock barely nodded at Miss Bingley.

An interaction of some sort was inevitable. Could Elizabeth disappear just for one moment now? The last thing she wanted was another unequal discussion with Miss Bingley, and the cut indirect seemed the logical answer to her dilemma—so she remained with her back to Miss Bingley to avoid seeing or being seen.

"Lizzy was here a minute ago, Miss Bingley." Of course, the person who most wanted to show Elizabeth as the queen of the occasion was the one who would find her—her mother. "I know you were such dear friends when you were last at Netherfield, and you must have seen one another here in town. She does not write to me nearly enough when she is here. Her letters are all for Jane. There she is, talking to Lady Matlock."

She closed her eyes. When she opened them, she could not help but twist slightly to face her nemesis. She was not so far away as to overlook Miss Bingley's annoyed scowl and Mama's cheerful wave. Elizabeth cringed although she could not say why, except that she could not countenance being at the end of any difficult interaction even from afar. She forced a tight smile and waved back to her mother. Had Miss Bingley dipped her head ever so hesitantly? Elizabeth's wave and forced smile were all she could manage whilst facing that aggravating visage, so she averted her gaze once again to the left side of Lady Matlock's face to have the back of her head to Miss Bingley. She shivered. She was not cold, yet every hair on her body stood on end.

"Was that a cut?" Elizabeth asked of Lady Matlock. "I do not want to raise her ire any more than I must."

"No, you waved, even if it was in response to your mother. She cannot say you cut her in public, but I am sorry you witnessed that gimlet eye. At least you did not have to talk to her," said Lady Matlock.

"Thank you for giving me the reprieve."

"She is now speaking to Fitzwilliam. You will be able to return to the receiving line shortly."

Elizabeth could not help herself and glanced over. Her curiosity was rewarded by the vision of Miss Bingley's replacing her menacing frown with a sugary smile at seeing Elizabeth's husband-to-be. The affected smile did not meet her eyes, which remained without sparkle or expression. After a short moment, Elizabeth turned back to Lady Matlock. "Though I should not let my courage fail me in the face of such a petty creature, I cannot help but feel poorly."

"Do not fret. I shall intervene if she tries to ruin your evening with her waspish ways. I guarantee she is out of Fitzwilliam's favour as well, so he will not tolerate her either. Come, return to Fitzwilliam's side."

"She is gone?" Elizabeth turned and perused the room. Sure enough, Miss Bingley now stood at the refreshment table where she picked up a glass of negus, her long fingers splaying out from the glass. The cramping in Elizabeth's back and neck remained whilst she tried to maintain a rigid, upright attitude rather than drooping from seeing the nasty woman. She blew a breath of air and gave a grateful look to Lady Matlock.

Lady Matlock nodded. "She will be seated mid-table. It is the best she can do."

"I cannot thank you enough," she said. "I dread being near her. Poor Jane—what she must endure being sister to the woman."

"I believe Miss Bingley may be the reason your sister delayed her travels to town until now. She would not have wanted to foist her upon you."

She shook her head. Jane's letters recently shared the secret of their hesitance to travel. "Jane has been ill before breakfast these last few months. It only passed a few weeks ago."

"Has she felt movement? Is she certain?"

"Yes. My mother is not aware. Jane does not want it announced to all and sundry, but I know she would be happy for you to know."

"It must have been difficult to hide her illness."

"Mr. Bingley was very good about limiting my mother's calls to later in the morning. The cold winter helped—it provided an excuse to stay at Netherfield and to keep my mother at home most days."

"I shall leave you to my nephew and find my husband."

They took the few steps over to Fitzwilliam, who greeted both with a subtle smile whilst remaining relatively dignified in appearance as per his wont. His evening wear added an air of sophistication to his serious yet especially handsome face, and for once, the unruly lock of hair that usually fell aside was tamed into a stylish mix with the rest of his curls.

"Thank you once again," Elizabeth said to Lady Matlock.

"Yes, I observed your tactics and thank you for assisting Elizabeth,"

Fitzwilliam said. "I shall find a better way to fend off Miss Bingley for future occasions."

With a smile and a nod, Lady Matlock stepped away as they continued to greet the remainder of arrivals at the party.

Soon enough, the guests had all arrived, and Elizabeth, as the guest of honour, took Mr. Bingley's arm into the dining room. Superb crystal chandeliers hung along the length of a well-appointed, impossibly long dining table, and liveried footmen waited to serve the guests. Elizabeth took her seat near one end of the table, facing Lord Matlock, with the gregarious Lord Powell to her side. Fitzwilliam sat next to Jane, with Lady Matlock and Lady Powell as his nearest companions. Miss Bingley would be nettled with her seat below the Bennets, but the Darcys had many high-ranked friends.

As she envisioned, amiable conversation with the two kind gentlemen dominated during the most exquisite meal she had ever been exposed to; this French chef was truly a find for Mr. Bingley. The flavours and aromas were heavenly, and the composition of each plate was a work of art. She was able to laugh, tease, sparkle, and open up her personality, relaxing, as was her preference, setting aside all cares, and merely enjoying herself. In between, she delighted in glances at heads bobbing with plumes and a colourful array of gowns all along the grand table in between the dapper men's costumes with their own choice of elegant coloured waistcoat. It was truly a remarkable sight.

Once the final course was completed, Jane stood and invited the ladies to join her in the withdrawing room. Mama, her satin-wrapped chest all puffed forward and self-satisfied smile shining, could not have been prouder. Jane's success was her success, and since the lady of the house was hosting a noteworthy dinner like this one, Mama could believe she had indeed done her job of raising a noteworthy lady.

In such a large party, Elizabeth was certain she would not be of interest to her future husband's long-time admirer. Instead, Miss Bingley would spend her time attempting to impress a friendship upon someone of high standing within the group to better arrange her hopes of invitations to all the best events during the next season. After all, she now teetered on the edge of that most unpleasant of positions: being considered too old to be a perfect bride. She had at most one or two more seasons before she was on the shelf, and the lady must be quite attuned to the expiry of her charms.

The Mist of Her Memory

Elizabeth's predictions were correct, and she was able to speak amiably among the curious but well-meaning ladies in attendance. Although some of the questions proved to be a little on the presumptuous side, none of the ladies attempted to undermine her as Miss Bingley had done. Were they simply not interested in Fitzwilliam for themselves or their daughters, or had they graciously decided to support her rather than make her life difficult? She had been informed some ladies of the *ton* would indeed make the attempt. Of course, tonight's guests had been selected because they were family and close friends, so they were predisposed to approve of her. It made it easy to have a friendly conversation.

The mother of a young woman with striking green eyes and hair much like Elizabeth's asked the duration of their engagement.

"Mr. Darcy wanted a short engagement, and we recently had the banns called. My mother so wanted an afternoon ceremony, but I am sure she will be able to show off her skills at creating a proper Venetian breakfast, as any good hostess can, and that will satisfy her."

"Your mother must be very proud of your match."

"Indeed she is, as she is proud of my sister."

"Ah, yes, two sisters to two best friends. It is often the way of the world," said the lady.

"If the couples are well-suited, indeed."

"Many young women would be curious with regard to the sort of woman suited to Mr. Darcy. He is known for being reticent, yet you appear to be delighted with the society of others," the lady said.

"He is only a bit uncomfortable in groups, and I have learned how to find pleasure in most situations."

"You will be a good influence on him. Much better than many," said Lady Powell, a small, quiet woman.

She was more than gratified. A glowing sensation covered her. "I thank you. But Mr. Darcy is merely in need of discussions with close friends to become lively."

"I noticed it at dinner, but I took it to be due to your encouragement," Lady Powell said.

"Your husband being a close friend is of no little inspiration to amusement in conversation." Elizabeth noticed Fitzwilliam enter the room in an animated discussion with that particular gentleman and Lord Matlock.

The rest of the gentlemen filed into the room, filling every corner with a faint scent of cigars and port. In the corner of her eye, she could see Miss Bingley's attention had abandoned the countess with whom she was speaking. The brazen young woman's steady gaze made its way over to Fitzwilliam as he came to stand by Elizabeth. How long would it take for her to join them for words of grovelling praise to her betrothed whilst sending disingenuous comments Elizabeth's way?

Sharing a look with her betrothed heated her to the core. He had such expressive eyes, and each time he glanced at her, they were blacker than black as if he wished to drag her away at that very moment for a long interlude of passion. They did not have many opportunities to kiss, but when they did, he demonstrated his deep feelings in a physical way that left her breathless every time.

Miss Bingley must have seen the look as her face turned so red it might threaten to burst as she glared straight at Elizabeth from across the room. Could one romantic glance trigger such jealousy? Elizabeth turned away so she would not have to face an enraged countenance.

"Did you fare well among the she-wolves?" Fitzwilliam asked in a low voice. His expression was soft and caring. He was not hiding his emotions at this moment.

"Indeed, I did. No one was anything but solicitous and a little inquisitive regarding this so-called mismatch."

"They believed you should be an earl's daughter like my mother?"

She smiled as she returned a loving glance as surreptitiously as she could whilst attempting to be light and imperturbable in her words despite his effect on her. "No, they seem to have noticed that I am twice as gregarious as you and wonder at the difference in sensibilities. I reminded them that you are their friend and they must be aware of your easy conversation among those with whom you feel most comfortable."

Fitzwilliam's initial expression was of humour, but his face became pained as he took notice of something over her shoulder. He groaned. "Oh, no. Here she comes."

Elizabeth turned her head. Miss Bingley was marching briskly towards them, a determined air upon her face.

"I suppose she would have to congratulate us on our engagement at some time. I shall just have to try to be positive." Even as she said it, she had difficulty believing the other woman would mean well or hold back her barbs. She braced herself as a warning prickle of tiny hairs on end covered her again.

"You horrid wench!" yelled Miss Bingley when she was nearly in front of them. Her arms went forward and she slammed her palms into Elizabeth's chest with a frightening degree of force. "Leave Mr. Darcy alone!" Sturdy as she was, Elizabeth was caught off guard and stumbled back. Fitzwilliam caught her by her arms and righted her again.

Conversations halted, and all eyes in the room turned towards them. Elizabeth's heart tightened within her breast and her palm flew to cover it as she tried to steady her quickness of breath. Horrid wench? How low and coarse! "P...pardon me?"

"Get out, strumpet! Desist in your arts and allurements!" bellowed Miss Bingley. "He wants me, but you have distracted him for all the wrong reasons!" Claws came at Elizabeth's face and a low-pitched growl filled her ears. Oh, no! It could not be!

Chapter 29

Earlier the same evening

Whilst the other gentlemen sat back with their port and cigars, Darcy rose from his seat at the opposite end of the table from Bingley and walked over to stand near the tall, multi-paned windows close to his friend. He ran the tips of his fingers along the rich dark wood of the wainscoting. How to approach what he needed to say? It was a difficult topic, yet he had no choice, for Elizabeth's sake. Even though her mind was stronger than it had been, she was still recovering her memories and had no need of mental anguish from the spiteful words Miss Bingley had subjected her to at Darcy House the last time the two were together. Darcy could predict Miss Bingley's future treatment of Elizabeth. She would hold onto the discrepancy in the stories about a holiday on the continent versus Elizabeth's illness and would gossip amongst the *ton* with the intention of humiliating Elizabeth in the eyes of the fashionable crowd. He had to act before it became a problem of that magnitude. Luckily, nothing untoward had occurred thus far that evening, but he had put off this discussion with his friend long enough. When he became aware that he had been holding his breath as Miss Bingley moved along the receiving line, he made up his mind to speak to Bingley as soon as possible.

Bingley saw Darcy, excused himself from his conversation, and walked over to him. However, he had other ideas about the substance of their private exchange.

"So, my friend. What do you know of the inmates in Clapham?" Bingley, along with Mr. Bennet, was one of the few who had been apprised of Wickham's situation. They had agreed to keep matters reasonably quiet and let the public record disseminate the information. All were determined to ensure that the time before the wedding remained a happy one for Elizabeth's sake. The family had mourned Lydia after she disappeared from the Forsters' lodgings in Brighton, but Mrs. Bennet would likely want a formal period of black or lilac once she learned the truth about her daughter's fate.

"Wickham and Sir Frank are each sticking to their blame of the other, and the magistrate has delayed in hopes of finding witnesses. He does not want to execute anyone in the case of a clear accident; though, at the very least, both are looking at manslaughter."

Bingley rubbed his neck. "How dreadful."

"It is. My tendency is to believe Sir Frank as Wickham was not consistent in his story to us. He still insists Lydia ran in front of the carriage after slapping him and that he only released her due to the slap but did not push or drop her—at least, that is what he claims."

"It is too bad they cannot catch him in a lie."

"I believe a well-placed person accompanies them in gaol in case he admits something to a fellow inmate that he would not say outside."

"Oh, an excellent tactic."

"Apparently, not at all uncommon either."

"Will he get the gallows, then?"

"If found guilty of murder, it is possible. But right now, it would be difficult to prove, and for manslaughter, he will probably not meet the hangman's noose."

Bingley shuddered, and Darcy could not help his similar sensations of a chill at the idea, though he was more practised at hiding those feelings since he had been receiving reports from Clapham all along. He took a large sip of his port.

"Bingley, I have a favour to ask that has nothing to do with the topic at hand."

Bingley drew himself to his full height, a genial grin lighting his face. "Of course. Name it, and it is done."

"It will not be easy, so you should be less eager in your agreement, my friend."

"Oh, this sounds serious. Go ahead, Darcy."

"As amiable as you are to all, Miss Bingley is the opposite. When your sisters called upon Georgiana whilst Elizabeth and Mrs. Gardiner were also present, Miss Bingley could not remain well mannered in Elizabeth's presence. Mrs. Hurst tried to settle her into something representing civility until I had no other choice than to ask them to leave. Now, you and Mrs. Bingley may invite whom you like to your home, but after your sister's disparagement of Elizabeth, I shall no longer come here if Miss Bingley is among those in attendance. Most importantly, I must disallow Miss Bingley's entrance to my homes."

"Are you not reacting in the extreme, Darcy? You know Caroline has a sharp tongue, but that is all. Despite this affront, Elizabeth has always proven to be a stalwart lady with an elegant wit. I am certain she can match Caroline any day. We certainly saw it when the ladies stayed at Netherfield when Jane was ill back in the year eleven."

Darcy crossed his arms. "You were not at my house during the last interaction. Miss Bingley tried her best to undermine Elizabeth in rather unkind terms, upsetting Georgiana and the other guests. I merely want to ensure that my wife is not embarrassed in front of her friends or suffers hurt feelings in her own home. Please, Bingley, do me this favour and speak to her and to the Hursts. I will not back down on this. She is no longer welcome at Darcy House or at Pemberley."

"Very well. I shall honour our friendship and hold back my sister. It should teach her a lesson or two about curbing her tongue. Hurst and I shall have her on our hands forever if she does not learn to be amiable enough to find a good husband."

Darcy passed a hand over his jaw. "You are correct."

"It is past time to join the ladies. Shall we?" At Darcy's nod, Bingley addressed all the men. "Refill your glasses and extinguish your cigars, gentlemen. Our beautiful companions await!"

The men did as they were asked and filed into the drawing room in groups, continuing some of their conversations as they went. Lord Powell caught Darcy along the way and made a pleasant joke about how a wife keeps a man in good spirits.

Barely a moment later, Miss Bingley howled and dove towards Elizabeth, pushing her away, whilst a stunningly rude bit of cant escaped the harpy's lips. Everyone in the room stared in shock. Good G-d! He caught Elizabeth as she stumbled, but her nemesis shouted in anger again, her hands curled into claws. She scratched the air far too close to Elizabeth's face for Darcy's comfort. Gardiner and Hurst shot forward and grabbed Miss Bingley's arms, pulling her backward. Mrs. Bennet's screams filled the air, followed by the protesting murmur of those voices too astounded to remain quiet any longer. Miss Bingley shook free of the men and leapt towards Elizabeth again, but they took better hold of her as a footman came forward to assist.

"You thief of men! You trickster!" she bellowed at Elizabeth with fervour as she fought against the men, who restrained her as best they could though she twisted and writhed like a serpent. "I thought I had convinced you to stay away from Mr. Darcy, but you will not cooperate! I should have killed you when I had the chance!" Miss Bingley proved to be much stronger than expected and very nearly escaped more than once. He could only guess that her strident rage was inspired by too much negus and wine.

"Oh, help me, help me!" screamed Mrs. Bennet. She fell into a faint, collapsing into her seat. Mrs. Gardiner and Mr. Bennet rushed to her side.

"She is fine. All she needs is her salts," said Mr. Bennet.

"Footman!" shouted Gardiner when the fellow baulked from Miss Bingley's attempt to bite him. "Fetch Ralph from the carriage and Bingley's strongest man."

Bingley had been standing frozen to one side as Jane clutched at his arm, both of their mouths agape at his sister. He finally spoke, a tremor in his voice, "Find Brian. He is the strongest. Be quick about it, Ross."

It was all happening so fast. What could Miss Bingley be thinking?

As the tall, strong footmen arrived in the room, Darcy gained Ralph's attention. "I believe Miss Bingley has taken ill. Mr. and Mrs. Hurst were about to accompany her to their home," he said quietly. "Can you please help her to her carriage and accompany her on the trip? She will need robust encouragement to leave us, so you must be firm. I hope you understand my meaning."

With a strained groan, Gardiner added, "She is strong. We can barely hold her."

Ralph nodded, and the two footmen took over detaining Miss Bingley. They were far less awkward about keeping her whipping movements under control than the other men had been and quickly subdued her rage-fuelled struggles. They began to lead her to the door, but she dug her heels into the carpet.

Hurst tugged on his cravat whilst Gardiner tilted his head both ways as if to relieve an ache in his neck. What had Miss Bingley's struggles done to the gentleman?

"You are a simpleton if you think you can dismiss me so easily," Miss Bingley said, her voice loud and throaty, its force rising with each word. She had quit fighting, but the gleam in her eye made every nerve in Darcy's body stand alert.

Miss Bingley stared straight at him with a malicious glare. Her voice changed to one that was sugary sweet. "After the way you looked at that cheap country girl when we were all at Pemberley, I knew I needed to work harder to gain your approval. I decided to join you on your morning ride and rose early so I could be dressed in time. Instead, you tricked me and left even earlier. The groom told me you were bound for Lambton to see Miss Bennet and the Gardiners, which did not bode well for avoiding an attachment between you."

Because of her lack of resistance, the footmen once again attempted to lead her to the door, but she went limp, and they nearly dropped her.

"Stop," said Darcy to the footmen, and they ceased moving Miss Bingley but continued their restraint. As they exerted themselves to hold her still once again, Darcy addressed Miss Bingley. "You followed me from Pemberley to Lambton?"

"Of course I did! I had to put a stop to your foolish notions of romance with that chit and redirect your attentions towards myself."

"Why did I not see you then? Did you get lost?"

"I arrived in time to witness a disturbance among the townspeople. They were shouting about money and the honour of an inconsequential tradesman's daughter while chasing some knave. Those men were so riled that they were ready to collect their pitchforks. Would that they were cleverer and used them against Eliza. You were nowhere to be found, so I tried to find a maid to direct me to the Gardiners' apartments."

Darcy touched his lips lightly to stop his mouth from gaping open. It would seem Miss Bingley would not restrain herself. At that moment, her expression resembled a wild beast rather than a human female. The others, including her own relations, had expressions of shock. "But you did not come in. I would have known if you were announced."

"I did not see you either, Miss Bingley," said Elizabeth, her folded hands shaking. His body went on alert. He had to protect her from any bitter words that could be directed her way, so he moved closer to her.

Miss Bingley addressed Elizabeth with a smug expression. "Blessed blow on the head. As luck had it, I saw Mr. Darcy when he came out. He was pale and crestfallen, and he was rubbing his neck. I almost left at that point, but I had to know whether he had offered for you." She cackled as if she were the devil himself—literally laughed aloud in a harsh, uneven, deep tone that hurt the ears.

Bile rose in his throat. The clearly unhinged Miss Bingley had seen her rival under vulnerable circumstances, particularly when he had come precisely for the purpose the insufferable woman feared: to propose to Elizabeth. "Good G-d. Elizabeth was alone."

"Indeed she was. She was looking out of the window at that noisy fight in the garden. When I grabbed her arm to turn her around, I shouted at her, told her you were meant for me, that we had been matched suitably years ago with only the formalities left. She had obviously been crying, and I felt something of triumph already." She chuckled again, a deep, grating sound. Abruptly, her laughter ceased, and she gnashed her teeth, eyes wild like those of an angry feral cat. The sudden silence was as threatening as her menacing voice, which soon continued. "But when I asked her to promise me that she would never enter into an engagement with you, she refused. She said, if asked the question, that she would say yes. I argued with her, shouted at her, but she would not budge. I had to do away with her." Her eyes darted about the room, not fixing on anything.

Elizabeth spoke at this point. "But it was a man's voice. Every time in my memory, it was a man's voice." Her voice was small and high-pitched, almost child-like. Darcy gently touched her arm to pacify himself as well as Elizabeth. She was trembling, so he placed his hands upon her shoulders. Miss Bingley's face pinched tight, and she struggled mightily against her captors.

Mrs. Hurst nervously clutched the bracelets that customarily rattled when she was bored. "You may not realize this, but when my sister becomes cross, she does not become shrill like many women. Instead, she becomes deep of voice, like a man."

"Indeed," said Miss Bingley in a low-pitched tone, exemplifying her sister's statement. "I remember how well it worked for my grandpapa when he wanted to intimidate someone, so I have learned to emulate such a voice."

Darcy blinked. The gruff voice was more akin to his own than to a woman's.

"But Grandpapa was mad!" said Mrs. Hurst. "Caroline, you must not copy a madman!"

Gardiner entered the conversation. "But how came you to be so strong? Although not as stout as some, Elizabeth is a robust lady. She cannot easily be overcome, I am sure. Her attacker grabbed her arms hard enough to leave bruises, particularly on her right arm, which was jerked from behind her. They also hit her and scraped her cheek, choked her, and finally threw her to the ground."

"Stupid rattle-pated cow was so overcome by her own concerns that I surprised her." Her mouth was turned up on one side in a sneer as she glared at Elizabeth with those crazed eyes. "I also shook her by the arms but to no avail. And yes, I choked her and struck her—hard. I am not so tall for nothing." She held up her large hands. "I am built on the scale of some men, and I am also strong for a lady, something I learnt from my grandpapa. I admired him a great deal and imitated the independence that assisted him in gaining wealth and importance. Thus, like him, I have never cared for servants except to inform me of happenings in the household. Instead, I take responsibility for my jewel case and the shifting of items within my rooms."

"But heavy shifting is for servants! You have a maid; you call footmen!" Mrs. Hurst cried. Her sister buried her face in her hands for a moment before looking Miss Bingley straight in the eye. "Heavens, Caroline, I was aware you were quite taken with Mr. Darcy, but I had no idea you would carry your rivalry to violence. I do not know you!"

"I love him with all my heart, and I know he loves me. That wanton bit of baggage turned his head for lust, and that is all." The collective gasp in the room at the vulgarity of her outburst was no surprise. "Such is the purview of men. Father married for lust and hated Mother. I had to stop Mr. Darcy from making the same mistake." She turned towards Elizabeth. "You tripped over the stupid chair and grasped it! I smacked you so hard, your head should have cracked open when you hit the ground, but the chair saved you. I could not countenance it when I heard you were still alive after all my efforts. You were supposed to die!" She once again flew forward and out of the grasp of one of the footmen, enough for one large hand to become freed. It darted out, ready to strike at Elizabeth, who had moved far too

The Mist of Her Memory

close in her curiosity about Miss Bingley's story.

Fortunately, Darcy's hold on Elizabeth's shoulders allowed him to tug her out of the way, and the footmen regained control of the cruel woman as her strike missed its mark and lost momentum. Darcy quickly placed himself between the two ladies and rose to his full height.

One glance towards Elizabeth turned into shock. Her eyes held the worst fear he had ever seen in human or animal. Elizabeth clutched at him, holding onto his coat, then his arms. He had to be strong for her. He put one arm around her protectively, regardless of its propriety.

"She is mad! She is mad like Grandpapa, Charles!" shrieked Mrs. Hurst.

"Bingley?" he addressed his friend whose eyes and mouth both gaped open as Mrs. Bingley wept silently at his side.

Bingley collected himself, swallowing hard and folding his arms. A stern look embedded itself upon his face, the harshness of which Darcy had never before seen in his gentle friend. "Caroline, you are banned from Darcy's homes and from mine. Do not think you can get away with this heinous act towards Miss Elizabeth. You will be properly punished, at the very least by your family, though I shall not stop Darcy or Mr. Bennet if either wishes to involve the authorities. Gads, I have half a mind to turn you over to the magistrate myself." He placed his fists on his hips and looked away.

Caroline was not cowed in the least. As she was almost literally dragged to the door by the footmen on Darcy's nod, she continued to vent her gall towards Elizabeth in a horrible, strangled, masculine tone. "You cheap slatternly excuse for a country chit! How dare you set your cap so far above you, and into territory where I had already laid claim? In Lambton, I saw you for the trollop you are and tried to off you then. But you are some sort of witch, coming back from the dead! Stay away from Mr. Darcy—do you hear me? I shall kill you! You man trap! You hussy! I *will* kill you, I say!" The sounds of the madwoman died away as the drawing room door closed behind her.

Chapter 30

Every nerve in Elizabeth's body remained so tightly and awkwardly strung, they would have created a harsh, unpleasant noise had they been plucked. And plucked they were by the terrifying, low-pitched voice that finally had a name: Caroline Bingley.

How could she ever have believed that a man had beaten her? G-d in His mercy somehow protected her by hiding certain specifics. Otherwise, her mind surely would not have been capable of tolerating the attack any more than her body was managing, and both threatened to collapse.

A wail filled the air. Was it Miss Bingley? That evil, fearsome woman was too near to her!

Her knees trembled under her while her fingers clutched Fitzwilliam's coat as an eagle's talons clutched at a branch. How revolting they looked, curled up like claws! Like the claws Caroline Bingley had used around her neck. Her grip tightened. One of Fitzwilliam's arms went around her shoulder, and she froze. Had she hurt him? The situation was so confusing.

Could she make herself small so no one could see her? Elizabeth huddled into her betrothed as much as possible and ducked her head into his cravat. Oh, to be little again, held like a child, and comforted until every bit of this tight pain flowed out of her like a rushing river and left behind the comfort of emptiness. But she was supposed to be grown, able to stand straight like a lady through any trial. A lady could call for salts if she was overcome, but she needed no salts. All she needed was both of his arms holding her as tightly as this single one. A deep sound rumbled in his chest under her face. He was talking, giving orders.

The Mist of Her Memory

The shouting and yelling continued but now, it was no longer in the room with her and had become muffled so the words were no longer discernible. She placed her hand over her face and released several shuddering breaths, but her fine, new kid glove was immediately ruined from the tears that soaked into it. Oh, heavens, she was crying, and in public! Huge, bone-wracking, mortifying sobs rent the air—and they were coming from her!

Fitzwilliam turned and clasped her close to his chest with both arms, clutching her tightly so the sounds she made—horrid, wet gasps interspersed with pained shrieks—were muffled at least a little.

"Hush, sweetheart, shhh. She is gone, and it will be well." His voice was quiet, directly in her ear, but she heard his words this time. She dared to look up into his eyes. They were that wonderful shade of green and light brown that was called hazel, and grief lay in their depths. His face crumpled as soon as he saw hers. She buried her nose in his cravat once again.

"Bingley, please excuse me. Mrs. Gardiner, would you accompany us to the nearest sitting room whilst arrangements are made for a carriage to take Elizabeth to your home?"

"Yes, Mr. Darcy, that is wise," Aunt Gardiner agreed.

Mr. Bingley spoke from a thousand miles away. "Of course. Please accept my family's apologies for this display. I am aggrieved and so, so sorry. I cannot say how remorseful I am that we did not see Caroline's true character before this happened. Please, this way." His voice cracked several times. The poor man was close to crying himself.

"Come, dear." Fitzwilliam shuffled her along whilst still holding one arm around her shoulders and a hand at her cheek so she could still hide her tear-stained face from the others. He was the best of men, and here he was, proving it before all their friends.

He reclined her on a lounge, gently extricated himself from her grasp, and stood close by where he could look upon her. His dear face with its tilted brows, so full of concern for her! Aunt moved next to her and took her hand.

"There, there," she said as she stroked her hand over Elizabeth's glove. "She is gone, and she will never be allowed near you again."

In the past, nothing would have seemed worse than the headaches, the haunting sound of voices, the pain of not being believed, and the heartache of hidden memories. The mild mental impairment she had suffered concealed the truth from her, and only now, when she was strong enough and safe enough, could she recall everything.

Nothing compared to the knowledge of the events that truly happened, the pain she would now have to bear. Nothing was worse than her recall of falling heavily and watching as Miss Bingley slipped behind the door that opened on Fitzwilliam's ashen face. Then the chair fell on her too as her head bounced on the floorboards. Pain radiated through her brain whilst she slipped from Fitzwilliam's grasp and something cool and wet spread over her lower legs. Blackness began to encroach on her vision just as Fitzwilliam uttered words of love, and then she knew no more. But tonight's revelation showed her it could have been so much more than intolerable. She could have been as fit for Bedlam as Miss Bingley was if she had remembered those details in her weakened state.

But now, between Aunt's tender caresses and the outpouring of love from Fitzwilliam's eyes, she managed to inhale deeply, calming herself, and at length, her sobs diminished. Nothing was more life affirming to one who had spent nearly the last year renewing her life than their love.

"Excuse me, sir, but the carriage is ready." A footman, the older one. Ross.

"Now, we shall go home and you can rest. We can find those sleeping powders that were so helpful when you first came to us," said her aunt.

"But Mr. Darcy. Fitzwilliam. Is he coming with us?" Her own voice, full of panic.

"No, dear. He will go home now."

She tugged her hand out from under her aunt's and sat upright, snatching Fitzwilliam's hand into hers. "No! I need him! I need to be near him!"

"Then it is a good thing you are marrying soon," said a voice laden with dry humour. Papa! He was standing at the door to the sitting room where they had taken respite from the party. "Do not upset yourself, my dear. Footman, have Mr. Darcy's carriage readied as well so it can follow Mr. Gardiner's. Mr. Darcy, you may accompany Elizabeth so you may spend more time with her. Now, Lizzy, please let go of Mr. Darcy's hand."

"Thank you, Papa." Her face heated as she dropped Fitzwilliam's hand as if it were burning hot. How could she have allowed all and sundry to see her as she had been earlier? They had watched her cry into Fitzwilliam's cravat, heard her mother's nervous exclamations and Miss Bingley's nasty harangue. A strong enough word did not exist to express her mortification. But their expressions had all showed caring and concern for her well-being.

The Mist of Her Memory

A few had wiped away tears of their own.

"How fares my mother?" she asked.

"Your mama has been revived with her vinaigrette," said Aunt Gardiner. "Our Jane is caring for her in her chambers. The party is all but over, so you need not trouble yourself over anything but your own comfort."

"Oh, the art of moving family members about when Lizzy has a once-in-a-lifetime set of her mother's nerves," said Papa with a light laugh. Thankfully, he made sport of things rather than judging her. She began to laugh too, but with her emotions still just below the surface, it caused her to burst into tears once more. Fitzwilliam gave Papa a black look and then knelt in front of her.

"Do not cry, my love." His voice was as gentle as his eyes as he said those words that had remained in her memory the longest. "You have spirit like no other woman I know, and I love you for it. You can beat Miss Bingley's game; I know you can. You recovered despite her efforts, and you can do so again."

What a relief recalling how well she had recovered these recent months despite not knowing who had hurt her or, indeed, whether it was real. She had doubted so many, including herself.

This time, when she blew out a breath, it was long and strong, and she was able to force a small smile in response to Fitzwilliam's encouraging one.

She was hale enough to survive this, and she had a man who trusted in her at her side forever. Her memory had proven helpful to her in the past, allowing her to remember the pleasurable side of that horrific morning. Throughout those terrible days, she always knew Fitzwilliam loved her. Those feelings were all she wanted to bring forth from the time spent in Lambton. Remembrance of the past as it gave her pleasure—yes, that should work.

The realization hit her all at once. Even though she had dealt with intense emotions today, she had evidence of her own strength in comparison with the past. "I did not swoon nor get a headache," she said with surprise.

"You did not, no matter how frightened you were, my beautiful, strong love," he replied, "and you will recover."

"With your help, I know I will be happy again."

Late May 1813
Longbourn, Hertfordshire

Tomorrow she would marry, but today, Elizabeth had managed to escape Mama long enough to indulge in one of her favourite pastimes: reading in the window seat of her father's library whilst he himself was absorbed with his own book at his desk. He had leaned back in his chair as was his wont, holding the book in one hand, his littlest and index fingers behind it so he could mark pages with his other fingers at any time. His spectacles were perched low upon his nose, and he would sigh every once in a while. Trust Papa to sigh when reading a history!

For her part, her toes were tucked up under her with a book open upon her lap whilst she warmed herself in the rays of the late afternoon sun. She was not one to be easily distracted when reading; yet this day, her heart was not in it since she was awaiting her betrothed and Bingley from town. She and her family had arrived home a week earlier, and then Jane had announced her pregnancy. However, Mama had learned of Lydia's fate that same morning, and her sister's happy news compared poorly to the anguish of losing a child. She did not blame Mama for her outbursts this time, but poor Jane was hurt that the promise of a baby could not lessen her mother's misery.

Elizabeth leaned back into her seat and let her eyes roam the outside world. Ripe with the blooms of spring and strewn with bright green elsewhere, the paddock was a happy prospect. Upon sighting two horses walking into the courtyard of Longbourn, her heart leapt in her chest, and she closed the book and slid to the floor. The thump of her slippers alerted Papa.

"They are here?"

"Yes."

"Then I do not have to listen to you sigh every second page."

She laughed. "I? You were doing the sighing!"

"Had you been reading about the plight of Hannibal, you would have sighed as well," he said with his usual acerbity. "But your novel does not demand so much a sigh as a fright—from the awful writing."

"You know it is not so bad." She strode to the door and entered the hall just as the gentlemen arrived.

Fitzwilliam's warm gaze made her heart dance a reel within her breast, but nothing was quite as stunning as the sensation of his lips on her bare hand as he bowed to greet her. That familiar butterfly sensation fluttered and danced within her lower belly. However, before they said much to each other, Mama scurried into the hall, followed closely by Jane.

"Oh, welcome, Mr. Darcy and Mr. Bingley!" Her hands flew into the air, darting about like a pair of nervous birds. "Mr. Darcy, I have your favourite dishes prepared, and one for Mr. Bingley as well! Can I offer you refreshments now or would you like to wait until after you have washed? I suppose you will want time to give your regards to Lizzy."

"Mama!" Elizabeth could not believe how forward her mother's speech was.

"Indeed, madam, I need to change my clothing and perform some basic ablutions before I am fit for company. At that time, Mr. Bingley and I would like to address you and Mr. Bennet, Mrs. Bingley, and Miss Bennet for what we have to say concerns you all." Oh, how she loved that deep, cultured voice. The special smile he gave her did not hurt either. His voice, his gaze, his smile, his strong arms—she could go on and on cataloguing his attributes.

"That is perfect, Mr. Darcy, sir. Anything you need," replied Mama as one hand flew to her chest whilst the other stilled in mid-air as if halfway through waving. "We can meet in the west parlour and enjoy the sunshine whilst you share your intelligence. Is one hour sufficient?"

"One half-hour should be more than enough time."

At the appointed time, they gathered together, the ladies taking seats whilst the gentlemen remained standing. Fitzwilliam stood just beside the settee where Elizabeth was settled.

"The first item we wish to share with you is that of Miss Lydia's final resting place." Fitzwilliam paused, probably anticipating Mama's wails regarding her youngest daughter's demise. He was correct to do so, but the weeping was not accompanied by complaints of heart fluttering and tears, and Papa's soft look calmed Mama soon after she began. These fits of pique took place every time Lydia's absence was mentioned around Mama, yet one could hardly blame her. Even though Lydia had been lost to the family for nearly ten months, her mother had not had the proper opportunity to grieve, and they all held pain in their hearts over the loss of a lively daughter and youngest sister.

"Based on Sir Frank's description of the location, we located her grave. She rests in a proper graveyard near Clapham. On Mr. Bennet's advice, we arranged to have a headstone commissioned to mark her final resting place."

"How awful to have to make such plans for a young girl of her age," said Jane, "but it is fitting that she be safe with G-d."

Bingley, who stood beside her, patted her shoulder. He cleared his throat and spoke next. "No doubt you are wondering what has become of my sister Caroline."

Elizabeth's spine stiffened, and tears sprang into her eyes at the mere mention of the name. She squeezed her eyes shut to control the emotions threatening to overwhelm her. She must be strong now and overcome her fears. *Think only of the past as its remembrance gives you pleasure…think only of the past as its remembrance gives you pleasure…*

"We thought of sending her to the Royal Bethlehem Hospital for treatment—"

"No, no, you must not send her to Bedlam!" Elizabeth blurted as she quickly leaned forward in her seat. "No matter how hard-hearted she has become, undoubtedly that place is so disagreeable, we cannot countenance a family member's internment within. Nobody ever wants any person to go thither, not even the worst sorts of criminals."

"Do not alarm yourself unduly," said Bingley. "We found a fine physician who engages in the study of diseases of the mind, which is surely what must have overcome Caroline to make her act so violently towards you in Lambton and also to speak so cruelly in London last week. Rather than make her an inmate in a place where people are much more flawed than she is, we have chosen to keep her at the Hursts' for now."

She shook her head vehemently. This was no better. "You are going to isolate her, lock her up in the attics. Whilst my memories were being recovered, I hated that I was unable to see anyone due to other peoples' fears for me. It is cruel to sequester a lady in that way, no matter what the reason."

"But Elizabeth," said Fitzwilliam, "your family kept you away from others for your own protection. You were not bitter towards any one person; it was simply your situation that they wished to guard. In Miss Bingley's case, it is for the protection of others—most importantly, you."

"She and I do not have to be at the same place at the same time." She turned to Bingley. "I think if she does not see me with Mr. Darcy, she should not act out again. She only became unhinged at your house."

"If that were only so, we could make some sort of arrangements for her to have limited society so that she would never chance upon encountering you," said Bingley. "Even that notion would stick in Caroline's craw, but I will not reward her by allowing her great freedoms when she has shown that her mind is unstable."

"But what will happen to her?" asked Jane. "It seems there is nowhere for her."

"Each day, the physician I mentioned will take her into a house he has specifically for those with deranged minds, and she will spend her nights locked in her bedchamber at the Hursts' house. This physician will use the latest curatives and methods of treatment to help her recover from this travesty of madness. I am not hopeful, however, since it seems she has the same madness my grandpapa had. He was locked in his apartments with the windows barred for many years. I am afraid, when this physician is unable to cure a patient, that he refers them to Bedlam. In the end, that may be the best place for her."

Elizabeth still could not be comfortable with the situation, no matter how deranged Miss Bingley proved to be. Could she think of any solution other than Mr. Bingley's proposal? "What about Mrs. Bastion? She knows about defects of the mind."

Papa interjected, "Your friend knew about head injuries from her own experience with her son's war injury. This madness runs in Miss Bingley's veins. She will have to be bled, take tinctures, and maybe even more."

Bingley nodded. "Precisely. The physician indicated, if she undergoes such treatments of a nature that she should not be moved, that they will be administered at home whilst she is restrained."

It sounded so disturbing, it was hard to believe, but then, Miss Bingley had meant to end Elizabeth's life. Even so, she could only feel pity for the woman.

Miss Bingley would rather die than be less than important among the *ton* or be cut off from people with whom she could gossip. To that end, Elizabeth's heart ached based on her own experience for needing to feel a part of society, though she was never as vindictive as Miss Bingley—or as evil. She was moved to request help for her nemesis all the same. "Can you promise me something?"

Bingley leaned in towards her. "I should hope so."

"Could you determine whom Miss Bingley might like to see from society to make her feel comfortable and allow her to have visitors in her sitting room? Even if you must subdue her so she does not hurt them, she would probably have a better chance at recovery if she feels a part of society—that is, the type of lady she has always been. I think she would like to dress up nicely and talk to her lady friends."

"If I can convince some of her old friends to visit her and can ensure their safety, then I shall try to use your idea."

A tight spot in her spine released at his positive words. "Thank you for your very human approach to this sad change of position and consequence for your sister." She smiled in her encouragement, a calm overspreading her that she had not felt for a long, long time. Finding out the truth and then acting with sympathy helped her recover more than time alone could ever accomplish.

"If we are done here, I would like the privilege of a private word with Miss Bennet," Fitzwilliam said.

"Of course. Would you like to go for a walk in the gardens?" Papa suggested.

"That would suit."

Jane and Bingley decided that they, too, would like to see the flowers nearby the house. The foursome made quick work of donning hats and gloves. To give the other couple their requested privacy, Jane and Bingley dawdled, looking at those happy azaleas that had earned Elizabeth's attention earlier whilst she had been waiting for Fitzwilliam's arrival. He led her briskly ahead of them until they stopped just beyond some taller rhododendron bushes. The sun was setting, leaving their giant puffs of flowers awash in warm tones.

"What caused you to have a need to speak with me today?" she asked.

"There is some silly tradition about not seeing you tomorrow, so I thought I might like to give you a small gift now."

"A gift? But you have already given me trinkets and baubles enough!" It was true; he had selected some exquisite jewellery for her to wear for the wedding: a matching set made of fashionable red coral with a beaded necklace and earrings plus an arm-band and an eternity ring made to look like a snake eating its tail—to represent the infinite circle of their love—and a full set of combs.

Fitzwilliam stretched his neck to peruse the area about them. They were a fair distance from the house, and the Bingleys had wandered to where they were out of sight. Clasping her hands in his, he pulled her towards him until they were a hair's breadth apart. "Just this," he said then brushed a sweet kiss across her lips.

As usual, his kiss made her legs weaken beneath her body, but he was prepared and pulled her into his arms. Her palms came up to press lightly on his chest, feeling the strength of the muscles beneath the fine, tailored layers of clothing.

"I like your gift!" she said in a near-breathless state.

He smiled, and his lips descended upon hers in a deeper, more passionate manner that left her aching for something beyond her reach, a state of being she did not know existed until she became engaged.

"How comes it that your kisses elicit these feelings of hunger within me? Hunger for what, I do not know. It is the same as hunger. A want to be fulfilled."

He growled, and his open mouth came crashing down upon hers again, urging her lips open with his tongue and rousing a fire low in her belly. His hands wandered across her back, signalling hot trails on the skin beneath her gown in their path. At length, he released her so they were once again joined merely by their hands. The rest of her body missed the closeness with a strength of desire she did not know was possible.

"Until tomorrow, my love, that will be enough."

"Tomorrow, this will be another pleasant memory for me to cherish. Today, it is an example of how wonderful a love can be between two hearts that have overcome so much difficulty and separation in the past."

"It is past, and now, we look to the future." He rubbed his thumbs across her hands, driving her to distraction once again. He leaned in to nuzzle her below her ear.

"Fitzwilliam?"

"Hmmm?"

"I hope you do not mind if I am as impertinent as when you first met me."

He whispered into her ear, his breath nearly causing her to swoon. "Do you plan to be?"

She leaned away from his teasing tongue that had curled into her ear after he spoke, threatening to make her forget her plans altogether. "I plan on telling you that Jane and Bingley are now watching us and giggling."

Fitzwilliam jumped back as if burnt. He grabbed at the collar of his coat as if to straighten it, even though it was in tidy condition, and she burst into peals of laughter. When he realized she was teasing him, he chuckled along with her, and they laughed until their stomachs were sore whilst they walked hand-in-hand back to Longbourn House.

Chapter 31

Late June 1813
London

Elizabeth descended the stairs in the most beautiful gown she had ever worn. This was not a new experience, as every gown she wore since becoming Mrs. Darcy had outshone the last, or so it seemed. This particular dress was pale lilac in the finest muslin over an incandescent ivory satin under-dress with Vandyke lace at the hem. White beads and drops ornamented the bodice and continued down the front in diamond patterns. The light-as-a-feather fabrics floated about her petticoats as she moved, and the drop beads chattered, tempting her to twirl whenever she got the chance. A Kashmiri turban adorned her dark locks.

Awaiting at the bottom of the grand staircase was her husband. Without a doubt, Fitzwilliam was the most handsome man of her acquaintance, made more striking by the black formal wear that fitted his perfect figure, a crisp white cravat in a waterfall design about his neck, and a silver-shot aubergine waistcoat adding the only colour.

He took her hand and kissed it, but before he could release it, she lifted their two hands over her head and spun underneath them to give herself yet another twirl. He caught her at the end of it and held her in his arms, nuzzling into her neck and making her giggle at a ticklish spot.

"I feel touched by magic tonight, my love," she said.

"Indeed you do appear magical to my eye. You are an enchanted confection, and I see a spot that needs to be nibbled." His teeth tugged at her earlobe, sending sensual waves across her skin.

"Please leave some of me for display at the ball, sir. It would not do for me to look like the cake that is missing a bite."

"You do know how to tease a man. Come, let us see what we can accomplish in the privacy of the carriage and still leave you looking like the best Gunter's has on offer."

As with any newlywed couple, she and her new husband took any private moment to engage in furtive kisses and gentle touches as they found it difficult to keep their hands off each other. It seemed as though little time had passed on this trip to the last ball of the Season when Elizabeth pulled back, her lips bright pink and her breath laboured.

The carriage stopped in the queue at the Broussard town house.

"I must confess I had something to discuss with you, but it flew right out of my head the moment you kissed me. Adequate time for honest conversation became scarce when you wasted so much of our ride trying to distract me, husband!"

A sinful yet boyish grin covered his face. "I enjoy distracting you!"

"And I enjoy the distraction. But now, we have no choice but to right ourselves and prepare to be seen by the cream of the *ton*."

THE BALL HAD BEEN A CRUSH, AND THOUGH SHE WAS A SOCIAL CREATURE, Fitzwilliam was not, and she sympathized with his fatigued reticence. Since she had refrained from dancing during the mourning period she and her family were observing, she was not tired. Even so, she suggested they depart shortly after one o'clock. It was not such an unfashionable time, even though the candles would still burn in the Broussard ballroom for more than another hour.

"I want to tell you a secret," she said as the carriage pulled away from the grand house.

"A secret! Is this something special between man and wife, or is it something you know and desperately need to tell someone?"

"A bit of both, I suppose. I could not bear to tell it to any other than you. No one else would understand, but after what we have been through together—" He smothered the words with light, brief kisses before she could continue. "You have been the best confidante of what has been in my heart for a long time."

His mien changed to include a furrowed brow. "You are suddenly very serious."

"In a way, it is a serious topic."

"Then let us discuss it in the privacy of our chambers." He pulled her into his arms where she settled for the remainder of the trip as the contented recipient of gentle kisses on her hair from time to time.

After a quick change into their nightwear and dressing gowns, they comfortably ensconced themselves on a settee in their shared sitting room.

"As I toured the house today, I came to be passing along the servants' corridors near the back entrance," she said. "There was a cloak hanging there, a heavy woollen thing."

"Odd for this time of year."

"I agree. But it reminded me of the same sort of cloak I had seen in Gracechurch Street whilst I was sequestered there and allowed no visitors or trips out of the house other than to the park with my family members."

"That must have been an exasperating time for one as sociable as you. I do not know how you could have borne it."

"I cannot deny how difficult it was to be set aside for so many months. As you say, I require a variety of people around me to make me energetic and content. With such a small circle, I was dejected and uneasy a great deal of the time, and I believe my aunt and uncle thought that meant I was not well enough for society. They offered me occasional trips to the booksellers' and limited visits and, eventually, private balls as I improved, but I missed you. Absence from those we love frustrates hope more harshly than despair." Tears sprang into her eyes as her fingers went gently to her throat.

His arm tightened about her. "I did not see evidence of that when I finally spoke with you. How did you manage your spirits?"

She withdrew a handkerchief to dab her eyes dry. She managed a smile. "My little cousins helped, as did my intention of convincing my aunt and uncle I was better, particularly when the headaches stopped. However, for a long while, it was trying—a true inconvenience."

"I am certain you were determined in a situation that would frustrate most."

"Oh, I do not deny my fair share of frustration, but I had reason to hope. You see, the broadsheets had declared your presence in London and a cloak hung upon the wall much like the one in our home. I planned to use that cloak to steal away from Gracechurch Street. My object was to call upon

The Mist of Her Memory

Miss Darcy and hopefully encounter you during the call to express my thanks for what I thought you had done for Lydia."

He pulled back to look her in the eye. "That is quite the secret, meaning to flee from captivity. I remember spending much time wondering what had happened to you due to all those rumours and tales. When Georgiana mentioned you were asking about me when she called, I was elated."

"Nothing gave me greater joy than to know you were visiting Uncle, though it disappointed me to have you so close yet unable to call on me."

Darcy dragged the tips of his fingers along the side of her face, and she leaned into the tender embrace. "It was a difficult spell to be apart from you, made worse by your injury. How the situation aggrieved me!"

"That is why it was so important for me to recall those memories stolen from me when my head struck the floor. I needed to be taken seriously and allowed to make calls to improve."

"Are you happy with what you have remembered?"

"Most of it. I wish I had not remembered Miss Bingley's evil actions, but in such cases as these, a good memory is unpardonable."

"So you intended to steal out of the house in Gracechurch Street and call on me to thank me for something I did not do? Are you sure it was not for my kisses?" he teased. A long, passionate one was planted upon her lips.

She lingered with her eyes closed for a moment after the kiss; then mischief captured her at the idea of going to his home for kisses back then. "Mr. Darcy! You had not yet declared yourself, so how could I expect your kisses? I did hope that, given an opportunity, you would make your addresses again. You see, the only words I recalled from Lambton at first were yours saying 'my love.'"

She was pleased at the number of memories she had uncovered and grateful for the joy of rediscovery. A secret knot in a tree near Oakham Mount with a booklet she had made and carefully wrapped in oilcloth opened up some of her past. When Mama surprised her by encouraging Cook to make a sweet bread Elizabeth treasured as a child but had forgotten, the scent and flavour burst open a new world of visions from her childhood. But she still had to be told what she did when she was eleven, who that person was, and which books were her favourites at that age. Of course, she had been told a great deal; nevertheless, more remained unclear in her head. Some memories came out wrong—almost like a wilful misunderstanding. What would her future bode if she could not remember the past?

The greatest concern about her memory had to be shared with her husband. "I am apprehensive that, if we have a child, I cannot tell him or her everything about their mama."

Fitzwilliam ran his hand over his mouth before responding in a kind and gentle tone. "A child only needs to know that he or she is loved beyond compare. Do not fret. What is important can be re-taught, and not everything is important. We shall make new memories between us and with our family once we are blessed with children. For now, I should like to dwell on your wonderful knowledge and intellect rather than the gaps."

"I have not changed, yet I am no longer the same. Does that make sense to you?" she asked.

"Of course it does. You are the same in essentials but have been affected by the loss of your memories."

"No matter the event, I do not want to forget ever again. It is much too discouraging. Let our remembrance of the past dwell more on pleasure than sorrow, but all memories must be cherished, for we never know how fickle they may become." She stroked his face from brow to chin. "Love is composed of a single soul inhabiting two bodies. We share the past as we shall share our future."

If any single faculty of Elizabeth's nature were to be called more wonderful than the rest, she would choose memory. There seemed something more speakingly incomprehensible in the powers, the failures, the inequalities of memory than in any other of her intelligences. Her memory was sometimes so retentive, so serviceable, so obedient. Yet at other times, it had been so bewildered and so weak—at others again, so tyrannical, so beyond control! Her recovery was, to be sure, a miracle in every way, but her powers of recollection and forgetfulness seemed peculiarly past discovery.

Was a good memory unpardonable? Was it something to fear? She moved closer into Fitzwilliam's warmth. In certain instances, she supposed it was. She could count on her recollections as facts better than ever before, but all in all, an underlying sinister edge lay in the stories that resided somewhere within her mind. She had to endure and balance it with gratification and hope for the future.

Yes, her future was bound to bring wonderful richness of experience with Fitzwilliam and their children. They would create their own set of beautiful stories to recollect whenever the past insinuated itself to cause her to relive her despair. New sights, new smells, new voices dear to her—they would make up who she was and who she would become. Love would overcome and compensate for discontentment both past and forward, and nothing in this world could give her more comfort than those prospects.

The End

Epilogue

August 1813
Pemberley, Derbyshire

Darcy looked up from the letter he was reading at the large mahogany desk in the library. His dear bride stood nearby, bent over her own letter from Jane. She reached up to brush away a curl that had fallen from her new stylish hair beneath the net and lace cap onto her forehead. His gaze ran up and down her body, drinking in her primrose morning dress and matching cape. Her uncle had procured a border of Indian needlework especially for her, and it currently wrapped about her delicate ankles. The draping of the cambric robe over the curves of her fine figure was a pleasure to his eyes. He shifted within his chair as his thoughts went towards how easily the costume could be removed. As if she sensed his perusal of her person, her eyes rose, and a dazzling smile enhanced her beautiful face.

"What does Colonel Fitzwilliam have to say?"

He cleared his throat to help dispel his ungentlemanly thoughts and respond to her question. "Are you comfortable? Would you like to take a seat? Because his news is not all happy."

She seated herself on a nearby lounge. "I think I can guess at least parts of what he relates. He will be telling you of how his arm fares after having the splint removed, and I suspect he has some sort of news regarding the futures of the men who were recently released from gaol."

"You are correct. The arm is weak, but he is practising use of it in hopes it will eventually recover its strength." Darcy referenced his letter. "Once again, he writes that he is thankful that was the worst of his injuries out of Vittoria as, since his return, he has heard of several fellows who eventually succumbed to their injuries weeks later with infections and disease. Some with broken arms required amputations."

"War is horrific!" She shuddered and shook her head. "I do not wish to know more." How fortunate, then, that she had not asked to read the letter, as the details were not for a lady's eyes.

"They did claim success in the fight, and if it is any consolation, Richard will be receiving a promotion as a result of his actions to support their strategy."

"That is wonderful news."

"He also writes of Wickham and Sir Frank as you mentioned."

"Have they completed their gaol time?"

"Yes, they served their sentences for manslaughter and paid their fines. Richard was at Newgate as they were released. His sister Maggie is on the marriage mart again since Sir Frank's misfortunes became too difficult for her and Lord and Lady Matlock to tolerate. He was not the man she imagined him to be."

"How sad."

"Although we cannot claim such a dramatic situation, I am grateful that we were constant to each other in the face of our relatives' disapprovals."

Her head tilted and her dark eyes glowed in warmth towards him. "At least my uncle was able to see reason. We do not take Lady Catherine's views seriously, and nothing proved enough to sway us."

"Are you pleased with your choice, my love?"

Her eyes twinkled and creased at the edges whilst her lips quivered. "You mean pleased with Pemberley? Of course. Who would not approve of it?"

He laughed lightly, something he had been doing a great deal more of since she had become a steady part of his life. He preferred himself like this, enjoying her wit and charm and learning to flirt in return. "Perhaps a miss from Hertfordshire who was in no mood to marry such a conceited and proud man?"

Laughter poured out of her like the sparkling water that rushed from the fountains in Pemberley's park. "Of course I am ecstatic with my choice of you. I waited long enough to have the pleasure of being your wife, and I know you are a caring man who is honest to a fault. I have no cause to repine." Her mirthful face changed remarkably to a more serious one, complete with a curl to her upper lip. "And what of Mr. Wickham? Has he found employment as a seducer or a gambler? He was quite skilled at both." Sarcasm dripped in her tone. Wickham's contrite confessions at the end did little to impress her even though he had been found innocent of killing her sister purposely. All indications pointed towards Lydia pulling free from his grip and either darting or falling into the path of Sir Frank's speeding curricle.

"No, but apparently his experiences being plied with drink to confess, followed by a month in gaol for manslaughter, did have a sort of sobering effect upon him. Furthermore, he met a man in prison who gave him interest in the faith."

"Let me guess. He will be applying to you for the living at Kympton again." The biting sarcasm again laced her retort.

"Nothing like that. He repaid his debts and the petty thefts using money the religious fellow gave him. It seems the fellow had a fortune gained from sugar plantations that he has since sold. Wickham returned to the ——shire Militia for court martial and was sentenced for his crimes, including desertion. He was demoted, marked with a 'D' upon the left side of his neck, and was placed in general service in the Royal African Corps in West Africa."

"Oh, my gracious, so far from home." She rubbed the back of her neck, and he made a note to kiss her there later. "I do not know whether to feel relief or pity. I am sure Georgiana will be happy once she hears." Their sister was at Matlock for the summer to give them some time alone as a newly married couple.

"Feel pity for the poor fellows in his regiment. I am certain his repentance will only last so long and he will be up to his old tricks in no time, that is, unless dice and cards are forbidden in the encampment."

"Speaking of pity, dearest," she said, "I have word of Miss Bingley from Jane."

"Do tell. Has her work with the physician resulted in any curative restoration?"

"Unfortunately, no. She has proven to be a danger to more than just me. She had been behaving as a sane person would, but they believe it was all an act. Just last week, when she was forbidden from leaving the house for the society of those she finds important, she attacked Mrs. Hurst with her sewing scissors. Then, she blamed me for her incarceration in Mr. Hurst's townhouse. Mr. Bingley and Mr. Hurst will not risk her hurting anyone again. Jane feels it is all a misunderstanding, but she did not argue when her husband insisted that Bedlam was the best place for Miss Bingley."

"Gracious! And how do you feel about that? You never favoured Bedlam for Miss Bingley. You were dead set against such an action when you voiced your opinion in the past."

"It still unsettles me, and Jane is apprehensive as well. But poor Mrs. Hurst required many stitches. She is lucky the wound healed well and did not go putrid. I cannot bring myself to feel sympathy for Miss Bingley any longer." Indeed, the situation was disturbing; the wound was not unlike those of soldiers who died on the fields of Vittoria.

Darcy traced his fingers along a line on his trousers, his eyes following their movement. "Elizabeth, I must ask you a question I am certain will bother you. I can imagine you already anticipate it, but I must understand how you feel right now."

Elizabeth's voice was calm and forthright. "Lydia died one year ago tomorrow. You wish to ask whether I am over my fears and anxiety regarding the situation in Lambton nearly a year ago."

His head snapped up. He had not anticipated such a measured response to the recollection of that horrible time. A shaky voice or a few tears would have been completely understandable, yet she remained perfectly composed. "Yes. I have arranged for a small prayer service in the chapel to remember her."

"Thank you, Fitzwilliam. I am grateful for all you do for me. I also thank you again for the grave marker. Papa writes that it is quite fitting for Lydia. I do hope to see it the next time we are up to town.

"Now, to answer the question not asked, you may rest easy that your caring nature and the time allowed to heal my injuries have helped a great deal. I do believe I am greatly improved. Many of my childhood memories have been regained, although my brain becomes tired and overwhelmed easily. I am not without anxieties in life, yet I no longer entertain lingering qualms regarding the attack. I am satisfied and lacking in remorse of any sort over the incident."

"That is very brave of you."

"I should not refer to it as bravery because I had no choice in my recovery. I lived in the manner required of me, given my ailment. Where there is choice, there may be bravery, but where one must forge ahead, reconciling one's illness becomes part of the perception of regular daily life."

Darcy smiled at his wonderful wife, and Elizabeth beamed back. They were blessed with their ability to love each other the way they had always wanted, as husband and wife and as partners. Through their hardships, they had become stronger individually and as a couple. Their time apart was a measure of their love as much as was each day they now had together, each time they said "I love you," and each time they demonstrated through words and deeds that the other was the most important person in their life.

The remainder of his days would be scarcely enough time to show her how wonderful their consequences were in spite of all they had endured and the grief that had threatened them through those days when her memory was all a mist. He too would share some of her philosophy to help him have the courage to get through those difficulties in life where choice was not available. He would always cherish his beautiful lady who had no regrets.

End Notes

From "stealing an heiress" to "transportation": legal issues in *The Mist of Her Memory*

READERS IN JANE AUSTEN'S ERA WOULD EASILY UNDERSTAND THE LEGAL expressions, precedents, and related sociological evils in *Pride and Prejudice* as well as in *The Mist of Her Memory*, but modern readers might find it an unusual mix of lingo and surprising penalties. In many Regency novels, the author automatically assigns transportation to the guilty party in any crime, not understanding what it means or realizing that such a severe punishment was not a universal solution in the courts 200 years ago. Jane Austen's readers would be familiar with the typical punishments of the day; modern readers may not be. These limited examples are intended to assist in understanding a few of these crimes and penalties.

When Mrs. Younge and Mr. Wickham conspired to have Georgiana Darcy elope with him in *Pride and Prejudice*, they were breaking a law colloquially known as "stealing an heiress," an act worth three to five years' jail time.[1] The age for statutory rape was under sixteen, making Lydia's sixteenth birthday in *Pride and Prejudice* significant, as it was a crime with a two-year jail term as a penalty.

In *The Mist of Her Memory*, Sir Frank and Wickham are both found guilty of manslaughter for Lydia's death under the wheels of Sir Frank's carriage. A case in the Old Bailey from October of 1811[2] states that a young boy died

---

1. Tomlins, Thomas Edlyne, *The Law Dictionary, Defining and Interpreting the Terms of Words of Art, and Explaining the Rise, Progress and Present State of the English Law*, (London: C. and R. Baldwin, 1810), 614 and 373, https://books.google.ca/books?id=aSmTHVqp4NQC.

2. *Proceedings of the Old Bailey, 30th October 1811*, (Sussex: Harvester Microform,

from sepsis caused by a broken leg a month after being accidentally run over by a "waggon of coals." The driver was found guilty of manslaughter and sentenced to a month in Newgate with a one-shilling fine. The original drafts of *The Mist of Her Memory* had Lydia pushed in front of the horses, the crime of murder because of Wickham's intent to hurt her. However, cold readers expressed that even though Wickham's disappearance was reprehensible, they hoped he would not hang. Interpreting legalese[3] of the Regency suggested that Wickham's releasing Lydia to dart or fall in front of the speeding carriage constituted manslaughter.

Miss Bingley's assault on Elizabeth resulting in battery, if prosecuted, could result in damages being claimed by Elizabeth or the Bennet family. In court, Miss Bingley would be subject to a fine "in accordance with the heinousness of the event" and would be required to pay court costs.[4]

In the Regency, with so many men active as soldiers in the Peninsular Wars, it was difficult to recruit for the militia, which was a domestic peace-keeping force. This was especially true for officers. Therefore, a blind eye was turned to militiamen who went missing for a short period of time.[5] Austen's early readers of *Pride and Prejudice* would have expected Wickham to be forgiven for his leave and to return to the ——shire even a month later after Darcy found him in London. Otherwise, it would have proven difficult to obtain the position in the regulars. In *The Mist of Her Memory*, this situation would have been the same in early August 1812 when Lydia was killed, indicating that Wickham would still have the station of an officer in the militia if he had faced judgement for Lydia's death immediately after it happened.

However, by April 1813 in *The Mist of Her Memory*, he had disappeared long enough to be considered a deserter.[6] The results of Wickham's court martial in *The Mist of Her Memory*'s epilogue are examples of penalties for

---

1984), 436, https://www.oldbaileyonline.org/images.jsp?doc=181110300018.

3. Tomlins, *The Law Dictionary*, 448.

4. Tomlins, *The Law Dictionary*, 55.

5. Austen, Jane, *The Annotated Pride and Prejudice: A Revised and Expanded Edition*, ed. David M. Shapard (New York: Anchor, 2012), 543n4.

6. Samuel, E. *An historical account of the British army, and of the law military as declared by the ancient and modern statutes, and articles of war for its government with a free commentary on the Mutiny Act and the rules and articles of war; illustrated by various decisions of court martials*, (London: William Clowes, 1816), 322, 335-37. http://books.google.ca/books?id=Bq1BAAAAYAA

deserters from the militia.[7,8] "General service" (i.e., service for life) and "marked with a D" were common consequences for militia members for desertion. Transportation for seven years (to a British colony for work that was effectively slave labour) was often the result for crimes such as theft or manslaughter in the British military and civil courts or, in certain cases, to avoid the penalty of hanging for murder. Trial and punishment in both civil court and courts martial for the same crime was not uncommon;[9] however, the militia was required to "deliver the accused person over to the civil magistrate" first or face court martial.[10] It's likely that Wickham also was cashiered, that is, subject to a military degradation ceremony.

---

7. "Statement of the Number of Soldiers sentenced to General Service, and to Transportation, by General Courts Martial, in the Years 1809, 1810, and 1811," *Journals of the House of Commons, Volume 67,* 675-676, https://books.google.ca/books?id=dxdDAAAAcAAJ.

8. "British Soldiers in the Eighteenth Century: Discipline and Punishment," Wikipedia, accessed 8 February 2019, https://en.wikipedia.org/wiki/British_soldiers_in_the_eighteenth_century#Discipline_and_punishment.

9. Henderson, Robert, "'Terror of Example' Crime and Punishment in the British Army in 1812, Part One: Capital Punishment," The War of 1812 website, accessed 8 February 2019, http://www.warof1812.ca/punish1.htm.

10. Samuel, *An historical account,* 489.

Acknowledgements

I was reading another author's acknowledgements, and they were about a quarter the length of mine, so I trimmed this section down so it's only about three times that other author's. Once again, I have a lot to be grateful for.

First of all, I'd like to recognise the marvelous beta team of Nina, Leslie, and Angela. You three are a dream team for a Regency romantic mystery/suspense book!

A beta team is a great start to editing, and lucky me, I was able to capitalize upon the "Lopt and Cropt" wisdom of Sarah Pesce for the book's content. Similarly, I was fortunate to work again with the inimitable and excellent copy and layout editor, Ellen Pickels, and the gifted cover artist and book marketer, Janet Taylor. I'm grateful to you all for making this so much better than it was when Meryton Press first accepted it!

My sincere appreciation goes to the authors Ken Follett, Mary Higgins-Clark, Robin Cook, V. C. Andrews, Michael Ondaatje, and multiple others' books for an understanding of the suspense novel that remained with me as inspiration.

Thanks also to Jane Austen. I could not have completed such a book without understanding how Elizabeth felt when things went totally sideways, or how the proud Mr. Darcy would behave when in love but misunderstood. It's all there in canon; I just had to write a dozen chapters where Austen had written a few paragraphs to exemplify those aspects of her characterization.

My family, close friends, and the Chat Chits and Chap are always asking how the writing is going and then offering wonderful encouragement and making me feel blessed that I can actually do this and be taken seriously about it! Similarly, the readers at AHA enthusiastically commented through the serial posting of the story and helped me fill some continuity gaps. Many thanks to all of you.

I wish to recognize AHA's Aureader and Jude as well as author Abigail Reynolds and dear friend and author Leslie Diamond. Each of them assisted in a small way with the content of this book. I'd also like to acknowledge the real people who inspired some of the scenes and words in this book—those overcoming adversity with invisible disabilities every day. Their experiences and comments have been drawn upon to add richness to this novel.

Finally, my heart is full when I think of the support from my life partner, also known as Mr. Suze. He's the reason I can so easily write romantic scenes that my readers adore. For this novel, he and my darling kitties gave me time and support like never before. We grow and learn as our love blossoms every day.

About the Author

A lover of Jane Austen, Regency period research and costuming, cycling, yoga, blogging, and independent travel, cat mom Suzan Lauder is seldom idle.

Her first effort at a suspense novel, *The Mist of Her Memory*, is the fifth time Lauder has been published by Meryton Press. Her earlier works include a mature Regency romance with a mystery twist, *Alias Thomas Bennet*; a modern short romance, "Delivery Boy," in the holiday anthology *Then Comes Winter*; the dramatic tension-filled Regency romance, *Letter from Ramsgate*; and the Regency romantic comedy, *A Most Handsome Gentleman*.

She and Mr. Suze and two rescue cats split their time between a loft condo overlooking the Salish Sea and a 150-year-old Spanish colonial home near the sea in Mexico.

Suzan's lively prose is also available to her readers on her blog, *road trips with the redhead* www.suzan.lauder.merytonpress.com, on her Facebook author page https://www.facebook.com/SuzanLauder, on Twitter @suzanlauder, and on Instagram as Suzan Lauder. She is a lifetime member of JASNA.

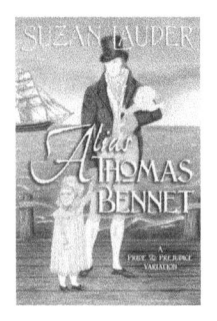

Book Club Questions

1. As is typical of many romance novels today, the point-of-view speaker in *The Mist of Her Memory* changes by chapter and is limited to the male and female protagonists. As a reader, what are the benefits of this style? What are the drawbacks?

2. *The Mist of Her Memory* is set in the Regency period, which dictates changes in comparison with a modern setting. Consider Elizabeth's head injury as one topic that may be different, and discuss. What advantages and disadvantages does the Regency setting offer for the discovery and punishment of the villains? What other areas are markedly different than today?

3. As a mystery and suspense Regency romance novel based on Jane Austen's *Pride and Prejudice*, *The Mist of Her Memory* is different than many readers of Regency romance or Jane Austen fan fiction are accustomed to. What drew you to read this book?

4. Many readers are surprised at the final outcome and the unmasking of Elizabeth's attacker. Discuss your suspicions during the story, why you suspected various characters as being the one who viciously harmed Elizabeth Bennet, and how that changed with new information.

5. Consider the new character of Mrs. Bastion. Discuss her role in the book. Similarly, consider the other new characters and their input.

6. Elizabeth and Darcy's romance is a key aspect of *The Mist of Her Memory*. Describe the growth of their relationship in parallel to solving the mystery.

7. The author originally had Sir Frank and Lady Margaret marrying at the end of the book because she had been so steadfast in her dedication to him. However, online readers balked, saying he did not deserve her. What is your opinion? Back it up by referring to the novel.

8. *The Mist of Her Memory* draws upon the characters and base plot of Jane Austen's *Pride and Prejudice*, but takes a markedly different path halfway through. Does the reader need to know Austen's book well to enjoy *The Mist of Her Memory*, or can it stand alone? Had the names of the characters been changed, would it affect the ability to enjoy the novel?

9. Elizabeth's time sequestered in the Gardiner home opens the novel. What were your first impressions of the Gardiners as her protectors, and how did that evolve as you learned more about the history of her affliction?

10. Elizabeth Bennet is considered an unreliable narrator due to her amnesia. Discuss this and other unreliable narrators you have observed, whether in this book or a similar book.